WARRIORS IN EXILE

H . BEDFORD-JONES

WARRIORS IN EXILE

H. BEDFORD-JONES

ILLUSTRATED BY
HERBERT MORTON STOOPS

ALTUS PRESS • 2018

© 2018 Altus Press • First Edition—2018

PUBLISHING HISTORY

Warriors in Exile originally appeared in the June 1937–October 1938 issues of *Blue Book* magazine.

THANKS TO

Everard P. Digges LaTouche and Gerd Pircher

TABLE OF CONTENTS

"WE, ABOUT TO DIE"

*"We, About to Die" is the first of a fascinating series
based on the records of the most famous and picturesque
fighting force of modern times—the French Foreign
Legion. Fiction these stories admittedly are, but so
vigorous and vivid that they outshine history itself.*

PORSON AND red-haired Casey and Kramer, all
anciens of the Foreign Legion, were having a drink and a
gam when I broke in. They made me welcome, though the
nearest I ever got to the Legion was back of its rear files in
Morocco.

"I tell you," Casey was saying excitedly, "there never was any
Foreign Legion before 1831! I know. I've got the Livre d'Or of
the Legion, and it gives the records!"

Porson calmly rolled a cigarette. He was a dark Alsatian, a
splendid chap and a scholar to boot.

"You're wrong, Casey. Our corps began in Algeria, yes; but
there was an earlier Foreign Legion, no less heroic, in the Egyp-
tian campaign."

"Bah!" kicked in Kramer. "You might as well say the Swiss
Guards, the old Scots archers and all the other mercenaries
were foreign legions! There was none that had our title, however."

"There was one that had the title." Porson held a match to
his cigarette.

"You're all wrong," I put in. "There's no such thing as the
Foreign Legion."

Maybe they didn't jump on me! Not Porson, however. He
knew I was right. He had the Croix, the Médaille, and a couple
of wounds from Syria. When the others calmed down a bit, I
explained my statement.

"Look up the records in your Golden Book, Casey. The

Legion was formed in 1831, and finally went out of existence in 1856, to be replaced by the *Regiment Stranger.* Twenty years later it took back the name of Légion Étrangère, but in 1884 was again cut up into Foreign Regiments, and the name of the Legion does not reappear until 1915. Today the corps consists of five Foreign Regiments again, and one of cavalry—"

"You're just nuts on technicalities!" Casey exclaimed hotly. "It's always been the one corps—"

"It hasn't," I broke in with wicked delight. "The original Legion went out of existence in 1835, was destroyed in Spain, and not until 1837 was the corps again organized."

It began to look like a row, until Porson intervened.

"Our friend is right, boys," he said placidly. "Look at the records for yourselves. At the same time, the corps amounts to the same thing, regardless of changes of name—"

"But he says the Legion doesn't exist!" shouted short-tempered Kramer.

"It does not," said Porson. "And I say it existed back in 1800, which is the original argument. In fact, the greatest glory that the Legion ever won, came before it was our present Legion. Just *a* Foreign Legion, mind you, not *the* Legion!" His white teeth flashed in a smile. "This was the genesis of our Legion,

my friends. Upon its men, its traditions, its heroism, was modeled our organization."

"You're opening your mouth too wide," said Casey shortly.

Porson gave him one lingering glance.

"Yes? The grandfather of my grandfather commanded that earliest Foreign Legion. I have seen his papers, his letters, everything. His story was a thing to marvel at. I, as a child, never believed the family tradition, until I investigated and found it to be true. It was the Foreign Legion who won the most desperate, bloody and momentous battle of the First Republic—a battle of which few people have heard."

Kramer signed to the waiter and had our glasses refilled.

"Tell us about it, Porson," he urged.

"It's a story, *mes amis!* The story of how one man succeeded where Napoleon failed. You all know how Bonaparte took an army to Egypt, cut up a few poor devils of Mamelukes in a make-believe battle, went into Syria and got trounced, lost his fleet, was facing disaster—and skipped out before a soul knew he was going. He left Kléber in command of the Army of Egypt: an army scattered all over the place, homesick and hungry and cut off, regiments shrunk to half their strength, no provisions, clothes or ammunition, a British fleet blockading the ports, and an army of sixty thousand Turks marching in from Syria. Do you get that picture? Kléber got good terms; he had to capitulate. When the Turkish army reached Cairo, he would turn over

the city to them and go home with the honors of war.

"From that picture, turn to the story of Colonel Hans Porson. He had gone up from the ranks during this campaign; we have a miniature of him at home—a stalwart, lean, dark man—"

"Like you," put in Casey. Porson showed his teeth again.

"Like me, maybe, but far ahead of me. His men loved him. His wife loved him. He had married a girl in Cairo, you see: a lovely blue-eyed girl named Leila, the daughter of a Mameluke bey. They lived in her father's house near the Ezbekieh gardens. I wish I could make you see that house, built around a courtyard shaded by great trees, sweet with plashing fountains, and gay with tiles and with delicate work of fretted ivory and carven woods—"

WHAT MAGIC lies in words! Before us rose a picture of Porson in that courtyard, a strapping, handsome man in tattered uniform and mended boots—only the officers had any boots at all in that Army of Egypt. And his young wife, looking up with anxious eyes.

"You have news, Hans? It is bad?"

"I've obtained quarters for you and the babe and one servant, in the citadel," said Porson abruptly. "You must be out of here before noon."

She stared at him, this man who commanded the Foreign

Legion that Kléber had organized.

"No! What do you mean? What has happened? You've been gone for two days," she said. "And now we must move into the citadel, before noon—why, that's only a little more than an hour from now!"

"I must be back at Headquarters then; you must be in safety." Porson wearily stretched out on a divan and closed his eyes. He went on speaking: "Nothing has happened; everything is about to happen. Let me sketch it for you. I myself am struggling to see it clearly."

"No news from the English admiral?"

"None as yet."

In the desperate effort to bring up his shattered regiments to some semblance of strength, Kléber had enrolled a corps of Copts, another of negroes from the Sudan, another of Greeks and mixed nationalities—the Foreign Legion, this, under Porson. Now, speaking slowly, painfully, Porson sketched for his wife the position of things.

"You have news, Hans? It is bad?"

The capitulation signed with the Turks and English had gone into effect. Some of Kléber's generals had departed. A scant twelve thousand men remained here at Cairo. The frontier forts

had been handed over to the Turks; their army was within sight of the city.

Then had come that terrible letter from Sir Sydney Smith noblest of gentlemen. As a matter of honor, he warned Kléber that the capitulation had been disavowed by his superiors, that the English would not acknowledge the treaty, that the Grand Vizier who commanded the Turkish army would not keep the terms. Kléber made one frantic appeal to Admiral Keith of the British fleet; no answer had yet come.

A SLAVE appeared, with coffee and fruit. Porson sat up, ate, swigged the coffee, and wiped his dark mustache.

"If Admiral Keith stands by the treaty, all's well," he said. "If not, it means massacre. Reports have come in that the Grand

When they reached the front lines these veterans rose with rolling oaths of wild delight; they vibrated an enthusiasm which left Kléber himself astounded.

Vizier has sworn not to leave one Christian alive in Cairo; men, women, children, are to be exterminated. He has sixty thousand men—some say eighty thousand. We've given up all defenses. We've scarcely any powder."

Leila was white to the lips. "But the English signed the treaty! They can't—"

"They can do anything they desire," Porson said bitterly. "Already Turks are in the city by thousands. None of us is safe. Get your things together. As soon as I see you safely in the citadel, I must go to the palace of Elfi Bey, where Kléber is waiting for word. I have an escort outside. Waste no time."

NONE WAS wasted. With what could be hurriedly salvaged, Hans Porson, Colonel of the Legion, drew his escort about his little family and conducted them through the streets to the citadel. Only the naked hungry steel of the escort saved them from the maddened populace; the Arabs, incited to fanatic fury by Turks who had entered the city, were mad for Christian blood.

Once within the towering gates, Porson kissed his wife, stooped above the child for an instant, then departed to Headquarters....

It was the nineteenth of March, 1800.

Kléber, that fiery, impetuous genius whom every man in the army loved as a brother, was asleep upstairs. In the courtyard were generals Reynier, Lanusse and Leclerc, awaiting what news might come; Porson fell into talk with them, and learned that the Grand Vizier's army was at Heliopolis, a scant five miles from the city. As they talked, a courier came in hurriedly and saluted.

"Citizen General," he addressed Reynier, "Nasif Pasha and six thousand Janissaries are occupying a village a mile this side of Heliopolis. The Grand Vizier is reviewing the cavalry of his vanguard, fifteen thousand strong, this afternoon; that means action tomorrow."

*The Legion led the storm; a Legion not of
men but of fiends, stopping for nothing.*

"Then the Turkish lines have moved up almost to our cantonments?"

"Yes, Citizen General. And as I returned, a boat was landing
at Boulak. I saw an English officer coming ashore. And the
Janissaries have openly proclaimed a massacre not only of the
French, but of every Christian in Cairo."

Massacre? No matter; only the English officer mattered now.
Here was the response on which hung life or death. Reynier
sent an aide to bring the Englishman. Kléber lay still in exhausted slumber. Reynier turned to Porson.

"When the letter comes, take it to him. Let the chief meet
it alone."

The words were gloomy. During these past days the insolence
of the Turks and Arabs had become insufferable. Already Egypt

was in their hands. That Kléber had scarcely ten thousand effectives, they knew only too well.

Porson waited. He and Kléber, both Alsatians, were old friends; therefore these others left him to endure the lion's wrath if the news were bad. Kléber, bitter enemy of Bonaparte, whose genius outshone that of the Corsican!

The guards saluted. The trim figure of an English naval officer entered—Lieutenant Wright of the *Tiger*. He looked at the grave, anxious faces.

"Messieurs, I bear a letter from my admiral for General Kléber."

Colonel Porson took the letter, turned, and ascended the stairs to the upper rooms of Elfi Bey's palace. He came to the door of Kléber's room, knocked and entered. Kléber had just risen. The flowing lock of hair that marked him out, stood up from his massive, energetic features. In silence, Porson handed him the letter.

Kléber tore it open; without change of countenance he read the epistle, which was in French, handed it to Porson, then turned and went to the window, staring out. Porson glanced at the writing:

> *Having received positive orders to consent to no capitulation with the French army except as prisoners of war... it is my duty to notify you that no ships will be allowed to leave this country....*

Kléber swung around.

"We're caught," he said quietly. "Even if the Turks gave us the promised ships, the English will not let us pass. And the Turks will do nothing."

Taking the letter from Porson, he sat down at his table, scribbled a few words at the bottom, and invited Porson to read them:

> *Soldiers, this insolence can have but one reply: victory! Prepare to fight.*
>
> > *Kléber.*

"Fight!" repeated Porson in a low voice.

Kléber stood up, and he was smiling.

"Fight! Have a thousand copies of this letter, with my notation, printed and distributed among the troops before six o'clock.
Here, have a letter written in Turkish to the Grand Vizier; send
off a prisoner with it, and demand immediate answer. Say that
he has kept no single term of the treaty, that the English refuse
to honor it, and that unless he retreats by daylight tomorrow
morning, I shall regard him as an enemy and the treaty as
abrogated."

"The generals are below," said Porson. "You will receive
them?"

"No." Kléber pointed to the maps on his table. "Leave me
alone. Under no circumstances am I to be disturbed, until we
get the Grand Vizier's reply."

Porson departed. In the courtyard below, the whole staff had
gathered. They read the letter and the notation, and their eyes
glinted.

"Ah!" Young Leclerc of the cavalry caught at his saber. "What
happened, Porson? What did he do when he read it?"

"He smiled," said Porson, and went forth on his errands,
gloomily enough.

As he worked, that afternoon, gathering news and getting
off the messenger, he knew the worst was at hand. This ultima-
tum to the Turk was theatrically superb—and was utter nonsense. The enormous Turkish army, occupying the whole plain
of Heliopolis, had more men in its advance guard alone than
Kléber's entire command could muster.

Massacre! Yes: for nothing else remained. The few French
wives and families, like his own, were in the citadel; but Cairo
was full of Greek, Italian and other Christian merchants; not
even the ancient citadel could hold out against the Turkish
artillery. Massacre, for every man, woman and child. His own
wife, his own child! Porson looked up at those towering walls,

and shivered. There was no escape from this land of Egypt. The end had come.

TOWARD SIX o'clock Porson was in the courtyard at Headquarters, with the other staff officers, when the reply came from the Grand Vizier. Kléber appeared on the stairs, saw the messenger, and halted.

"The answer has come? Read it, Colonel Porson."

Porson obeyed. It was short, ominous: *"A Grand Vizier never retreats."*

There was an instant of dread silence—and then, despite the frightful tension, a laugh went up. For upon that silence Kléber had uttered one scornful word: a word which does not see print either in French or English.

"I'll make him retreat, and quicker than he wants!" went on Kléber. "Comrades, there need be no discussion. What shall we do?"

"Fight!" cried the impulsive Leclerc, and the others joined in.

Kléber smiled slightly.

"General Verdier! Put the wounded and convalescent here, to hold Headquarters. At midnight I join the front line; the army marches. Can you hold the citadel with three thousand men?"

"Two thousand," said Verdier briefly. "Take the rest."

"Agreed. How much powder must you have?"

"Take the powder. We have bayonets."

Kléber beamed. "Keep enough for the cannon on the citadel. Colonel Porson, can this Foreign Legion of yours be relied upon to lead our march?"

"More than that." Porson saluted. *"Morituri te salutant!"*

Kléber clapped him on the shoulder. "We who are about to die—ha! Perhaps, and perhaps not. I'll tell you one thing, my friends: whether we die or live, we'll show these Turks one hell of a fight! And now let us eat, drink and be merry; for tomorrow—we accomplish the impossible!"

Porson, and many another, finished the speech otherwise in the course of that evening. When their first enthusiasm died out, when reality settled upon them, Kléber still clung to his calm assurance, but it was unshared by his staff.

"The fact remains," Porson said to him, when they were alone together, "that we have a scant ten thousand men."

"You forget what sort of men they are, comrade," rejoined Kléber, smiling.

TOWARD MIDNIGHT, under a clear moon, Porson and the others rode beside Kléber to the camp, leaving Cairo glittering and fermenting under its silver citadel. When they reached the front lines, with the distant lights of the vast Turkish camp stretching off across the plain, a surprise awaited them.

To Porson, it was an acute surprise.

He had snatched one brief farewell with Leila, with the baby to whose tiny loveliness he was devoted. He knew, and the other staff officers knew, that they were marching out this night to death. All illusion was dead. Ten thousand ragged, barefoot, hungry men, ill armed and equipped; and yonder, sixty thousand at the least—the dreaded Janissaries, the elite regiments of the whole Turkish Empire, with an enormous park of artillery.

But here in the camp came swift astonishment. These skeleton brigades, these veterans of Italy and the Rhine, rose up with rolling oaths of wild and fierce delight. Scarcely could Kléber command a way through the throngs to his own tent. These crowding figures fairly vibrated with an intangible force, a burning enthusiasm, an almost frenetic emotion, which left Kléber himself astounded. The other officers scattered. Kléber, before his own tent, took the arm of Porson, with a low word.

"What does it mean, my friend? Could you feel it, or did I imagine it—the wave of power, like a living force, uplifting these men?"

"They know they're about to die," said Porson quietly. "But they know that you, unlike Bonaparte, will share their fate. That's the answer."

"Not all the answer." Kléber turned him around gently until they faced the city, and pointed to the sky. "Perhaps I'm a little mad tonight; it seems to me the earth and air are filled with strange things. Do you see anything there?"

Clouds had veiled the moon, stopping her brilliant flood. Above the city hung a murky glow that vibrated, that moved in waves, that seemed instinct with life and motion. A reflection of torches, of lights in the streets, Porson declared.

"No." Kléber spoke so softly the sentries could not hear. "That's what you see; but I see something else. Just as you see a death-march ahead, while I see a march to victory—and each of us denies the other's vision. Look! I can see them as plainly as I see these camp-fires. Marching men, regiments, squadrons like waves! And all one, my friend, all of them beneath one flag. Not the tricolor; it is a flag I cannot distinguish. A legion, a great united corps, the legion of a dream—"

He broke off, face uplifted, staring. Then he sighed a little, and turned.

"You think I am a little touched in the head, *hein?*"

"I think you need a good sound sleep," said Porson dryly; and Kléber laughed.

"Very well; wait! At such a moment the heart speaks; repressed desires, hidden ambitions, secret thoughts. I trust you as I can trust no other man. Wait, then, and see! Perhaps I can have a destiny, a star, as well as that prating little Corsican. Good night, my friend. Sleep, if you can."

KLÉBER WAS gone into his tent. Porson went on to the camp of his own corps. The orders were to sleep until dawn, then march.

He moved among this Foreign Legion of his, talked with the men, did not attempt to hide the situation from them; they knew it anyway, and did not share the wild élan of the French.

Here were no veterans of the republican wars, but men who fought for an alien flag. Strapping blacks from Nubia, who had found under the tricolor not slavery but liberty, equality, fraternity. Copts, slim brown fellaheen who fingered unaccustomed muskets. Greeks, animated by age-old hatred of Turkish tyranny. Not a few deserters from Turkish regiments, mingled with Levantines, Mameluke warriors bred to arms, Italians, even Arabs.

PORSON AND his drill sergeants had welded these men into soldiers. Now they greeted him with brief words, with straining eyes, with a certain grimness he could well understand and share. Their families were in the citadel, yes; but for taking up arms against the Turk, they would be exterminated root and branch if the Turk won.

Nicolas Pappas, head of the Greek corps of fifteen hundred;

Ma'alem Yacoub, who had led his five hundred Copts through Upper Egypt under Desaix; Barthelemy, who commanded the Mamelukes and the 21st demi-brigade of blacks—these three met with Porson in his tent. They spoke frankly, freely, bluntly.

"My Colonel, we are alone," said the Greek, a massive, powerful man. "Not as one officer to another, but as one man to another, tell me what we must expect tomorrow."

"Death," said Porson quietly. He stuffed his pipe and lit it. "I have already told the commander that we shall lead the way. If you desire to let another corps have the place of honor—"

"Not I!" snapped Nicolas. "I answer for my men. That is all." He rose and strode out. Barthelemy gave Porson a twinkling glance, and came to his feet.

"Don't change your dispositions on my account, my Colonel," he said. "You'll find that my corps follow excellently where you lead, either here or in hell. Pleasant dreams!"

He too swaggered out. The dark Copt, Yacoub, shrugged slightly.

"By Allah," he said in Arabic, "what word can you give me for my men, effendi?"

"An invitation to help me loot the Turkish camp!"

Yacoub broke into a laugh, touched his forehead, and departed. Porson laid down his pipe and extinguished his little oil lamp, and slept....

Before dawn, in the darkness, the word was passed. The brigades formed in squares, each square surrounding light artillery loaded with grape alone; the guns were to be used only at close quarters, because powder was scarce. Kléber spoke to Porson; his orders were simple: Advance, and keep advancing. Ignore the cavalry, cut off the Janissaries whose camp was dead ahead, drive straight through at the Grand Vizier—and no halts.

No drums, no trumpets. Porson gave the word, and in the dawn-grayness the column moved out at a steady pace. The Turkish lines were almost within earshot. Over the plain rippled the tumultuous murmur of thousands wakening. A challenge went up, a *tambour* beat sudden alarm. Then, like a thunderbolt, the Legion was into the enemy's lines.

On and on, with a volley here, another there, with bayonets stabbing, with Leclerc and his cavalry slashing on the flanks; din and uproar rolled ahead, the massing Turkish regiments crumpling under the impact. Daylight, and as the ranks of Janissaries formed up, Porson and the Legion were into them. Cold steel here, a momentary pause, a surge—and then forward relentlessly, leaving the most dreaded fighting corps in the world to perish under the bayonets that followed.

As the sun rose, the little French array was completely lost to sight under thick powder-smoke drifting across the plain. The Janissaries and the entire Turkish vanguard were destroyed. Nasif Pasha, who commanded the immense cloud of Turkish cavalry, took for granted that this column would be overwhelmed by the main army, and sent out his orders. Away swept those regiments, spurring out and away for Cairo, and ere noon were hurling themselves upon the defenseless city in a carnival of pillage and massacre.

Kléber, ignorant of this, drove forward.

N O W T H E thrust became a battle. The Grand Vizier rolled back his lines and opened on the French column with his immense park of artillery; but already the French were upon him. Leclerc's dragoons slashed into the lines, and the Turkish gunners were sabered. The guns fell silent.

Kléber drove ahead with steady pace. As the day wore on, wave after wave of Turkish infantry came surging at the squares, to be met with a hail of grape, and then to break and vanish as the French bayonets went forward. Wave upon wave, advancing and shattering.

Desperately gathering what remained of his cavalry, the Grand Vizier hurled the squadrons forward in a furious charge. Grape met them as they thundered in, sundered and smashed their ranks. As they halted, Leclerc cut them up. As they rolled back, the French followed them, ever advancing, never pausing.

The blacks of the Legion tasted blood full deep; the Copts stood like veterans; the Greeks fought like devils. Porson was proud of his men this day.

Broken with the dying afternoon, the Grand Vizier saw his artillery lost, his cavalry smashed, his enormous army a wild rabble of men. Falling back, he attempted to rally his regiments; but Leclerc hit him with the dragoons; and Reynier, with the reserve brigade, hurtled into him.

WITH SUNSET, Kléber and his victorious squares occupied the camp of the enemy. There, amid fantastic luxury, these men who had gone since daybreak without food or drink, dropped in utter exhaustion.

After a little they began to pillage, to gorge themselves, to seize on powder and supplies. Here were stores of all kinds for the having. To Porson, it was like a dream, a soldier's dream come true. A wild frenzy of delight seized upon the whole army. The impossible had been accomplished. Ten thousand had shattered sixty thousand. But Kléber was not satisfied.

"Rest until midnight—then march on," he told his staff. "Four hours of rest, then continue. Otherwise, the Grand Vizier will reform his army at Belbeys; we began the work—we must finish it!"

He turned, startled. Amid the delirious rejoicing on all sides, a sudden silence began to spread and spread. Voices dropped. Men looked at one another in wild and terrible surmise. Kléber sprang to his feet and stood listening.

Across the night came steady pulsations: the distant mutter, the vibration, of cannon. Verdier—and the two thousand men who held Cairo's citadel!

Information was coming in. Prisoners began to talk. A frantic Copt, half mad with terror, arrived from Cairo on a foam-lathered horse, with the first definite word of Nasif Bey and the thousands of Turkish cavalry in the city.

"The city is taken; massacre is let loose!" he wailed. "They have killed all the wounded, assaulted the citadel, taken it; the populace is in revolt—"

THE GUNS muttered again, giving him the lie. Sudden panic seized on everyone. About Kléber pressed the staff; Reynier and the other generals urged instant return. He was adamant.

"We have beaten the Turkish army; now we must destroy it," rose his voice, calm and unshaken. "We must push straight forward to Alexandria and the delta, re-occupy all the forts, and win Egypt back at one stroke. General Lagrange, I confide Cairo to you. Take three brigades, and march.... Colonel Porson! At midnight your Legion will lead the advance on Belbeys."

Porson saluted, and in agony of mind sought out his own command. The frightful news had spread through the army. About him clustered his officers, his frantic men. Only the black troops slumbered. The others crowded upon him, demanding instant return. When he ordered an advance at midnight, there was instant flame.

"We've done enough, Citizen Colonel!" cried Nicolas Pappas hoarsely. "Now it's time to think of our wives. My men return to Cairo."

"And mine," added Yacoub. "Our brothers, our children, are being slaughtered there. Before God, have you no compassion, no human feeling for men whose wives and children are dying?"

Porson looked at them in the flickering firelight. He was very pale, and drops of sweat ran down his lean cheeks.

"Three brigades are returning to the city; we are advancing," he said. "If your wives are there, so is mine. If your children are there, so is my child there. We cannot save them now. But if they are dead, we can avenge them. Be ready to march at midnight. The Legion leads the van."

They stared at him.... He had spoken the truth. His own wife and child were back there in the hell of massacre. If they were in agony, so was he. Suddenly the powerful Greek turned to him, embraced him, and emitted a roar.

"Where you go, we go!"

"You are right, Citizen Colonel!" Ma'alem Yacoub seized his hand and pressed it. "Forgive my words. Kill! March, comrades—march and kill!"

And at midnight the army pressed on. Morning found the town of Belbeys ahead, with the Grand Vizier and his reformed regiments making a stand. The Legion led the storm: a Legion not of men but of fiends, stopping for nothing, slaying with the cold steel, breaking the Turkish ranks, sweeping all irresistibly before them.

Through the day the battle endured, until Belbeys was taken, and again the Grand Vizier fell back with his broken remnants, thirty thousand strong. A brief halt, and through the night Kléber pressed on. With daybreak, he fell upon the Turks, who had rallied for the last time.

Now all was confusion; the attack was rapid, counting no costs. Kléber and his hussars rode over the low sand-hills and slap into a horde of Turkish cavalry. The hussars were broken. Reynier sent a regiment of dragoons to the rescue, but not before Kléber was wounded and half his men dead.

This was the finish. The Grand Vizier and five hundred horsemen spurred for Syria, and reached it. Twelve thousand Turks withdrew in a body; Belliard and two regiments destroyed them. The wild desert Arabs, who hated Turks only one degree less than Christians, swooped down in clouds and gave no quarter. The army of Turkey was gone.

Then, with all Egypt won again, Kléber turned upon Cairo, where Verdier still held out in the citadel, and gave that rebellious city a lesson of fire and sword. Loot, vast supplies, powder, ammunition—suddenly Kléber, the idol of his army, found himself powerful and strong beyond all measure.

ONE DAY while the shattered city was being repaired, Porson and Leila and their child sat with Kléber in a Mameluke palace beside the rolling Nile flood. Kléber loved to play with the child; and to Porson he could unbosom himself as to no other person. Noon was approaching. Kléber had just come in from a review of the Legion, and was in high spirits, his luminous eyes agleam with energy.

"Hans, your Legion has given me a great dream," he said abruptly. "For you, for Egypt, for myself. As you know, with Bonaparte in control of France, my safest place is here. And we're utterly cut off from home."

He paused, and Porson nodded. So far as Kléber was concerned, any return to France was impossible; Bonaparte was bitterly jealous of him.

"The army has come to like Egypt—after our victory," went on Kléber dryly. "I like Egypt. And Egypt belongs to us. We've no more to fear from the Turks. A small English expedition is coming from India; we can destroy it. Now, Hans, I've been talking to the army and others. Your Legion has shown me what to do. We have the nucleus of such a Foreign Legion as the world has never seen! A native army, officered by French, with enough of our men to form a solid backbone. Instead of separate corps of blacks, Greeks, Mamelukes and so on, we'll form a single corps—a vast Foreign Legion inured to the sun, to the climate, to everything! There's a dream for you—and Egypt ours!"

In those blazing indomitable eyes Porson read the truth.

"The Just Sultan—that's what the natives call you. And now you translate the title into fact, eh? Egypt is ours, yes; you mean to keep it?"

"Yes," said Kléber in a deep voice.

"As Bonaparte has seized France, you'll seize Egypt—good! Will the army consent?"

"The army will consent," Kléber replied. "I've sounded out some of the generals; some I'll send back to France, with any men who want to return. Among the others, I'll divide up all Egypt. The thing will work. Those who stay with me will have something to fight for—an empire worth fighting for, by heaven! The Army of Egypt passes. The Foreign Legion remains: the Legion, itself a vast army, with you at its head. You've shown us how such men can fight when properly led. Good! Such a Legion will be invincible. I have five thousand Mamelukes ready to join the ranks tomorrow. With French officers, Hans—you see?"

"I see," Porson said slowly. "I see a dream Legion, Kléber, a dream empire; it has but one drawback. With you at its head, all things are possible. But if anything happened to you, there's not one other man who could take your place."

Kléber broke into a laugh and rose.

"No fear! Nothing's going to happen to me. Draw up your plans, talk with Nicolas Pappas and the others; make the scheme, mind you, a vast Legion to welcome all creeds and colors of men. By heaven, we'll form a new country here, a new nation! We'll have a fighting machine that can smash any invasion, a country reconstructed, born again! Why, the horizon is illimitable! A horizon of glory, my friend! *Au revoir.* I must meet the others at Headquarters for luncheon. You'll come?"

Porson shook his head; and in that shake of the head spelled destiny. For if he had gone to luncheon with Kléber—

THE VOICE of our enchanter fell silent; Casey looked at Kramer; and we all looked at the dark, powerful man who had made us vision that ancestor of his and the dreams and glory of a forgotten campaign.

It was Casey who spoke out.

"Aw, hell! There wasn't any such Legion formed, Porson?"

"No." And Porson smiled slightly. "An hour after that talk beside the river, Kléber was struck down by the hand of an assassin; and all the glory of life had passed over the horizon. There, my friends, is the story of the first Foreign Legion, and the story of the Legion of a dream that never came to pass."

"Ha!" exclaimed Kramer, his eyes shining. "I'd like to have been there, me—back in that campaign! I never heard of it before. You were right, Porson, you were right; here's to the glory of that first Legion, the genesis of our own corps!"

His glass came up. The others came up, clinked, clinked again.

"Vive la Légion!"

A TOUCH OF SUN

*"A Touch of Sun" is not literal history, but a story of the
old Foreign Legion flaming with the actuality of battle.*

I RAN INTO a queer birthday party the other evening;
it was the birthday of the Foreign Legion.

My three cronies had added a fourth to their number for the
occasion. Red-haired, hot-tongued Casey, the saturnine Kramer,
and the dark Alsatian Porson gravely introduced me to a new
arrival named Falkenheim. He was a sad-eyed, inconspicuous-
looking man, but it turned out that he had served through the
campaigns of Morocco, Madagascar and the Sahara; he was
older than the others.

"Falkenheim has picked up the most devilish interesting
thing you ever saw," said Kramer. "However, we'll come to that
later. *Anciens* of the Legion, attention! This is the ninth day of
March. I shall read you the decree of Louis Philippe, King of
the French, issued in the year 1831—"

Although not a Légionnaire, I came to my feet as the others
stood stiffly at attention. Kramer, in a dry parade voice, read off
the decree which had organized the corps which for over a
hundred years has been rather loosely termed the Foreign
Legion:

" 'We have ordered and ordained as follows: First, a legion
composed of foreigners will be formed. This legion will take
the name of Foreign Legion—' "

When Kramer had ceased reading, he reached down to his
glass and lifted it.

"My friends! I give you the corps whom we respect, whose

traditions we have upheld, whose name we have been proud to bear!"

The glasses clinked. All four men spoke out as one:

"Vive la Légion!"

We dropped into our chairs, relaxed and made merry, with a welter of talk. Our new friend, Falkenheim, had plenty on the ball; he proved to be some sort of nobleman, but nobody asked any questions, and he volunteered little about himself.

"That old original Legion," spoke up Casey, "must have been a hell of a corps, from all I've heard! They tell some queer stories about it, back at headquarters."

"They may well!" And Falkenheim grinned. "When the battalion disembarked at Algiers, thirty-five men deserted the first day. A few days later an entire company got drunk and mutinied. They court-martialed two and put the rest of the company in jail. It was something to see!"

"You talk as though you'd been there," Kramer observed.

"I was."

Casey stared at him, wide-eyed.

"What are you, the Wandering Jew or something? You're nuts!"

"A touch of sun, *cafard*, the madhouse blues!" Falkenheim chuckled. "Maybe. Anyhow, the Legion back in those days would have made us blink, I can tell you! There were seven battalions. The First had mostly Swiss veterans; the Second and Third had Swiss and Germans. Spanish were in the Fourth, guerrilla fighters. Italians in the Fifth, and Belgians and Dutch in the Sixth; the Seventh was made up of Poles, veterans of the recent Polish revolution. They segregated 'em in those days."

"And the uniforms!" chipped in Porson. "They had red kepis a foot high."

"Shako—that was the name for it," said Falkenheim with a nod. "With a star on the front. That was about the only mark of the Legion. And the knapsacks—good Lord! In column, they even had to pack firewood. The first-class privates had sabers, and they had muskets of the 1822 model. However, they had so much sunstroke that they took to sun-helmets, and the rats ate the old red shakos."

"Who told you?" shot out Casey, scowling at him.

"Pan-Andrei. He used to be a prince in Poland, but he ended up in the Polish battalion. The French held just the fringe of Algeria then, and the Legion was scattered all over the place, marching and building and fighting, and Abdel Kadir started out to polish them all off. That was in 1835—"

"Is this a history lecture?" put in Casey.

"No, it isn't," spoke up Kramer with a touch of reproof in his voice and eye. "It's a story out of the Legion's book, my friend; an unpublished one, at that. What do you think Falkenheim has found? He got it down in Algeria years ago and kept it. It's the diary or notebook of this fellow Pan Andrei of the original Legion!"

"Is it about the Legion?" questioned Porson.

"No, it's not—that is, it's got a reverse English twist to it," Kramer said. "But I'm going to ask Falkenheim to read the thing to us. I tell you, it's remarkable! This Pole brings the old days to life; he's vivid. Open it up, Falkenheim, and don't pay any attention to these rascals—"

There was a warm exchange of compliments in the slang of the Legion, under cover of which Falkenheim dragged into sight a fat bundle of spotty Arabic paper sheets, covered with hen-tracks. Polish writing, he said; he could read it, and he did.

PAN ANDREI was the name this prince had taken, probably his own name. As our friend translated, it was plain to be seen that Pan Andrei was no hero of romance. His Polish battalion was stationed at Oran; and after two years of helping the French hang on by their toenails to the strip of Algerian coast, Pan Andrei went all to the bad.

He must have been a crack soldier at the beginning, for he rose to be a *sous-lieutenant* and was saber champion of the corps. Probably a touch of sun hit him, for he went down like a shot and hit the bottom. These are inferences only. One gathers that he had met the girl Khatifa and her father Murad Bey while he was still in the service. Probably they had assisted him to get away.

WHAT A fascinating, terrible human document it was, from first to last!

Pan Andrei broke jail, killed an Arab guard, and got away. Once in safety, he sat down and occupied his time by writing, among other things; his first words were frightful curses on the French. He had come to hate them with a bitter, virulent hatred. From a deserter, he became a renegade, then a mortal enemy— this man whose brain had been touched by the sun.

The three of them made a fascinating picture there in Mascara, beyond the reach of France. The girl, lissome and slender, too slender for beauty in Arab eyes, utterly devoted to her husband and father; a great heart, this girl had! Murad Bey, the stout Turkish soldier, a fighter like all his race. Algeria had been wrested from Turkish hands, and the remnants of Turkish soldiery were scattered among the Arabs, helping their determined resistance to French rule. Murad Bey, a strapping fellow with keen eyes and handsome features, looked at his new son-in-law and smiled.

"So you have no regrets that life begins all over for you?"

Pan Andrei shook his head, glanced at his wife, and his wild gray eyes softened. He was lean and hard, mustached, sunburned to Arab hue. He spoke Arabic fluently. With his thin curved nostrils, his harshly handsome features, he even looked like an Arab.

"It is my third life, Murad," he said quietly. "Far away in Poland, I lost everything, thanks to Russia. I began again in Algeria; there, under the French, I lost everything once more.

Now I've begun afresh. With Khatifa's love, I've found a new life that shall endure."

The girl placed a lump of charcoal on the bowl of a water-pipe, handed one of the tubes to her father, gave the other to Pan Andrei. He had taken an Arabic name, that of El Mohdi, the Well-conducted; but it was only used by the Arabs.

"More than love," she said, a flash in her liquid eyes. "We're friends, comrades, soldiers! With war all around us, with rapine and destruction everywhere, I'm not sitting at home and watching what happens. Father, Andrei says I may join his squadron."

Murad Bey pulled at the pipestem.

"The event is in the hand of Allah," he observed. "Women of the Osmanli race can fight. These Arabs do not like to see their women in the field. I do not like to see you, my daughter, trying to fight like a man. But it is as your husband says."

"I drop the *alif* from my name, and become Khatif," she replied. "I serve Andrei as an aide. And in the garb of a man. Who will know the truth?"

"If he has agreed, it is settled," said Murad Bey. "After all, should husband and wife be separated?"

Pan Andrei smiled at the girl, a lean hawk-smile, wonderful to see. She was part of his own terrible hatred of the French, she and all these people around. And he, in his snow-white burnouse, was about to bear witness with the sword to this hatred.

Under the ancient crumbled walls of Mascara, Abdel Kadir's capital, Pan Andrei wheeled with his desert horsemen. He taught them drill and saber play; and because no two men could stand before that glittering saber of his, they feared and respected him. At his side was always the aide, Khatif, clad in Touareg burnouse and wearing a black Touareg *litham* or face-cloth.

The Arab chieftains came and saw, and marveled. Frequently the fierce, impetuous Abdel Kadir himself, hope of the whole Arab race, watched the drill. If any suspected the identity of

*His way was blocked, an officer halting him.
"You're the trader who just arrived?" said the
officer bruskly. "You're wanted at headquarters
at once." El Mohdi shrugged. "Who am I,
to understand the speech of infidels?"*

Khatif, as some must have suspected, no word was said. After all, she was the daughter of a Turk; it was none of their business. And in these days of death and raids and rapine, women fought here and there with the men.

Raids everywhere, as French fingers crept out across the land, along the coast, into the valleys. With spring, the name of El Mohdi began to be noised abroad. His mobile squadron struck, and struck again, and was gone. Parties of French workers, road-builders, soldiers, felt his saber. His squadron met a company of Arabs in the French service and slew the last man of them. The French began to curse his very name, but none of them knew that he was Andrei, the deserter from the Legion.

As a soldier, he was superb. As a husband, he was devoted; his love for Khatifa was an absorbing, perfect thing. But as a man—the Arab sun in touching his brain had made of him an Arab. He aided Murad Bey in training a force of twelve hundred infantry. Abdel Kadir was gathering an army; the French were to be destroyed. This lean, hard man who radiated vigor and energy was the life and soul of the Arabs. He showed Abdel Kadir how to strike the detached garrisons and move on Algiers. The Turkish engineers supported his words. The plan of campaign was perfected. Murad Bey's regiment, composed largely of Turks, became a deadly instrument.

"Attack Oran first, cut it off, then move along the coast!" said El Mohdi. So it was agreed. Some one must go into Oran, learn the dispositions there. Spies? Few could be trusted. French gold was everywhere.

"I'll go." Bearded to the lips, gray eyes grim, El Mohdi spoke up. "By Allah, French gold cannot burn my fingers! Also, I speak French."

He was the ideal person; but he did not go alone. By his side rode Khatifa, now in woman's garb. They took the brown road into Oran with a caravan of camels, laden with trading-goods from the south. Every man was picked for his fidelity.

They came into the city, where the hills run down into the

*"To the east is a defile
through the hills—"*

sea, and the long harbor opened. El Mohdi's papers were all in order, taken from other traders detained in Mascara. He passed the French outposts without a hitch. Ahead, in the street, a file of men were approaching, a column. He threw up his hand, halted his men, his camels, his wife. He sat his saddle, staring at the files swinging down at him.

Grenadiers of the Legion, as the scarlet epaulets testified; queer stuffed-looking figures, with their cummerbunds or cholera-belts carefully inside their trousers, being considered in those days as underwear. Knapsacks piled high and topped with the enormous tent that would shelter two men. Tin canteens a-swing, muskets at the carry.

The hawk-face of El Mohdi tensed and hardened. No need to look for the number of the battalion. A Polish marching song reached him, voices lilting roughly under the hot sun. The Polish battalion! He knew every one of those approaching men. He sat his saddle, gray eyes shrouded under the hood of his white *jellab.* They looked up at him, looked at Khatifa on her camel, sang out hearty greetings and gay jests, and marched on past. Not one of them dreamed that this bearded Arab was the Pan Andrei they had known.

El Mohdi gestured, and led his little caravan on to the great *suk,* the marketplace for caravans.

Leaving his men to unload and park the animals, he swung off through the streets with Khatifa follow-

"Pan Andrei!" A gasp broke from Lébert.

ing just behind him like a dutiful desert wife, shrouded to the eyes. His brain was busy with thoughts of that Polish battalion marching out—whither? As he drifted about the streets, he was aware of bugles lilting, of other battalions on the move. The entire Fifth of the Legion, the Italians, French regiments as well.

His way was blocked. An officer, two Arabs in the French service, halting him.

"You're the trader who just arrived? We've been looking for you," said the officer briskly. "You're wanted at headquarters at once."

El Mohdi—who was not using this too well known name—shrugged and looked at the two Arabs.

"As God liveth, who am I to understand the speech of the infidels? What does the man say?"

The Arabs explained. Upon learning that a trader had just arrived, the general wanted to question him personally about the roads and other matters. El Mohdi gave Khatifa a curt order.

"Go back. Tell the men not to unpack, for we leave ere sunset. There is no market for the goods here; I shall go on to Mostaganem."

He nodded to the two Arabs and fell in behind the officer. They led him through the hot town and on up to the Kasbah—that great castle which the Spaniards had built above the city, when they sojourned here. Impassive, veiling his knowledge of French speech and ways, El Mohdi strode along silent; but his gray eyes probed everywhere.

Something was up—something big. Troops in movement, aides dashing about, officers in campaign kit. He was conducted past the sentinels and on into the pleasant old courtyard, where fountains and orange-trees lightened the heat of early June.

At one side a gay group of officers and ladies were talking. He was led to the far end, where General Trezel and a number of his staff were conferring about a table loaded with maps. They looked up, eying him sharply. He remained impassive, eyes downcast. He could have named each one of those officers. Trezel was an old army man, a stubborn fighter, but not at all overequipped with brains.

O N E   O F the officers who spoke fluent Arabic, took him in charge.

"You came here from the south, from Mascara?"

"From the Sahara, effendi. I passed through Mascara."

"By which road?" said the officer in French. El Mohdi's face remained blank. There was a smile; naturally, the fellow spoke no French and had not fallen into the trap. The officer repeated his query in Arabic. El Mohdi replied at once, described the condition of the roads, and made frank answers to all questions. Then a shock reached him as General Trezel, turning to speak with an aide, gave brusque directions.

"The artillery are ready? Then give the orders. Remember, we're supposed to be marching for Arzew. I'll follow with the cavalry. We'll march at dawn and catch up with the army by noon."

El Mohdi with difficulty paid attention to the interpreter. Marching for Arzew, yes! Then a swift face-about, and down the other ieg of the triangle for Mascara. It was a forced march, an attack on Abdel Kadir—

"You came through Mascara," the officer was demanding. "How many men has Abdel Kadir there? Are they in the city or camped outside?"

"Outside, effendi." El Mohdi, by this question, knew he had hit upon the truth. He lied, swiftly and promptly, underestimating the force of Abdel Kadir by a third. "He has less than eight thousand men in all."

"Their condition?"

"It is not good, effendi. Many of his chiefs are leaving him. He has very little powder. The Berber troops are going home to get in their spring crops."

When this was translated, the general emitted a snort.

"So? With twenty-five hundred men, I'll guarantee to wipe the rascal out. Ask him about that fellow El Mohdi—Wait! Here come the ladies. Hold him."

El Mohdi stood aside, as the ladies and officers bore down on the general. Fine ladies, one or two of them just from France; and one among them not from France at all.

Upon the impassive El Mohdi, dark bearded features shielded under his white wool hood, fell a touch of wizardry; he wandered in the aisles of dream, standing as though paralyzed. So indeed he was. Her face, her face! And her voice, as she stood in talk with the general. Not six feet from him! Yes, she was

real. And now Trezel was bowing to her, speaking to her, so-
licitude in his manner.

"Madame la Princesse, I am deeply grieved that we can give
no news of your husband. The report has just reached me—"

"You mean, he is dead?" asked the Princess calmly.

"We do not know. He escaped from prison and disappeared.
He must, of course, be dead. He was known only as Andrei, or
Pan Andrei. I regret to say that it is believed he was affected by
the sun—"

By the sun! El Mohdi strangled a wild and insane impulse
to break out laughing. His wife, his princess, coming here in
search of him! And they had told him she was dead. Those
Russians who wounded and captured him and exiled him!

"Perhaps," she was saying quietly, "if the word is published
that the Czar has granted him a pardon and restored his estates,
it would reach him. I have, as you know, seen the King in Paris,
and have obtained his discharge from the French service. But
I must remain here until I'm certain whether he's dead or alive."

General Trezel bowed again, murmuring compliments on
the devotion of this splendid wife. But El Mohdi could riot
restrain the smile that curved his grim lips—a smile sardonic,
thin, disillusioned. She had let out the secret with those words.
Not for love of him, as the French thought; no, he knew better!
This cold, proud woman had no heart, no love: merely ambition.
If he was dead, the estates were hers. If he was not dead—

"I shall exert every effort, Your Highness," said the general
earnestly. "I am leaving at dawn to crush this rebel Abdel Kadir,
push our conquest to the south, and so master the trade and
caravan routes. However, I shall this evening issue orders, and
the moment any news of your husband the prince is obtained,
it shall be imparted to you. Meantime, you will allow me the
honor of placing suitable quarters at your disposal—"

She was very lovely, very cool, very calm. The general himself
escorted her to the farther doorway. As they passed, her rather

haughty glance fell upon the figure of El Mohdi, crossed with his gray-slitted eyes, swept on without recognition.

HE RELAXED; a slow, deep breath escaped him. Pardoned by the Czar, his estates restored, his rank of prince—

He laughed a little in his beard, and the dream passed. What of all that? It was gone; it was another life that had ended years ago. Prince Andrei had died, back there; this cold, haughty, cruel wife of his was not seeking him for love, but for knowledge of his fate and her own future. Probably in love with Orloff still, eh? Well, Orloff was welcome to her. Pan Andrei, the Legionnaire, was dead also.

Allah! What a contrast between that woman, a princess, and this Turkish girl who loved him, rode with him, was going to bear him a child within a few more months! Here was life— warfare, hard riding, privation, and love that sweetened it all. Here was the proper destiny for a man; not back there on the estates of a prince.

The general returned. The interpreter officer beckoned El Mohdi.

"Tell us about the leader of the rebels called El Mohdi. Where is he?"

"With Abdel Kadir, effendi."

"How many men are with him?"

"He has three squadrons of cavalry, effendi. They do not like him; they nearly killed him two weeks ago. I saw him as I came through the camp. He was badly hurt."

"Who is he? Where from?"

An officer had come into the courtyard, had saluted, was waiting. El Mohdi knew him, started slightly. Captain Lébert, of his own old company, the First of the Polish battalion. He responded almost mechanically to the questions.

"They say, effendi, that this man is a Turk from Egypt who has trained these squadrons with hard discipline. That is why they do not like him."

The Arab horsemen broke and rode off. Another
charge—to bring up against bayonets, this time.

"Ah, at last we're learning something about the fellow!" exclaimed the general. "So, Captain Lébert! My messenger caught
you!"

Lébert saluted. "Just beyond the gates, my general. I returned
at once."

"A curious thing, Lébert. About this fellow they called Pan
Andrei, of your company. You remember him?"

"Very well, my general."

"His wife is here. Madame la Princesse—the man was a
prince in Russia, you comprehend? I thought you might have
picked up something about him."

"I heard of her arrival just before we marched, this afternoon."
Captain Lébert glanced at El Mohdi, and the glance was like
a swordstroke. "May I inquire, my general, whether the man
Andrei is still wanted as a deserter?"

"No. His Majesty has been pleased to grant his discharge
and cancel his record," said the general. He turned to the in-

terpreter. "By the way! Ask this fellow if he heard anything of such a man among the rebels. Describe Andrei."

El Mohdi listened impassively to a good deal of talk about Pan Andrei, and shook his head.

"There is no such man in the rebel camp, or I would have seen him."

CAPTAIN LÉBERT spoke. "Who is this Arab?"

"A trader who just came up from the south. We've gained quite a bit of information about him," said the general. "That's all, I think; let the fellow go."

"With your permission," said Lébert, "I'd like to ask him a few questions about the water-holes beyond Arzew, my general. I can speak quite a bit of Arabic, and if I accompany him, might worm some information from him. He speaks no French?"

"Not a word." Trezel laughed. "Go ahead, by all means, and

luck to you! Now, Colonel Oudinot, you'll command the cavalry when we leave—"

El Mohdi and Captain Lébert walked out together, passed the Kasbah gate and the sentinels in silence, and looked down over the deep, narrow valley stretching below the walls and around the town.

"Well, *mon ami?*" said Lébert quietly. "It appears there's nothing against you, and a princely title waiting for you back in Russia. It wasn't my place to say anything in the face of your private desires—"

El Mohdi laughed harshly. "No, damn you! I will say for you that you're a gentleman, Lébert. Until today I've hated you bitterly. You rode the devil out of me when I was under you. However—let it pass. I thank you for keeping silence."

Lébert inspected him keenly.

"I'm not so sure I did right; but let it pass. I rode you, did I? Yes, and there was a devil in you. That damned touch of sun! It turned you from the finest soldier in the outfit, to the worst damned botch of a man I ever saw."

"Perhaps," said El Mohdi. "At all events, I'm happy."

"Your destiny is your own to choose," said Lébert, and turned away.

EL MOHDI slapped his way down to the town and the market place, his slippers raising the dust; he hitched the *jellab* over his shoulders as he walked, in true Arab style. So Madame la Princesse waited for news of him, eh?

Let her wait and be hanged, then; she'd get none! Pan Andrei was dead, but she'd get no confirmation of his death. Better still, in another fortnight he might send her a letter as visible proof that he was alive. How that would burn her cold treacherous heart! Bah—let the woman alone. Let the past go. Let the dead bury their dead. He was El Mohdi now; he had everything in the world Pan Andrei lacked. So be satisfied with it! And now to glut his hatred of the French, follow his new destiny behind Abdel Kadir, sweep them out of Algeria!

It was close to sunset when he came to where Khatifa and his men waited. Good! The animals still loaded, waiting; no one missing. An eager light in his eyes, he joined her, beckoned the chief of his men, and spoke rapidly.

"We must leave at once. I've learned everything. Trezel marches against the chief—he has only twenty-five hundred in all. Get off! Once outside town, abandon the camels, take the horses and push on at all speed."

They pushed out into the sunset, out into the starry spaces, out past the olive groves and the marching files of the French battalions.... Presently, safely away, the camels were abandoned to the care of one man, and El Mohdi pushed the horses on, with Khatifa spurring at his side, and a wild eagerness flaming in his heart.

They thundered on and on, pushing the foam-lathered horses past the salt lakes, on toward Mascara. Almost a triangle, those three towns—Oran and Arzew on the seacoast, Mascara south in the Berber country. Behind, the stroke was being launched; but now it would fail....

A patrol of Arab cavalry in the dawn. A quick exchange of horses. El Mohdi and Khatifa spurred on for Mascara.

There he poured out his tidings to Abdel Kadir and Murad Bey and the other chiefs. His words set a spark to them all.

"Twenty-five hundred men, no more. Meet them at tomorrow's dawn, destroy them! Oran is left defenseless. Take the city. Turn and sweep for Algiers—and destiny is yours!"

"If Allah wills," said Abdel Kadir piously; but he was in a glow. "Rest for an hour, then lead your squadrons. Ride north to the forest called the Forest of Mulai Ismail; occupy it. I follow with the cavalry. Murad Bey, march with the infantry as soon as the sun goes down a little—"

An hour's rest. Khatifa lay faint and weak, exhausted by that pounding ride. El Mohdi looked into the eyes of Murad Bey.

"She must remain here; in her condition—well, I can take no chances. You agree? Good. She has done too much already.

During these next months, she must rest, she must think only of the child."

One last embrace they exchanged; then he was gone....

THE SQUADRONS, his squadrons, swept out and spurred hard. Behind, more slowly, came the infantry, slogging along beneath the June sun. Night found El Mohdi posted along the fringe of trees, his scouts out. Toward morning two of them rode in. The French were coming, were making short halts, forced marches.

The infantry came in and dropped exhausted. Abdel Kadir, with his cloud of Arab horsemen, arrived. With the dawn, El Mohdi rode out, led his squadrons along the road, cut up a few advance posts of French cavalry, and drew back.

SUNRISE FOUND the French army at hand. Trezel did not hesitate, but sent Oudinot with the cavalry ahead to clear the road. The main force of Abdel Kadir remained out of sight. El Mohdi, his white burnous thrown aside, his saber flashing, held his men in leash until the dragoons and hussars were in among the trees—then he launched them.

"Allah!"

WITH THE yell, they struck. Carbines banged out; the French cavalry, unable to maneuver in this forest, wheeled vainly. The first squadron struck that glittering mass. The second hit it from the flank. El Mohdi led his third squadron in at the gallop. *"Allah!"* they cried. And the French lines crumpled.

Colonel Oudinot vainly strove to rally his men. El Mohdi sought him out, found him, crossed sabers with him; Oudinot died there. That flashing saber brought death through the French ranks. The crumpled ranks took to flight.

Artillery opened. Trezel flung forward his brigades, covered the retreat of his cavalry, and under a hail of grape the charge of the Arabs ceased. Murad Bey brought his infantry forward, but already Trezel bugles were blowing the retreat. The French had carried no provisions on this forced march, had anticipated no pitched battle; and suddenly finding themselves so vastly outnumbered, they partook of discretion.

El Mohdi sought out the green banner of Abdel Kadir, flung himself from his steaming horse, spoke swiftly to the chief. Bare-headed, splashed with blood, he was a figure of savage energy.

"They must retreat through the defiles at Macta—send me there! I can ride around them, reach the defiles first. Every horse

will carry double. You follow; I'll guarantee to hold them until you come up and strike."

"Allah aid you! Go!"

There was fast mounting and riding. Those Arabs knew every foot of ground. The horses carrying double, El Mohdi skirted the retreating French column, encumbered by their train of baggage and their wounded in wagons. He came ere noon to the higher ground, where the road wound through deep defiles toward Arzew, and took post. If the French were silly enough to follow the road, instead of taking some other way, they were lost.

His scouts brought in the word; they were coming. He waited grimly, his men disposed among the trees, along the heights. The heat was terrific, but he paid no heed. Giddiness seized him. Some one would have given him a burnous, to shield him from the sun, but he refused curtly. The columns were coming— walking straight into the trap!

They came; and the fierce hatred of El Mohdi was assuaged in blood as powder-smoke ringed the upper ground. A company of infantry came charging up to clear the way, and fell back shattered.

Then hell broke loose in those defiles. Abdel Kadir and his horsemen came up, burst upon the rear ranks, smashed them, captured the wagons, massacred the wounded.

The unhappy column reeled back from those defiles of death. The artillery at last came into action. The Arab horsemen, unable to stand against the guns, broke and rode off. Another charge and another—to bring up against bayonets this time. The companies of the Legion, the Italians and the Poles, stood like living walls to keep Arab sabers from the disorganized mass that had been an army. They, and the guns, broke those charges.

The Arabs drew off and waited. Night would finish it surely and certainly. The disorganized huddle of troops dared not attempt the defiles again, and did not know any other way to go. The guides had fled. Only those two battalions of the Legion stood like a wall, waiting. Abdel Kadir drew back his men, until night should come down.

EL MOHDI sat up and blinked at the afternoon sunlight. He had failed there on the hillside. Slowly he came to his feet and examined himself. No hurt; but his head ached intolerably, he was dizzy and weak. Ah! The sun, of course. He passed a hand over his head, shaven in Arab fashion except for one long lock of hair.

He was alone; his men had retired. He had not been missed, or else he was thought dead. No matter.

Below was the French camp. Order was coming out of chaos. The lines nearest him were forming a bivouac, throwing up an earthwork. He stared incredulously; the fools were stopping here! The minute night came, the Arabs would be upon them. The artillery would be useless then—

A sound of singing pierced into his brain, and he stood as though frozen. Polish voices, Polish songs—the songs he himself had sung with these veterans, during the pitiful and hopeless revolution, years ago! Those bitter days of struggling, of fighting through utter cruel disaster, all swept back on him in an instant.

He was Pan Andrei again, of a sudden—the impulsive, sentimental, illogical Polish spirit in him leaped to life. The army of France was nothing; the new life and future he had carved out, was forgotten. There before him were faces of men he knew, Poles with whom he had fought far in the north, comrades who had sought liberty in vain beside him. Brothers in exile. They mattered; nothing else did.

Scarcely aware of what he did, he found himself staggering toward those lines. The Polish voices, the simple old folk-songs he had learned as a child, were ringing through his brain. Those country-men of his must not die....

The voices fell into silence at sight of this figure reeling toward the lines, this blood-splashed Arab. An officer stepped out with curt demand. Pan Andrei halted, and a queer, hoarse laugh broke from him.

"Mon capitaine!" He stiffened in salute. "Pan Andrei—reporting. Two miles to the east, *mon capitaine,* is a wide defile through the hills. The enemy have not occupied it. The cavalry may advance and seize it. You can march at once and reach it before sunset—"

"Pan Andrei!"

A gasp of recognition broke from Captain Lébert; a joyous eager shout went rippling up from the men of the Polish battalion.

But Pan Andrei heard it not.

He heard nothing at all, for he had quietly crumpled up and fallen on his face. And what was left of the army, went on to safety....

There ended the story as Falkenheim read it off to us. With a gesture of finality, he shoved away the bundle of papers, and reached for his glass, and drank. We sat staring at him, wrapped up in the scenes he had painted with the brilliant sunlit colors of Algeria, until Porson spoke up.

"Yes, I've heard something about that disaster. The French don't play it up, of course—"

"Hey! Look here!" Casey, who had been scratching his red thatch and frowning, suddenly exploded in words. "How could that guy Andrei put all that stuff into his diary, will you tell me? About how he died, and all?"

Falkenheim regarded him with a quiet, shrewd smile.

"Perhaps I put that in myself, *mon ami.* At all events, that's what happened. A touch of sun—it does queer things."

"Right you are," Kramer assented, with a curt nod. "A damned human touch to it, there. Remember how that Swiss chap deserted from the Second Regiment in the Saharan campaign, got sunstroke, and came marching into headquarters all by himself, thinking he was with the column? Yes, the sun does some queer things."

Porson was refilling the glasses.

"What I'd like to know," he intervened quietly, "is what became of Andrei's wife, and the expected child."

Kramer leaned forward, and gave him a deep, dark glance.

"That question, or one like unto it," he said with bitter gravity, "has wrung the heart of many a Legionnaire within the past hundred years—and seldom or never does it ever receive an answer.... Well, comrades—"

The other glasses lifted to clink against his.

"Vive la Légion!"

THE LEGION IN SPAIN

"The Legion in Spain" sets forth a stirring drama of this famous fighting force in the war-torn Spain of 1835.

THAT CRABBED and old Spanish mountaineer Gaspenjo with his white hair and wrinkled face, could certainly curse; and the language furthered his aims. The old scoundrel was guiding me over the mountains of Catalonia, for a fat fee. The revolution was just then breaking, and I wanted to get out; and Gaspenjo was getting me out. He was old, but agile as his tongue, and I was rather surprised to find that he possessed not only the traditional Spanish pride, but a certain amount of education and culture. Uncouth as he was, he knew his history like a book.

"And why not?" he said, on the day we rode up to the lonely bleak mountain hut that he called home. We were to break our journey there. "My family, señor, have shared in this history of ours. A hundred years ago, when things in Spain were almost exactly as they are today, my father and his brother were in the thick of it."

"Your father?" I repeated. "A hundred years ago? That's stretching it."

"No," he said gravely. "I am not young; my father was young then. I'll show you his picture presently. He was in the French army, in the Foreign Legion. The Legion kept its name in Spain, you know, even if it was only a regiment without a flag."

This tiny detail showed his real knowledge. Curiously enough, the Foreign Legion ceased to be part of the French Army in 1835, when it was loaned *en masse* to Queen Isabella, to help defend her throne against the Carlists. And it had no flag, for its regimental *drapeau* was taken back to Paris when it left Algiers for Spain....

We rode on to the stone hut. No one was there; old Gaspenjo lived alone. The one big room inside was smelly but comfortable; and before darkness closed down, Gaspenjo had cooked an amazingly good meal over the corner fireplace. His wine was truly admirable. We ate, drank, smoked and relaxed.

"A hundred years ago," he said musingly, "and the situation about what it is today. Don Carlos trying for the throne, against the child Isabella; and red war without quarter. Father against son, brother against brother. My father was in the Legion, though his only brother was with the Carlists."

"What got your father into the Legion?" I asked curiously.

Gaspenjo shrugged.

"He enlisted in Algeria—there was a Spanish battalion then. Every battalion was a nationality; Spanish, Polish, Belgian and so on. But Colonel Bernelle, who brought the Legion here, broke all that up; and a good thing too. He mixed up all the nationalities except the Poles, and formed them into three squadrons of lancers. I tell you, those Legionnaires did some fighting in Spain! Over four thousand came from Algiers, and only five hundred went back."

HE STARED into the fire, his seamed, wrinkled old features wreathed by smoke as it issued from his lips.

"My father was back in his own country. The Legion was fighting all over this hill-country against the Army of Navarre, the Carlists; it was like home to him. Nobody knew he was here. He had run away after a duel, you see. It was about a girl, as usual. And now he was back, older and different, a big man. They called him Don Jorge, and because he knew all the hill roads, he was useful. There was killing everywhere, as there is killing today. A hundred years ago, in 1836, it was the same."

His voice drifted out and died on meditation. In the silence,

our horses were snorting uneasily in the shed against the wall.
We rolled fresh cigarettes and poured more wine.

"A fine fellow, Don Jorge; they all said so," resumed the old
rascal. "He and his friends in the Legion suffered. No pay, no
provisions, no support. The day came when fifty men of the
First company, and a squadron of the lancers, were sent to
occupy the village of Taraburi. It is over yonder in the next
valley. We shall go through it tomorrow morning. An important
place in its position. My father had come from there, and now
he was bound there again, and he wondered if the people would
know him. Bad luck if they did, for they hated the Legion
anyway, and would hold him as a traitor. But he acted as guide,
and Captain Breval joked with him and with Captain Korski
of the lancers—joked with him about El Picador."

His voice drifted away once more. The moon was high and
cold outside, high and white as it had been on that night a
hundred years ago, when distant voices of wolves made the
horses fidget uneasily, and men joked about El Picador.

Miguel's pistol exploded—
the bullet fanned the face
of Don Jorge. The latter's
carbine discharged,
almost without volition.

ONLY THE Legion, swinging along the lonely hill trail, would jest about that Carlist rascal—about El Picador and his lance, and his ravaging hell-bent crew, who strung up every man of the Legion they captured, and thrust him through with the lance, neatly but horribly. It was one of the horror stories that have hovered above the Spanish hills since the days of Napoleon.

Not that they were to be blamed, you understand, or the Legion either; retaliation sprang quick and sharp, as it does today. Then as now, men had a cause, and slaughtered for it with relentless ferocity. When men have a cause, they become gods, and do the work of devils—which is rather the same thing, when you reflect that Satan came from heaven originally.

So jested Captain Breval as he rode through the cold night, Korski at his stirrup, and Don Jorge striding along between them.

"Look out that this Picador doesn't catch you, Don Jorge!" said Breval, with a laugh. *"Ma foi,* I'd like to see the two of you at it! They say he's a big fellow like you."

"Give me a chance at him, *mon capitaine,* and you'll see something." Don Jorge showed his white teeth through his beard, as he laughed. "But no danger. From what I hear, it's quiet enough in these parts. Another half-mile, and the road widens; then it's a straight shoot down to the valley and the village."

On ahead, scout videttes clattered. Behind, the column slogged, more lancers in the rear. Queer men, these Legionnaires; not the men who had left Africa behind. If the Spaniards had forgotten to feed or pay, they had also forgotten to clothe. The Legion had to take its uniform, like everything else, from the enemy: strange flat bérets, like Scotch tam-o'-shanters; leather cartridge-pouches at their belts, pouches destined to make the Legion famous in later years; huge leather musette-bags slapping their hips; Spanish *espadrilles* replacing their French boots.

Don Jorge, peering at the scattered village lights far below, was thankful for the uniform, the heavy reddish brown beard, the powerful frame; no one would recognize the stripling of two years ago. His heart leaped to every twist of the road, to every hill crest in the moonlight. Was Ysadora still there? Had she forgotten him in these two years, or perhaps married another?

"Halt!"

The word rang. One of the lancers was waiting. In grim silence he extended his long iron-tipped lance. Captain Breval and others pushed forward to where a great oak partly overhung the road. A mutter grew and spread. A thing was hanging there, slowly spinning on a rope. Into the moonlight its face turned. The mutter increased.

"It's Private Sablonowski," spoke out Captain Korski. "He was captured in that scrimmage last week—unhorsed and taken. What the devil!"

A paper with a scrawl was pinned to the dead man's back. *"El Picador!"* Nothing more. No more needed.

NO MORE jesting about El Picador now, as the column went on, with parties scouting the way. So El Picador was here, in these parts, had left this sign as a warning to the Legion! Captain Breval spoke quietly to Don Jorge.

"You know these people; you can talk with them. With the morning, you're relieved of all duty. See what you can learn about this Picador fellow—who he is, where he comes from, whether he's around here. Understood?"

Don Jorge assented.

Yet after all, these people were his own people. El Picador he could hate savagely for his cruelty; not these people here, in his own village. He was not back here from choice, but by order. He was not fighting Spaniards by choice. However, El Picador was a monster—easy enough to string up that devil if he were caught! And his brother might tell him something: his brother Miguel, who would be living at the old homestead of their father just beyond the village. His own flight had let Miguel inherit everything; they had never been downright enemies, although no great love had been lost between them. Well, to-morrow would tell!

With morning, he strode up the well-remembered street, a stranger here. Few men in the town; the women, the old men, cursed the French. No Spanish troops had come along—this was a quick stroke to prepare the advance coming later....

Angry eyes, blank looks, met Don Jorge. He could have called this one and that one by name, had he chosen; he knew every one of those he passed; but none knew him. The troops, with outposts placed, had scattered, billeted on the place, commandeering food and drink and quarters.

On through the last houses—ah, that was the house of Ysadora! He caught his breath; he halted: there was Ysadora herself, coming toward him. Older, more lovely, a black lace shawl about her fine head. He could feel his heart pounding as she came, as she looked him in the eyes, as she passed on. With an effort, he did not look back, after one last sidelong glance. If she still loved him, he muttered, she would have known him again. Two years—well, at least she was unmarried! Perhaps, though, she loved another now.

He went his way to the lonely old house on ahead, the house of the Roca family that had been. Now it was desolate and gloomy and unkempt. There was an old servant sweeping before the door—old Pedro. The heart of Don Jorge warmed as he looked at the wrinkled face, but Pedro stared blankly at him, in open terror.

"Is Don Miguel here?" inquired Don Jorge. The old man nodded, shrinking from him, crossing himself furtively.

"Inside," he croaked. "Inside. Come."

He scurried in. His thin voice cried: "Don Miguel! A foreigner here—one of the accursed French. He asks for you—he will burn the house and murder us—" Laughing, Don Jorge waited.

Laughing, Don Miguel came—a stalwart man like himself, his face shaven except for mustache and side-whiskers. Don Jorge stared at the face. His own face, had his beard been so trimmed! His own face—except, perhaps, for a glint in the eyes that was not his: a glint of craft and cruelty.

"Well, señor?" asked Don Miguel politely. He was well dressed; a gold ring glittered on his finger, a heavy gold ring with an old crest cut in it. Their father's ring. Curious how white that powerful face was, thought Don Jorge; not the face of one who served under the African sun all the long day. Curious—

Something jerked at him. All in an instant, his whole course of action was changed: the words on his lips died; the recognition in his heart was stifled. This man did not know him, did not suspect his identity! Yet except for the beard, they were alike as two peas.

Don Jorge bowed. "Señor, I regret to inform you that I have

*Ysadora herself! He could feel his heart pounding
as she looked him in the eyes, as she passed on.*

been billeted upon your house," he said. "I am Private Murieta
of the Foreign Legion."

"Indeed? It is an honor that I am given a guest who speaks
our tongue so well," said Don Miguel politely. "The house, señor,

is yours; all in it is yours. I have but the one old servant; I place him at your disposal. Pedro! Show the señor to the spare room; he is our guest." He bowed to Don Jorge. "You will excuse me? I am engaged with the village notary—I am to be married next week. I beg you, consider the entire place as your own. It is a great honor."

AS DON Jorge tramped up the creaky stairs behind Pedro, he wondered. White features—yes. His own features would be white as those, did he rid himself of this beard. Too white, too white! And the politeness, the welcome to a hated Frenchman, the glint in the eye! He knew that glint of old, he knew what it boded.

"Thank the Lord, I did not speak first!" he muttered in French, and turned to old Pedro, as he glimpsed the room assigned him. A corner room, the room that had been his own in past years, until his flight. He, who should be master of this place!

"So your name is Pedro?" he said gruffly. "Come, I am a friend. Your master is to be married, he tells me. Some lucky girl in the town?"

"But yes, yes, caballero," stammered the old man. "Doña Ysadora Prieta—"

DON JORGE recalled nothing more. Somehow he got rid of Pedro, was alone, and sank on the bed. Two years were swept away; the room around him just as it had been, fetched him back to himself, as he had been. The thought of Ysadora, the face of her, burned at him. Miguel to marry her? And the mud on Miguel's boots?

Riding-boots, fine leather boots; but splashed with mud. That, and the white face, had checked his words. Curious, with what a shock they had been checked! He looked around the room again, and presently sighed, laid aside his belongings, and went down into the sunlight. Old Pedro was there, warming himself, and Don Jorge gave him a cigarette and a smile. He caught the almost frightened stare of the old man, and his brows lifted.

"Well? What is it, Pedro?"

"The saints forgive me, señor! I thought for a moment you must be of this house. The look in your face—"

"A Frenchman of this house? Nonsense! So Don Miguel has not been at home much of late, eh?"

"The less the better," muttered Pedro, with a proverb none too polite that made Don Jorge chuckle in his beard. "Ah, he's not like his brother, the dead one! Young Don Sebastian would have been the true Roca for you; a caballero of the old blood, that one! But he's dead and gone."

"And your master is marrying. So the lady is in love with him, eh?"

Pedro shrugged and evaded direct response, suddenly suspicious of questions, conscious that he spoke with a Frenchman, an enemy. The whole country hereabouts was all for Don Carlos.

Looking over the place, Don Jorge glanced into the ramshackle stables, where two unkempt and shaggy horses were tied. One, a powerful beast, had recently been washed down and curried, but none too carefully. Along the hoofs, Don Jorge could see welts of that same yellow mud, caked hard.

Thoughtfully he went into the village again, and so to his headquarters. The hideous twisted shape of Private Sablonowski lay ready for proper burial. Don Jorge uncovered the corpse. The worn brogans and legs were heavily splashed with that same mud, whose peculiar color came only from the vale of Zuburi, twenty miles away, Don Jorge knew.

He went his way, avoiding any talk with those who had known Don Sebastian Roca in the old days; now, above all things, he did not want recognition. Not that it was likely, if his own brother and old Pedro did not know him again. Still, he was taking no chances. Miguel was with El Picador, knew who that slaughterer was, belonged to that murderous crew; of this he was convinced.

*"I regret to inform
you that I have been
billeted upon you,"
said Don Jorge.*

It was like Miguel, he thought, to play the fine gentleman, be most polite to the French, and steal out on guerrilla raids with a few days' growth of beard to mask his features. Home again, a quick shave and change of clothes, and no suspicion. Most of the townsfolk would know it, naturally; they would be proud of Don Miguel, the patriot who helped to slaughter the hated French! Things were done that way, in Spain.

But Don Miguel was his brother. No getting around that. And Don Jorge, to be blunt about it, sympathized wholly with the rebels who fought for Don Carlos, and with his own people here. Certainly he had not enlisted to fight against his own brethren. He had been pitchforked into it with the Legion, against his will.

"Which was a dirty trick," he reflected later, as he strolled about sunning himself and eying Don Miguel Roca. The latter was talking pleasantly with Captain Breval, and allow-

ing Tonto to
paint his por-
trait. Tonto, for-
merly of the
Belgian battal-
ion, was an ac-
knowledged
artist—the only
one in the
Legion—and
did excellent
portrait work.

Don Jorge
smoked,
watched the
scene, and bal-
anced duty
against honor.

"I don't love
Miguel, but he's
my brother," he
reflected. "I
don't love the
cause I fight for,
but it's my duty.
If I could do it
honorably, I'd be
under arms for
Don Carlos and
the patriots this
minute; but I
can't. El Picador
may be a patriot,
but he's a
damned scoun-
drel; I'd love

*"The house, señor," said Don Miguel
politely, "is yours; all in it is yours."*

nothing better than to get my sword into that murderous rat who tortures my comrades. Certainly, I sha'n't go snitching on Miguel, even if he does have everything that should be mine—"

No, the scales swung about level. He could make up his mind to nothing.

Suddenly the balance swung. Late that afternoon he was watching the squadron of lancers drill, enjoying his own absolute freedom from duty. Clusters of the townsfolk were scattered about, but none close by. Then he heard his own name spoken softly.

"Sebastian!"

Startled, he glanced around. Ysadora stood there looking calmly at him, and his heart turned over. He was unable to speak, to move, to think.

"I knew you when we met this morning," she said quietly. "The figure may change; the face may be hidden; youth may become man: but the eyes do not change. Have you no word for me? Have you forgotten me?"

"Dios!" he gasped. His voice was dry, husky. "Could I ever forget? But I'm not the one who is being married next week."

SHE CAME closer to him, unsmiling, cold, proud. But behind icy pride was seething emotion; if it did not show in her voice, he could read it in her great dark eyes, burning under the lace shawl and the wealth of silky hair.

"And whose fault is that?" she asked quietly. "You were dead. Miguel had the proofs of your death. Before you died, you had married an Arab woman in Algiers—"

"What?" he cried, and a flash leaped in his eyes. "No, no! Miguel would not lie about that! My death perhaps, but not my honor. He'd not put me to shame!"

"Well, he did," she said slowly, looking into his face. "It was a lie, then?"

"A lie," said Don Jorge, breathing hard. "An accursed lie!"

"And yet your honor is not so clean and white," she said

bitterly. "You're in French uniform. You're killing your own people, Sebastian. And you a Roca! There, at least, Miguel is a step ahead of you."

"True," he replied. "But I'm doing something. He's merely living at home, getting married, enjoying our father's wealth!"

If he thought to tempt some utterance out of her, he was mistaken. She only looked at him and laughed; she was wary, this girl. Spanish blood may be all fire, but only when the ice is broken.

"Then," he said, "you love Miguel now?"

Her bosom rose and fell sharply at the question. "I do not," she said. "But I would sooner marry him than a Roca who wears the uniform of an enemy."

With this, she turned and left him; and when he passed her again in the street, she looked at him as though she had never seen him in her life. French uniform or not, his secret was safe with her; he knew this.

SO MIGUEL had not only lied, but had spattered his name with mud! Almost did this tip the balance; almost, not quite. Don Jorge was a true Roca. There was steel in him. His brother was a scoundrel, but this would not excuse a blot on his own honor; and if he betrayed this brother to the French, it would be a blot in his own sight that he could never remove. This thought tipped the scales back again.

That same night, Don Jorge lay long awake.

From boyhood, he knew the creak of the old stairs; he heard them creak as he lay, but no light showed. He went to the window. A horse was led out of the stables and away. He went into the room his brother Miguel occupied; no Miguel there. With a shrug, Don Jorge went back to bed; but in the morning he did not shrug. Miguel was here again, affable and polite. At the edge of town, however, two men of an outpost lay stabbed; a third, who had been captured, was strung up and pierced by the mutilating lance of El Picador, in rather horrible fashion.

Captain Breval, furious, sent for Don Jorge, who was equally furious. This man pricked to death had been his chief friend in the Legion.

"The enemy are nowhere near, but El Picador is," snapped Breval. "Well? Have you learned anything?"

"I'm on the track of something," said Don Jorge, a growl in his throat.

"Good! You're safer than any of us, in that house; won't have your throat cut there. Don Miguel is a splendid fellow. Well, get some news quickly!"

"Within two days, *mon capitaine.*"

A splendid fellow, yes; he was the perfect host at dinner that evening, fluent and courtly, while old Pedro served them. Don Jorge studied him. No need of a muffling beard, now that the work was close at hand. The unshaven face was only for longer rides. There was a bandage under the right leg of his pantaloons; he walked a trifle stiffly. One of those three dead men had left a mark on one of El Picador's crew, evidently.

"Do you know, Don Jorge," said Don Miguel in his stately Castilian, "there's something hauntingly familiar about you. I can't quite place it."

Don Jorge, who was careful not to use his own voice around here, grinned in his beard.

"You compliment me! But I've never been out of Galicia in my life, until I enlisted with the French. A health to the king— yours or mine!"

A man had come into the kitchen; his voice sounded, was gone again. Presently old Pedro, removing the dishes, spoke softly to his master in the local Catalan patois. Don Jorge caught the words: *"Midnight. Spring of the Dead."* Don Miguel merely nodded carelessly and went on talking about literature.

Ojo del Muerto! Don Jorge knew that lonely little spot, only two miles outside town. The Dead Man's Spring. A tiny little fountain, dignified by local legends from old Moorish days. Loving couples used to go there. Romance was all around it, but no buildings were near by. It was a lonely fountain in a lonely little valley. Midnight, eh? El Picador had appointed that meeting-place for another murder raid, perhaps....

Don Miguel had bought the portrait painted by Tonto, and surveyed it with vast admiration; it was an excellent likeness too; though it flattered his strong features a trifle, and failed to catch the odd glint in his eye.

HALF AN hour later, Don Jorge was talking low-voiced with Captain Breval. He gave his information, or rather his guess, without saying how he had come by it.

"You know the place? You can guide us there?"

"Certainly, *mon capitaine*. And I have one request to ask. I may be wrong, but I have reason to think that in El Picador's company is a man who is my own brother. Let him chance the risks; but if he should be captured, I ask for his life."

Captain Breval frowned. After all, this man of his was a Spaniard.

"Granted; that'll clear your conscience, eh?"

"Perfectly, *mon capitaine*."

"Then pick twenty men. Carbines, sabers, pistols to each man. Be ready in an hour's time. I'll join you in front of the church. Take the best horses."

The Polish lancers grumbled, but yielded up their horses on demand.

Midnight; in the clear sky a high-sailing white moon.

The small glade was open, but thickly grown on all sides by huge ancient oaks. Against the hillside was a little broken shrine; there the fountain bubbled.

By twos and threes, men collected here toward midnight. Shaggy figures, men of the mountains, each man with his fusil. A dozen of them in all, standing around and talking, smoking, waiting. Suddenly a murmur went up. "El Capitan! El Picador!"

IT WAS El Picador himself who came now, riding a power-ful horse; a large-bulking figure, massive, cloaked, huge hat pulled over his head, and in his hand the long lance with glit-

tering point which gave him his nickname. Without dismount-
ing, he waved a hand—

The brush on the hillside crackled. Men faced about, muskets
swung up.

"Surrender!" ordered a voice. "Surrender, and—"

A musket crashed; a yell went up. From the oak trees flashed
spurts of flame, jets of smoke. Half the band were wiped out at
that volley. The others fought savagely, silently—asking no
quarter. But not El Picador.

With one flying leap of his horse, El Picador was gone ere
the first discharge rang out—gone at a gallop, leaning over in
the saddle. He lurched wildly, almost fell, caught himself.

*Two men of an
outpost had been
stabbed; a third
was strung up
and pierced by the
mutilating lance
of El Picador, in
horrible fashion.*

A moment later Don Jorge, not awaiting the result of the ambush, sped awa' in his own saddle, following that massive leaping shape as it lessened. He knew the hill trails, he knew for which one of them El Picador was making. The crash of shots fell away into dim echoes as he spurred among the trees. Two or three others were after him, but he left them behind. Even Captain Breval fell back as the oak-branches whipped his face and threatened to unhorse him.

A mile fell behind. Don Jorge was closing up now; he had El Picador clear in his vision, was not fifty feet behind. A yelp broke from him.

"Halt and fight it out!" He was using the Catalan patois in his excitement. "Halt, you murdering devil—"

El Picador drew rein and wheeled his horse, lance leveled.

"Who are you?" he shouted, leaning forward and peering at Don Jorge. "Why, the saints upon you! You! *You!*"

The big hat had fallen away. Don Jorge, his carbine ready, sat his panting horse and stared. His brother—Don Miguel! And now, by his voice, Miguel knew him.

"So *you* are El Picador!" Don Jorge exclaimed, reeling under the shock of it. "You, Miguel—a gentleman by day, a murderous slayer by night!"

"And you, Sebastian!" The other broke into a hoarse laugh. "No wonder you seemed so familiar, eh? And pretending to speak only Castilian, with your damned lisp and your talk of Galicia—*arrgh!* Sneaking in and spying on me!"

The lance leveled, he struck in spurs and came like a thunderbolt. His left hand whipped up a pistol; it exploded—the bullet fanned the face of Don Jorge. The latter felt his carbine discharged, almost without his own volition; his frightened horse reared and took the shock of the charging horseman, took the lance in the throat.... Then they were both down in a wild jumble of hoofs and death.

Only the horse of El Picador came out of that jumble, shivering and standing motionless, rolling a wild eye at the thing dragging from one stirrup. Don Jorge rolled over and scrambled to his feet. His horse was dying, the lance still fast in the poor brute's throat. He himself was unhurt. But his brother—

After a moment he straightened up and crossed himself, and murmured a prayer. The guilt, the blame, was not his; the stern steel of the Roca conscience had no spot. He had not even aimed that carbine, yet the heavy ball had shattered the whole face of Don Miguel, had killed him instantly. Another ball had been in him also—that alone would have killed him in an hour more, for the hurt was mortal.... No, there could be no blame here.

Then, suddenly, Don Jorge started, stirred into life and action.

FIFTEEN MINUTES later Captain Breval and two of his men rode up to the spot. There was nothing in sight except the dead horse and the dead man. They dismounted, and a torrent of hot curses lifted on the moonlight. Captain Breval looked at the uniform of the Legion, the slumped figure whose face was black with blood, and turned away with a shiver.

"Poor Don Jorge!" he said. "A fine fellow; he'd have been a corporal tomorrow, if he'd lived. No use going after that damned El Picador now—we can't find him on these hill trails. Put Jorge into a saddle, and double up; by the Lord, we'll give him a Legionnaire's burial, at least!"

Captain Breval did not feel too badly about it. If he had missed El Picador, he had bagged most of El Picador's outfit, who were left to the kites. Don Jorge was taken into the village, and was buried next morning with full military ceremonies.

Don Miguel attended the funeral, as did many others. He was freshly shaven, and was dressed in his best, and expressed himself with great courtesy to the officers; the death of his guest left him very sad, and he brought a huge wreath of flowers for the grave. After the ceremony, he sent for Tonto, and asked him to do another portrait, to which the grinning Tonto agreed gladly.

On his way home, Don Miguel came face to face with Ysadora. He saluted her with the formal courtesy of a hidalgo; she was white to the lips as she stared at him.

"What does it mean—all of it?" she demanded fiercely.

Don Miguel twisted his mustache and smiled.

"You have, of course, heard that these accursed French ambuscaded a number of guerrillas last night? And one of them has just been buried yonder—"

"None of your sardonic jokes, Miguel!" she broke in. "Yes, I've heard; and I've heard which man it was. Why, you devil! I believe you knew all the time that man was your own brother Sebastian—oh, you heartless fiend!"

DON MIGUEL smiled again and looked her in the eyes.

"My dear Doña Ysadora, may I offer you my arm? A little promenade in the warm sunlight—yes? I wish to discuss with you my plans for action against the French. I may confide in

you that in future they are going to be more like the actions of
a soldier, less like those of a murderer."

Even her lips had whitened now. She stood shaking, over-
come by so powerful a thrust of emotion that but for his supporting arm she might have fallen.

Don Miguel laughed softly.

"So the eyes never change, eh? Nor the heart either—with
some men."

Her fingers clung to his arm. After a moment she uttered
low words.

"And I—I never knew the difference. I thought you were
Miguel—you have his air, his carriage—all but his eyes."

"For that I may thank the good God, and our worthy father,"
said the young man cheerfully.

"And by the way, I'm having another portrait of myself
painted by that Legion artist. That will make two portraits of
your husband, to delight your eyes."

T H E   W O L V E S howled again on the cold moonlight, the
horses stirred. My wrinkled old Gaspenjo rolled a fresh cigarette
and lit it from the embers of the fire. He leaned back and puffed
contentedly.

"So that's the story," he said. "Don Miguel did fight the
French very honorably, and lost his money and lands because
Don Carlos was beaten, so that in the end this barren place was
all he had left. But it was enough. And in his later years he
begat me, who am the last of the Roca family."

"I thought your name was Gaspenjo?" I said curiously.

He shrugged.

"Oh, that's another story," he said in dismissal.

"But you mentioned pictures—portraits of your father and
your uncle. Not the same ones this Tonto, of the Legion,
painted?"

"The same ones, señor," he said. "Poor Tonto, my father used
to say, died like a brave man. He died at Barrastro when the

Legion, reduced to a single battalion, was practically wiped out, and their colonel with them."

He rose, opened a cupboard, and took out two portraits in cheap frames which he handed me. He stirred the fire a bit, and by the flickering light I looked at them.

They were assuredly not art. Each one showed a grim, powerful face with mustache and sideburns, a face abounding in vitality, energy, even cruelty. The two faces were identical so far as I could see.

"Which of them," I asked, "is your father—which your uncle?"

Old Gaspenjo hitched up his shoulders, sucked at his cigarette, and replied with the eternally hopeless and careless response of his country:

"*Quién sabe?* Well, perhaps the good God knows; but I don't. After all, what does it matter?"

THE GRANDSON OF POMPEY

"The Grandson of Pompey" tells a story of
beleaguered men in desperation—of the
Foreign Legion at its gallant best.

I WALKED INTO the restaurant one evening to find my three friends, all veterans or *anciens* of the Foreign Legion, gathered about a bottle. The red-headed Casey was pugnacious; the thin, saturnine Kramer was very dignified; Ponson, the dark Alsatian, was animated.

They made room for me, ordered more wine, and blinked at the old brown sheet of paper I laid down.

"That," I said complacently, "is something you Legionnaires ought to look at twice, my friends! You think so much of the traditions and legends of the Legion—"

"It's Arabic," blurted out Casey. "I'm no Arab!"

Kramer held it up and inspected it. Arabic, yes; it was a letter from the hand of the great Emir who had fought the French in Algeria to the death.

"Abdel Kader," said Kramer stiffly. "Ha! I can read it. After his capture! He thanks Napoleon III for the gift of a portrait— bah! If you had one of his letters stirring up the great Kabyle rebellion of 1840, that'd be something!"

Ponson seized a pencil and began to jot down letters on the menu.

"I know something better," he cried quickly. "Miliana—the grandson of Pompey—the Fourth Battalion of the Legion—do you guys know about it?"

Casey lifted heavy eyes. "Miliana—that's the town below

Algiers on the hillside. Sure, I been there. I had a girl there; her old man was in the quartermaster's department."

Ponson gave him a bitter look. "And that's all the name means to you! But to the second Legion it meant—"

"Second Legion?" exclaimed Casey. "You mean 2nd Regiment Étranger—"

"I mean the second Legion! The first corps was loaned to Spain and destroyed; then the Legion was organized afresh—"

The scrap was on—a furious discussion about the history of the famous corps. True, the Legion had been mustered out and sent as a body to Spain, on loan, as it were; a permanent loan, for it was practically wiped out, fighting the Carlists. A new Legion was formed in Algeria, where the French still had only a precarious foothold along the coast.

Then was begun the work at which the corps has excelled ever since—road-building, construction, organization of a conquered country.

"When you look at the map today," said Ponson, still jotting down letters and trying to reconstruct something, "it's funny to think that Miliana could have been a frontier town—it's so close to Algiers. But it was. And back in 1840 the Fourth Battalion of the Legion, which had only one regiment then, occupied it and garrisoned it…. Ah! Now I've got the thing."

He laid his pencil aside, and grinned.

"I suppose you birds would say there's no such thing as an honorary Legionnaire, eh? I don't mean honorary members of the association of veterans, like our artist in New York; but honorary members of the Legion itself—"

Then there was a real howl. These men who had fought and slaved away the best years of their life, had an intense pride in the corps. They denied furiously that such a thing was possible. But I knew better, and nodded at Ponson.

"You mean that chap Lord Teignmouth or something?"

"I don't know his name; Milord Pompey, he was called. That's the name he went by. He was pottering around Algeria. He was one of those terrible Englishmen who speak Greek and Latin like natives. He was always poring over some old inscription. When he got to Miliana, he was in his element—a lot of old Roman cities were around there; and even now you stumble over the ruins if you walk a mile."

"Any Americans in the Legion then?" demanded Casey.

"I don't know. There were some English, anyhow. There was one in the Fourth—a big, lazy blond with yellow mustache. He was Private Smeeth; there was no *Compagnie d'élite* then, or he would have been in it. The best soldier, the worst drunkard, the most unvarnished scoundrel, in the whole regiment. He spent half his time in a cell or at punishment—"

"Never mind about him," growled Casey. "I tell you, there's no such thing as being an honorary member of the Legion. *Arrgh!* It's enough to make anybody sick."

Ponson chuckled blithely and went on:

"You know, when the Kabyle war broke out, it came in a hurry, all along the line. Back in those days, Miliana was a great place of pilgrimage for the Algerines. They came from all parts to kiss the shrine of some saint or other."

"They still do," I broke in. "Sidi Yusuf is the name—one of those local saints who sprang up all over the place."

"So," resumed Ponson, with a nod, "the first place that the rebel tribes wanted to get back, was Miliana. Not that it was much of a place—just a village, then, with red tile roofs to mark it out. It had an old wall around, which Arabs had built from Roman ruins; you could find anything in that wall—pillars or capitals or tombstones. Perched on the hillside, half a mile above the glorious plain which the natives called El Chudary or the Green, it had a swell view.

"And one fine day, that whole plain was filled with Kabyles, horsemen by the thousand. The war was on. Miliana was invested tight as a drum—and no artillery. Milord Pompey was there, and no getting out for him. Lieutenant-colonel Illens turned all the natives out of the place, repulsed a couple of

"There's your stone, Grandfather!" he said, gasping. "Blood on it now.... A good fight, sir!"

assaults, and settled down to stand a siege with the twelve hundred of the Fourth. He held a dress parade—and you should have seen it! That's where the English milord got in bad with the Legion."

Ponson started to laugh. Sober or not, he had us all interested; and his description of that dress parade was a classic. It occurred in the abandoned marketplace of the village. Except for the outposts, in the gardens and vineyards around the town, and up the creek that watered Miliana abundantly, the whole battalion was lined up on parade.

Illens and his staff took along Milord Pompey to inspect the ranks. He was an old fellow with gray hair and spectacles. Twenty-five years previously, he had fought the French at Waterloo; and being a real live lord and a great man, he was treated with extreme respect. He was harsh-spoken, abrupt, and about as amiable as a bear with a sore head.

THE JUNE sun was hot, and Milord Pompey showed up with a green umbrella, which drew titters from the ranks. And what ranks they were! The élite companies had red epaulets, granted in memory of the assault on Constantine three years before, which were pinned on their vests—no coats under that sun. Some wore red pantaloons; some had white cotton ones. Most fearful and wonderful of all was the headgear.

You could see red shakos, leather tar-bucket hats, sun-hats with long vizors, some with neck-flaps, some without. As Milord Pompey stalked along beside Colonel Illens, he uttered caustic comment in his perfect French.

"There is a remarkable uniformity about one thing, I observe," said he. "That is, the entire battalion has buttons that are alike."

Some truth in that; the buttons with a star, the only mark of the Foreign Legion at that time, were alike. Some one spoke out from the ranks.

"And its muskets are all bright, you old fool!"

"Who spoke?" snapped the Colonel. "Advance three paces."

Private Smeeth advanced, saluted, stood at attention.

"An insult to a guest demands an apology, which I make," the Colonel said. "Insubordination demands ten days of heavy labor on the fortifications, which is your privilege."

Milord Pompey peered at the man and went up to him.

"It seems to me," he said stiffly, "that this rascal must be a poor soldier."

"On the contrary, milord," said Colonel Illens, "he is a good soldier; but he is a rascal."

"That is obvious in his features." Milord Pompey stared at Private Smeeth, who looked him in the eyes, with a thin suspicion of a smile. "Yes, an arrant rogue by his looks; a dissolute scoundrel, obviously. Eh, fellow? Is it not so?"

Private Smeeth saluted. "Monsieur, it runs in the family," he said. "My grandfather was a scoundrel; so am I. But I'm not a hypocrite, as he was—and is."

The listening officers saw Milord Pompey turn white with fury, but could not account for it; Smeeth's words had been polite. They had not yet guessed the relationship between these Englishmen.

The review went on. Milord passed sarcastic comments that made the Fourth furious. The battalion, however, did not hear what he said to the officers when the ranks had been dismissed.

"Messieurs, if we had to fight these Arabs for a month,"—and he waved his green umbrella toward the sweeping plain below, where the white robes fluttered,—"we could not have better men. Their uniforms are rags; but I cannot imagine more superb soldiers."

The heart of Colonel Illens, who loved his men and his battalion, warmed to the harsh old Englishman from that moment. Milord Pompey—so he was known everywhere. He had a theory that the family of Pompey the Great had been buried in one of the Roman cities hereabouts, and this was why he was in Algeria, or so he said. He collected all the old inscriptions he could find, and if he had any other business here, he did not mention it....

During the first two or three weeks of the siege, Milord Pompey continued poking among the ruins and making a nuisance of himself generally, regardless of bullets. Tribesmen by thousands were around the village. After the first few assaults

"An arrant rogue, by his looks; a dissolute
scoundrel, obviously. Eh, fellow? Is it not so?"

were repulsed by the fusils—1822 model—of the Legion, the
siege settled down to a continual fusillade and sniping. All roads
were closed; the revolt was general in Algeria, and Colonel
Illens could only hang on to his position like grim death.

Luckily, provisions did not lack, and the water-supply was

assured; but the hot sun and the effluvia of the Arab village suddenly began to fight for the Kabyles. Dysentery broke out, and a terrific scourge of fever swept the living and killed off the wounded quickly. The advance posts had to be held at all costs; with daily assaults on these, a daily hail of musketry pouring into the town itself, the Fourth began to shrink—and was in its agony before anyone realized it.

IN THE midst of all this, Milord Pompey and his green umbrella came one blazing afternoon to the most exposed section of the town wall. A minor attack there had just been repulsed. Half a dozen dead and wounded Legionnaires were being hauled off; others along the wall were engaged in sniping. One of them was Private Smeeth, unshaven and powder-grimed, who regarded the old Milord with a grim smile and flung him a bitter word. Bullets buzzed like hornets, but Milord Pompey refused to stoop.

"Hello, old hawk-face! I suppose you think you're showing

off, with your stiff neck and your umbrella; but you're not. You're safe as safe. The natives won't fire on you; green is their sacred color."

"Hm! The event proves you wrong." And the Milord showed a bullet-hole through his umbrella. "Why didn't you answer my letters, you graceless rogue? Why did you refuse to let me buy your discharge?"

"I'm satisfied," said Smeeth coolly. "I've no more use for you than you have for me. You're a cold-hearted scoundrel who could watch his only son die rather than lift a finger to help him or his wife. To hell with you!"

"Perhaps I've paid for my own actions," the old man said harshly. "I cannot ask forgiveness from the dead, but I can atone to the living. That's why I'm here, Reginald. I want to ask only your pardon, your—"

"My name is Private Smeeth, Fourth Battalion of the Legion, to you," said the younger man. "Kindly remember it, and save your crocodile tears for those that want 'em. That's all I care to say to you."

"Indeed?" Milord shook with anger. "I suppose you hope an Arab bullet will take me off so you can come into the title, eh?"

"To hell with you and your title!" said Smeeth, and chuckled. "Look at that stone down yonder, at the base of the wall below me! It ought to interest you, Milord Pompey. It seems to have your nickname on it, unless I've forgotten my Latinity."

He turned his back, put his reloaded fusil over the parapet, and banged away.

"Got him!" he cried exultantly to the next man. "Not bad, comrade, eh? We may never see Algiers again, but at least we're depopulating this section of Kabilia at a good rate!"

Milord Pompey was below the parapet, on his knees, examining a great block of stone built into the wall there. It was laid in sideways, but the inscription on the stone, only partially defaced, could be made out. With pencil and paper, the old

Milord was feverishly copying it. The men above jested and laughed at him, but he was quite oblivious to their sneers.

At dinner that evening—for he messed with the officers—the beak-nosed old Englishman peered excitedly about.

"Gentlemen, I've made a discovery, a real discovery!" he declaimed with unwonted enthusiasm, and passed a paper around the table. "This inscription is from a tombstone, a *cippus* as it is technically known, built into the wall of the southern angle. It goes to prove beyond a doubt that the grandson of Pompey the Great was buried here, and possibly the great-grandson as well. My theory, messieurs, has been proven! What a force, what a beauty, is lent the touching epigram of Martial upon the misfortunes to this family, of the man who had the entire Roman world at his feet!"

There was a polite smile, a faint lifting of brows. Colonel Illens and his officers, their circle rapidly thinning, had but faint interest in this Englishman's theory, and none whatever in Pompey the Great.

"We happen to have the entire Arab world at our feet just now," said some one dryly, "and it's devilish unpleasant."

"Oh! That reminds me!" Milord Pompey turned to the Colonel. "I beg that you'll have the goodness to assign me some post of duty. It will afford me great honor to serve under your command, *mon colonel.*"

This sudden courtesy and desire to be of use astonished them, but the offer was accepted; Milord Pompey was assigned work with the ambulance section.

He flung himself into it with a devotion, a stern self-denial, which amazed everyone. He handled the wounded, the sick, with a tenderness no one would have suspected in him. As the days dragged on to July, and the agony of the Fourth Battalion slowly developed into a death-rattle, the value of his services became ever more pronounced.

The walls were held; the outposts were held; but at fearful cost. Up the long sharp slopes, in among the vineyards and

*"I've no more use for you
than you have for me. To hell
with you and your title!"*

gardens, on the rocky hill above, the Arabs were everywhere. Day and night their bullets hailed into the devoted town. Only the odd chance that Miliana, almost alone in the whole country, had tile roofs on its houses, saved the place from fire and from that riddling storm of lead.

The circle of officers lessened. The battalion shrank. The whole place was one vast hospital, for fever and dysentery never slackened. The heat was horrible. Milord Pompey rigged all the available canvas and carpets into sunshades; bullet-riddled as they were, these afforded the sick men some relief.

Each day the outposts had to be re-victualed and relieved. These outposts, which held off the Kabyle waves, simply had to be held, regardless; and they were held. But the necessity of a tiny column going out to each one, every day, became more and more terrible. The twelve hundred had shrunk to half that number—and of those, not three hundred men could bear arms.

Private Smeeth, in all this, bore a charmed life. When an assault came, his was the rallying voice; when an officer fell, it was Smeeth who took over. The day came, indeed, when he was acting captain of his company—not much of a company, however. His herculean strength never seemed to diminish; and sickness, like the hot lead, passed him by.

On the morning when he brought his dying lieutenant to the hospital, he ran into Milord Pompey, and grinned at him.

"I hear you're making yourself useful, Milord. It must be rather a strange experience for you, eh?"

The shaggy brows drew down at him. "Strange that you can jest, with death all around you, sir. None of us are going to get out of here alive. Will you not listen, at such a time, to my words?"

"Yes, as you listened to my father's words," said

"I suppose you hope a bullet will take me off so you can come into the title, eh?"

Private Smeeth. "Not the twelve plagues of Egypt would soften your hard heart; and I've all the respect for my dead father that I lack for you. And nothing could give me any respect for you."

He turned his back and went back to his post, at the south angle. That had become his accustomed station. It was the most exposed point of the walls, but Smeeth was a remarkable marksman, and he had developed a technique of killing off the Arab leaders in every attack which more than once saved the place. This was the one point at which the enemy could come, for the outposts protected the rest of the walls from direct assault; therefore the outposts, at this angle, were subject to daily attack.

On the parapet beside his grandson, Milford Pompey
emptied death into the horde of white-robed figures.

Still the battalion shrank. Colonel Illens and a handful of officers survived. Men lacked for bare defense. When it came to visiting the outposts with food and water and reliefs, the prospect became more terrible each day. The few civilians were under arms. The surgeons, the ambulance section, the officers, took fusils and acted as guards when the little columns went to the outposts. Musket in hand, the Colonel himself became a soldier.

Milord Pompey was bandaging a wounded man under the parapet of the exposed angle, when Colonel Illens came up and stood wearily, drawn and haggard, to inspect the point. No

officers remained. The sergeant of the guard approached and
saluted.

"*Mon colonel,* Private Schultz has mounted his last guard.
There is no one to take his place. I need a man."

The Colonel made a helpless gesture. The harsh-faced old
Milord straightened up and saluted stiffly.

"My colonel, I claim the honor," rasped his voice. "I am well.
Let some of the slightly wounded look after their comrades.
Give me a fusil."

The Colonel embraced him—to his frowning annoyance.

Thus, with a fusil and one of the old casquettes of the Legion
to shield his head from the blazing sun, Milord Pompey
mounted to the parapet. The alarm sounded; gaunt tottering
figures flooded up. The Kabyles were launching an attack at this
exposed salient.

The fusils ripped out volley after volley. White robes littered the slopes down below the wall. The attack was repulsed. As Milord Pompey reloaded, he found himself face to face with Private Smeeth, and smiled grimly.

DAYS PASSED. The death-rattle of the Fourth was passing into the final convulsion. The twelve hundred had become as the dust. Over eight hundred lay in shallow graves below the wall. A scant hundred and fifty men were able to stagger to duty; yet so fierce remained their fire that the Arabs delayed a final assault. Not yet had the outposts been taken—and until these fell, the walls could only be reached at the exposed southern angle.

Untouched by bullet or sickness, Milord Pompey mounted guard with the rest, used his fusil with the best of them; his bony old frame under its Legion casquette seemed impervious to sun or fatigue alike.

He, like those who remained, like Private Smeeth and the officers, was no more than a living shadow. With lack of sleep or rest, with continual *alerts,* with incessant fighting, the men had lost human semblance or volition; they could fight mechanically, no more. Frequently, they had to be taken by the arm and led to their post and made to sit there, gun ready, vacant eyes fastened on the ground outside. If an attack came, they fired like automatons.

They had to fight, watch, tend the sick and wounded, relieve the outposts—everything. A bare hundred and fifty of them. Half the surgeons were dead, but that was balanced neatly by most of the battalion being dead also.

COLONEL ILLENS, three officers and Milord Pompey messed together one noon. The haggard, hollow-eyed Colonel regarded the old Englishman with amazement.

"Mon Dieu! What a man you must have been at half your age!" he exclaimed. "If you can do better than any of us today—"

A thin smile cracked the gaunt old face.

"I am merely making up for some of the things I've missed,

mon colonel. At half my age, I might have been what Private Smeeth is today: the best soldier in the whole battalion."

"You Englishmen are magnificent!" murmured the Colonel. Milord Pompey inclined his head.

"It takes a Frenchman to recognize the fact, Colonel."

All very polite and very Gallic—but the alarm sounded. A new attack was on the way, at the south angle. Milord and officers alike seized muskets and hurried out to the threatened point. The outposts were being attacked also; it was general— a desperate effort to overwhelm the defense.

On the parapet beside his grandson, Milord Pompey loaded and fired as coolly as any veteran there. Wiping his spectacles now and again as sweat smeared them, he exchanged jests with Private Smeeth, emptied death into the horde of white-robed figures, watched the flood come almost to the very walls ere it broke and eddied back again.

The attack was broken, but bullets still came, buzzing like wasps, or hitting the stones and sailing away in screeching ricochet. A few more dead, a few more wounded for the fever to finish off. The tension relaxed. Weary men slumped down in repose. Messengers came on the run; all was well at the outposts.

MILORD POMPEY glanced at the Colonel, who was receiving the reports, then turned as a hand clamped on his shoulder. He looked into the eyes of Private Smeeth, who was extending a hand.

"Shake!"

"Eh?" The old Milord scowled as he took the extended hand. "You mean it?"

"I never expected to see the day when I'd salute you, but I do it now," and Smeeth suited action to words. "We've been good comrades these last few days; when I said I'd never respect you, sir, I lied. I offer my apologies."

The harsh old features broke suddenly into radiance.

"My boy, my boy!" He caught the other in his arms, stared

into the unshaven face. "Humph! This won't do. We're acting like these Latins—can't have such a thing." And he drew back. His face was still radiant. "Then it's—er—all right?"

"Quite all right, sir. Or should I say—Grandfather?"

"Thank heaven!" muttered Milord Pompey. Then, hearing his name, he swung around to find the Colonel speaking. He saluted smartly.

"Private—*Mon Dieu,* but that English name is terrible!— Private Pompey," exclaimed the Colonel, "I am proud of you. You, monsieur, are an honor to the Legion, and the Legion is proud of you! I shall recommend that you be placed on the records as a member of honor of this battalion—that is to say, if you'll write out your name for me."

A thud—a sharply choked cry, a slithering rush and fall. Men came running. Milord Pompey flung himself from the parapet, and with the Colonel hurrying to help him, leaned over the figure that had fallen.

Private Smeeth put out a hand to the stones beside him. His fingers slipped on something wet. He laughed suddenly at the two faces above him.

"There—there's your stone, Grandfather!" he said, gasping a little. "Not a bad touch of irony, eh? Blood on it now. The grandson of Pompey, isn't it? A good fight, sir, a good fight. Pompey was lord and master of all the world—same as you, in a way. And his grandson died in a ditch—same as me—"

He laughed again—and died. He had three bullets, all through him at once.

Colonel Illens looked at Milord Pompey, who stood very erect, his harsh beaked features set hard; and suddenly the Colonel lifted his hand in a salute. The other men around imitated his action. No word was spoken. The gesture was a tribute to that indomitable old man who stood with stricken features.

And yet, strangely enough, there was something of a radiance still lingering in the man's face, as though not death itself could take from him the happiness that had come to him a moment before those bullets struck.

THIS WAS the story that Ponson told us; and when he had finished it, he handed over the menu on which he had scribbled.

"I believe they've broken down the old wall at Miliana now, in building a modern town, and they've changed the name of it, or rather its spelling," he said. "But I copied that inscription years ago. I remember every line, every letter of it, perfectly. I can point you to the records of it; the thing is real."

"But what about the siege?" I questioned. "How did it come out?"

The others smiled at my ignorance. They knew the traditions of their corps, the stories of its exploits.

"Oh, it came out as the Legion usually comes out,"—and Ponson shrugged. "A day or two afterward Changarnier's column relieved the place. Practically everyone left alive went into the Blidah hospital—but there was no surrender."

The menu was passed around and came to me. I stared at it, plucking up my scanty Latin. Yes, it was the tombstone of Pompey's grandson, no doubt of that—almost all the inscription was there to read, abbreviated in the Roman fashion:

Q. POMPEIO CN. F. QUIRIT. CLEMENTI PA.... DI-IVR EX TESTAMENTO. Q. POMPEIO F. QVIR. RO-GATI FRATRIS SVI POMPEIA Q. P. MABRA POSVIT

But I thought of the grandsire, not of the grandson, as I lifted my glass to clink with the others at the toast of redheaded Casey:

"To the honorary member of the Legion—*salut!*"

LEATHER-BELLIES IN THE CRIMEA

*"Leather-Bellies in the Crimea" vividly presents a little-
known but desperate adventure of the Foreign Legion.*

CASEY, THE red-headed soldier of fortune who had
once been in the Foreign Legion, stared at me and Kramer
with a ghastly fear in his eyes.

"It's awful! I can't stand to think of it," he blurted out.

He must have been on a spree for days, by his looks. Casey
was not a wholly lovable or admirable person; but after all, he
was an *ancien* of the Legion.

"What's happened?" Kramer demanded in some alarm.

"I just woke up to it; you know, how a fellow does." Casey
swigged his drink, and looked at us again. The fear was in his
gaze and no mistake. "It's seventeen years since I quit the
Legion. Seventeen! That was back at the end of 1920. I was
with the French mission attached to Denikin's army in South
Russia—you know, the Bolshies blew us all to hell like a stack
of dry leaves."

That campaign was, and still is, one of the nightmares of the
French army.

"What about it, to make you get the wind up now?" I asked.

"That's the point." Casey nodded toward a corner table.
"Come on over there and I'll tell you something—a ghost story,
by heaven, that's true! Yeah—seventeen years; it just doesn't
seem possible. Only, when I look at myself and see how this
red thatch of mine is thinning out—"

I knew, or thought I knew, what the queer look in his eyes
meant. Casey, the reckless devil who feared nothing, was afraid

now: afraid of getting old. Some men are like that, when they stop to think of it.

Kramer and I got him seated at the corner table; he was pretty shaky, had reached the point where he wanted to talk his head off. We ordered drinks. Casey got out a coin and began to spin it—a big silver coin of Czarist Russia. He watched it spin, and it fell with the eagles up. He gave us a queer glance.

"Now I'll tell you something funny," he said, meaning it was not at all funny. "I had an uncle once."

"Back in Ireland?" I asked lightly.

Casey shook his head.

"Nope. We're Liverpool Irish. I never saw my Uncle Teague; he had skipped out and disappeared long before I was born. He was a tough one. He was the oldest, and my dad the youngest of a long string of kids. He went off to the Crimean War and never did come back. We used to have a picture of him in the parlor."

"The Crimean War," Kramer said skeptically, "was around 1856."

"Yeah," Casey scowled. "My dad was born in '50, and I was born in '90, when he was forty years old. I was thirty when I quit the Legion—hang it, stop reminding me how old I am, will you? I'm trying to tell about that picture of Uncle Teague."

"I thought it was a ghost story," was my comment.

"Well, it is; a hell of a story, too. Uncle Teague had a flat nose and a scar like a V right on the end of it. He was in a fight with a drunken sailor who bashed his nose and nicked it with a knife. That was one reason he took the Queen's shilling and skipped. He didn't like the army, and deserted about the time he got to the Crimea, and that was the last ever heard of him. But we had that picture in the parlor, and I used to look at his bashed nose and the scar when I was a kid. Got all that straight?"

"Fairly so," I said coolly. I didn't much care for Casey, or for anything about him.

"I don't know just how to tell you this. It looks screwy; maybe it's all screwy," he went on, spinning that silver coin again. Again it fell tails—eagles up. "A hypnotist, or some of these psychology sharks, might explain it. Anyhow, I'm going to tell you just what happened, and what I saw. I was bumming around with Captain de Silz, of the aviation, another volunteer; this was at Eupatoria, on the eve of the evacuation. Everything was in chaos. General Wrangel was somewhere at the front. The French fleet lay off the coast. White Russians, crowded into the Crimea, were slaughtered by tens of thousands; typhoid was everywhere. That night the chief of staff sent for me and Captain de Silz—I was a volunteer in the aviation unit too.

"He told us that one of us was to be sent in the morning to find Wrangel with dispatches; we both volunteered. He laughed and said to settle it between ourselves before morning. So we went off and had a drink, and I went to meet a girl I knew; and neither of us cared a damn whether we went or stayed.

"In the course of the evening I got knocked on the head, and woke up to find myself in one of the Cossack tents on the outskirts of town. I was tied up, too. That was an old trick—to murder one of the Allied Commission men for the sake of his money and boots. So I knew I was a goner."

Casey broke off to empty his glass and signal for another drink. He resumed:

"A huge jabbering was going on. By light of a lantern, I saw half a dozen Cossacks crowded into the place. Suddenly they all let out a wild yell and squatted down. One of them was old, white-haired, flat-nosed. He spun a big silver coin; they all let out another yell; then they trooped out. The old fellow came over and sat down by me, and chuckled. He said he had won me from the rest, and I realized that I was hearing broken French from his lips. And in the light of the lantern, as I stared up at him, I saw that he had a nick, a scar, in the end of his flat nose—a scar like a V. It was just like the picture of my Uncle Teague."

Casey scowled at us; as though awaiting contradiction, but we remained silent.

"All right," he went on. "The old fellow said he had saved me because I was in the Legion uniform. He had been in the Legion once. And he said that when dawn came, I could go back safely to headquarters. Until then, I must wait here. And he settled down to talk, fingering that big silver coin. It fascinated me. Maybe I was hypnotized, maybe not; explain it as you like. I'm not trying to explain it. But I saw something as I lay there—I saw a whole story, like I was in on it. And either this old fellow was the ghost of my Uncle Teague, or maybe he was Teague himself; I dunno. Anyhow, this was what I saw."

And he told us.

A MAN was standing in a wet trench, with snow all around, and the chill of Russian winter on him. His blue tunic and baggy red pants were frayed and patched; he wore a blue-and-red képi; his mittened hands clung to his rifle as he stared out over the snow, and he was in big wooden *sabots—sabots*, not shoes! He was a strapping young fellow with a heavy beard and a big flat nose with a scar on the end of it. At his waist was a

long flat pouch of leather—the famous cartridge-pouch of the Legion.

These were the trenches before Sebastopol.

Sad, glowering, cursing his luck, Private Casey of the Legion stamped his *sabots* and hugged the tattered greatcoat closer about him. He was the type of man who rebels at discipline; and he was in the most highly disciplined corps in the world, as he had found to his sorrow. Little they cared whether he were a British deserter or not—they needed every man they could get.

Here was Mullins approaching: Mullins, three years in the Legion, who had the adjoining beat—a big beefy Englishman who got on famously with everyone.

"Hello! Toes froze yet?" exclaimed Mullins genially. "Relief

*"Tails!" she said, turning away. "Tails! Tails!" With a
laugh, Casey nodded and pretended that he understood.*

any minute now. Going to see them Russky friends of yours
tonight? I'd like a look-in, s'elp me!"

"Aye, it's a bit o' Paradise after this hell," Casey said sulkily.
"They'll be glad to have you, me lad, and if you've a bit o' clink,
they'll turn out some grub to warm your backbone. That slush
they give us—ugh! Why in hell I ever jumped into this French
outfit, I dunno."

Mullins grinned. "I do. Thought it'd be soft work, eh? But
cheer up, Casey; you make a fine upstanding Legionnaire, and
you've picked up French wonderful. I hear the British regiments
are worse off than us; fair starving, they be, and half sick. We've
men enough to lighten the job, but not them. Well, remember

about tonight! It's ag'in' the rules, but I can fix the boys on sentry go. Anything to get warm, says I; and them Russkies keep warm. See you after retreat."

Casey nodded sourly, shouldered his musket, and growled curses afresh. True, it was flat against orders to sneak off to that Russian village back of the headquarters at Kamiesh; but little he cared for that. They were friendly folks, those Russkies. Most friendly of all, and free with his vodka, was the big Cossack peddler and his daughter with the eyes of fire; to Casey, that girl was as the magnet to iron, and all the more so because neither of them could understand a word the other spoke. Her father, the peddler, spoke a little French and even better English—a strange thing in a Cossack. But then, it was even stranger for a Cossack to be a peddler, had Private Casey known it. The other Russkies could only jabber and grin, but this one could talk, and his vodka was strong; and his daughter—well, her name was Irene, and when Private Casey pronounced it in the Russian way, a glow came into her face and a new light into her eyes.

Here was one person who saw no ugliness in a flat scarred nose. Cossacks did not bother about looks, anyhow.

THE RELIEF came at last; and Casey slid and clumped through the snowy mud with a bitter eye cocked at the cold bleak sunset. There was good stuff in Casey, good fighting stuff, or he would never have made the fighting line with the 1st Regiment Étranger; there was some bad stuff in him too, maybe a bit more than is in most men.

It was the fourth of November; and Private Teague Casey cursed anew as he realized that the winter was not even well begun yet. He looked forward at the rest of it with a sort of terrified horror. The Irish have never liked winter; even in the ancient days they could never comprehend the pangs of hell until it was pictured as all ice and snow—after which, they were quickly converted. And small blame to them!

As for slipping away that night, he was supremely unworried.

The 19th and 39th of the Line had the adjoining posts; the English were beyond; and Casey's silver tongue could get himself out and in unless an officer happened to be around. He would chance that. A Legionnaire, as he had found, could get away with anything. Nor did he have any fear of being picked up by the English he had deserted. In this uniform, with this beard he was growing, he could evade recognition by his own mother.

Yes, it was safe enough. There was no danger; there had been no attacks along here; the big guns had done all the work thus far, after the autumn fighting was over. Men were always foraging for something to burn, too.

Casey cursed the camp as he trudged into it—he was cursing everything today. Here, he had some reason. The camp had been a quagmire, now happily frozen over; but there was no warmth in it at all. In those days soldiers, especially the two regiments of the Foreign Legion, were not pampered by Y.M.C.A. boys and nurses and aid societies and whatnot. It was root, hog, or die.

Casey nodded to the other men. Most of the Legion went in for chin-tufts and long mustaches with waxed ends, like the Emperor Napoleon; others, like Casey, were contented with plain whiskers, as luxuriant as possible. Mullins and a few others shaved clean. But Casey looked more like a Russian than anything else—and knew it.

MULLINS SHOWED up with a few twigs and sticks, found somewhere. The tent that they shared was ditched around the outside, banked around the bottom, and like most of the others, had a tiny fireplace made out of jam-tins. They built a small fire and tried to warm themselves.

"You said it," broke out Casey sullenly. "Them Russky boys—they're warm, anyhow; that's more'n we are. They got food; all we have is thin bean soup. For tuppence, I'd clear out of this army. I got into it to fight, and all we've done is starve and freeze and dig trenches."

"The Legion got its belly full at the Alma, in September."

"You mean, the élite companies did. I was digging trenches then."

"Lucky you got 'em dug before the ground froze, lad. Look here, forget such bally nonsense!" Mullins exclaimed earnestly. "You've nowhere to run, anyhow. This is Russia. You can jump into the sea or get a Cossack lance through your gizzard—no other choice."

"We'll warm up tonight, anyhow. Who's got the guard?"

"The 19th. I know all those lads; leave it to me."

FROSTY MOON in a frosty sky, *sabots* clumping the snow, bitter wind blowing off the sea, they risked much that night for an hour or two of warmth; yet once away from the position of the Legion brigade, discipline was slack and many a forager was out.

They came into the little village. Casey knew the way; he was

recognized, and presently the two shivering men were en-
sconced in the steaming warmth of a room occupied by no
more than a dozen or so others. Peasants, all except the Cossack
and his daughter Irene, huge bewhiskered amiable folk, who
grabbed at the coins Mullins dug out, and then went into bursts
of laughter, repeating one phrase over and over as they pointed
at the huge leather cartridge-boxes attached to the belts of the
two visitors—pouches whose very existence was traced back to
the days when most of the Legion had died in Spain, twenty
years before.

"What do they say?" Casey demanded of the Cossack Ivanov,
who roared with laughter like the others. He winked.

"Leather-bellies—that's what we call the Legion."

"Yeah! I've heard that before now," growled Mullins. "*Ventres
de cuir*—the Russkies have been calling us that ever since we
landed. What about some grub?"

Still laughing and joking about the cartridge-pouches, the honest peasants produced and shared what food they had.

Casey had eyes only for Irene. As he held her hand and looked into her beaming face, those hard features of his took on a new and unwonted expression. He spoke to her, low-voiced, the while she listened uncomprehending, giggling. Her father, meantime, big Cossack square hat shoved back from his eagle-eyed bearded features, was talking with Mullins, offering him vodka, laughing and jesting jovially.

Then, to the astonishment of Casey, the girl put her fingers on his wrist and leaned forward, and uttered one English word. It must have been the only one she knew.

"Tails!"

"Eh?" He stared at her. "Say it again—"

"Tails!" she said, turning away casually, as she made a gesture of caution. "Tails! Tails!"

Casey did not know what it was all about, but the gesture warned him, and with a puzzled frown, he determined to keep his mouth shut. Then she gestured again, made as though to spin a coin. "Tails!" With a laugh, Casey nodded and pretended that he understood. He was still puzzled.

Ivanov, the Cossack peddler, turned to him, and Casey accepted the vodka and tossed it off blithely. It was warm here, warm and steaming and expansive. Mullins, who had picked up a little Russian, was laughing and joking with the peasants.

"What about it?" said Ivanov in a low voice. His English was queerly clipped, quite impossible to reproduce, but it was good. "Have you thought it over?"

"I have that," murmured Casey. "How do I know it's not a knife in the back that I'll get?"

"Bah! Irene loves you; I've nothing else in life—except Holy Russia." And the big Cossack darted one glance at the girl which revealed all his heart. "If she wants you, she shall have you, my son. Besides, you're a man worth while. But mind you, it's marriage for a lifetime! I offer you a place, friendship, companions; not wealth, but honest work. Here I'm a peddler. Among the Don Cossacks, I'm something else."

"Done with you," said Casey. "How do you know I'll play you fair?"

Ivanov laughed in his beard. "I've seen you look at Irene— that's all I need to know. It's no easy life with us, if that's what you're after."

"No," said Casey. "I'm after a life where I give the orders."

IVANOV'S HAND crashed on his back. "Good! That's Cossack life; that's what I saw in your face! It's agreed, then. A free man among free men—the brethren of the Don! You must have a horse, clothes, arms; you can't leave here a French soldier."

"I'm not leaving now," Casey said quickly. "Tomorrow night."

The other stared at him. "No, no!" he said urgently. "That may be too late."

"Not until then." And Casey gestured toward Mullins. "I must go back with him."

"Bah!" Ivanov passed a finger across his throat. Casey caught his arm and glared into his eyes.

"Careful! None of that. He's my comrade—until I go."

For a moment the Cossack stared at him. Then the bearded features relaxed in a wide grin.

"Ha! A gamble. You have money for horse and clothes?"

"You know well I haven't a sou."

"Right. Then listen! I'll spin a coin with you. If I win, you go here and now, and your comrade to the wolves. If you win, it's tomorrow night—and I'll provide the horse and clothes. Agreed? One spin of the coin?"

As he spoke, Ivanov drew out a big silver coin and flipped it in air.

Into Casey's brain flashed the memory of the girl's words. Somehow, she must have known her father meant to spin the coin—spin it, not toss it. Teague Casey was nobody's fool. He understood in a split second: a crooked coin, of course.

"Spin it!" he said. The Cossack stooped and spun the coin on the hard earthen floor. "Tails!" exclaimed Casey sharply. "Tails, I win!"

Ivanov leaped up, hand to dagger. Before Casey's grin, his face changed. The coin fell tails up.

THERE WAS an instant of silence. Ivanov glared at Casey, flashed one glance at Irene—then his white teeth showed through his beard in a laugh. He caught up the coin and pressed it into Casey's hand.

"I should have known that nobody can fight love," he said simply. "Keep it for luck, my son. Now, another drink! So those English lines above you are pretty thin, eh?"

The fiery vodka burned Casey's throat. The coin burned his

*Looming bearded figures; a click, a stab—and on
to the next.... Into them again—the wave was
halted once more, not by men but by crazed fiends.*

pocket. The eyes of Irene, shining like stars, burned his very
soul; and exultation surged in his veins.

"Thin as butter," said he. "They scarcely have enough men
there to relieve the guards. Half their camp is down with
disease."

Ivanov tapped him on the shoulder and spoke at his ear.

"Better go now, before one of your patrols comes around.
Tomorrow night, here at this place, remember. All will be ready,
my son. And if I were you,"—his eyes drew into glittering

pin-points,—"I'd be sick tomorrow morning—really sick! Good night."

The two Legionnaires went stumbling back toward camp. The high white frosty moon had thinned. Snow-mist was in the air, a high vapor.

"Bli' me!" said Mullins. "I have me doubts about yon peddler man of yours, comrade. He asked too many questions, he did. About the positions, the guns, all of it. A blinkin' spy, I say."

"Nonsense. He's coming to peddle his things in the lines, when he gets the permission," said Casey. "A spy isn't lugging his daughter along."

"Right you are, my lad, right you are. A fine lass, from what I could see of her. But what's to come of it, I ask you?"

"That's what I'd like to know," said Casey darkly, and hugged his secret to himself. One more day, and he was done with it all. Then off for the steppes, a wedding, a free man's life!

When he rolled up in the cold tent, he was happy for the first time in months. One more day of it! Then he wouldn't exchange places with General Canrobert himself, by heaven!

He completely forgot, until too late, what Ivanov had said about playing sick next morning. With no reason mentioned, it had made no impression upon him.

The day came up gray, with masses of fog sweeping in from the sea, filling the ravines and blanketing the heights. The meager breakfast was over, the business of the day was in hand, when a spattering of rifle-shots was heard from near and far, all along the line of outposts.

From the adjacent British positions, volley after volley began to crash out. The French bugles blew frantically; the drums took up the alarm; to right and left the French 1853-model rifles, transformed carbines, began to ring out. Officers were desperately trying to get some men forward. Casey and Mullins fell in, and three companies of the 1st Regiment trotted off to the wide ravine that led toward the outposts.

"It's an attack under cover of the fog," panted Mullins.

"Listen—hear them volleys? The British positions are catching of it hot and heavy, my lad!"

"And we haven't a brigade in shape to move up, from what I hear," Casey put in. "That means we've got to hold 'em. Holy mother o' God! Would you look at that!"

His gasp was reëchoed through the ranks. For a moment the fog thinned, lifted slightly. Coming for them in silence through the mist, filling the entire ravine, was an enormous gray mass, wave after wave of Russians. Then another swirl, and the fog was down again, cloaking everything.

An officer came dashing up. "The Legion must hold them until the brigades can be moved up!" he cried. "Fix bayonets!"

"Leather-bellies it is," said Mullins in French; and the words spread with a laugh through the ranks—then the ranks were charging into the fog and the tremendous gray sea of men there.

The first company was swallowed up in an instant. The second followed, and was engulfed. Casey went plunging in with the third and last company—and next moment that gray mass was halted and writhing.

Three companies against an army!

It was a mad pandemonium in which all order was lost. The Russians gave back; frantically the officers got what remained of the three companies formed up, and as the gray wave rolled on again, the Legion met them halfway. Flash, stab, jerk to clear the bayonet—to Casey, it was all a chaos of furious fighting such as he had dreamed long since but never met before.

Looming bearded figures; a rasp and a click, a stab—on to the next! Cold steel, and the leather-bellies sheer madmen in the midst. The wave rolled over them, writhed horribly, was halted again; fewer leather-bellies emerged now. Mullins had a blood-streaming face as he stabbed. Casey lost a *sabot*, cursed frantically, found it again, and went on.

Over them the wave rolled anew, and once more halted in agony as the cold steel of the leather-bellies pierced into its vitals.... Halted and rolled back, broken and in confusion.

Another officer, his saber dripping blood, was yelling frantically.

"A demi-brigade of the Legion's coming up—hold them! Form up, form up—"

Casey looked around. Forty or fifty leather-bellies were rallying, waiting, panting and leaning on their weapons. Then it came as before, that huge gray mass rolling forward; and the order—and the charge.

Into them again; the wave broke, eddied around, was halted once more, not by men but by crazed fiends who fought like mad. A wild yell, and two companies of chasseurs were in on the flank. Then, on the other flank, a wilder yell—here was the demi-brigade of the Legion hurtling forward into the midst of everything, trampling corpses and wounded, plunging through the mist with the cold steel.

Casey tore into the thick of it. The Russian ranks had closed up, halted, were firing. The bayonets ripped them apart. A clicking rasp of steel, and the two lines wavered, surged back and forth. There was Viénot, colonel of the 1st, in the midst of it all with his saber flashing. Casey stabbed a passage to him; a little knot formed there, and the mêlée centered around it.

MEANWHILE, TO right and left, along the French and English lines roared the volleys. The Russians, covered by fog from the dread artillery fire, were making a violent attempt to smash through the thinly guarded lines. Success meant an overwhelming victory, the allied positions crumpled and broken, the camps and headquarters taken—and only the leather-bellies, with the chasseurs aiding, held up that column of victory, preventing the allies from being driven into the sea.

Now came the remainder of the Brigade Étrangère; both regiments of the Legion, every man of them able to bear arms, striking into the Russian column with a ferocity, a brutality, that smashed those serried masses and rolled them back. Still the fight was stubborn, as fresh Russians poured up, but the Legion yielded no foot of ground.

And suddenly a terrific fusillade split the thinning mist, a
hoarse yell went up—here was the Brigade of Lourmel, firing
as it charged. The reserves were up at last; three French brigades
were hurled at the Russians. The movement was flung back, the
gray masses crumpled. The artillery began to crash as the fog
lessened, and the sullen Russian column fell back whence it
had come, defeated.

CASEY, UNABLE to lift his wearied arms, stood panting
in utter exhaustion. A voice among cries and groans of the
shapes that littered the ground touched his ear. He stumbled
toward it, and looked down at the beefy Mullins. A glance was
quite enough.

"Hold it, me lad!" gasped the dying man. "You've done—good
work. Leather-bellies, huh? They'll have something—to remember leather-bellies by—this day—"

So he died. Noon had come and gone, Casey found to his
astonishment, and the battle of Inkermann had passed into
history....

The afternoon was a nightmare of labor with the dead and
wounded. The Legion had suffered frightfully. The later hours
came down with a bitter freeze, and Casey huddled for warmth.
The hot blood had cooled in him now. Mullins had gone, and
this obtuse but friendly tongue had been his one link with
sanity. The eyes of Irene were beckoning to him, glinting at him
out of the gray sunset.

Colonel Viénot passed by—he so soon to be cut down by
Russian lead at the head of his men—and spoke briefly, curtly.
When he had gone, Casey looked after him with a scowl, and
spat, and rubbed the scarred end of his flat nose. Corporal?
Corporal be damned. He was no bloody hero. That morning's
fight had brought on its reaction, and all heroism was sapped
out of him in this terrific cold snap. Teague Casey wanted
warmth above anything in the world—warm food, warm shelter,
warm arms. And they were his for the having.

He took out that big silver coin, and twirled it between his fingers, and watched it spin, a grin on his lips.

"Tails it's go; heads it's stay and be made a corporal!" he muttered. The coin fell, and the eagles were up. "Tails it is!"—and Casey pocketed it.

That night Private Casey of the Legion, Corporal Casey to be, departed. That he had deserted, was unthinkable; he was set down as missing, and that was the end of it.

A S H E told us this, and came toward the close of his own tale, red-headed Casey peered at us with weaving head, and his tongue was thickened. He emptied his glass again and resumed his story where he had left off.

"Now, was the old fellow talking to me the ghost of my uncle Teague, or was it himself in the flesh? I dunno," he said in maudlin accents. "And why did he take a shine to and throw vodka into me by the quart until I was pretty near drunk? It was him did all the talking. I had no chance at all.

"Along in the gray of dawn, he took me out and led me back into Eupatoria, and never quit me until we were close to our billets. Then he halted and shook hands with me, and shoved the big silver coin into my hand. And here it is in proof that I'm no liar when I tell it."

He spun the coin, and looked at it with morose and terrible eyes. Something in his look, in his face, startled me. Suddenly, without knowing why, I realized that I had been wrong in my first thought. It was not that Casey was afraid of old age. He was afraid of something else—some memory, some thought in his brain. And then, lifting his head with an effort, he told us what it was.

"I told you about Captain de Silz," he said. "It was him or me to go into that hell up-country, with those dispatches; and neither of us cared which got the job. I asked him which of us was to go, and he shrugged. So I took out this coin, and I spun it; and 'Heads!' says he, as you might expect. Then, while the coin still spun, he spoke again: 'Heads goes, tails stays here—'

And as he spoke, the coin fell with heads down, as it always does. So Captain de Silz laughed, and shook hands with me, and went out; and that was the last ever heard of him, too."

Casey's head drooped. He could hardly keep his eyes open.

"There y'are," said he. "That's what I can't stand to think about. Seventeen years ago, and him off dead somewhere, and me worse'n dead with my red hair thinning out, and age coming on, and—and—"

He sighed, and with the deep breath lolled forward on the table, and his head sank down on his arm. His hand was covering the silver coin.

Kramer looked at him, then looked at me, and shrugged slightly.

"Poor devil!" he observed, but there was a thoughtful look in his eyes. "Or should I say 'Poor Legion!' that such a man should be known as one of its veterans? Well, remorse rides him hard, obviously; and tolerance is a great thing. And I suppose none of us is an angel."

"The whole thing was nonsense, something he made up," I said. "That yarn was no more than a drunken rigmarole, Kramer. It never happened at all."

KRAMER LOOKED at me. "No, my friend; it did happen. It was real. I've no doubt that the old Cossack he saw was really his own uncle."

"What makes you so positive?" I questioned curiously.

"This fellow,"—Kramer gestured toward the sodden Casey— "doesn't know much about the Legion. He has a superficial knowledge, yes; he's not the sort to probe into its history and traditions, as you know. Yet his hypnotic vision, or whatever it was, contained a wealth of detail that was correct; and above all, one thing that can't be found in the records. One thing that happens to be true, and yet something that practically no one knows."

"You mean, that the Russians called the Legionnaires leather-bellies?"

Kramer laughed a little, and shook his head.

"No; that old army stuff is known to everyone. The more I think of it, the more I'm astonished by Casey voicing the one fact above all others. It's the very last detail that anyone would think of."

"And what the devil is it, then?" I asked.

"That the Legion wore wooden *sabots* in the trenches of the Crimea."

LIFE, NOT COURAGE, LEFT THEM

*"Life, Not Courage, Left Them," is a fire-vivid story
of the Legion's gallant part in the strange adventure
of the French and Maximilian of Austria in Mexico.*

KRAMER DREW rein, looking up at the big live-oak on the higher ground, and the broken iron railing, with the defaced and ruined stone slab. He glanced at his Mexican guide, then at the village some distance away, then at the hobbling figure of an old man who was approaching. The guide spoke.

"That is old Juan, señor. He always comes when one visits the monument."

Kramer dismounted. "Take the horses to the village, enjoy yourself for an hour or two, then return," he said. "I'll go back to Vera Cruz by the night train."

The guide departed, with the horses.

Kramer made his way toward the shade of the live-oak, mopping the perspiration from his face; here in these Tierras Calientes it was always hot. His features were striking, and peculiar. Slanting forehead, long nose, long narrow chin, almost like a caricature. Not a face to forget by any means. It held strength, and virile savagery.

"So this is the spot!" he murmured, halting. This broken and half-ruined stone, surrounded by remains of the iron railing, had once been some sort of monument.

A few words chiseled in the worn stone slab were still legible, but only a few. Here and there, peeping from weeds and cactus, bits of stone showed that a building of some kind had once

stood here; the adobes were gone in the rains, no trace of wood remained, and only fragmentary foundations.

Leaning forward, Kramer tried to decipher the words graven on the slab. They were French words; odd to find French words on a stone slab in Mexico!

SOIXANTE.... ARMEE LES ECRASA.... PLUTOT QUE LE COUR.... ABANDONNA....

Kramer turned as the hobbling figure appeared—an old, incredibly old, bent man leaning on a stick, a cheap poncho over one shoulder, little shoe-button eyes glinting in a brown face that was one mass of seams and wrinkles.

"So you," said Kramer, "are Juan. I hear you witnessed what took place here a long time ago."

"Plague take your Emperor," said the curé stoutly. "I'll say no mass for him or for you!"

Juan came close, peered up at him, took the cigar he offered, and emitted a shrill cackle.

"Yes, señor. I was the altar-boy down in the village, in those days. After the Emperor came and they said mass that day, I ran away and stayed with them. You see, they needed an interpreter. And they were kind to me, and very gentle."

Kramer's thin lips split in an incredulous smile.

"Legionnaires gentle? That's a new one."

"It is true. There was little Pepita, my sister; that night before the high mass, when they all got drunk and little Pepita was in the corral among the horses, two of them fetched her out unhurt. Why, señor, they were tender as women! You know, they were here often, going back and forth on the Puebla road, guarding convoys. That was how our Mexican army knew where to wait for them and find them."

Kramer sat on a gnarled root of the oak, and old Juan squatted down beside him, puffing at the cigar. Wasps droned about; on the brown lower pasture toward the village, a few scrubby cattle grazed. The hot and listless landscape was much as it had been some seventy years ago. The village church with its high bell-tower was the same, the scattered houses were the same; except that here by the huge old live-oak had stood an ancient hacienda, a stout and massive house with sheds outlying.

DOWN THOSE dusty roads came dusty men, with convoys of mules and wagons; marching troops, who sang as they trudged—alien songs, the marching song of the Legion ringing out from the bare brown hillsides, and the gay lilt of *"Partant pour la Syrie!"* and something about the *bidon*. Gaunt bearded men, hatted with wide sombreros, rifles and bayonets aglint, huge packs towering on their backs; such men as marched a hundred and fifty miles in thirty-two hours—men who accomplished the impossible, men who made a jest of the incredible and put it behind them.

The second company of the first battalion came and went most frequently, back and forth on a portion of the road from Vera Cruz to Puebla, so that their faces were known in the village. On a Saturday night they marched in, and did not march out again; word spread abroad of some great event about to happen, parties of gold-laced officers appeared, more troops came through. That Saturday night the sleepy little village was on edge with the great news. The Emperor himself was coming, the Austrian, the legendary personage whom half Mexico fought and the other half stared at in awe....

Victor, sergeant of the second company, drank deep that night in the village *fonda*. He spoke Spanish fluently and he was a great favorite with the Mexicans, for he ever had a laugh and a song, a cheery greeting, a certain courtesy gratifying to

Spanish blood, however abased it might be. The Caballero, they called him, as a compliment.

In the *fonda* that night was the scowling village *curé*, who did not love the French invaders, also many another Mexican. Spies were here, of course; all up and down the land a guerrilla warfare was waged, armies were gathering, outlying parties of soldiers shot down. It was a merciless war, without quarter asked or given. These Mexicans were fighting for liberty. The French were fighting for an empire.

"Ha, my good priest!" cried Victor jovially. "Yours will be the honor of saying mass for the Emperor tomorrow morning!"

"Plague take your Emperor," said the *curé* stoutly. "I'll say no mass for him or for you, except over your dead bodies." With this retort he strode out, while the French roared with laughter.

Deepest of drinkers, gayest of comrades, was this Victor. His lusty oaths would make the rafters ring. In his lean wiry body was the strength of three men. When all others flagged, he kept going. Captain Junod was wont to say that if he lost Victor, he would lose the whole company. And tonight, crouching wide-eyed in one corner, little Juan the altar-boy watched and listened with all his ears to the swaggering talk and the bellowing oaths of these heroes who had fought the Moors overseas.

Arnheim, the big Bavarian who was Victor's chief friend—*corps et chemise,* as the Legion saying went—shook his head sadly over his wine.

"The corps isn't what it used to be," he said, wagging his grizzled blond beard. "Ten years ago it was the Legion; and now what is it? Merely the Regiment Stranger. The Emperor took away our name, gave us carbines instead of rifles, changed our uniforms, sent us to fight for Maximilian of Austria—"

"*Tiens!* Stop your grousing," spoke up another. "Uniforms? We're regular turkey-cocks! I'm going to transfer into the cavalry squadron and get my red pants back."

THERE WAS a burst of laughter. True, the cavalry squadron kept the red *pantalons,* the képi, the saber, but had no epaulets. Jests flew thick and fast. These marching companies were grenadiers, as the red grenades on their collars testified; but they wore white cotton trousers and blue vests, only the officers keeping to the *ténue* of the old Legion left behind in Algeria. And the hats—good Lord! The rafters rocked with laughter.

"Remember the nice little straw hats they served out to us?" cried Victor. "They lasted just one hour, if that long. Ha! These sombreros are the proper thing for this climate. And these carbines do good work. Blue sashes forever—here's to them!"

Upon the toast to the blue cummerbunds of the Legion, broke in a frightened screech. Little Juan echoed it from his corner, as his mother ran in with a torrent of excited Spanish that brought every man to his feet.

"Pepita! Little Pepita! The horses are fighting and she's in the corral—"

Out they poured, half of them not knowing what it was all about. Behind the *fonda* was a corral filled with horses and mules, who had taken to kicking and fighting. And in that hell of flying feet was the child Pepita, a year older than Juan. He ran with the others, and it was he who brought a lantern and held it up.

INTO THE corral leaped half a dozen of those wild bearded men, cursing, hitting out, savage as the frightened animals they fought. Out of the *mêlée* they dragged the senseless child, who was not greatly hurt; she and Juan and the mother were hustled into the tavern and surrounded by a crowd.

The rough fingers became gentle, the oaths were stilled, musettes were explored for tidbits; gifts and tokens showered upon all three. Juan found himself on the knee of Victor, who heard his proud boast and regarded him wide-eyed.

"What! An altar-boy? I salute you, comrade!" The bearded face softened, the wild hard eyes became warm and tender. *"Mon petit*, you do well to serve God while men kill one another; stick to it. We're friends, eh?"

"Always!" exclaimed the boy eagerly. "I don't want to see you

Victor

killed, even if you are French devils. My father's dead. Don't you want me in your company?"

"You! Hm!" Victor turned gravely. *"Hola,* Arnheim! Could we use a recruit or not? We can't take him away from his altar service; that's important."

"We could use an interpreter," said some one seriously. "We can't all chatter this parrot talk like you, Victor."

"That's an idea, *ma foi!"* Victor held up a finger to the boy. "I'll speak to the Captain. After mass tomorrow, before we leave town, hunt me up. Remember!"

Later that evening Victor had his chance, when Captain Junod summoned him.

"The Emperor will be here at eight, or before, sergeant. Mass at eight. Round up that *calotin* of a *curé* in good time; parade celebration. Decorate the church a bit in the morning. And be

The senseless child was surrounded by a crowd;
Juan found himself on the knee of Victor, who asked
gravely: "Arnheim! Could we use a recruit?"

sure to have the drummers and buglers ready for the salute at
the elevation of the Host. Do you know when that comes?"

Victor saluted gravely. "I believe, *mon capitaine*, that I know
the time. But we have no dress uniforms here—"

"What is good enough for the Legion to fight in, is good
enough for the eyes of Emperor Maximilian," said Captain
Junod. "Confound these cartridge-boxes! Half the company
has leather ones, half use their musettes—there should be some
regulation!"

Victor seized his chance. He spoke of the boy. The mother
had approved. Juan could be of great use to them, on the road

as they were. Captain Junod listened, frowned, and nodded approval.

"I'll see the mother tomorrow. If all's well, we'll use the lad."

MORNING FOUND the church decorated, the guards on hand, the Emperor in his carriage, the staff and generals in their gold lace—and no *curé*. True to his word, rather than say mass for the hated invader, he had taken to the hills. And there was not another priest within twenty miles.

"Your fault, confound you!" Furious, Captain Junod halted before Sergeant Victor, on parade with his company outside the church doors. "Why didn't you make sure of that rascal? His Majesty is waiting—"

General Bazaine was coming over to them impatiently. Victor saluted and took a step forward, his narrow pointed features lifting a trifle, his beard jutting out.

"If you'll permit me, my captain, I will say mass for you."

The men within hearing stiffened. The general, who had heard the words, came up white with rage, shoved Junod aside, and faced the sergeant.

"So! You dare to jest, do you?"

"No, *mon général,*" said Victor calmly. "I was a bishop before I entered the Legion. Under certain circumstances a bishop is always enabled to say mass. It is the business of the Legion to provide the proper person for any emergency, *mon général.* I offer myself."

A gasp ran along the files. Victor a bishop—a bishop! Even Junod stood stock still, gaping; then he turned to Bazaine and saluted briskly.

"Mass will be celebrated, my general. Sergeant! Come with me."

He led Victor into the church. The company of the Legion grinned, exchanged low words—and that ended the matter for them. Being what they were, they did not refer to this matter again. Some among them, perhaps, had been even greater than bishops in their time.

Nor was there any jesting while that mass was intoned. Pop-eyed, little Juan served the altar; in the vestments of the absent *curé,* Sergeant Victor did his duty; and Juan afterward swore that at the benediction—when he should not have been peeping—he saw tears on the bearded cheeks of more than one Legionnaire. It was something the boy always remembered vividly, as boys do remember some things.

But neither he, nor the men of the Legion, spoke of this matter in future. Juan, proudly numbering himself among these heroes, could share their virtues if not their vices.

IN FACT, the boy became the mascot of the company in no time. He wore a miniature uniform, which was made for him by a tailor in the company of fusileers, so that it had green epaulets instead of the red epaulets of the grenadiers; but he was charmed with this distinction. In his baggy red trousers, his blue tunic and cummerbund, he looked like a little monkey, but he was of extreme service when surly peasants or prisoners had to be interrogated. And he, at least, was faithful to his salt where many of his compatriots turned their backs and fled, or cut a French throat and ran for safety in the hills.

The Legionnaires—in actual fact they were no such thing, being named the Regiment Étranger—were dying in numbers from plague, yellow-jack and sun, but not fast enough to suit the Mexicans. Backed by French arms and power, Maximilian was seizing a throne in this year of 1863; he might hold the cities, but everywhere the stubborn, savage, merciless half-Indian men of Mexico were swooping in guerrilla raids from the hills, cutting communications, smashing outposts. And in the background, Diaz and Terrazas and Nuñez and other Mexican leaders were gathering their forces.

Such things did not worry little Juan; he was a boy, Victor was his great hero, Captain Junod was his demigod, and all the others of the second company were his comrades. He lived with them, for them, among them, and inside a month's time he was chattering French like any one of them.

Victor was bearded, like most of the others, with a big chin-tuft like that of Napoleon III. One day, in lighting his pipe with a firebrand, he set fire to his whiskers and burned them off, amid roars of laughter from the others. So, for a while, he went clean-shaven, and this intensified his strangely jutting features. One day, under the burning sun, with fever strongly upon him, he sat uttering strange words while Juan listened, staring at him with awe and puzzled wonder. A bishop? Yet it was true. And now he was certainly talking Latin such as the *curé* talked at times, for Juan comprehended some of the words.

Again, he spoke tenderly, softly, mentioning a woman's name, a sparkle of tears on his roughened cheeks. Juan's eyes widened. A bishop should have nothing to do with a woman; but then, a bishop should not be a Legionnaire—and an uncommonly rough one at that.

The days drifted on. Up and down the roads tramped these

undeniably odd figures of men, with their wide hats, short carbines, flopping epaulets, and white cotton *pantalons*. Each Sunday and holiday, Juan somehow managed to find himself at home serving the altar, for Victor insisted upon this sternly; the village *curé*, back at his post, scowled and stormed at him, but there was no one else to fill the place.

SO CAME one glorious week-end when the entire company, sixty strong, laid over in the village, waiting for a Puebla-bound convoy which they would take over. There were no gentry here-abouts, therefore there was no *baile;* but plenty of people came in from the hills on Sunday for the more popular fandango that night. The convoy was in, and here were queer soldiers of all kinds—chiefly *voltigeurs* of the Legion, or what had been the Legion.

Captain Junod had his hands full that night; what with fights, drinking and women, the Legion had its hands full likewise. Furious, Junod consulted with the officers of the escort whom he was to relieve, and induced them to lead their men back toward Vera Cruz at midnight. He regretted it bitterly enough a few hours later.

He got his men up and off with the wagons, at daybreak. Not a soul was visible in the village. Even the *fonda* was de-serted. Victor beckoned Juan.

"Where's Pepita? And your mother?"

The boy shrugged. "Gone. How should I know? We men don't worry where the women have gone."

Victor broke out laughing. A bugle spoke. The column formed up. Breakfast was over; the march lay ahead. Arnheim was adjutant; the Regiment Stranger did not have adjutants who were commissioned officers.

Just outside the village lay a defile, steep and narrow, com-manded by slopes thick with cactus and brush. On ahead was rising ground, with the old deserted hacienda of Carillo off to the right. Once it had been a fine house, of stone and adobe, but now it was unroofed and empty.

The curé, rather than say mass for the hated invader, had taken to the hills.

Juan was perched on a wagon as the column came through the defile. He caught a muttering from the Mexican teamsters; suddenly one of them pulled in his team, leaped clear of the wagon, and was gone like a rabbit into the brush. Another followed him, and another. All along the hillside came flashes and glints of steel. A rifle cracked, and the man next Captain Junod fell with a bullet through his head.

Pistols, old muskets, ancient guns of every kind, opened up in a tremendous fusillade; luckily, it did slight damage, for few of the Mexicans had rifles or carbines. In a flash, Captain Junod saw that this was a raid of the enemy in force, that he was cut off from any return, that his one chance of getting his men through lay in abandoning the wagons. Perhaps the guerrillas would be so eager for plunder that they would let their prey escape.... Captain Junod little knew his Mexicans.

The orders went out. Juan jumped down and darted amid the files. Victor caught sight of columns of Mexicans off to the left, closing the road ahead. He shouted at Junod, who peered through the drifting smoke and nodded.

"Forward! Once in the open, form a square. *Forward!*"

Under a scream of lead and slugs, which for the most part went high, the second company deserted the wagons and went on. Junod, with Victor beside him and little Juan pressing close, coolly eyed the road and the ground ahead. That the column was cut off, became more obvious with every moment. Mexican horsemen, a cloud of them, showed on the farther road.

"What is that place yonder?" demanded the captain, pointing.

"The old Hacienda Carillo, *mon capitaine,*" piped up Juan excitedly. "The well turned bad or it was bewitched. No one has lived there for a long time."

THE TWO lieutenants came up. Another man was dead, several were wounded. The three officers conferred shortly; then the bugle sounded.

The square formed up with precision. Ahead, the mass of horsemen was bearing down in a wild and maddened charge. Bullets had ceased to scream now. From their ambuscade, the Mexicans were pouring down to loot the wagons—in passing. Only in passing. These men were after blood, not loot. From right, from left, from the rear, rose the shrill Indian yells, as the enemy closed in.

Quiet, unhurried orders. The carbines went up. Thundering down the road came that mass of cavalry. Victor's voice crackled out; the four sides of the square began to belch smoke and bullets. Juan, peering forth as the smoke lifted a little, saw the front ranks of the cavalry go down, the others pile up on top of them. And the volleys went on, crashing out, smashing the charge on every side.

The bugle shrilled again. Forward! Orders rippled. Juan, white and frightened, heard the screaming men yell and curse, as the files passed the tangle of death that barred the road, and turned to the upper ground. Halt! The cavalry were re-forming, were bearing back for another charge. From the rear, more masses of horsemen were now appearing. The square took shape.

"The hundreds are becoming thousands," said Victor coolly, and passed his water-bottle to Juan. "Here, my son! Give Dindon a drink."

Dindon—they called him turkey-cock because he looked like one, with his scrawny neck. He was down, coughing out blood, two slugs through his chest. Juan knelt beside him and helped him to gulp at the bottle, and saw him die as the volleys began to crash again. A drifting reek of acrid fumes set the boy to coughing. He took a swig from the bottle, and blood smeared his chin—Dindon's blood.

"Ha! That's taught 'em a few things!" yelled Victor. "Juan! Where are you?"

Juan found him and stuck close to him. Captain Junod spoke briefly with the sergeant.

"Hold the house yonder—eh, Victor?"

"*Ma foi!* Thousands, no mistake about that," said Victor. "Yes, *mon capitaine.* The house, by all means. This is no skirmish, but a battle!"

"Take a dozen men, secure the place, do what you can for defense. We'll come more slowly."

The wounded, of course. He knew his business, this Junod. Victor yelled at the men and started out; beside him pattered the boy, whose first terror had passed now into a fever of excitement. Everything was unreal, terrible, magnificent.

"We'll show 'em!" he said. "We'll show the cockroaches, won't we, Victor?"

Victor laughed, the men laughed and ran for the hacienda.

They made it safely. There was a patio surrounded by half-ruined sheds; the building itself was enormous. Muskets banged;

powder-smoke spewed forth—the enemy were in part of the huge place. One of the men doubled up and collapsed. Victor set to work barricading the two great doors opening on the patio, closing window openings, pouring lead at the Mexicans in sight. To drive the enemy out of the whole place was impossible.

"Your job, Juan!" In the midst of everything, he paused, his hand on the boy's shoulder. "Collect all the water bottles; take charge of them. Save the water for the wounded."

JUAN BUSTLED about. As the column came in, he collected the canteens and proudly assumed charge of them. Wounded there were, yes, but as yet not out of the fight. A wound had to be mortal before it kept a Legionnaire from handling a carbine.

Now there was a tremendous scattering—loads dumped, men running to walls and windows, knives and bayonets at work hacking loopholes. The Mexicans still occupied a portion of the rambling place; they were in the sheds along the patio, they were coming up by hundreds.

"A white flag!" shouted Victor.

The firing ceased, but not the bustling work. A Mexican officer came into the patio with a white flag. He could speak no French. Juan piped up, translating his command to surrender.

Captain Junod, brushing dust from his tunic, smiled.

"Never."

Just the one word. The Mexican withdrew. From huts, from brush and trees, from everywhere, began a furious storm of musketry. Bullets ripped through adobe and windows and chinks.

The second company wasted no powder. The wounded reloaded; the others fired from every point of vantage. Junod mounted to the roofless crest of the structure, and after a time came back to the main room of the place. He summoned the adjutant. As Arnheim came, a bullet went through his brain.

The boy's first terror had passed into excitement now. "We'll show the cockroaches!" he said. "Won't we, Victor?"

His body was dragged aside; other bodies were lying here now, Juan was helping the wounded tie up their hurts, and was passing the precious water around. Captain Junod went up to Victor.

"It's worse than we thought," he said coolly. "Thousands of them; we have an entire Mexican army upon us. Summon every man who can be spared."

Word was passed. The men came crowding in. Captain Junod eyed them and his voice lifted in cold precision.

"My comrades, we are fighting an army. The Legion does not surrender. I think this is quite understood, but there may come a moment when some of us hesitate. Swear after me—"

He lifted his hand, and the sonorous words came from his lips. No melodrama about it, no theatrical phrases; short, curt sentences that burned. Hands lifted, and the oath was sworn. It was carried out to the others at loopholes and windows. Presently the report came back. Every man had sworn; even the wounded added their voices. No surrender—a fight to the death!

Junod lifted his arm to speak again. The arm jerked—then again. On his gold-laced sleeve appeared a gush of scarlet. Over the neck of his white shirt spurted a red stream. He collapsed in the arms of Lieutenant Baudry, dead.

Calmly, Baudry took charge. The firing continued, incessant. The carbines of the dead and wounded served, when the others became too hot to use. Juan was busier than ever now.

Noon came and passed. Suddenly men stiffened, faces lifted, movement ceased; clear and high, the sound of bugles, and then the pulsation of drums, sounded. Two of the men scrambled up to the roof-edges. Victor stood awaiting their report. Every man thrilled to it, and Juan stood gaping, listening, eager-eyed. Troops! Another column of the Regiment—

One of the men scrambled down. The other fell headlong with a ball through his head.

"Three new battalions of Mexicans coming up," was the report.

THE HEAT of the day was terrific.

There was no more water. One o'clock, two o'clock; Baudry got a bullet through his heart, and Lieutenant Berg took charge. The floor was littered with dead and dying now.

The men had long since cast aside hats and vests. Shirts followed. Naked to the blue sashes, black with powder, unrecking of wounds, they fought on. Juan guarded the water jealously for the wounded, his own mouth too parched for speech.

Victor was everywhere, watching everything, and lending a hand to everyone. His gay, eager laugh rose high, though hoarsely.

"Victor!" One of the Bavarians, with a bullet through the body, called feebly. Victor went to him. Blond-bearded, blue-eyed, the dying man looked up at him. "I fear God, comrade; give me absolution."

Victor choked and came to his knees, and hid his face in his hands. After a moment he lifted his head, and the two of them spoke together, and presently the Bavarian died, smiling.

AFTER THIS, others of the men called Victor to them, or went apart with him for a moment.

Juan, awed, wondering, remembered that he had been a bishop. Always, the men who spoke with him came away smiling, or different; like people who came out of the shrouded confessional, the boy thought.

"Lieutenant! Where's Lieutenant Berg?" yelled some one.

"He's dead," came response. "What's the fuss about?"

"They're firing the sheds, out there."

Fire! Upon the reeking shambles came new heat, new suffocating clouds of smoke. Under cover of the fumes, charge after charge was made; outside, the dead were heaped high, the charges were repulsed, but each charge left a few less men inside. The afternoon was passing. Victor, conscious of a hush, a cessation of the fire outside, took stock.

Fifteen men remained on their feet. And Juan, unhurt. Victor went to him, wiped sweat and blood from his eyes, and grinned at the boy.

"Out of that uniform—no talk!" he croaked. "Here, Charles! Get that gaudy Mexican blanket out of Emile's pack and give it here."

Amazed, but obeying the command, the boy stripped. Victor threw the gaudy native blanket about him, took his hand, led him into a little back room where a pile of boards and refuse was heaped about one window-opening. No firing came from this direction; the window was placed high above the ground here.

"You alone, Juan, have not sworn the oath—"

"But I'll swear it!" cried the boy eagerly. "I will, Victor—"

"You will not! I command you!" snapped the man. "Remain here. I've an important bit of work for you, comrade," and he pressed a folded paper into the boy's hand. "Take this. It'll soon be dark and you can get away. The Mexicans won't hurt you, now that you're not in our uniform. Give this paper to one of our officers, some day."

"I will, Victor. What does it say?"

"That the second company was composed of good soldiers."

"Yes, Victor…. Won't you give me your blessing, please?"

The rough, harsh man with the queerly pointed features leaned down and kissed the boy, and made the sign of the cross above him—then abruptly shoved him out of sight under the debris and was gone.

A lull, in the sunset. The voice of a Mexican officer rose clearly to the few grim men who waited here. His harangue needed no interpreter; they caught enough of the words to understand it. Victor went from man to man. Outside, the sheds had burned down, revealing blackened pits beneath one and another.

A burst of yells went up. A man at a loophole turned.

"Here they come, Victor!"

YES, THEY came—came with a rush.

The carbines banged out, pitifully few. From the rear of the house, the barricades were burst down. Mexicans flooded in. The doors were burst down, bayonets flashed, knives glittered, swarthy Indian faces were alight with slaughter.

Through the hell of it stormed Victor. Somehow, he was outside, five men after him; the rest were dead now. The six broke through the whole mass of men outside and gained one of the fire-blackened pits, recessed in the hillside. Bayonets fixed, they remained there. Moments passed. Attack after attack rolled upon them, but they were protected from the rear and the flanks. One man fell. Another pitched forward. Victor stood in the forefront. He was alone now, streaming with blood.

The Mexicans drew away. He dragged himself out and faced them, shook his fist at them—his carbine was broken.

There was a spattering explosion, and the bullets lifted him, and he dropped back among his men.

Then the sun was gone, and darkness came down, and the boy Juan wormed his way out of shelter. Hundreds of men lay dead here; the odor of blood was sickening. As he got away into the scrub, a flickering light arose. Looking back, Juan saw that the hacienda was fired and was blazing high....

The voices died. The croaking tones of old Juan, recalling the days of his boyhood, drifted and died into silence.

Kramer looked out. Something was stirring far down the road; the plodding figures of a man and two horses. His guide, returning for him.

"So this is the spot!" he murmured.

"This is the place, señor," said old Juan, and pointed to a huge burst of cactus a little distance away. "The cactus, there, comes out of the old pit. That is where my comrade Victor died. It is hard to tell, now, where the hacienda stood."

"But you remember."

"I remember, señor," mumbled old Juan. "He gave me his blessing, and he was a bishop. It is something I do not understand, señor. For he spoke of a woman and of a child, I think; it was when he had fever, one day. Yet a bishop does not have anything to do with women. It is indeed very strange, very strange."

"That man—you called him Victor?" Kramer lifted his head and looked at the broken old stone slab with its writing. "He had another name."

"Perhaps he had, señor; most of us in the Legion had another name," said old Juan. "Yes, you look like him. You have his face. I could almost imagine, as I told you about it, that you were the comrade whom I loved. He was not your father?"

"My father's father," said Kramer softly, and rose. "That is why I came here today, Juan. I have been a long time coming."

He went over to the slab and looked down at it.

The sun had changed. Now its slanting rays brought out the old carving in the stone, made shadows where there had been nothing, brought to light the broken letters. And Kramer, looking at them, could make out one sentence of this slab that had been laid above the Second Company:

LIFE, NOT COURAGE, LEFT THEM.

THE FIRST AMERICAN TO
FIGHT IN THE LEGION

"The First American to Fight in the Legion" is
fiction—but fiction based on very probable fact, and
written with the flaming reality of truth itself.

T HE F I R S T American ever to serve in the Foreign
Legion, you ask? Now you're asking something. Who
knows, who cares? Yet the thought has its interest; it piques the
attention. The records of the Legion are silent, but other records
exist. Attic records. Those old letters Ellis Clarke wrote home
to Wisconsin, lying in a trunk up in the attic all these years.
Even after he was mustered out of the Union cavalry, down on
the border, he wrote his mother pretty regularly, and she trea-
sured the letters....

He was writing home that night outside Matamoras, when
the orders came in regard to the Hacienda of Santa Ysabel.

Clarke was a pretty hard citizen, and so was Bill Hicks. They
were quartered together in an adobe hut, and Clarke was writing
beside the fireplace in the corner—a little, high fireplace used
for both cooking and heating. It was the end of January, 1865,
and the warmth from the fire felt good to the hut's occupants.

Both men wore the Union blue, stripped of all insignia except
the name of Cortina on bands around their caps. Like scores
of others, they had flocked across the border to take a hand in
the Mexican scrap, now that things were quieted down over
the line. They were with Cortina's irregulars, fighting tooth and
nail against the Austrians, French and the Mexicans who supported Maximilian on the throne.

"So you're Cap'n Clarke, and I'm Lootenant Hicks, huh?"
Bill Hicks took another swig from the tequila bottle, and

smacked his lips. "Gorry, that's hot stuff!... Say, the old Third Wisconsin would sure as hell open their eyes to see us officers, huh?"

Clarke glanced up, grinned, signed his name to the letter, and laid it aside.

"Suits me," he said. "We're going to clean up on these French yet. After four years of soldiering back home, the farm don't look so good to me. Officers, you bet! And the way these boys can fight is an eye-opener, Bill."

H E   WA S   a rangy, hard-bitten man of thirty, bowlegged from the saddle, with a reddish mustache, thin lips and chin, and bitter gray eyes. Bill Hicks was lumpy, heavy-set, a hard drinker and with the general morals of a jackrabbit, but a darned good man in a scrap.

"Well," said Hicks, biting at a twist of tobacco, "I hear tell the French have got new regulations to shoot all guerrillas like us, so watch your step, feller. I met a guy in town today from the 71st New York. He says a lot o' Johnny Rebs are with the

French. Say, let's you and me mosey into town and look up a couple of them señoritas—"

The door swung open. A Mexican saluted, and spoke eagerly to Clarke.

"Señor Capitan! General Cortina orders that you take your company, mount, and ride at once for the Hacienda of Santa Ysabel, twenty miles south. A guide is being provided. A column of French and Mexicans are moving to attack the hacienda, and the garrison there must be reinforced. It is one of our most important positions."

"On the jump," said Clarke. "Send this letter for me, will you? Thanks. We'll be marching in twenty minutes, señor."

And in twenty minutes the jingling company of irregular cavalry, with Clarke and Hicks and the guide riding ahead, were trotting out of camp—a hundred motley troopers, mainly Mexicans, with a few negro soldiers out of the regiment at Clarksville, and a scattering of Americans.

IT WAS natural that, the war between the States at an end, footloose Americans should flock over the line and join up with

the republicans fighting against the Emperor Maximilian. Not
the cause of liberty attracted them, but the good pay and the
chances of loot, and the pretty girls and the hot liquor. They
were no fancy heroes laying their swords on the altar of liberty—
not by a darned sight. They were out to raise hell where no law
existed except that of the revolver; and they did it.

"Funny about these greasers," observed Bill Hicks, at Clarke's
stirrup. "I been getting a line on things. Seems like they're scared
as hell of the French boys, who know how to put up a scrap.
The Austrians are no good except to shoot down. Them greasers with the Emperor aint worth a hang. But the French—
they're good. That new law about shooting all guerrillas don't
hearten our boys a lot, neither. And they don't like that durned
Foreign Legion the French have got. Ever hear of it?"

Clarke grunted. "Yeah, I got a cousin in it, or had. Jim was
no-account. Just before the war broke, he robbed somebody
and lit out. Last we heard from him, he was in their Foreign
Legion, over in Algiers. Dead by now, I reckon. We used to be
pretty thick, him and me. He was sure a bad one, but there was
something about him you liked. Say, Bill—this hacienda we're

The Legion was breaking; one man, ill,
was in the captain's saddle.... A battalion
of staggering, stumbling men.

heading for: they tell me the garrison there is probably lousy with loot from all this part of the country. Keep your eye peeled for pickings, and we'll work the riffle together."

"You bet." Bill Hicks chuckled softly.

Twenty miles; but the road was a mere cattle trail. It was past three o'clock when Clarke, to pay safe, sent ahead three of his blacks to scout the last few miles.

The dawn was graying when a pulsing beat of rifle-fire reached them. Clarke halted his men and reined up beside Hicks. They knew instantly what had happened: the French column had reached the hacienda ahead of them. Came the scurrying thud of a horseman at full gallop. One of the scouts hammered up and drew rein.

"Cap'n, boss!" he exclaimed. "We's too late, suh!"

"How many of the French, Arkansas?"

"We 'lowed about a hundred, suh. And a lot o' Mexican cavalry."

"Bad news for us," muttered Bill Hicks. "This gang of ours aint itching to fight no frogs, you bet. Do we ride back?"

"Like hell!" said Clarke. "Take fifty men and the guide. Circle around. I'll give you half an hour start, then come on with the other fifty. Hit that column from the south; I'll come in from this side. Scatter out your men. The greasers will run; and between us and the garrison we'll nip the French."

"Got it," said Bill Hicks laconically, and was off.

A BRIEF halt for breakfast, and Clarke rode on—his men none too eager, as the rifle-fire told them that the French were there already. The hacienda came into full sight as they topped a rise. It was a scant mile away; the full day had broken by this time. Clarke halted his riders and rode out to view the cluster of buildings with its high surrounding wall.

A garrison of two hundred men there under a Colonel Mendez, who had a reputation for butchering every Frenchman he could lay hands on. The walls were spurting smoke. In front of the hacienda gates was an outflung force of white-clad men who had taken cover, thrown up trenches, and were firing carefully, slowly. Parties of Mexican cavalry had circled about the hacienda, their horses dashing madly, their gunfire spitting wildly. Arkansas had estimated their numbers very fairly, Clarke found.

"Dismount!" He snapped out his orders. "Advance on foot behind me; scatter out well. You horse-guards, ride 'em back and forth over this rise, like cavalry spreading out."

He rode forward deliberately; he wanted to be seen. Almost at once, a bugle shrilled. The parties of Mexican horse began to form up; at this moment, rifles began to sputter on the other side of the hacienda. The scattered force of Bill Hicks came into sight, advancing rapidly.

Yell upon yell pealed up from the Mexican horse. In vain the French bugle voiced its silver call. It was all too plain that the column was caught between two fires of an overwhelming force; and amid a cloud of dust, the Mexican cavalry took to its heels. The French, now caught between the hacienda and the new-comers, deserted by their allies, frantically fell to work throwing up new entrenchments at their rear.

Clarke, riding in, squinted at them and cursed admiringly. They knew their business. A dozen wagons with them were being lined up; the animals were shot and their bodies dumped; as by magic, a hollow square was formed.

"Damned good troops!" said Clarke, and dismounted.

He met the grinning Hicks. The fire of the French continued steadily, keeping down that from the walls before them; then Clarke's men spread out and opened fire against the square; it was a deadly fire. They advanced like Indians, taking cover behind every rock and cactus-clump.

"Bill! Stop the firing," Clarke said suddenly. "Got a handkerchief?"

"Had one my ma give me, but lost it at Gettysburg," said Bill Hicks.

"Stop the firing, you horse's neck!" snapped Clarke.

Hicks obeyed. The rifle-fire dwindled. That from the French died out. Clarke stripped to the waist, took a rifle from the nearest man, and waved his shirt on it. He stepped out, and the firing died from the walls of the hacienda.

As Clarke advanced, a Frenchman leaped from the wagons and came out to meet him, a figure in white cotton, blue vest and huge straw hat.

"Hey, you!" called Clarke. "Savvy any English? *Habla Español?*"

"Talk English," responded the other.

"All right. I got five thousand men coming on—only got a thousand here, but the rest are behind, with Cortina himself. Surrender and do it quick, and you'll get terms. Refuse, and Cortina will wipe you out."

"Well, I'll be damned!" came the response. "If you aint the

*"Hey, you!" called
Clarke. "Savvy
any English?
Habla Español?"*

same big liar you always was, Ellis Clarke! Hello, durn you!
Thought I knowed your walk."

Clarke stared, his jaw fallen; then he uttered a yell and caught
the hand of the other, and pumped it.

"Jim! Why, damn your hide, I was talkin' about you only last
night! Say, this is great. Who's in command of your outfit?"

"Right now, I am," said the other, grinning all over his lean

bronzed face. "Every officer dead or laid out. Want to surrender
to me?"

Clarke sobered. "No joking, Jim. I aint got quite so many
men as I said, but I want to save your necks. I can't do it unless
you give in."

"Go to hell," snorted the other promptly. "Listen here, Ellis:
I got what's left of three companies of the Legion, first battalion. The Legion just aint learned that surrender talk. Say,
what in hell are you doing in Mexico?"

"Same as you, only with the other side, I reckon," said Ellis
Clarke. "Damn your stubborn hide, will you surrender?"

"I will not, nor my outfit neither."

"You fool, you haven't got a chance!"

"All right, all right." A rifle cracked somewhere; a bullet
buzzed, and Jim Clarke turned. "Your folks are getting impa-
tient. Sorry we aint got time to talk. Say, you got a chew of
tobacco on you?"

"Sure." Ellis Clarke handed over a twist. Another bullet sped
from the hacienda walls. "Change your mind and do it quick—"

"See you later!" And his cousin went hastily for the wagon.
A cheer rang out from the French—a long cheer, a wild, lusty
roaring cheer. It was answered by shrill Mexican yells from the
hacienda garrison and Clarke's troopers.

LESS THAN two minutes later the rifles were again smashing out. Clarke, telling Bill Hicks about meeting his cousin,
stared gloomily at the scene.

"What with our fire on their rear, they haven't got a ghost,"
he said. "They can't keep down the garrison's fire now—look
there!"

True. The high walls of the hacienda were spurting and
streaming smoke, for the defenders of the doomed square below
were unable to maintain a punishing fire; and from those walls
bullets rained into their little compound unhindered. Ellis

Clarke cursed furiously as the moments passed, as the French reply dwindled.

"They got their bellyful now, maybe," suggested Bill Hicks. "You always got to give furriners their bellyful, and then they'll hear to reason. Once Mendez fetches out his men from inside, it's a throat-cutting. Want to try again?"

CLARKE NODDED. Hicks sent out the word; and the troopers, who had suffered heavily enough, let their rifles cool. Again the white shirt waved, and again the jetting smoke from the hacienda walls fell away to nothing. Clarke walked out, and was relieved past measure when his cousin appeared, a bloody rag about his head, his straw hat gone.

"Thought maybe you'd stopped one," he observed. "Looks like the last chance, Jim. I only got a hundred men here, some less now, thanks to your lead. If Mendez comes with his outfit to rush you, it's all up."

"Butcher Mendez, huh?" Jim Clarke spat. "Well, I got you down to telling the truth anyhow, Ellis. Fact is, we only got twenty men on their feet, and most of them are hit. What's your offer?"

"Prisoners."

"Nope. We march clear with our arms, or we stick to hell and back. Yes or no?"

Ellis Clarke saw the great gates of the hacienda swaying, as supports were removed and bulwarks hauled away.

"Done," he said, and turned. "Hey, Bill! Fetch in the gang, hotfoot. Quick, damn you!"

"What's the big idea?" demanded Jim Clarke.

"Mendez is coming now. Might have trouble. Go wet down your friends and get 'em in one corner. If there's any gunplay, I'll start it. Say, Jim, what's your name?"

Jim Clarke grinned. "Faber, Jim Faber. Sounds German. Sergeant Faber, that's me!"

The gates trembled, moved, swung open. Already Hicks and

the troopers were coming up to the wagons on a run. Ellis Clarke met them as they came, and held up his hand.

"The French keep their arms, and march clear. Loot what you like before Mendez gets there, but don't touch any Frenchman, or I'll kill you."

Then he headed them into the doomed little fort of bodies and wagons, where corpses sprawled and the sand was black with blood; and in one corner Jim Faber herded the desperate, wounded, thirst-maddened remnant of three Legion companies. Leaving Bill Hicks to keep his own men in hand, Clarke mounted on a dead horse and faced the line of Mexicans streaming from the hacienda.

"Halt!" he shouted. "Halt, or we fire! This is Captain Clarke—"

"Ah, señor!" Mendez himself came swaggering forward, a rangy, half-Indian man with gold braid scattered all over his uniform and sombrero. "We are friends. I met you in Matamoras. You came in the very nick of time with your brave *soldados!* Bring out the Frenchmen so they may be executed."

"I've given them terms." Clarke met the hot, swarthy eyes. "They're my prisoners; rather, they go free. Their camp and wagons are yours—"

"Go free?" A torrent of curses poured from Mendez. "By the saints, I say they shall not! I am your superior officer; I order you to retire with your men and leave the accursed French to me."

"You want to shoot them?"

"No, hang them; every one. I have sworn it. I shall do it—"

Clarke whipped up his revolver and shot Butcher Mendez between the eyes. It was done coolly, calmly, deliberately.

THEN IT was touch and go, and no mistake. When Clarke walked on in among them, the stunned rebels fell away from him; when he spoke to them, they listened. This move won the game. Another officer came forward, and Clarke spoke to him coldly.

"Get on with your looting and don't interfere with me. I saved you, drove off the Mexican cavalry, and took care of the French. You can fill the boots of Mendez."

"Agreed, señor," said the officer. "But when General Mendez, brother of the señor colonel, hears of this, you'll talk differently. It's his affair, not mine."

"And where is he?" sneered Clarke.

"At Monterrey, señor. With General Escobedo."

"Far away from here." Clark laughed and turned on his heel. "I'll be ready for him."

His own men and the garrison looted freely; the French were not molested. Clarke joined Bill Hicks and Jim Faber, and gave the latter a level-eyed look.

"Jim, throw up these damned French and chuck in your bag with us. What say?"

"Nope. Thanks all the same, Ellis. I got a man's job. Sorry I missed your little war up north. Got a better one here. You aint doing so bad yourself, I notice."

"Hey, Cap'n!" said Hicks anxiously. "What in hell did you go and do that for? Now we'll all be strung up for killing Mendez—"

"Stop your bleating," snapped Clarke. "Nothing of the sort, Bill. These fellows are killers. I've got 'em topped, that's all. His brother the General will go out for my hide, and nothing more'll come of it. You'll see; gun law is what counts."

And gun law counted. Clarke went about his business, and the awed Mexicans gave him free going. The man who had shot down Butcher Mendez got anything he wanted, now and later. It was a bloody land, and only the strongest, the most merciless, could survive. Ellis Clarke's chill gray eye had judged aright.

The few French, with a couple of wagons and escorted by Bill Hicks and fifty troopers, went their way. Clarke exchanged a last hand-grip with Jim Faber, sergeant of the first battalion of the Legion, and walked into the hacienda to make himself

*"Jim! Say, this is great!... Damn your
stubborn hide, will you surrender to me?"
"I will not, nor my outfit neither. The Legion
just ain't learned that surrender talk."*

at home in the quarters of Mendez. A day later he had sobered up enough to write another letter home, telling about it.

After that, Ellis Clarke became a colonel under Cortina, and then dropped from sight. He was not a man to admire, not even a man to like; but he was the only sort of man who could win respect among the wild guerrilla bands. Other Americans came over to the rebel cause, looted and killed and burned, and got nowhere; in fact, Sheridan came after them and clapped more than a few of them in jail.

CLARKE WAS lost to view. The rebels had scant organization; one day they were in the saddle; the next some French force had them on the run. The United States had not yet interfered. Maximilian was supreme. The rebel leaders were fighting, but no one knew much about them. They fought each other and the French. Diaz, the strong man of them all, was in a French prison, hard and fast. Juarez was playing for time. One or two brief letters from Ellis Clarke got across the border and were mailed home, but they gave no detail of his movements.

Then, from the east and the south, a flying French column headed for Monterrey to smash the rebels there. Other columns

"Leave the accursed French to me," Mendez said. "I shall hang them, every one. I—" Clarke whipped up his revolver and shot Butcher Mendez—it was done coolly, deliberately.

were ordered to concentrate with it at Monterrey, where a few French were besieged in the citadel. It was a sudden, vicious burst of energy. The orders were imperative; march night and day, march as men never marched before—but get there!

Captain Saussier, with the first battalion of the Legion, was holding the La Blanca hacienda, ninety miles away. Besides his

Legion companies, just brought up to their old strength by the Legion reserves newly arrived from Africa, he had the mounted squadron of the Legion. The hacienda was an important outpost. He himself was a dry, hard, tough little man, who had seen the battalion killed off almost to the vanishing-point before the reserves came in.

THAT NIGHT, before the courier arrived, a squadron detachment brought in a scarecrow whom they had found sitting on a dead horse. He was clad in rags; he spoke no French; they could not understand his Spanish; he carried only a United States army model revolver. He was a bony-featured man with a glittering cold gray eye and a nearly healed bullet scar across his forehead.

Once at the hacienda, he ate like a famished wolf. They led him into the old ranch-house, where Captain Saussier was conferring with his top sergeant, reported briefly, and the Captain eyed the ragged creature with his shaggy hair and wealth of beard.

"You are a Mexican?" he inquired in Spanish. "A partisan? A guerrilla?"

A ghastly laugh shook the lean scarecrow.

"No, Señor Captain," he rejoined in execrable Spanish. "Ask Sergeant Faber, there, what I am."

A sharp exclamation broke from the sergeant. He peered into that haggard face with its mask of beard; a cry escaped him, and he turned.

"Mon capitaine! This is the man who saved us, at Santa Ysabel—the American who commanded that force, who shot Butcher Mendez!"

"Good," said Saussier. "Take him out and shoot him. A guerrilla caught with arms has only one fate."

"But it was he who saved us!" protested the sergeant, forgetting all discipline. "Besides, he's no guerrilla. Have I permission to speak with him?"

"You seem to have forgotten that any is needed," said the Captain dryly. "But speak."

Sergeant Faber obeyed. Clarke, shrugging, replied briefly. He had left the rebels a month ago—General Mendez had given him that bullet-scar over the eyes.

"For once," he admitted, "I bit off a hunk I couldn't chew, Jim. They got me. All I want now is to get Mendez under my rifle-sights. The devil hung poor Bill Hicks in front of my eyes, understand? If I can get back to Monterrey and reach him, general or no general, I'll put a hunk of lead into him before they get me. Why, damn it, Bill Hicks was with me three years in the old Third Wisconsin!"

Captain Saussier listened, twisted his mustache, and nodded.

"Very well; order rescinded. Feed him. We'll decide later what to do with him. Get him some clothes. He may be eligible for enlistment in the Legion. We'll see."

It was half an hour later that the courier came in, having ridden his horse nearly to death.

The orders he brought were simple; leave the squadron to hold the hacienda, march to Monterrey and join the main column before the city. The urgent words were brusque, imperative, electric. They had reached the right man. Captain Saussier glanced at his watch and sent for Sergeant Faber.

"How soon can the battalion march, knapsacks filled, pouches crammed?"

"In twenty minutes, if the Captain desires."

"In twenty minutes, it will be nine o'clock; we march then. Rations for three days; full equipment; no wagons. At six o'clock in the morning, day after tomorrow, the battalion must take part in the assault on Monterrey. We have thirty-three hours to get there."

Faber saluted. "*Mon capitaine,* the battalion needs only thirty-two hours."

"Prove it," snapped the Captain.

March in twenty minutes; show old Saussier they could reach Monterrey—with full equipment—in thirty-two hours. Ninety miles to march. The men blinked. They looked at one another, wagged their beards, they grinned, and dived for their equipment.

CLARKE STARED at his cousin. This last half-hour had made a new man of him; new clothes, a shave, food. He was himself again, gaunt and iron of body.

"You're insane!" he blurted out. "Your captain's a madman—

you're worse. No troops on earth can march that distance in such time, even without knapsacks. You fool, it means three miles an hour—on an average! I've soldiered with the finest army in the world, and it can't be done."

Jim Faber grinned. "Never soldiered with the Legion, have you? Nope. You boys up in Georgia and so forth couldn't do it, sure. The Legion can do it."

"It's impossible, I tell you!"

"Sure. The Legion does the impossible; that's why it's the Legion."

"You're a fool. Your men will bleed their feet off."

"Nope. The Legion has iron feet, old man. Not like your Third Wisconsin, who'd holler if they got a bunion."

A flame of anger rose in Clarke's face.

"Monterrey? By God, I can march the legs off any frog going—"

Faber swung on him. "Get this straight; we aint frogs. No French in the Legion. We're all God's refuse who can't go back—that's why we go forward. If you want to see what real soldiers are like, come along to Monterrey."

"I'll take you up on that," barked Clarke. "Monterrey, huh? Gimme a rifle?"

"Well, if you can carry it. Of course, you're not used to—"

Clarke shook his fist under Faber's nose. "Gimme a rifle! I can carry any damned thing you fellows can carry and walk the legs off you, French, German, Swiss or what have you! You and your big brag—I'll make you swallow it! By God, an American can show these frogs what's what! Any man who's soldiered under Grant and Sheridan can wipe up the ground with you amateur Injun fighters!"

Faber grinned, and with expert hands lashed his canvas roll into place above his filled knapsack.

"Cartridges and a rifle—that'll be enough for you. We've got no baggage wagons this trip. Rations, too; blanket. Got to take 'em all if you go with us."

"I'll take 'em double, damn you!" shouted Clarke.

Single was enough, however—quite enough.

At nine o'clock, on the dot, the column marched; Captain Saussier was that kind of man. And Ellis Clarke marched too.

When his first heat died out, he was soldier enough to realize to the full what an iron training and discipline lay around him. And as they marched, Jim Faber gave him a sly word.

"One thing helps, Ellis; no hills to climb. It's downhill all the way to Monterrey. How do those boots feel?"

"Pretty good," grunted Clarke, who had replaced his high heels with an old pair of brogans. "One thing, though. When your outfit does get to Monterrey, it'll be too done up to fight."

Jim Faber merely repeated this as a good joke to the man next him, and laughter rippled down the ranks in the darkness. As the column swung onward, bets were freely made on all sides as to how long this American would last; he was regarded with good-humored tolerance, with friendly liking; even, it might be, with a little pity.

FOUR MILES an hour, he figured, or a fraction over; a good stiff gait, this marching pace of the Legion. After a breaking-in halt, it went on and on—a swinging tramp-tramp-tramp, jingle and clatter, haze of dust in the throat. Knowing himself fully as tough as any of these men around him, Clarke pulled in his belt and settled down to it.

Hour after hour—eight hours of it with scarcely a break. Then, in the gray dawn, a halt; ranks were broken. Clarke dropped like a log and lay until Jim Faber kicked him awake.

"Fall in! Sun's coming up. Here; put down this cold coffee."

The bugle shrilled. On again, and into the blazing morning.

Daylight now, and all was different. The officers rode with the guides, the men swung along; never a break in that slogging tramp. Luckily the hot season was not here; even had it been, these veterans of Africa would scarcely have minded.

An hour, another, another. Clarke was beginning to crack

under the undeviating strain. Long unused to such marching afoot, he was not inured. He was aware that Jim Faber was trying to occupy his mind, as they slogged along in the dust together, telling him about one man and another. This one a German prince, that one a broken Spanish grandee, another who was the son of an English lord, and so on.

Other men tried to help him out—hints on his stride, on bandaging his feet, on the carriage of his rifle and pack. Teeth set, harsh brown features drawn and streaked with dusty sweat, Clarke hung on, praying for the respite that did not come until noon. Already the march had been incredible; from now on, said the German prince with a guttural laugh, it would begin to grow tough....

Noon, the bugle's voice, and he dropped where he stood. The Captain and his officers consulted maps, nodded, washed down a bite to eat and lighted cigars. Clarke ate a bit, bound up his feet, and was presently aware that the Captain had sauntered up and was speaking to him. He rose and saluted stiffly. Jim Faber interpreted.

"He says you're looking fit, Ellis, and how do you feel?"

"Like walking the legs off any frog on earth," said Clarke defiantly, "and if he wasn't on horseback, he'd learn a few things."

Faber softened the words into a florid French compliment. A grin went around, among the men who understood English. The Captain nodded and passed on.

Clarke was asleep again when the bugle spurred him into ranks.

THAT AFTERNOON it began to get bad. The men smoked; Clarke chewed, which was a new thing to many of them, and it helped him. He marched in a grim desperation, his whole body a consuming misery of ache. He was gratified to see that these Legionnaires were beginning to break. At least, he would not be the first to drop out! He waited, to speed a gibe and a laugh after the first who left the ranks.

Instead, he found Saussier speaking to him. Faber again interpreted.

"He says do you want to take his hoss a while?"

Clarke, astounded, wiped the sweat out of his eyes and gave Saussier a glance as he strode. He was suspicious of some joke.

"Shucks, Jim! Tell him I aint got my second wind yet. I'll wait till some of these new recruits have eased their feet a bit."

FABER TRANSLATED that literally. Captain Saussier nodded and went on. Clarke's reply was passed along the ranks. More laughter. The men swung along, the enormous knapsacks weighing them forward, rifles weighing them down. One company had carbines, to the vast envy of the others; every ounce counted now.

A man, ill, was in the Captain's saddle; Saussier was swinging along with the men. He spoke with them, moved from rank to rank, brought up intimate details, heartened every flagging spirit. Spirits might flag, but not the steady undeviating pace.

Just the same, the Legion was breaking. They all knew it. Clarke knew it. He was a mere numbed machine now, in a mental agony and physical stress; but somehow he kept going. The bearded faces around were gray and tortured as his own. A man fell out and began to vomit, but after a time he regained his place, gradually catching up and falling in again. The Captain beckoned him, ordered him into the saddle, and fell into step beside Jim Faber.

"Sergeant," he said crisply, "you were correct. We're going to do it in thirty-two hours; we're well ahead of schedule now. If you were in command, what would you do?"

An admission of defeat, this asking advice. Saussier knew they were ahead of schedule, yes; he also knew they were cracking up fast. And the night was fronting them, and the last long stretch of leagues to Monterrey.

"If the Captain pleases," said Jim Faber through cracked lips, "I would halt for an hour and a half, at sunset. The column could go straight on, assuredly; but half of it would be missing at dawn. With a halt, we'll not lose a dozen men and can keep up the pace."

Saussier nodded.

Sunset. The men were staggering now. A few had fallen out, others were lagging behind. Clarke, his features contorted in a snarl of desperation, was on his last legs. When the bugle blew, he did not hear it; glassy-eyed, he kept on. So did some of the others. Men had to stop them, pull them down. They all dropped sprawling in the sand and were asleep as they fell. The officers acted as guards and let them sleep. The laggards came stumbling up and dropped with the others.

During a full hour, the camp was a picture of total inertia. Then the noncoms were awakened. The men were stirred and kicked into life. Fires twinkled in the gathering darkness and warmed the pallid stars. Soup and coffee were heated.

Clarke tied up his bleeding feet grimly.

"You're not the only guy with blood in his shoes," said Jim Faber. He nodded toward a stir at one side. "That Englishman I was telling you about—there he goes. He just didn't wake up. Can't dig much of a grave with bayonets, I reckon."

"You don't look so skittish yourself," said Clarke. But Jim Faber laughed.

"Oh, I'll last. Say, you'd better join up with this outfit. You'd make a real Legionnaire."

"We'll see. Got to find that Mendez first."

"Want to ditch your rifle? You can get another at Monterrey."

Clarke snarled an oath of refusal. The bugle's silvery command floated out. Stiff and weary, aching in every muscle, Clarke suppressed a groan and fell in.

The march went on.

ON LEADEN feet the terrible hours dragged past. Bodies broke, spirits broke, iron wills broke; under cover of darkness, pride broke. Gaps appeared here and there where men had fallen out. Now it was a nightmare for all concerned. The steady swinging pace was maintained, however. Ellis Clarke kept his rifle. And at the midnight halt, when one or two men clapped him on the back, when deep voices gave him accolade, he felt a thrill of warm pride as he sprawled and closed his eyes....

Then on again.

On and into the dawn; a battalion of staggering, stumbling men. From ahead, a challenge; the lights of Monterrey in the grayness. Voices, French voices. The French camp, men swarming around them, hot drinks and food pressed on them. Ninety miles in thirty-two hours? Impossible!

That march was entered on the army records; for the impossible had been achieved.

After the assault started, Sergeant Faber saw nothing of Ellis Clarke; the latter simply vanished from sight. Jim Faber and his friends went on a hunt, and two days later, Clarke was located in hospital.

HE LOOKED up at Faber, gaunt, unshaven, his gray eyes alight.

"Hi, Jim! Well, I got that blasted so-and-so."

"Who?" asked Faber.

"Mendez, durn him! I got him, plugged him twice. One of his aides plugged me, but I got him. Say, I been writing Ma a letter. Get it sent off for me, will you?"

"Sure thing." Jim Faber took the letter. "Ellis, the cap'n says to fetch you along and sign up. The boys are all for you, too; they been hunting the town over to locate you. We can have some swell times if you'll throw in with us. What say?"

The gray eyes shone happily. A wilder light sprang in them.

"That's swell! You bet I will." Clarke turned his head, looked past Sergeant Faber. "Say, Bill, you'd better throw in with us. Jim, you know Bill Hicks? Shake hands. Bill's the best judge of liquor I ever laid eyes on. Gen'ral Sheridan says you and me are all right, Bill, but we aint soldiers. He's a damned liar. I reckon you and me had better go on down below the border and mix in that muss they got there. I hear tell we can get to be officers right off. You say the word, Bill—"

Jim Faber started back, sudden sweat springing on his cheeks. The gray eyes had closed, the voice had abruptly ceased.

With that last letter from Eliis Clarke, Jim Faber enclosed a short message of his own. It was the last scrap of paper on the very bottom of that bundle of old letters, tied about with thread and kept in the attic trunk. And it ended with four words which were crude and beautiful and eloquent:

"He Marched Out Happy."

ONE NIGHT IN MAGENTA

"One Night in Magenta" gives you a spirited
story—and a vivid picture of the Foreign
Legion's little-known campaign in Italy.

I WAS TALKING that evening with Ponson, the dark
Alsatian, in our familiar café, when I noticed that we had
a new waiter at our table, a man who was evidently an Italian
by origin, and who seemed a very pleasant fellow. Then my
attention came back abruptly to Ponson, who had a notion of
writing a history of the Foreign Legion. He had spent fourteen
years in the Corps and was saturated with its history and traditions. None of our other friends showed up that evening, I was
admitted on sufferance to these gatherings of Legion veterans;
and now Ponson was appealing to me for assistance in his
proposed history.

"It's very odd," he observed, "that the Legion has had contacts
with practically all phases of life except one—the commercial.
I have a bibliography of every book known about the Legion.
Plenty of memories, memoirs, experiences and so forth, but no
popular history of the corps that will bring in its legends, touch
on its great deeds, introduce the human element of these men.
And nowhere is there any relation to trade and commerce."

The dark eyes of our waiter flashed down at us.

"Pardon me, gentlemen; you speak of the Foreign Legion.
Will you permit me to say that you're wrong? I know of one
instance, at least, where the Legion did have contact and relation with things commercial."

Ponson gave him a sharp look. "What do you know about
the Foreign Legion?"

The waiter smiled and hunched up his shoulders in a shrug that was both whimsical and apologetic.

"Nothing, of my own knowledge; much, from what I have heard. That is to say, it is about the Legion in Italy, under Napoleon III, when he beat the armies of Austria there. If it had not been for your Foreign Legion, the entire commercial history of the world might be different today."

"You must tell me about this," said Ponson sharply. "When do you go off duty?"

The waiter glanced at the clock: "In five minutes."

"Then join us as soon as you're free. Bring an extra bottle of wine."

Our unknown friend departed. Ponson lit a cigarette.

"This may be worth while; it may supply a missing gap! Do you know, that Austrian war and the activity of the Legion in it is a very vague subject? Difficult to get in any proper light, in the right perspective. So many great events were happening about that time, in 1859 and after, that it's been neglected. And as for the Legion—*pouf!*"

"This chap," I suggested, "may be a false alarm."

"True. And he may not. It'll do no harm to see."

PRESENTLY OUR waiter reappeared, dressed in street attire. At Ponson's invitation he pulled out a chair and sat down. Did you ever notice the queer difference in a waiter, once he lays aside his apron and jacket and becomes as other men?

Well, this one looked different now. He was amiable, pleasant as ever; but new things appeared in his face: a weariness, a defeatist expression; the world had used him hard. He accepted a cigarette, sipped his wine, and began to moralize.

"They talk about the terrible conditions all over the world, the hatred, the killing, the slaughter of whole classes in Spain and Russia and elsewhere—but that has always existed," he said rather sadly. "We see it with different eyes because of radio and telegraph, perhaps; it has always been like that, only it seldom comes home to most of us. The instinct of the race is always to take and kill, or to turn and rend. Once ordinary respect for law is cast aside, men kill."

"What has that to do with the Legion in Italy?" I inquired. "There was no butchery in that war."

HIS BROWS lifted; his gentle eyes rested on me.

"There was hatred—Italian, Austrian, French, Swiss."

"Swiss?" I frowned at him. "Why, the Swiss had nothing to do with it!"

Ponson intervened with a nod.

"He's right. The Emperor formed a Swiss Legion, which became at the time of the war in Italy the 1st Regiment Étranger. Some odd things about it, too. This corps had not been to Africa and did not carry the big leather cartridge-pouch of the old Legion. Also, it wore green, not blue. A peculiarity of Swiss mercenaries is that they must wear a color of their own. The French have always gratified the desire. In the museum at Berne you can still see the uniforms of the Swiss general who commanded this brigade of ours, and they'd make you smile."

Our waiter shrugged. "Well, I know nothing of all that," he said; "but a Swiss was in the Foreign Legion, and he hated the Austrians terribly. His name was Basseti. He was a young man and had been a chemistry expert of some kind in London, assisting the famous chemist Perkin; but sorrows and illness had driven him from England, so that, thinking life would always be unkind, he was now in the Legion. I have a picture of him—I'll show it to you later. You know those days of marching in Italy, before the battle of Magenta?"

Ponson broke into a laugh.

"I've heard of 'em, yes. The Emperor flung out his line to circle around, in a march of a hundred kilometers, to take the Austrians in flank. They had a damned poor system of making the front and rear ranks couple up at night—the men marched fifteen hours a day, and covered only six or seven miles!"

"Magenta is only about six miles west of Milan," said the other. "Before the drive started, weeks before, Basseti was captured and taken into Milan; but he managed to kill a guard and escape at night. Peasants helped him on his way, and he got into Magenta. Eight thousand Austrians were garrisoned there, and Basseti went into hiding. He was trying to reach the French army again, but no one knew where the French were. The Italians who were hiding him turned him over to Dr. Torini, and there the story really begins. And remember, above all things, the hatred."

"What hatred?" I questioned, as he paused.

What hatred? The hatred of the Italians, now forming into a free nation, for their Austrian oppressors. The hatred of Austrians for French, of French for Austrians; the hatred of bad for good, that comes with the loosing of law and the storm of men and rushing armies—the hatred of the oppressor for him that is oppressed.

HATRED AND fear blew in the air of Magenta, these days.

Austrians were billeted in citizens' homes throughout the town. Anyone suspected of revolutionary sentiments was arrested; houses were searched; everyone was under suspicion—all except a near-sighted scientist. No one suspects a near-sighted man.

They excitedly told Basseti this, as he lay under a mass of hay in a loft.

"Come quickly! Torini says it's safe for you with him. An Austrian officer's in his house, but he says to bring you. You'll be his assistant."

"Torini?" Basseti stared at them in wonder. "Not the chemist, Dr. Torini?"

"The same, the same. Hurry! The Austrians are searching farther down the street—they've heard of a stranger. They'll shoot you as a spy if they catch you."

An escaped prisoner, a soldier in the French service—yes, capture meant a firing-squad. Basseti's Italian was none too fluent; under close questioning, he could not hope to evade.

The Italians assisting him hauled him out into the dark streets. They hurried him along, avoiding Austrian patrols, hiding now here, now there, and at last shoving him into a dark doorway that stood open.

*"So you have no
interest in politics—
only in chemistry,
eh?" Wettstein asked.*

A woman's hand found his and led him on through darkness, and so into a lighted room.

She looked at the young Swiss—in rags, unshaven, haggard; he looked at her—alert, blooming, lovely, a girl of twenty. They smiled at each other.

"You're safe," she said quietly. "This room is yours. Everything you need is here. The clothes will fit you. Shave, dress, sleep—Father will see you in the morning. Do you know anything about chemistry?"

"Something," croaked Basseti, repressing his smile.

"You're to replace Father's assistant—he's in Milan now, and won't be back soon. We have an Austrian officer here; you must beware of him. We'll say you returned from Milan this evening. That'll be all right, but you must know something of chemistry."

"I do. Is your father Dr. Torini, the famous Torini?"

"Yes." She stared. "How do you know of him?"

"Why, I studied under

Perkin in London—your father's friend!"

The girl clasped her hands. "It can't be—it's too good to be true! Wonderful! But I must run; Captain von Wettstein is waiting for me. You'll find food and wine there in the cupboard. Good-by. Good luck!"

She was gone, and Basseti was alone; but no longer alone. Her presence lingered; her eyes, her smile, remained with him, her voice like a cello.

Shaving, bathing, eating, Basseti was lost in wonder at the chance that had brought him to this house of all in Magenta. He was a soldier of the Legion; but he was also one of those men who have somehow retained a faith in God. Perhaps it was this belief which impelled him to attempt desperate things with a laugh. It is always your studious, quiet fellow who can face forward into hell without a whimper.

MORNING FOUND him downstairs and talking with his host Torini—a pinched, inoffensive man

It seemed obvious he could be nothing but an inoffensive and inept student.

with straggling beard and thick glasses; the last man to be suspected of being a patriot and the center of revolutionary activity in Magenta. A few words, and in upon them came Captain von Wettstein, brusque, bluff, overbearing, a very deadly man in his way, being a great swordsman and hating all Italians—except one.

Torini calmly introduced his assistant and ordered him to the laboratory.

"I'm working with those aniline crystals sent me from London," he said to Basseti. "Be careful not to disturb anything; get your notes in shape for me."

It was all very matter of course, as though Basseti really were his assistant just come home from a routine trip to Milan.

Basseti left the room, and found the girl Maria waiting outside.

"Come," she said simply, and conducted him to the laboratory.

There she showed him where everything was kept, gave him an apron, and he began to clean up the place. She left him quickly; not before one look, one smile, passed between them. Shaven and rested, he looked very different from the ragged refugee of the previous night.

The laboratory was a small room, built onto the house in the gardens. Basseti knew nothing whatever of the newly discovered aniline dyes with which Torini was working. All over a workbench stood little earthen pots, filled with crystals and with powders. At that time, very little was known about these coal-tar products; the colors to be produced by them, in conjunction with mordant agents, were as yet largely unsuspected or unproven.

Here were bits of wool, tufts of cotton cloth and pile, little vials of acids—everything with which to experiment on various materials with the various crystals and their agents. Basseti looked over the notes of experiments, but could make little of what was going on. At a step, he turned to see Wettstein, slender and elegant in his uniform—a thin, pinched face, intently malevolent eyes, youth aged by dissipation.

"An interesting place, this where you work," said the Austrian affably. "So you are Swiss, I understand? From what part of Switzerland?"

Basseti told him, quite truthfully; he understood perfectly that Wettstein was perhaps not suspicious, but was merely careful. Switzerland! He spoke of it, spoke of his stay in London, his studies. So frank and open were his replies, so obvious did it seem that he could be nothing except an inoffensive and inept student, that Wettstein nodded and accepted him at face value.

Him, a soldier of the Legion, hunted as a killer by all the Austrian police!

"So you have no interest in politics—only in chemistry, eh?" Wettstein gazed around. "What is this apparatus for?"

Basseti explained this and that. In the midst of his talk Dr. Torini came in, listened, and went about his work.

The Austrian officer, with a careless jest, departed. At once Torini turned to his assistant.

"You know what you're about. My daughter tells me you studied with Perkin in London. Good! We are professor and assistant—nothing else. Remember, one word amiss, and not only are you lost, but I and my daughter as well. Close your lips, your heart, your brain, to any thought except that of chemistry. You understand?"

"Perfectly, my master."

"And slump your shoulders a bit. Right! Also, beware of that Austrian." Torini turned to his work-bench. "Now, about these aniline powders and crystals: I am experimenting a little with these new dye bases. We get new and amazing results every day, but ceaseless labor is demanded. Twice I've discovered a marvelous color, only to find it useless—"

The days passed uneventfully, on the surface; but below, with a growing tension, an ever-increasing suspense, a swift growth of emotional forces. Wettstein, except for his garrison duties, was like one of the family.

BASSETI REALIZED perfectly what was happening. He had the gift of vivid imagination; not only the situation but its possibilities lay open to him, and appalled him. To leave here, to reach the French army as he had hoped, was impossible; the Austrian army completely encircled Magenta, and occupied the entire railroad line and the Ticino River beyond. Rumors of action, of battles, flew thick and fast. No one knew what was occurring or where the French were.

And within this house grew the makings of a terrific explosion.

Torini, in the utmost secrecy, was head of the Italian local activity—an intricate network of secret agents, momentarily paralyzed by the presence of the whole Austrian army. Maria, rather than her father, conducted the actual work. Captain von Wettstein held a high rank in the Austrian secret police—and was ardently wooing Maria, after the fashion of a gay Viennese. Torini was, perforce, blind to this, as he was apparently half-blind to everything else excepting his work.

Normally, Maria was fully capable of handling the arrogant Austrian; but the times were out of joint. She dared not antagonize him, lest he summarily clap Torini into prison in order to have the father out of the way.

"You see, it's Italy we must think of; my father must remain at liberty to carry on our work—such things as giving you refuge here," she said to Basseti as they sat talking one evening in the garden. "Father deliberately refuses to see what's going on. I don't want him to see too much and lose his head. After all, Wettstein is still tractable; and I can afford a kiss or two for the sake of Italy."

Basseti's deep eyes flashed. "Perhaps your father isn't the one in danger of losing his head," he rejoined slowly. She looked at him gravely in the starlight.

"Be careful! I haven't asked you to interfere, my friend; you've

"Chemistry occupies
us, my friend—
nothing else; one never
knows what ears
may be listening."

questioned me; I've been frank. Any outbreak from you would endanger us all. I learned today that they have sent your description everywhere and have put a price on your head—you killed a guard, remember. They don't forgive such things, these Austrians."

"And there are some things men don't forgive," said Basseti gloomily.

She laughed lightly and left him; she was going to an officers' ball with Wettstein that evening.

Basseti did not laugh. He was frightened by the necessity of self-control.

Those days were hard for him. It was difficult to keep occupied day and night in the laboratory with Dr. Torini, to fasten his mind on work with the same grim intentness that the older man displayed, and to forget that under this very roof Wettstein was pursuing his affair with Maria. Torini gave him the example, yes; but that helped little.

UNDER THE surface Basseti was explosive. And he was fiercely and frankly in love with this girl; from that first meeting, the flash had sprung between them. Hunted, with a price on his head, he must be circumspect not only for his own sake, but for that of the family sheltering him. Yet at every meeting with Wettstein, he was conscious of the bristle, the clash, between them. A subconscious enmity had sprung up that boded ill....

The days passed with tightening tension. Dinner, on the first of June, was an electric meal, the very air surcharged. Wettstein was prodigal of news, sneeringly triumphant. The French were close, within a few miles; a battle was imminent, a victory in which the Austrians would emerge the masters of Europe.

Torini, blinking, colorless, without opinions, went back to the laboratory. After a little, Basseti followed, fists clenched, deep fury in his heart and eyes; the laughter of Wettstein, the ogling, the deliberate forcing of himself on Maria, was maddening to Basseti. He marveled that the girl could endure so much. He himself, in passing, exchanged one look with the Austrian, and veiled his eyes.

He tried to discuss matters with Torini, but the latter refused point-blank.

"Chemistry occupies us, my friend—nothing else. One never knows what ears may be listening. Now get that sulphuric acid ready; somewhere we must find the right agent for this dye, and then who knows? A new color may be born!"

"Dyes and acids be damned," muttered Basseti, but forced himself to obey....

Noon of the next day: Wettstein appeared and joined them

at luncheon; he was excited, filled with energy, with news. It burst all restraint.

"We have the accursed French where we want them!" he exclaimed vibrantly. "We've been retreating; now Kuhn, our chief of staff, has taken over command. For another two days, Kuhn will continue to draw back—then suddenly hurl every division forward and cut through the extended French line and annihilate them! The old cavalry strategy; it can't be beaten. Is it not splendid?"

"It sounds well," Torini agreed mildly, blinking across the table. "By the way, did you get the address of that chemical firm in Pesth I wanted?"

"Chemical firm? When the fate of nations is to be decided at your very door?" the Austrian snorted. "*Gott,* what a man it is! No, I forgot all about it."

Basseti caught the eye of Maria, understood the look she gave him. Humbly he rose and excused himself. In the hallway outside, she joined him, a flush in her cheeks.

"You heard—you heard?" he exclaimed, twisting his fingers in futile despair. "You must get that information through to our army at once, today, tonight!"

She shook her head. "No. It's impossible. Our system is paralyzed."

"Then I will," he said brusquely. "I must, I must!"

"How?" she demanded. Basseti shook his head.

"I don't know. There must be some way of getting through the Austrian lines."

"Only by the bridges across the Ticino," she replied. "That is impossible. Those bridges are guarded by their whole force, against the French advance. Please, for my sake, contain yourself, have patience!"

"For your sake,"—Basseti suppressed a groan,—"I would move the world—but I cannot see our army lured into this trap and do nothing about it. Tonight, something may turn up."

And that night, something did—though not as expected.

THE THREE of them had just finished dinner. Wettstein, flushed by wine, by the assurance of victory, by impending battle, was in no mood to delay his personal triumph. To Dr. Torini, to Basseti, he was affable but haughty; for Maria, he was all smiles and jests. As she was passing him, he caught her by the arm and seated her on his knee, and laughed.

"Tell me," he said to Torini, his arm about her waist, "have you a grindstone in that laboratory of yours?"

"Eh?" And Torini blinked through his thick glasses. "A small one, yes."

"Good. You,"—and Wettstein gave Basseti a curt gesture,— "go to my room, get the saber that's lying under my bed, and put an edge on it, a keen edge."

"What?" Maria, laughing, touched the saber he wore. "But here it is!"

"No; the other is my dress saber, with a gold hilt." And Wettstein twisted his mustache. "I want to use it tomorrow or the day after on these accursed French, when we have them in our trap. I have special permission to leave the garrison and join

*It was a fight to the death, a battle from house
to house, with no quarter asked. Death struck
on every side, but left Basseti unharmed.*

my cavalry regiment for the occasion. So, my Maria—shall I
bring you back the ears of Napoleon the Little, eh?"

BASSETI ROSE and went on the errand; but as he left
the room, he exchanged one look with the Austrian, and this
time he did not veil his eyes or what lay in them.

Trembling, he got the saber and took it to the laboratory.
The edge was not good, but the point was all that could be
desired. He laid the weapon on the big bench, and stood
hunched in desperate thought. There must be some way—some
way! He forgot about the task assigned him. He went back to
the doorway, heard a quick, light step, and saw Maria, almost
running. She scarcely paused; but he glimpsed the tears on her
face, the quick frightened breath of her bosom.

"No, no!" she gasped, as he would have stopped her. "In the
garden—later."

She was gone. Basseti went back to the work-bench under the lantern and scowled at the gold-hilted saber. He could imagine what must have passed; Wettstein must have gone beyond all bounds. And no interference from Torini? Strange! That man was by no means so impassive as he seemed....

"Attention!" barked a voice in French. "Attention!"

Drill, day in and day out, of the Legion—it is a terrible thing. It affects the nerves, the brain-reflexes, the muscular reactions, as it is meant to do, until a man becomes an automaton who moves at the word of command, and moves instantly.

So with Basseti. At the word, he stiffened, came to attention, even before his mind could realize that it must be a trap. He turned, and looked into the eyes of Captain von Wettstein. The Austrian was standing in the doorway, bared saber in hand; a thin, cruel smile flashed over his face and was gone. He advanced toward the staring Basseti, who knew himself lost.

"So, you are a soldier! A French soldier. That is to say, a spy."

"I am not a spy," said Basseti simply.

Wettstein eyed him.

"No? My man, when you looked at me as you left the dining-room, the truth flashed over me. You answer the description of that Frenchman who is hunted for killing one of our soldiers; an escaped prisoner. You appeared here at the correct time. You posed as the assistant of Dr. Torini. So, then! He has been shielding you here. You know what that means for him—"

A S   H E spoke, the Austrian advanced, the point of his saber extended. Basseti backed before him, until he could back no farther. He stood against the workbench. Almost under his hand was the gold hilt of the other saber.

For an instant he cringed, shrinking back, apparent terror in his face.

"No, no!" he cried, as the steel point advanced at him. "Don't kill me—I'll tell you everything!"

"Indeed?" Wettstein halted, smiled again, and twisted his

mustache. "Very well, you are under arrest. And everyone in this house is also under arrest—"

With a movement so sudden that the eye could not follow it, Basseti had seized the saber under his hand and taken one swift sidewise step. The blade whirled and came with a clash against that of the Austrian. Startled, astounded, Wettstein turned about and thrust. But as he did so, the point of Basseti's steel passed through him, transfixed his heart, drove into the wall behind him, and held him pinioned as he died.

One convulsive movement. The Austrian's hand swept out his saber, lost it, struck the dye-pots and paraphernalia on the work-bench, and then fell again. The saber rattled on the floor.

Next instant Dr. Torini appeared in the open doorway, a revolver in his hand. He stood there for a long moment, motionless, blinking at the scene, at the staring and speechless Basseti. Then he lowered his revolver.

"Apparently you were a moment ahead of me," he observed mildly. "I congratulate you."

Basseti came to life. Words erupted from him, a torrent of eager words. The older man listened, shrugged and gave consent.

"It is a perfectly insane thing to attempt; but why should you not attempt it?" he said in his calm manner. "You speak German; at least you'll have a chance to die in action, which is more than I can hope for with my feeble sight. Yes, by all means. I'll bury his body in the garden tonight; his horse is in the stable—yes, it might be done. Hm! You've made a mess of my experiments, but that can't be helped. Here, I'll lend you a hand with his clothes. Leave him where he is until we get them unbuttoned."

And this man of science fell to work, as calmly, as coolly, as he had come here to kill Wettstein. To his ex-assistant, it was amazing.

So, in another ten minutes, Basseti was garbed in the officer's uniform of the dead man, the gold-hilted saber now at his hip. Only then did he recollect his tryst, and after a word to Torini, passed out into the gardens.

"Maria?"

S H E   C A M E to his voice, sighted him in the starlight, halted. Basseti broke into a laugh and seized her hand.

"Behold! Never mind what's happened, Maria; I'm off in five minutes. With the uniform, the passes, the papers of Wettstein, I may win through. Wish me luck!"

"You!" She trembled suddenly. "But where is he, then? What's happened?"

He told her, with a shrug. She stared at him in the obscurity; he was indeed a vastly different man now, in looks and deeds—and future. She gasped:

"But you know—you know what it means! If they catch you, if anything goes wrong, you'll be shot—"

"Then wish me luck, and nothing will go wrong." He drew her closer; she flung herself upon him passionately, vehemently, all restraint melted in fear. They still stood there in each other's arms when Dr. Torini joined them.

"My children, you are optimists," said this strange man dryly. "You, my son, may not live out this night; but, if by any chance you do live, I shall honor you. Here are all Wettstein's papers. Get off, and get off quickly. I'll help you saddle his horse."

Another fifteen minutes, and Basseti was riding through the town. He passed the gates, holding down Wettstein's pass to the lantern of the guard; then he was on his way for the Ticino and the bridges.

I N   T H E early morning of June 3rd, a detachment of French cavalry sighted a lone rider approaching, a man naked to the waist, in Austrian uniform breeches, a broken saber in his hand. This was Basseti, who had rid himself of his upper uniform lest it bring bullets upon him. The squadron surrounded him, and he saluted.

"Private Basseti, third company, 1st Regiment Étranger, reporting for duty!"

He poured out his news. If true, it was important; but he was greeted with open suspicion, and was sent back under guard. It was past noon when the Legion was encountered and not until then was his identity established; and it was later still, when messengers were sent dashing off to find Marshal Mac-Mahon and the emperor.

Thus, it was not until the next morning that the word he bore really went into effect; and then the French columns were hurled forward in a smashing attack, just as the Austrians were moving up to take the initiative.

But the first blow, struck the hardest, was decisive.

The Austrian lines were broken, their columns crumpled, the whole line of the Ticino and the bridges was taken. Straight at Magenta, toward noon, was hurled the second brigade, with the Legion well in advance, as always. Espinasse, that old Legionnaire, had the brigade; Chabrier, hero of a score of African campaigns and of the Crimea, was colonel of the Legion.

Down across the brooks and vineyards they drove, to see, too late, a tremendous Austrian column pouring upon them.

"Drop knapsacks! Fix bayonets!" rapped out Chabrier, and turned to the bugler. "Sound the charge!"

Basseti, in uniform again, his heart burning at sight of the little town where destiny awaited him, was in the van. The Austrian rifles crashed once. Gaps broke in the line. Chabrier was down under the bullets, and a howl of fury broke from his men as they swept past his body. Then they were into the masses of Austrians—into them with a rage, an insensate ferocity that staggered the whole Austrian column.

More of the enemy regiments poured up. The Legion wavered; but now the Zouaves were charging in, and the Austrians broke. Basseti found his bayonet streaming red, found himself charging with the rest, on and on, until the Austrian defense stiffened and determinedly formed anew.

On through the vineyards they fought; then Espinasse came up with the other troops as the afternoon was fading into dusk. Forward again, on into the town beyond—and the garrison of

eight thousand Austrians awaiting them. Here it was a fight to
the death, a battle from house to house, with Espinasse dead
and no quarter asked. Basseti was on fire now, as death struck
on every side but left him unharmed; down the street, on to
the next house, into the garden with the bayonet, into the house
itself where rifle-flashes split the darkness. But never the one
house he sought, the one garden he knew so well.

EIGHT O'CLOCK, nine o'clock—the hell continued
unabated. Suddenly Basseti knew where he was, recognized the
street, gathered half a dozen men around him. The Austrians
were breaking now; the street, the next street, was cleared.

With a rush, Basseti was through into the street beyond,
running full tilt. Here was the doorway, here was the garden
wall.

Basseti's voice lifted hoarsely.

"Maria! Maria!"

Their rifle-butts pounded the door. She opened, in the darkness; Basseti was clasping hands with her, pressing her to him
while his comrades crowded in.

"Friends—they'll watch the street. Take them to the windows,
Maria; they'll keep all safe for you. Give them wine. Where's
your father?"

"In the laboratory," she panted; "working. Go to him, quickly!
I'll follow—"

He was already on his way, laughing excitedly. What manner
of man was this Torini, to be working in his laboratory while
a battle raged all around?

When he broke in, Dr. Torini was stooping over the work-
bench. Glancing around, peering and blinking, Torini finally
recognized his assistant in this powder-smudged, breathless
Legionnaire.

"Oh, it's you—alive, eh? That's good," he exclaimed. "Come
here, come here at once! Arrange things on the bench exactly
as they were before you left—hurry!"

"What the devil's wrong with you?" demanded Basseti. "Did you bury Wettstein—"

"Never mind all that." Torini waved his hand. "The acids, the dyes—everything, just as they were! Look at this; it's the most marvelous thing I ever saw, and I've not been able to discover what agent was used—when Wettstein disarranged everything, it must have happened then—"

He held up a long tuft of wool. At first, Basseti thought it dipped in blood; then he perceived that a dye had colored it, a marvelously vivid scarlet-purple hue.

A laugh seized him, until he saw that Torini was in frightful earnest. Swiftly he went to the bench and arranged everything there, the dye-pots, the acids, everything, as he had last seen them. He remembered the dying gesture of the Austrian—the outflung hand crashing things to chaos. He comprehended that in this accident, something had happened; some combination of crystals and acid and wool—

He flung himself into it with a will, then glanced up.

"Do you know we've won a battle? At least, on our front—"

"Battle be hanged," exclaimed Torini, blinking. "Here, the wool was lying exactly here—you can see where the red dye spilled! It's an unknown shade, absolutely new and glorious!"

H E D R E W himself up against the wall. It was just there Captain von Wettstein had stood. His hand swept out to the work-bench. A cry broke from him.

"Ha! I never suspected it—look, look! There are the crystals, there's the acid, the wool—yes, it's a combination I haven't tried—"

He stooped forward eagerly. Basseti turned to the doorway, saw Maria there, and gayly joined her. Her lips touched his, then she drew back.

"Come! We have bread and cheese and wine. What sort of a discovery did you make that got him so excited? Is it true there's a tremendous battle going on?"

"And if I haven't lost my senses, we've won it," said Basseti. "But I've won more than anyone else this night—"

So he had, indeed, as Maria made very clear to him.

Later, as the two of them sat with the Legionnaires, talking and eating and drinking and preparing to make themselves comfortable until dawn, Dr. Torini burst in upon the lot of them. He was excited, transported with delirious joy, and held up a dripping skein of wool.

"Look at it!" he cried out. "The most wonderful color ever seen, the royal Tyrian purple of the ancients—all from a crystal and a bit of acid! And the wool takes it perfectly, cotton takes it perfectly—eh, Maria? Who's that you're kissing?"

"My future husband, and I think with your consent!" replied the girl, amid a burst of laughter from the interested Legionnaires. One of them bawled out loudly:

"Here's a name for your color, good doctor! The name of your town, the name of this day's victory—Magenta! *Vive la Légion,* comrades, and a health to Magenta!"

O U R   W A I T E R had finished his story....

He sipped his wine, lit a fresh cigarette. His rather sad eyes touched upon us; the eyes of a waiter who sees everything upon his table except the people sitting there.

"Upon my word," and I turned to Ponson, "I have heard some story about magenta dye having been discovered during or just after the battle—why, there's the hookup you were looking for! The Legion and commerce, certainly!"

Ponson nodded. "Right. Is that story true, my friend?"

The waiter smiled a little and produced from his pocket an ordinary old black leather daguerreotype case. He opened the case and handed it to us.

We looked at the daguerreotype of a slender, erect head, a thoughtful face, a man's face. No uniform, but such a face as Basseti might have owned, that man with fire inside him.

"Basseti, yes," said our waiter, nodding to our glances. "Doesn't that answer your question, gentlemen?"

"I don't see how," Ponson said sharply, as he returned the little picture.

The waiter pocketed it and shrugged.

"It should," he replied, and smiled at us as he came to his feet. "You see, gentlemen, my name is Basseti too. Good night."

DUST OF DEAD SOULS

"Dust of Dead Souls," ninth in this unique series,
vividly pictures the tragic adventure of the
Foreign Legion in the Franco-Prussian War.

WHEN NEWS of the *Hindenburg* disaster broke, I
was in Algiers.... Europe and Africa being tremendously air-minded, that calamitous news made a real impact.
People talked about nothing else. My chauffeur talked about
it, as he ran his rickety taxicab up the steep hill above the
cemeteries, to the glorious church of Notre Dame d'Afrique
on top of the headland. Two white-clad monks out on the
church steps were evidently discussing it, too, with a little old
gnarled, white-haired man who waved a newspaper in one hand
and in the other held a stick, as a man holds a sword.

As my driver pulled up beneath the trees at the side, he jerked
a thumb at the old bent figure.

"*Regardez!* A veteran of the Franco-Prussian war, m'sieu; the
Colonel Wiart. He's getting on to ninety, they say, and spry as
an Arab boy!"

Not quite, perhaps; those little brown animals have the very
devil in them. Old Wiart went into the church. Some kind of
service was going on, and I followed him. The Black Virgin
above the altar was lighted up, which seldom happens, and I
studied her with some interest. This was a place of pilgrimage
for all Algeria, and the walls were covered with votive objects
of all sorts, from ship models to plaster casts and crutches.
Among them were not a few medals. One, set high up, appeared
to be a cross of the Legion of Honor, set behind glass.

I was looking up at this when Wiart came out. As he passed, he followed my glance, and I saw him smile and nod.

"Pardon me," I ventured, "but you seem to recognize that cross. Of the Legion, I think?"

We had a few words; he spoke English perfectly, and seemed pleased by my request. We walked over beneath the trees and sat down at the verge of the great drop. Off to the left, the seminary, the villas and buildings running westward; below, the cemeteries; to the right, all Algiers dropping down its sweeping hillsides to the sickle-curve of the bay—and beyond all, the Mediterranean. A lovely spot, white with sun and green with the soft verdure of Africa, and vivid blue with sea and sky.

"Dust!" old Wiart snorted. "These scientists say that the blue of the sky comes from dust. Then it is the dust of men long dead."

"That's an idea, anyhow," I said. "A charming conception."

"These poor people who died with the *Hindenburg* airship—they are up yonder." And he pointed with his stick. "They are the blue we see; the dust of souls. Conception? Not at all. It is fact. You asked me about the cross of the Legion, inside there. I'll be glad to tell you the story. It is about a sergeant in the Foreign Legion, and what happened on the 15th of January, 1871."

What all this had to do with the cross and its ribbon up there in the church wall, I did not see. The old fellow had a way with him, however. He mentioned Sergeant Wiart of the Legion, and this puzzled me; an old veteran, thirty years with the Foreign Legion—his father, I reflected. This man, approaching ninety, could not have been much more than a lad of twenty, back in 1871.

"You know," he went on, accepting a cigarette and brushing back his white mustache as he held it to my lighter, "Bourbaki was the great hero, in those dark days. He had begun his career with the Legion in Africa; he was the finest soldier in all France; he had even refused a throne. Well, Bourbaki commanded the

*"Have you need
of anything,
Sergeant?"*

Army of the East; he was the hope of all France, when 1871 began. He had already beaten the Prussians once. Now he had one hundred and fifty thousand men and was advancing to relieve the siege of Belfort. Do you know why he lost his entire army and emptied a pistol into his own head?"

I shrugged; who knew, or cared, about those days of 1871? The old man caught my gesture, and sighed. Then he took a pencil and pad of scratch-paper from his pocket, and made a sketch. He dashed down a face, a ragged uniform, a man—an entire personality. The result was one of those astonishing trifles which say more than words can convey....

A grizzled, unshaven man of iron, this sergeant of the Foreign Legion, wearing odd bits of various uniforms—anything to keep out the wintry blasts. The vivid intelligence of his face was held in check by his inbred habit of discipline, of respect for his superiors; if you ordered Sergeant Wiart to march and die, he might know you for a blithering idiot, but he would march to death in silence.

During the horrible march to capture the heights above Sainte Suzanne, this sergeant knew better than anyone else what it was all about. The Legion had been almost wiped out in previous fighting; now the gaps were filled by two thousand young Bretons. This entire army was composed of recruits, backed by a steely nucleus of a few old regiments.

The Foreign Legion was given one day in which to capture those heights. It was a mere detail of the marvelous plan Bourbaki had evolved to crumple the whole Prussian invasion; a plan so perfect that, despite all defects and failures, nothing could stop it. Bourbaki had spotted the one vulnerable point. General Cremer was to be hurled forward like a spearhead, all opposition rolled away—and the Prussian disaster would be inevitable.

AS THE Legion found, the plan was evolved from maps. The army had no intelligence service. Sergeant Wiart snorted through his mustaches that the Legion had to do what an entire division could not do—and it was literally true. But the Legion did it.

All that day, the Legion struggled ahead. Prussian batteries played upon them. Prussian troops occupied every height of

Wiart saluted.
"Support—for
the Legion."

land. Bridges no longer existed. The weather was bitter cold. There was no food; all service of supply had failed. The wintry air, throughout the whole Lisaine country, was hammering with artillery, spiteful with rifle-fire, clouded with the reek of powder.

Sergeant Wiart prompted the green officers, cheered up the

men, scoffed at hunger and bloody feet. To him the colonel turned for some knowledge of what lay ahead. With admirable precision, Wiart sent on the advance scouts, sent back the word they bore, watched the Legion struggle grimly forward.

With afternoon, the plateau was dead ahead—the heights dark with Prussian battalions. They had reached the objective; they had only to take it. The harassed colonel and adjutant summoned Sergeant Wiart, who saluted stiffly.

"There is no reserve ammunition, sergeant. How is the supply?"

"Practically exhausted, my colonel."

"Have you heard anything of supporting troops coming up?"

"There are none."

"It is incredible!" muttered the colonel, his worried gaze searching the valley behind. "Already we have lost—how many, adjutant?"

"A few over five hundred, my colonel," said the adjutant, and grimaced.

"Very well. The Legion has been ordered to take those heights and hold them. The quicker we do it, the better."

The bugles shrilled. The orders rattled along the lines. Wiart had caught up a rifle, and fixed bayonet as the click of steel lifted on the wintry sunlight. Smoke rimmed the snowy heights ahead. Sergeant Wiart surveyed his weapon approvingly. Old model bayonet, new model rifle; the "fusil, 1866 model"—the famous chassepot.

Jests broke out. Wiart's voice crackled into the chorus, dominating the others with its rasping, blasphemous profanity until the Legion howled with joy, all except the dark Breton recruits, who were religious fellows. There was nothing pious about the Legion in general, or about Sergeant Wiart in particular. He was noted for his hatred of anything clerical. He was as savagely blasphemous as his wife, in Algeria, was devout.

Oddly enough, the thing he most revered in life, aside from his wife and son, was the Cross of the Legion of Honor. He had won it years ago, and was wont to mourn over his wine-cup that the first Napoleon had not chosen another emblem than the Cross….

A sudden order rattled. A wild yell burst forth; then Wiart was up and going with his company.

Fire rippled along the heights. Balls screamed and sang viciously, or thudded home. Grape shrieked and whistled; the cannon ahead were blasting away. Men stumbled, slipped in the snow; the charge left a bloody wake, yet, with never an answering shot, the figures wavered on and upward.

The heights came closer. The Prussian faces, bearded and staring, appeared through clinging smoke. Breastworks, by God! And then, suddenly, it was hand-to-hand work.

The sergeant was up and over. Wily old veteran that he was, he fought carefully and coolly, plunging the point home, warding threatening steel away. The guns were taken, the positions carried; the Prussians broke. The ferocity of the Legion swept everything before it, until the entire plateau was captured.

Now it had to be held.

THE COLONEL paused beside Wiart, who was calmly bandaging a ragged gash across his upper left arm.

"So you caught it, eh?"

"A mere scrape of the bark, my colonel."

"You're able to travel. Go back to headquarters; give this note to General Barolle, chief of staff, and augment it by word of mouth. We must have cartridges, food and supports. Meantime, we shall hold the plateau as ordered. Now, sergeant, lift the lid off hell if you like—but reach headquarters!"

Sergeant Wiart saluted, caught up his ragged coat, and started.

A dead Prussian provided a sound pair of boots, and emergency rations. A mile farther back, kindly fortune provided transport. A gallant and portly Bayonne wine-merchant, who had squeezed himself into captain's rank and cavalry uniform, was frantically trying to find his regiment, when the ragged figure of Wiart came upon him, with revolver leveled. The major dismounted, cursing hotly, and Sergeant Wiart swung up into the saddle with a grin.

"Curses don't hurt a Legionnaire, old sowbelly," he retorted.

"I'll have you shot for this, you scoundrel!"

"You'll find me at headquarters," said Wiart, and rode away.

Now he began to meet stragglers, officers, a torrent of marching men and transport. To anyone else, it would have been an involved and confused mess; to Sergeant Wiart, the news he picked up began to make the whole campaign look simple. Suddenly a shout halted him. He turned, to see a young staff officer, a captain, riding toward him. His scarred, brown features broke into joy. His gray mustaches quivered. Stirrup to stirrup, the two men embraced warmly, with open emotion.

IT WAS the first time Sergeant Wiart had seen or heard of his son, since leaving home.

"Ah! You're a fine fellow—and a captain!" Tears glittered on his unshaven cheeks. "Magnificent! On the staff, eh? What staff?"

"Headquarters, my father. I'm one of Barolle's aides."

"Good! We ride together," and Wiart explained his mission. Voluble speech flowed from them both; joy at their reunion, wonder at the chance of it. The old sergeant called it luck; the young captain called it providence. He did not share his father's atheism.

As they rode, their speech was torrential. Neither had heard from Algeria in weeks; with France prostrate and struggling vainly, everything seemed in chaos. Everything, except here. Under his son's explanations, old Wiart understood the strategy of Bourbaki, and approved it. Simple enough; roll back the Prussians to right and left, let General Cremer smash through with his army corps to Belfort, and the war was over.

"But it's not so simple," said Captain Wiart, a worried look on his young face. "The chief of staff, Barolle, is a wonder. But

Within a quarter-mile of the hill, he drew rein. His errand had come too late.

General Bourbaki has a favorite aide, one Colonel Perrot, who has practically superseded Barolle; he's a flashy fool."

"Bah! Old Bourbaki knows his business," growled the sergeant confidently. "I knew him thirty years ago when he came to the Legion as a shavetail. He's all right."

It was dark when they rode into the village that housed headquarters. The captain procured food and wine for them both, reported, and took in the sergeant's note. Old Wiart noted with some astonishment that there was no particular tension here; couriers and aides were dashing about, but the general air was one of complacent assurance.

"Bourbaki knows how to run a battle!" he muttered. "Calm efficiency—that's the ticket!"

Barolle appeared, a tall, thin man with the absolute precision which marks the born chief of staff. With a dozen words he appraised and ticketed Sergeant Wiart.

"No food, no ammunition, no supports—this must be remedied. God knows where the various corps are. Make yourself comfortable, until I see the general."

The sergeant followed into a large room, blue with tobacco-smoke, littered with tables, maps, officers hard at work. Barolle vanished. Sergeant Wiart took a chair and relaxed gratefully.

"Poor Barolle!" remarked somebody. "They've raised hell with all his dispositions—"

The voice hushed abruptly. From an adjoining room came a laughing, jovial colonel, his face flushed, his eyes bright with wine.

"Captain Marcel! Send a telegram to General Belancourt at Verlans, instantly! At ten in the morning, he is to advance on the Mont Vaudois heights with every available man; instruct him that his job is to divert the enemy's attention from the main attack against Hericourt."

A dead silence fell. It was broken by the officer addressed, who spoke in dismay.

"But, my colonel, we do not know that Belancourt has yet reached Verlans! In fact, we received a report that the Prussians are there in force and have mined the bridges—"

"Nonsense!" exclaimed Colonel Perrot. "Belancourt was

ordered to capture Verlans before six tonight; it has been done. Officers of France never fail. We've just had word that the Legion has taken the Sainte Suzanne plateau, as ordered. You see?"

With a twirl of his mustache, he turned and disappeared. Sergeant Wiart saw the flash of horror in the faces around.

"Colonel Perrot is always right," some one muttered. "He counts the kilometers on a road—good! It should be marched in an hour. He does not stop to ask if the Prussians hold it, or if it is still a road."

"Anyhow," said another, "we know that the great thing is accomplished: General Cremer has gone forward, the Prussians are pierced, the way's open to him!"

"And there's hell to pay everywhere else," retorted the first officer.

Sergeant Wiart got out his pipe and lighted it, to choke down the spasm of emotion that gripped him. To his wise, cynical old eyes, the curtain had rolled back, revealing terrible things. A chief of staff superseded by an aide—that was bad enough. Worse, a telegram sent to Verlans on the assumption that a French general was there, because he had been ordered to be there! A telegram, not in code, revealing the whole strategy of the morrow's battle! If that telegram reached a Prussian general*—well, Sergeant Wiart went cold at the very thought. He looked about for some sight of his son, but the young staff captain was nowhere to be seen.

Colonel Perrot reappeared and summoned an aide.

"Make out a formal order, which the General will sign. Order Colonel Chauvez to march at once with the 115th Infantry and the 23rd Zouaves, to support the Legion at Sainte Suzanne. When it's ready, Captain Wiart will take it."

The aide saluted, and hesitated. "It is not known yet," he blurted desperately, "if Colonel Chauvez and the reserve corps has reached the river—"

---

* *As it did .—Editor.*

"It will not be a battle but a massacre, my son."

"Certainly he has reached it; he was to have been there by four this afternoon," said Perrot brusquely. "Here's an order for the quartermaster-general. Have food and ammunition sent the Legion at once, by a forced night march."

Perrot disappeared. Sergeant Wiart again saw the officers look one at another, and from somewhere came a low, bitter comment:

"A fat chance the Legion has! Every corps living on its knapsack, and not a wagon of food to be found within twenty miles! And who knows where the ammunition is?"

Sergeant Wiart shivered with a chill that swept through his very soul—though he had always denied having a soul. A courier came stumbling in, and presently another; he could guess that they bore bad news. Telegrams were arriving. A funereal aspect settled on the big room, an air of consternation and dismay.

Suddenly it changed, all in a moment. The muttering talk ceased. General Barolle appeared, and his presence transformed the whole place; the man's energy, his strength of character, was like a tonic.

"Sergeant! General Bourbaki wishes to speak with you."

OLD WIART went into the adjoining room and stood at attention. More than anything in the world, just now, he wanted to see his son again; but orders were orders. A table was littered with maps and reports; orderlies at work with Captain Perrot;

other officers all about. At the table was Bourbaki himself, with three other general officers.

"Ah! A sergeant of the Legion, and looks it!" exclaimed Bourbaki. He was swarthily handsome, for his father had been a Greek officer. "Here's a glass of wine for you. What's your name? Haven't I seen you somewhere before now?"

"Thirty years ago, *mon général.*" Wiart downed the wine, put the glass on the table, and stood at attention again. He gave his name, pronouncing it in the German fashion.

"I seem to remember you," Bourbaki said, frowning. "Thirty years ago? Where?"

"When the General joined us as a lieutenant at Algiers. He got into trouble about that Arab girl—"

Bourbaki broke into a roar of laughter, in which the others joined.

"So, I remember you now! Well, well, make yourself comfortable at that corner table, help yourself to food and wine; no ceremony, old campaigner! Rest a bit, eat, then return to your leather-bellies and congratulate them. The Legion has reached its objective, if no other corps has!"

"No other corps has!" Those words sent a jolt through Sergeant Wiart, but he settled himself at a corner table and began to eat and drink. An aide came in with a message. Bourbaki read it and uttered a delighted exclamation.

"Messieurs, all goes well! Cremer has driven the enemy from Chenebier. The Lure road is open before him. He has only forty kilometers to march, and France is saved!"

There was an outburst of voluble, joyous voices. Only one among them all uttered a hesitant word of disagreement.

"Forty kilometers? But, Bourbaki, that is a march!"

"Bah! Five years ago in Mexico, the Legion marched thirty leagues in a day. And Cremer can certainly throw his corps forward a mere forty kilometers, when the fate of France hangs in the balance! He must do so. He shall!"

Sergeant Wiart was actually stupefied by the fact that Bourbaki spoke in earnest. True, the Legion had marched something like a hundred and fifty miles in thirty-two hours; but not through ravened country, with every road mined, every bridge blown up. When Bourbaki rushed off half a dozen telegrams and couriers, the sergeant noted the messages, then wiped his gray mustache and fumbled for his pipe; his appetite was gone.

"The devil!" he told himself in dismay. "Army corps scattered everywhere. No information about the enemy. A general attack to roll back the Prussian armies, cut their rear, cripple them— and not a third of the job accomplished! And the old man gives an aide full charge of operations while the chief of staff is a mere messenger-boy. Well, if Cremer goes through, we still win the day, for nothing can save the Prussians then. If he doesn't go through, the Army of the East will be wiped out like a burst of smoke."

With his thirty years' experience, he saw this in one flash— not of intuition, but of shrewd intelligence. He knew his business. At least, he had definite news that was good. Cremer had smashed through the Prussians and had a clear road before him. He tucked away his pipe and rose. Bourbaki caught sight of him.

"Leaving, Sergeant? Have you need of anything?"

Wiart saluted. "Food. Ammunition. Supports. For the Legion."

"There's a soldier for you, gentlemen!" And Bourbaki chuckled. "Well, my friend, I've sent food, ammunition and supports. You'll probably join them *en route* back, for Chauvez and the reserves are down at the river, ahead. Perrot! Write out a pass for my friend the sergeant of the Regiment Étranger."

Colonel Perrot scribbled the pass.

AS SERGEANT Wiart took it, the door suddenly burst open. Into the room hurtled an aide, pale, eyes staring. He struck against old Wiart, knocking him aside, and thrust the telegram in his hand at the General. He tried to speak, and could not.

Bourbaki seized the message. As he read it, his eyes distended.

"Mon Dieu! Mon Dieu!" he gasped. "Manteuffel and his army of sixty-five thousand Prussians are advancing on Cremer's flank—an army supposed to be sixty miles away!"

The blood died out of his face; he was suddenly an old man, tragic, broken, hesitant, his fire exterminated. It was a frightful moment. Every man present knew what it meant; but only one man, of them all, knew what was to be done. Sergeant Wiart. The mad words rose in him—"Tell Cremer to hammer through!" They were on the very lips; and he might, in his momentary madness, have uttered them, had not General Barolle at this moment come into the room and saved him from the breach of discipline.

"Barolle!" The General swung around. "You know? You have heard? It is not true?"

"Apparently it is true," said Barolle calmly. "You have not asked my advice. Pardon me for presuming; it is to tell Cremer to advance more quickly."

Sergeant Wiart could have hugged the man, general or not, for those words.

"My God! It's impossible. We haven't any force at hand to meet Manteuffel—except Cremer's army," broke out Bourbaki, purple veins rising in his forehead. "He must halt, retire, and stop the gap. Once Manteuffel breaks through, our whole army is lost!"

"But my general!" said Barolle coldly. "If Cremer goes forward, if the army of Manteuffel does not strike his flank—then every Prussian in France is lost!"

"If! *If!*" cried out Bourbaki in a tragic voice. "Who could take such a chance? This is the one army remaining, the hope of all France—No, no! Send the order to Cremer at once, instantly!"

Barolle saluted and retired.

Sergeant Wiart went stumbling out of the room, out of

headquarters, out to where he had left his borrowed horse. His pass took him through the sentries. He mounted, kicked in his heels, and sent his horse scrambling away.

He perceived, quite clearly, the truth of this whole business. The chances were ten to one that Cremer and his army would have gone through without sighting a Prussian—but the General dared not take that chance.

"And now, what happens?" reflected Wiart, as he rode under the cold stars. The crepitation of distant artillery fire crept down from far snowy hills. "What happens? Only one thing can happen. Cremer halts, checks the veterans of Manteuffel with his young recruits, and perishes. Meantime, the other Prussian armies are rolling in from all sides. The Army of the East is destroyed, its retreat is cut off, it ceases to exist. One of the great tragedies of history is happening around us."

The night was bitter cold, and growing colder, but not nearly

*They had reached the objective; they had
only to take it.... The charge left a bloody
wake, yet the figures wavered on.*

so cold as the heart of Sergeant Wiart, when he thought of the
Legion awaiting him, up yonder on the heights. Not even his
explosive roll of oaths could give any comfort. And by midnight
the stars were hidden behind clouds, with a threat of snow.

THE HEIGHTS of Sainte Suzanne were only a couple
of miles farther, when Sergeant Wiart overtook two wagons
plodding along, with a little column of men. An Arabic oath
crackled out; he responded with incredulous clelight. Tirailleurs!
Next moment a horse reined in beside him, and he was clasping the hand of his eager son.

"Your mother prates about miracles," he said dryly. "Is this
one?"

Captain Wiart laughed, and let the little convoy draw ahead lest they overhear him.

"Something of the sort, my father. I was ordered to take food, ammunition and supports to your corps. Well, I have bad news for you. There are no reserves, it seems. There is no food or ammunition. They have not come up with the army, and the Prussians have cut off the rear. I picked up a wagon of rations, another of ammunition, and a hundred tirailleurs under a lieutenant, who was lost; he consented to obey me and here we are."

"Excellent," said the Sergeant coolly.

WITH AN access of emotion, his son caught him by the arm.

"My God! Don't you realize what it means?"

"I realized that long ago. They've recalled Cremer to meet a fresh army of Prussians. If he'd gone on, their whole rear would have been cut. As it is, he's turned back. Their armies are around us. We have only one possible retreat—across the Swiss frontier, to be interned. That is to say, if we can reach the frontier. To-morrow, my son, all the upper air will be filled with the spirits of dead Frenchmen who have rejoined their Creator."

"What!" exclaimed the other. "You have not suddenly become religious?"

"Not likely," and Sergeant Wiart sniffed. "But I believe that when a man dies, what we call his spirit rejoins the Vital Force of nature, which you call God. It is quite simple, and satisfies me. Now, never mind theology. I'll take these wagons on, and you get back to headquarters in a hurry."

"No. I go with you," said Captain Wiart.

The old sergeant flew into a furious cursing rage. He had no idea that the Legion would or could retreat. In any case, a few more hours would see the army a chaotic rabble striving desperately to reach the frontier, Prussian rifles and Uhlans and artillery hailing death into them from three sides; the head-quarters staff would certainly be safe, and the Legion would as certainly be in the thickest of the hell. He said nothing of this, naturally.

"I stay with you," calmly repeated his son. "It's the first time we've met; and we can stay together now. Later, tomorrow, I can find my way back to headquarters—if there is one. Anyway, Colonel Perrot told me to inspect the conditions here and bring back a report later. That will cover my—"

"As your father, I tell you to clear out!" stormed the sergeant angrily. "It's no place for you. There'll be no report. We're retreating at once, you fool!"

"I thought you said the Legion would not retreat? You certainly said so, when we first met and were talking."

"It's none of your damned business what I said," furiously exclaimed old Wiart. "Get out! I order you—"

"I refuse. I'm your superior, an officer, and an aide of the General. March!" The younger man chuckled, then sobered. "Pardon, *mon père;* stop swearing and move on, will you? So far as I'm concerned, the argument's ended. Let's catch up with the wagons."

He urged his horse on, and the sergeant followed....

When they rode into the camp on the heights, Sergeant Wiart went straight to the colonel, who wakened to receive his report. Here was one man to whom he could speak his heart. The colonel was an old-timer. They were friends. In the blackness and chill, rank could be brushed aside.

SERGEANT WIART crouched beside the silent figure under the shelter, and told of everything he had seen and heard and feared. The colonel said nothing at all until he had finished. Then:

"You old fool, I hoped you'd stay gone!"

"Thirty years in the Legion, *mon colonel.*"

"I might have known it. Instead, you bring back a son and want me to send him off. I shall do nothing of the sort. We'll need him. I suppose you think the Legion's going to stick here unsupported—against all the armies of Prussia?"

"It's the sort of thing the Legion does, certainly."

"Not here. My orders are to fall back if unable to hold the heights. Turn in and sleep. We march at six in the morning; the food and ammunition you have brought will save us. Tomorrow the army will be destroyed, and the next day, and the next—"

He hung his head and muttered into his beard, in black despair and heartbreak. Old Wiart crept off, turned in among his comrades, and slept. He was dead beat.

Morning gave a gray sky, and the thunders of artillery from all the horizon; the Army of the East was encircled. A hero, who had suddenly turned into a broken old man, had flung away the whole splendid strategy of success. Sergeant Wiart found his son and sat apart with him, accepting the destiny he could not evade. He saw utter destruction for them all, and was desperate.

"F R A N C E I S dying," he said to Captain Wiart, despairingly. "Men are dying. Half the army may reach the frontier and safety; the rest will perish. It will not be a battle but a massacre, my son. It is cold up there!"—and he glanced at the gray sky. The younger man smiled slightly.

"You're still thinking of the Nature Force or whatever you call it?"

The sergeant nodded, gravely. "Yes; but I am not certain of anything. There is always a chance that your mother may be right about these things. Suppose I die, suppose what makes the life in me evaporates and goes up there, back to rejoin the divine force whence it came—well, after all one may reconcile that with Christ, or Allah, or what one likes. At all events, I have made a vow to the Virgin of Africa."

Young Wiart stared in sharp surprise.

"Yes." Old Wiart spoke with simplicity. "One never knows; your mother may be right. I have asked the Black Virgin—you know, the one in the church above Algiers, where your mother went on pilgrimage—I have asked her to bring you home safe; and if she does, I've vowed my Cross to her. You remember that. You tell your mother."

"I?" Sudden tears suffused the keen dark eyes. "I, Father? You speak as though you weren't coming back home."

"I don't think any of us are, my son; I hope you are." Sergeant Wiart put out his hand to meet that of his son. "Good-by. There go the bugles. God bless you—well, I'm a damned old fool for saying so, but I mean it anyhow—"

They embraced, captain and sergeant, as the bugles spoke. Rifles were crackling; bullets were in the air.

The Legion began its retreat. If the advance had been difficult, this retreat was a horrible nightmare. The Prussians were everywhere. The hills were masked by smoke, the ground shook with the tremendous blasts of artillery fire. The colonel went to old Wiart and pointed down the valley.

"You remember that sharp, steep hill we passed on the way up—the little one? Take your company and get there; hold it, while we check these damned Uhlans who are coming down on us. If the enemy gains that hill, we'll all be cut off. Otherwise—"

"Understood," said Sergeant Wiart. He passed the word to his men, and they were off at the double.

The main body fought on grimly. As the morning wore on, it became more apparent that the colonel had hit the nail on the head; if the Prussians held the little hill off the road, they had the entire corps at their mercy. Smoke and rifle-fire now ringed that hill, however. Sergeant Wiart was holding it against a blasting attack.

The column slogged on, the Prussians were checked and fell back, only to come again as fresh troops reached them. Captain Wiart had field-glasses, and as he rode, trained them on the little hill. The colonel came to him.

"Your horse is fresh enough. Will you take word to Sergeant

Wiart to retire his men at once? We're past the danger-point now—we can't be cut off, thank God!"

The captain saluted and thrust in his spurs, and was gone with a rush, across the snowy fields and away from the road.

He was within a short quarter-mile of the bald, bare little hill, when he drew rein. He was on a little rise of ground. His pulses suddenly leaped, as he sensed something wrong. Then he saw what it was: the firing had ceased. He drew out his glasses, focused them, and saw a flood of Prussian uniforms over the crest of the hill. His errand had come too late.

His heart stopped. Then, through the glasses, he discerned a little knot of struggling movement, off at one side of the crest. Figures were clumped there. For an instant, his glasses brought up a face and figure he was certain that he recognized. And then all was quiet; the group was dissolving.

THE GLASSES slipped from his stiffened fingers, slid away. His straining, distended eyes lifted; sudden astonishment came into his face. For directly above the little hill, the gray sky showed a spot of blue. The blue widened. It became a circle of clear, open sky—and it was gone again. Only for the fraction of a moment. But enough to convince Captain Wiart, to send him riding back with fear and mystery stirring in his heart.

"And now the scientists have come along to say much the same thing," said the old gentleman sitting beside me and looking down at Algiers and the Mediterranean. "It is very strange. The blue sky is only dust, they say. Well, it is not nearly so nice a thought as the one my father had! And there was something to his belief; perhaps that was why the gray sky opened and a little bit of blue showed to me, when he died there on the hill under the Prussian bayonets!"

I DID not argue with him, of course. If the old chap believed it, if the thought pleased him, why argue it away? Besides, to be quite honest about it, I was by no means sure that I could argue it away even if I wanted to do so!

"Then," I asked, "that story explains why the Legion of Honor decoration is hanging up there on the wall, silk collar and all!"

He nodded. "Bullets found me; but I reached home safe, though a little crippled. Still, that was not the fault of the Black Virgin. So my mother did as my father had desired, and his Cross hangs there as you see it. I had to leave the army, because of the bullets that crippled me. It was the great sorrow of my life. I had hoped to get transferred to the Foreign Legion, you see."

"That's all very well, about soul-dust making the sky blue," I observed. "When you apply it in general, to poor folk such as those who perished with the German dirigible, it's a nice thought. But what about people who go down under the sea with a ship and stay there? You can't expect their vital essence or spirit or whatever it is, to get up through the water, can you?"

I had him there. He gave me a slow, serious glance, and then he pointed to the big block of stone out in front of the church, on the very tip of the high headland; the stone with its inscription for very pious folk, about the souls of those who were drowned in the sea below.

"No," he said, "I can't. But maybe the Black Virgin takes care of them, m'sieur. For, look down there!" And so saying, he swept his stick out at the Mediterranean. "What makes that ocean so blue, if it's not the same thing that makes the sky overhead blue?"

Well, I was never good at theology!

A CROWN IS EARNED

"A Crown Is Earned" follows the fortunes of the
Foreign Legion—and of a royal Legionnaire—
against the Chinese Black Flags.

LANGLADE WAS in jail, over in Yuma. The sheriff told me about it, as we talked.

"It's a damned shame, honest! The old boy was drunk, and he lifted the roof—sure; a fine was slapped on, and of course he didn't have a cent. Then we found out he'd been in the Foreign Legion, and he's not a bad sort at all. The judge is off on vacation, and I can't get the fine remitted for another month or so, and that jail is hotter'n the hinges of hell."

"How much is his fine?" I asked.

I was headed East anyhow, and being alone in the car, gladly agreed to give Langlade a free ride out of the State. So I paid his fine, and he climbed in, and off we went. There was no blarney about Langlade. He asked why I did it, and I said on account of the Arizona heat.

"Heat! They don't know what heat is in these parts," he said. "I was in the Tonkin campaign, and that was hot. It was wet, too. Why, for six months I never once took off my uniform to sleep! That was the time Bernard got his crown."

"Was the Legion in Tonkin?" I asked innocently. He snorted.

"It still is, a lot of it. You run out to the cemetery in Saigon, sometime—a cemetery that would do for London or Paris! We had some queer ducks in the Legion back in those days, too. Bernard was one of the queerest ever, and the finest."

Langlade was a crunchy little old man, bullet-headed, scarred, well over seventy but spry as a whip. He had a snappy, blasting way of speech—a man of no sympathy at all, hard as nails, bitter at life, accepting a kindness with no more thanks or gratitude than he would have accepted a kick. Pretty much a man on all counts—the kind of man an easygoing chump like me would like to be if he could.

All the way to the New Mexico border, Langlade made only occasional remarks. He mentioned Bernard once or twice; the two men had been buddies in the Legion, years ago. Langlade was getting acquainted with me, in a cautious way, and I encouraged it, for I was getting curious about this fellow Bernard.

We got into Lordsburg for dinner. He was going to stop there, he said; he had some notion of getting a job in town. We went into a hash-house and sat up at the counter together, and as we ate, he suddenly let out a cackle and pointed at an advertising sign against the wall. It displayed a gaudy scarlet crown, some trademark.

"See that crown?" Langlade observed. "That's the kind of a crown Bernard used to rave about. He had one tattooed on his arm—got a woman in Oran to do it, before we went out to Tonkin. He was royalty of some kind, a German princeling, I'd say at a guess. Sober, he was just a solemn, handsome, genial youngster. Drunk, he became another man, a crazy devil. Once or twice a year he went on a bender, a big one; a bad habit for a young chap, too. Then he would mostly talk German or English and rave about that crown. No one paid any attention to his ravings, of course.

"We landed at Haiphong, forty days out from Marseilles; and before we transshipped on to Hanoi, Bernard was in a mess. Even me, I never saw a man so drunk. And I must explain that, when he was really liquored up, Bernard was another person entirely. Some people are like that: one man sober, another person drunk. When he was sober, Bernard was a real prince— quiet, with a sweeping blond beard, neat as a pin, fine big blue eyes that could hold a twinkle at times, and utterly precise and reliable…. Come on, let's go outside and look at the stars."

I paid for the meal, and we strolled out, with the bright glitter of Arizona's stellar display twinkling down at us. We wandered around, found a deserted spot to sit, and lit cigarettes.

"IT WAS a night like this, with the stars of Tonkin overhead, that first night in Haiphong," said Langlade. "I ran into Bernard, got him into a side-street, and wrestled with him—literally. Here! Look at that fellow, and you'll see Bernard—"

A man with two mules was rolling along. A desert rat, a prospector, bearded, and bawling some maudlin song. Langlade spoke under his breath. The old prospector's figure took on youth. His grayish beard yellowed. His slouch hat became a casquette—and I saw Bernard, the Legionnaire. The white sun-helmet fixed the date; it was in those early '80s when the hapless Legion was at its first job in these parts, before the brass-hats realized that a white sun-helmet in the jungle made a swell target for Annamese rifles.

It was in the jungle, at night; the fourth company of the Legion was ending its march to join the expeditionary force attacking Sontay. There was fighting every mile of the way. The entire battalion of the Legion had come from Africa to a new land, only to find half Asia awaiting them. The Annamese, vicious fighters who hated whites with a hatred that would never die; the Black Flags, bandit chiefs of the hills; Chinese themselves, regulars down from across the border.

THE JUNGLE, under the bright stars. Bernard wakened. His companion, young Langlade, saw his leonine head uprear, heard his voice come softly.

"What is that sound?"

"A saw," said Langlade. "We march in ten minutes. Get ready."

Langlade was cool, imperturbable; he laughed at the horror in Bernard's face.

For, sitting up, Bernard saw what was going on ten feet away under a lantern. A tirailleur, his leg badly fractured by a bullet, was stretched out on a pile of baggage. He was chloroformed, but agony convulsed his bearded, livid features as the surgeon worked over the leg.

Now and again a rifle-shot rang out. Somewhere a blaze rose lurid against the dark sky. Orders were passed, low-voiced; the march was to be resumed at once. A sergeant came by, detailed Bernard and Langlade to carry the wounded tirailleur when the surgeon was finished. Still Bernard stared at the scene, biting his lips, horror in his wide blue eyes.

"No time to lose," said the surgeon calmly. The leg was off; it fell, a white blotch, to the ground. The artery was ligatured; the job done, the bandage applied, the senseless man was made fast to the only available means of transport. His good leg and his arms were bound to a long, fat bamboo.

"Come along!" said Langlade, and Bernard rose. Each of them

"Count me in on it," said Langlade.

took one end of the bamboo, and lifted the wounded man. The column was moving again. As they filed off with their burden, Langlade kicked the white blotch off into the brush. Bernard cursed him.

"You need not have done that! You—"

He directed at Langlade, in the lead, a torrent of guttural

German curses. Langlade laughed, and shot back a riposte.

"You're in Asia now, yellow-beard! And wait till you see what's ahead of us; you'll soon lose all your fine notions of gentility, M. le Prince! Crowns, indeed; you'll get a crown that you're not looking for, in this jungle."

It was the first time that Langlade had ever taunted his friend with this crown business. They had a furious give-and-take over the senseless burden, until an officer savagely shut them up. Langlade, to tell the truth, was scared stiff.... Jungle fighting was something new, and the tales of terror had spread all through the column.

He admitted it freely enough at dawn, when they were up with the other troops and in camp.

"Sorry," he said frankly, as he and Bernard dropped in exhaustion. "I've had cold devils crawling up my spine the last two days, for a fact. These stories about torture and mutilation, these Chinese we have to face—well, I've been afraid."

Bernard reached out and touched his hand. "Spoken like a brave fellow, Langlade! Forget the whole business."

Oddly enough, this little affair drew them closer together

"When we get there," he hiccuped, "you shoot; I'll work!"

and evoked from Bernard a new and very sober confidence. They were moving on Sontay, a supposedly impregnable citadel and the chief fortress of the Black Flags. The outlying stronghold of Phusa blocked their way, and while the Legion kept aid from issuing from Sontay, the Algerian tirailleurs carried Phusa.

SAID IN few words, done in the course of a barbaric night of savage fighting. Bernard and Langlade, with little to do, could see the Algerians fighting up the hillsides and through the bamboos—there was light enough, though not from the stars. The Chinese had fired huts here and there, and every now and again, sallying in among the Algerians, went at them with the cold steel.

"They say those Chinese get seventy-five piastres for every head they fetch in," said Langlade. "Wait till the tirailleurs carry the place—you'll see some killing done in return!"

"I wish we were doing it," said Bernard wistfully.

Langlade gave a cluck of surprise.

"What! This from you, who faint at the sight of blood?"

"Don't be a fool," said Bernard pleasantly. "They tell me all these places have rulers—kings and emperors. Is it true?"

"Allah alone knows!" Langlade spat out the Arabic phrase. "This country is new to most of us, and filled with wild stories. They've got a couple of emperors in Annam and Tonkin, sure, and kings scattered all over. Why?"

"I want to loot a crown," Bernard confided to him. "Listen, my friend: When I was a boy in Germany, a prediction was made that I would win a crown in a distant land. It was sure to come true. You comprehend? I could not inherit one for myself; too many stood in the way. When I am drunk, I know well that I've talked of it to you. Not to others. A crown! Well, now the prediction is coming true."

Langlade stared in the lurid night. "A crown? You mean, get one as loot?"

"I don't know," murmured the other. "Loot a mere gold

crown? No, no, not just that. Win one—that was the prediction. We've heard a lot about men who have deserted and become chiefs or rulers. Look at that Englishman in Borneo, who's a rajah. With all these native states between here and China, up in the hills, over toward Siam—I tell you, it could be done! If I looted a crown in one of these places, it might become very possible."

"You're off your nut," said Langlade with decision. "Look here! The Algerians will mop up these Chinese before morning. Then we go at Sontay. It's full of Yacs, as our men call the Black Flags. The citadel has a hundred cannon, ten thousand Chinese regulars, ten thousand Black Flags, and five thousand Annamese armed with American repeating rifles. You'll see something before we step inside, and it won't be crowns either! So talk sense."

"All the same," said Bernard, fingering his yellow beard, "I tell you it was predicted that I'd win a crown in a distant country—"

The man believed in the prediction. As though his mention of it to Langlade had unlocked a secret place in his heart, he did not hesitate now to speak of it.

LANGLADE, WHO had been puzzled at the man and his hidden past, was a practical sort of fellow who took no stock in prophecies. He had long since figured Bernard as some sort of German noble, perhaps a prince. Such a thing, in those days, was nothing rare in the Legion.

But now, under the stars and the fire-glare, as they listened to the bullets going *clack-clack-clack* among the bamboos, Langlade knew that his friend was one of those simple, terrible men who see things with the eyes of children. And he made an effort to waken Bernard to the truth.

"Before you talk about winning a crown," he said, "you'd better start in by winning the Médaille Militaire! That's a necessary start, my friend."

"Oh!" exclaimed Bernard. "I believe you're right!"

Some moments later, Langlade realized that his friend was missing, with rifle and bayonet....

Action intervened. The Legion companies were deployed on a wide front to throw back a sally of Chinese regulars from Sontay. The red rippling fire of rifles slanted across the night and into the dawn. Toward four o'clock, the enemy attacked in force, and failed.

WITH DAWN, the Algerians were inside Phusa, concentrated on exacting a bitter vengeance for their mutilated comrades. The Chinese and Black Flags beat a sudden retreat, and flooded into their walled city with its hundred cannon and its impregnable citadel. Langlade, too busy to worry about a lost man, saw nothing at all of Bernard until, as the mess fires were smoking into the sunrise, murmurs of amazement from the wearied ranks drew his attention.

Then he saw Bernard ambling along, huge, shaggy, joyous, spotted with blood from head to foot, rifle and bayonet dripping red. He had gone out alone to take part in the clean-up, and had half a dozen slight wounds to show for it.

"Now," he said to Langlade, as he halted and puffed, "I have the Médaille Militaire! You'll see."

He learned otherwise, soon enough. When the officers got through with him, he came back to Langlade, shaking his head with a puzzled expression. He was no simpleton, but the heat and the fighting had made another man of him.

"I did wrong, yes," he said with a sigh. "However, I meant well. And now you can see for yourself that I don't faint at the sight of blood. I needed to fight, to find out for myself how it would be hand to hand. Well, I'm not a coward, at least! And they tell me mandarins in the citadel wear caps which are the same as crowns to these yellow devils."

His white sun-helmet was gone. Like other men who had lost theirs, he took one of the round Chinese hats and wore it; a few moments of the terrific sun was enough to knock a man out, for it was different from the Algerian sun. Langlade eyed his friend with real worry. The man was changed. Perhaps the morning sun had already touched him.

All that day they moved in on the city. Between the wide moat and the wall were planted bamboos, almost impenetrable, while the moat was defended by outer works masked by bamboos. Word had spread that an assault was to be delivered, that the town was to be taken by storm next morning. Meantime, the outer defenses had to be cleared.

It was savage, stubborn work, but the Legion was saved for the morning's job.

Toward noon Bernard, who had been ordered out with a reconnaissance squad, showed up with an excited glitter in his blue eyes.

"Now I've learned something exact!" exclaimed the blond German, flinging himself down and lighting his pipe beside Langlade. "I heard the lieutenant say we were to attack the west gate. Three huge black flags are there, with Chinese writing on them in gold. I'm going to have one of those flags."

"Has your mania turned from crowns to flags?" demanded Langlade.

The other gave him a quick, laughing glance.

"Mania, eh? Is that what you think it, my friend? Come, I'll be frank with you: I had a family at home, you understand? I was not good enough for them; I was the black sheep. I could not stand the folly, the hollow mockery, of glittering uniforms unearned, of court functions, of bowing and scraping servitors—nothing earned, nothing real!"

His profound bitterness, his burst of confidence, gripped Langlade. Here, he knew, was his first real insight into this blond German, into the man's past and future, into his hopes and failures and ambitions.

"All that sickened me," went on Bernard, rumbling German oaths into his beard. "I rebelled against it; and I was chucked out. I slipped away and went to Paris, and joined up with the Legion. They hope I'll be killed quietly. My father, a harsh, cruel man, hopes I'll never show up again to disgrace him, as he calls it. Well, what about that crown? I tell you, I mean to earn it! I've learned what a man's life is, in the Legion. I've learned what's real, what's worth while. Yes, I've had crazy notions about deserting and becoming some sort of a native ruler—who hasn't? But here's what I really want."

He sucked at his pipe for a moment, and all the glitter had left his eyes. They were somber and earnest, like his voice.

"I've told you more than anyone else knows or suspects," he said. "Now for what I really want to do. I want to send home a crown, you understand? A real crown. One I've looted or captured or won; I want to send it home to that harsh man, as a token of my contempt, if you like to call it so. Or, if not a crown just yet, then one of those Black Flags yonder. The highest trophy obtainable, something I've won with my own two hands, the way my ancestors won their lands and titles. Not by in-heritance, but by fighting. If I can do this, it'll put me on a higher level than those who sit at home and polish decorations they've done nothing to earn.... Or do you understand this foolishness?"

Langlade nodded, a thrill of comprehension in his heart.

"Understand it? Yes," he said quickly, a most unwonted touch of warmth deepening his words. "Yes! You're a poet, a knight errant! And I thought you were just some German princeling."

Bernard's lips twisted in a smile.

"Perhaps I'm a little of all three, Langlade. I'm telling you all this so you may comprehend what that old boyhood prediction means to me—the crown I'll win in some far land. This is the land, no doubt about it. Or perhaps up in China. And I suppose you still think it's foolishness?"

Langlade shook his head.

"I'm proud that you wanted me to understand! I'd take a run-out powder with you tomorrow," he said. (Yes, the Legion had precisely that bit of slang, long before it was ever transferred to English.) "If you said let's go and look for a crown up in the hills, I'd go. That's the way I feel."

Bernard gripped his hand.

"Oh, I'm not completely mad, unless drunk," he said, and grinned. "We know each other, you and I; we'll hang together. Well, I'm going to have one of those flags to send back home, no matter what it costs!"

"Count me in on it," said Langlade.

AFTER THIS, he regarded his friend with new eyes. Undoubtedly, he reflected shrewdly, there was more to the story than Bernard had admitted. A woman must be somewhere in it, since a woman was in every life-story behind those bearded bronze masks of the Legion. However, that was none of his business, and he shrugged it away.

That afternoon, that evening, rumors flew through the lines. The morning assault was postponed until next afternoon, when the mopping-up of the outer defenses would be finished.

Then the Legion was to lead in the assault upon the city.

Sontay had four gates, each one set in a tower, midway of one wall; the bamboo palisades outside the gates were formidable obstacles in themselves. Word went around that Lieutenant Poymiro, during the reconnaissance, had discovered something else, and Bernard confirmed this report: A small postern to the right of the west gate where entry might be made. Then it was learned that the marines were to attack this possible opening, and sullen fury filled the whole battalion of the Legion.

"That's right!" growled Langlade. "If something easy shows up, give it to the others, and let the Legion take the toughest assignment!"

Bernard laughed. "You should be proud of it, *mon ami!* They're going to issue axes and hatchets, I understand. We'll beat the marines inside, be sure of that!"

Night came on, and the bright stars. Dawn drew down, and with morning the operations began, but the Legion was held inactive. Orders came along. At two o'clock the Legion was to

The huge bamboos were shattered; Bernard hurled himself at them, and a gap was made by his weight.

assume combat formation and sweep everything clear outside the west gate. When the "Charge" was sounded, they were to go in—just like that. Meantime, the Algerians would be making a false attack at the north gate.

TOWARD NOON, Bernard disappeared. He did not show up until the battalion was forming; then he came rolling in, drunk as a lord, with his canteen chock full of navy issue brandy. He had been visiting with the marines, and regulations being relaxed, had made the most of the plentiful cognac. Langlade gulped down a stiff drink, and off they went.

Split up into squads, with the fourth company in the lead, the Legion went at the job. The walls, the thickly grown bamboos, the palisades, rolled out clouds of smoke; balls and bullets hailed forth in a rain of death. In a series of rushes, the Legion spread out and attacked. Men died; officers died. Some of the squads were wiped out.

Under Lieutenant Maquard, a burly man with a jaw of iron, the squad containing Bernard and Langlade worked its way forward. From time to time Bernard swigged at his canteen, brushing aside the remonstrances of Langlade. The big German was fighting drunk, and carried an ax worth a dozen of the hatchets issued to the other men.

"When we get there," he hiccuped, "you shoot; I'll work!"

It was nearly five when they were ready—fifty yards from the wall and the thick palisade. Everything had been cleared up behind. They were across the moat, past the clumps of bamboos. They maintained a heavy fire on the wall, and Bernard kept on punishing the brandy, until he flung away his empty canteen.

"You see them?" He pointed to the three huge black flags above the gate, showing now and then through the powder-smoke. "One of those, *mon ami!* Just one."

"Bah! Let's have all three!" exclaimed Langlade, who had not neglected the cognac himself. "Listen—*listen!*"

A thin, fine voice of bugles. Lieutenant Maquard came to his feet—it was the charge, the order to assault.

"Vive la France!" he yelled hoarsely. "Forward!"

The men leaped up. Half a dozen of them went rolling, under a hail of balls. Maquard was already dashing forward. Langlade was after him, Bernard and the others lumbering into speed. Maquard was at the palisade, hacking at it with his saber, when Bernard came up with a wild yell.

"Out of the way!"

Ax in hand, the big German hurled himself at the bamboos. Others joined him, their hatchets at work, while Langlade and the files to right and left maintained a heavy fire on the wall and parapet above. Upright, careless of bullets, Bernard slashed like a madman. The lashings of the palisade, thick withes of bamboo, were finally cut through; the huge bamboos themselves were shattered. Bernard hurled himself at them, and a gap was made by his weight. The lieutenant was up and over him, the first man inside.

Until the breach was widened, few could follow. Langlade shoved in among the first. Bernard had discarded his rifle, and was swinging the ax, a man gone berserk. Langlade joined him, bayonet and bullet at work. The Chinese fell back. As more Legionnaires burst in, the Chinese gave way and fled.

With a roar, Bernard turned to the parapet, Langlade at his elbow. The two of them were alone, for the rush of attack had swept on into the city. Bernard was making for the flat, solid roof of the gate-tower, where those three black flags waved. Here was a mandarin in fantastic armor; here were Chinese regulars; here were Black Flags in their round straw hats. Rifles cracked. Yells went up.

Straight at them hurtled Bernard, Langlade leaping beside him, firing as he ran, bayonet ready. The ax crashed down, and a spurt of blood dyed the blond beard crimson. Chinese closed in. Langlade darted forward with his bayonet; the ax whirled and bit afresh. Spears slithered at the two; swords glittered;

rifles banged. Before that rush of insensate ferocity the throng opened in terror.

An officer leaped at Bernard. One back-stroke of the ax crushed helmet and head together. There was the mandarin, bleating horribly, his gorgeous dragon-robes and queer armor spotted with blood. He went down under Langlade's thrust. The two of them were at the bamboo standards now, where waved the three black flags with their golden characters.

Then the Chinese came in. Ax drove; bayonet thrust; but the two were borne back and back, long halberds and spears thrusting at them. One of the waving standards was pulled down and carried off; another followed. With a roar of fury, Bernard struck aside the halberds and flung himself into the thick of the press.

A frightful yell arose, a wild cheer. The marines were through the postern gate, just beyond. The enemy, thus taken in rear, broke and fled. Bernard, dropping his ax, leaped over the fallen bodies and grasped at the one remaining flag. An Annamese, wounded, came half erect and whipped up his rifle—but Lanjlade fired first.

"Thanks, thanks!" And with a wild laugh, Bernard tore loose

the standard, reached for the gold-decorated flag, and ripped it from the bamboo. A blaze of triumph was in his face. "Look! We have it, *mon ami,* we have it!"

"And for the love of heaven, put it out of sight!" panted Langlade. "The first officer who sees it will send it to headquarters as a trophy!"

Bernard was prompt to see the sense of this, and presently had the silk flag folded away beneath his blue cummerbund.

Langlade, meantime, went to the officer, callously separated the crushed head from the crushed helmet, and from the wreckage of the helmet he extricated a gorgeous peacock plume. He

Bernard, swinging the ax, was on the flat solid roof of the tower where those black flags waved. Langlade, beside him, darted forward with his bayonet.

tossed the sopping object at Bernard, then sought the dead mandarin and produced a black silk cap with coral button. This he handed over likewise.

"Not a bad haul!" he observed. "Mandarin cap—that's a crown, anyhow. So is the peacock feather, or what's left of it. Put 'em with the flag, and you've got something worth sending— Hey! What's wrong? You're a hero, old fellow. Not hurt?"

Bernard smiled faintly. He had picked up a spear and was leaning on it heavily.

"Heroes be damned!" he said. "I'm going to be sick. It's the cognac. And the effect's all worn off—"

Langlade grinned. "Worked off, you mean! All right, be sick, and make a good job of it. I'll just see if there's any loot on these fellows."

A surge of figures, and to the bloody scene atop the tower came half a dozen of the Legion, with a tricolor to set in place. The city was taken; darkness was approaching; the job was ended. An officer appeared, bearing one of the two flags that had escaped.

"Ha! Hot work here, eh?" he observed. "It'd mean the Médaille if you'd only taken one of those other flags!"

"Too bad," said Bernard, straightening up, and Langlade chuckled.

WEEKS WORE on into months, with the Legion cleaning up all over the place. France was at war with China now; there was talk of various expeditions, to Formosa and Foochow and elsewhere.

Bernard was all afire at the thought of China itself ready to yield him new trophies. He talked often of the crown that had returned to his mind as a fixed idea; he had no secrets from Langlade.

The two of them applied for transfer to the northern expedition. Bernard had found that the Chinese did not use crowns, but this made no difference to him, for there were other insignia of royalty to be had. In a savage little jungle fight he killed the chief of a band of Black Flags, and took from the body a queerly shaped slab of reddish brown stone.

A scientist from headquarters heard about it and tried to buy the stone from him. It was ancient jade, said the scientist; Han jade, such as was only found in tombs these days. And this bit of jade, shaped like an ancient sword, was the royal insignia given by the emperor to a viceroy.

Bernard disdained all offers.

"Look you—the Emperor's insignia!" he said to Langlade that night, joyous as a child as he played with the reddish jade. "No crowns in China, eh? Well, here's just as good. And if I could get this in the jungles of Tonkin, what'll I get when we loot some big place up north? Back this goes by the next boat to my precious father!"

And back it went.

Back, too, went Bernard to the hospital base at Haiphong. He had come down with the insidious jungle fever, which turned his immense frame into a skeleton. So the two friends were parted.

Some days later, destiny descended on Langlade. In a night skirmish, by one of those queer freaks of luck which do happen, a Black Flag slug hit the cartridge-case of the next man, glanced, and took Langlade through both thighs—luckily without touching the bone. So Langlade also went to Haiphong.

When he got there, he was a walking casualty. Of Bernard, at first, he could find no trace. After some days, however, he traced his friend, and promptly sought him out. It was evening when he came into the ward where Bernard lay. A man in fever had just struck the sister attending to him; orderlies were rushing in to hold him down—and the man was Bernard.

The nun who had been struck ordered the men to be gentle.

"*Pauvre enfant!* He doesn't know what he's doing," she said. Then, as Langlade came up and she heard his name, she gave him a curious glance. "Oh! He was asking for you; he spoke of you often, every day."

"Eh?" said Langlade, startled. "Why do you use the past tense, sister?"

"The doctor says he won't live until morning."

So Langlade looked at the blond German for the last time, and had no joy of it; Bernard died in the delirium of fever, muttering harsh German words and fighting the orderlies who held him down.

Nothing particularly sad about it. As Langlade said, all men must die, and one of the curiously interesting things is the story of how other men die and go forth in search of what lies beyond.

UNDER THE blazing stars of New Mexico, Langlade's voice died out with this bit of philosophy, and we smoked together in silence. Amazing, I thought, to hear this yarn of other days in such a setting—this story of yesterday in another world, this tale of a forgotten war in an unknown jungle, here across the Arizona border.

"So," I observed, "your friend Bernard never got the crown he had sought so long and far! The prophecy he mentioned never came true, then."

"But it did," said Langlade, emotion in his brusque voice. "That was the queer thing about it all. You see, I did not attend his funeral, because fever caught me; and the same day he died, I was down with the shakes. However, I was in funds. The looting up-country had been pretty good, and I was well supplied with money. So I had the Sister of Charity who attended me fix up a handsome wreath for poor Bernard. It was no mere bunch of faded flowers, but a large wreath of those things they call immortelles—the kind that last forever. You know?"

"Yes," I said. He took a fresh cigarette, lit it and went on.

"IF YOU ever get a chance to look at the records," he said, "you'll find a singular thing happened. One of the Legion named Bernard was removed from his temporary grave. He was dug up. And I was there when he was dug up. Why was it done? Because a German cruiser was sent to get his body. Yes, damme if it's not a fact! Nobody knew much about it, but I've heard it said that he was a nephew or some near relation of the Kaiser. Anyhow, they sent the cruiser and took him away. He was carried aboard with no end of ceremony, too."

"And that's the end of the story?"

"Not quite." Langlade's voice took on a cynic touch. "That prophecy—it did come true, you see. Those Germans do things methodically. When they dug Bernard up, they took the wreath that was still on his grave, and put it on the coffin; I saw it done. Thus, he went back with the crown he had won in a distant land, just as the prediction said."

"A crown?" I repeated. "But you said it was a wreath—"

Langlade tossed away his cigarette.

"I said wreath, yes, because we're speaking English together," he said. "But as you should know, the word in French is *couronne—crown*. It had never occurred to him that the prediction might have meant a funeral crown.... Good night."

THE CRIME OF THE LEGION

"The Crime of the Legion" takes you to Formosa
and a half-forgotten savage campaign.

T HE TALK fell upon wars and rumors of wars.
About the table were gathered half a dozen men, here
met in New York; all were former members of the Foreign
Legion—*anciens* of the Legion, as they called themselves, who
met every so often to gam and drink and recall old days. Here
was the dark, calm Porson, the red-haired Casey, the excitable
Kramer, and others, notable men of the past, who now followed
all sorts of queer occupations to earn a living in America.

And when they talked of war, they knew what they were
talking about.

"It's all very well," grunted Kramer, "for you fellows to say
that war is war; but it's not. Times have changed. In our day, it
was considered dishonorable for a nation to make war without
a formal declaration of war. Nowadays, the first thing anybody
knows—*boum!* Airplanes overhead, and bombs falling."

"Right," said Casey with a nod. "A declaration of war is made
with bombs."

"Wrong, if you think that's anything new," put in Porson,
rolling a cigarette. "Why, even before our time, France did it."

Eyes went to him in shocked surprise.

"France?" said some one. "No, no, Porson! Not in modern
times, at least."

Porson smiled darkly. "Maybe you don't call 1884 modern
times? But if you knew the history of the Legion as you should,
you'd know better. France was trying, with all kinds of weapons,

to make China stand by a treaty—and was about a year doing it. That's how the Legion got into Formosa."

FORMOSA, EH? The name has vanished from maps, these days, since Japan grabbed the island and proceeded to remake it; but it has not vanished from history. More than one face around the table took on a frown. The arms of France had been soundly trounced on one occasion in Formosa—a subject best avoided.

"If," said somebody, "you're thinking about that affair at Tamsui—"

"I'm not," Porson promptly intervened. "The Legion wasn't there; that's why the marines got what they got. I was thinking about the hill fighting outside Kelung, in March of '85, when the Legion and the Bat d'Af worked together—"

The Bat d'Af! That stirred tongues, but mostly of curses. The *Bataillon d'Afrique*, that unhappy penal corps composed of the most hardened and obdurate rascals in the army, is nothing to get sentimental about. Plenty of men in the Legion could go back, or climb high; but the Bat d'Af, already in hell, had no Abraham's bosom in prospect anywhere.

"And," Porson added, "I was mostly thinking about Papa Weber."

"Papa Weber?" exclaimed a voice. "Why, I knew him! When I first joined up—that was back in 1897—he was at Bel Abbes; the grand old man of the Legion, they called him. He died a little while after. They said his heart was broken because he was unable to go on the Madagascar expedition with the Legion."

"His heart," said Porson, "was broken long before that. Yes, he had been in the Legion nearly thirty years, I heard. An Austrian, and some said a nobleman; no one ever knew for sure. He had refused time and again to be made an officer. He was a mystery—a tall, splendid old fellow, a great gentleman, a great criminal."

"Criminal?" spoke out some one indignantly. "You shouldn't say that of him, Porson! He's not forgotten. Even now they talk about him as the perfect Legionnaire, the man without fear and without reproach. Why, Papa Weber—"

"The noblest of men may be a great criminal," said Porson. "It all depends on the point of view. Let's get back to Formosa. That winter, if you remember, the French army in Kelung was hemmed in by immense Chinese forces. The French held the town and harbor, but the Chinese had them blocked there. Steep hills came up all about the town, cut by tremendous valleys. Lacking reinforcements,—the Legion had not yet arrived,—the French held on desperately. Then the Legion came—the fourth battalion of the second regiment, a thousand picked men. They landed and were assigned quarters in the Chinese town; a little creek separated them from the quarters of the Bat d'Af.

"Due to the rigorous climate of Formosa, the Legion kept its red pantaloons and its kepi without any neck-cover; thus looked like ordinary troops except for the white cartridge-box across the chest. Papa Weber, with his graying beard brushed out, was the lordliest of them all. And next door, so to speak, was the *Bataillon d'Afrique*."

NO NEED to describe those next-door neighbors. Zephyrs, they were nicknamed; one and all criminals, hardened to the privations of the Sahara, kept in bounds by an iron discipline and by merciless punishments, holding their lives cheap. They were drawn from military prisons and civil prisons; they were the lowest of the low, but when it came to such superhuman exertions as the besieged French must undergo, they were the very men for the job.

So, for that matter, were those of the Legion.

The day after their arrival, Papa Weber was strolling about, getting the situation in his mind. The heights occupied by the Chinese were only fifteen hundred yards distant. Fighting, thanks to the rain and bitter weather, had languished into outpost skirmishes. The high upland overlooking the town and harbor was broken into various peaks, which had been given

names by the French—the Eagle's Nest, the Bamboo Fort, and so on.

From the Bamboo Fort flew a flag which had captured the imagination of all the troops, the flag of old China. It was a narrow triangle of yellow, three feet wide at the base, and tapering for its length of fifteen feet—yellow, with the blue Imperial Dragon cavorting along its folds. Mounted on an enormous bamboo, which had given the Chinese position its name, it was already a subject of bets galore among the men.

Papa Weber, spick and span, big pipe tucked into his grayish beard, came upon a group of his own men and of zephyrs engaged in a hot argument, punctuated by curses and blistering oaths. A corporal of the Bat d'Af was the central figure of the group, and was heaping blasphemy upon the Legion with no uncertain tongue.

With a fight imminent, Papa Weber shoved his way forward in order to keep his own comrades in hand. Sight of his broad chest with its Cross and medals drew a jeer from the zephyrs, as the voice of their corporal lifted acidly:

"Bet? I'll bet anything you like, anything on earth or in hell! The Bat d'Af will pull down that flag, and not the Legion. The Legion won't be anywhere near. I'll bet money or pay or wine or women or—"

"Why not let me propose a wager?" The voice of Papa Weber, deep and grave and solid, checked the rabid outburst of the corporal. Then, as the two men crossed glances, a sudden startled silence held them.

He was not old at all, this Corporal Garnot. Crop-headed, his face all high, sharp angles, his blue eyes pools of vicious light, he seemed stamped with crime. A hard, lithe bundle of muscle, he was.

IN THE sharp silence, those around perceived that these two men knew one another. Old Weber took the pipe from his mouth and spoke.

"So! Perhaps you're afraid of my wager?"

"Not of it nor of you," spat out Garnot. "That flag goes to the Bat d'Af!"

"It does not," said Weber. "It's an honorable flag. It's the flag of an ancient race. It goes to honorable men."

"Like you, I suppose?" sneered the younger man.

"Precisely. And I'll wager you, if you like—a bet between you and me. The loser goes down on his face before everybody and licks the boot of the winner; licks it clean."

Either the words, or the supreme contempt in them, stung Garnot almost past bearing. His face flamed; fury shook him.

"Done with you!" he returned. "You'll crawl, medals and all, and I'll daub my boots with cow-dung before you start licking them clean."

"You would," said Papa Weber. Just the two words, and they lashed like a whip. The corporal leaped at him, but two of the zephyrs pulled Garnot off before a blow could be struck. Replacing his pipe, puffing a blue cloud, Papa Weber turned his back and strode away.

With him was the comrade he loved most, another Austrian, a big bearded fellow like himself.

"I think, Karl," said Weber slowly, as they paced along, "that man is the most evil person in the world."

"A man doesn't get his corporal's stripes in the Bat d'Af by being an angel," said Karl. "You'd better look out for trouble. He's following us. If he picks a fight—"

"No danger," said Papa Weber, without so much as looking.

CORPORAL GARNOT was, indeed, following them. He was alone, and as he approached it became evident he was in calmer mood. Karl offered to intervene and draw the other off, to avoid a row, but Papa Weber shook his head.

"No. Stand by. You do not understand; but it had to come. There will be no fight."

So Karl remained as a witness to the scene. Papa Weber turned and regarded Garnot calmly; the younger man halted.

"I thought you were in South America," Weber said in German. With a sneer, the other made reply in French.

"None of that; I've spoken French since I was a kid, and you know it. No, I'm not in South America and never was. That was just a yarn."

"Obviously," said Weber. "You killed your mother. I suppose you know it."

"I'd rather it had been you, you old sanctimonious goat!" snarled Garnot. This was the first intimation Karl had that the two might be related. "You, with all your talk of a great family and high name back in Austria—and a private in the Legion!"

"That's all I have left. It's enough," said Papa Weber gravely. Garnot thrust his face closer, his eyes vicious.

"Listen: I've found out a few things. I know who you were in Austria, and why you left; it's not such a pleasant story, either. I don't blame you for sinking your identity in the Legion. Going

They waited; they could do nothing
else—day and night the rain kept up
interminably, blocking and operation.

to make trouble for me, are you? Two can play at that game, you'll find!"

Papa Weber faced him impassively.

"Don't let your evil spirit carry you too far," he said slowly.

"Yah! That sounds like you," snapped Garnot. "Evil spirit, eh? Well, I'm going to pay you back—pay some of the debts I've owed you for a long time. If you'd stepped up to the scratch, I'd never have gone to prison. But no; you wouldn't do it."

Weber said nothing. The younger man straightened up and laughed; it was not a nice laugh to hear.

"You think that because you've disowned me, it's all over? Far from that, my good man. Far from that! Before I'm through, I'm going to make you and your damned Legion wish I'd never been born! And I'm going to collect that bet, and when it's collected the whole Legion will know that you're responsible for me. And that's not all, either."

With a flick of his shoulders, he swung away and strode off. Papa Weber looked after him calmly, then scratched a match and held it to the bowl of his pipe.

"*Ja!*" he said, turning. "It is worth something to be in the Legion, Karl. Now let us go on and find out about these American rifles the Chinese have—the ones that shoot so fast. Lee— is that the name? Or was it Winchester?"

KARL ASKED no questions about the scene just ended. It was evident, none the less, that this Corporal Garnot must be the son of Papa Weber; he was a curious man, this Karl, but he knew better than to ask his friend any questions. Weber was slow to be moved either by drink or by wrath, but once moved to action, he could be terrible.

A week passed, though not with inaction. Weber, veteran campaigner that he was, had no illusions regarding the situation; the officers, indeed, talked freely with him. The Chinese had proved they could fight, and their circle of positions held the French powerless. The ground, more perpendicular than level, was covered by a six-foot jungle of brush, cut only by winding trails.

"If the Chinese had artillery," said Karl one night, "they could blow us to hell. And rumor says they're getting Krupps."

"They are," Papa Weber confirmed grimly. "That's why we must act. Within three days you'll see something happen. It means work, a campaign of days in the brush, with grub and cartridges on our backs; no animals can follow the trails yonder. We'd need at least twenty thousand men for the job, but we've got two thousand who are better—the Legion and the Bat d'Af. It won't be done at one crack, either."

"Since you know everything," said Karl, who admired Weber with all his heart, "you must know how we'll attack."

"There's only one way, *ja!* They've neglected to seize the flat hill we call the Table; at least, they've no defenses there. It dominates the others. Once we have it, we can roll back their lines, outflank them, attack the Bamboo Fort and the others. A very simple matter."

Simple! Karl gasped. He, six years in the Legion, was no fool. To occupy the Table meant days of campaigning on almost impassable ground, against a determined and well-armed enemy. The Chinese were Fukien and Pichili men, picked regiments of the Imperial army. And no artillery could be used, except a mountain-gun or two the men might carry on their backs.

"I think," added Weber, "we'll get the orders Monday, and move out Tuesday."

He was right about that; but thanks to Corporal Garnot, he was also wrong.

AS THE days passed, it became more and more difficult to restrain the zephyrs. Those hardened, hopeless men, now on the fighting line with the chance of winning the *galons* of first-class privates, within sight and sound of the enemy, chafed terribly at their idleness. Naturally, they knew nothing of the headquarters' plan of immediate action.

On the Monday morning an impudent, swaggering zephyr came into the lines of the Legion and halted at the door of the Chinese hut in which Karl and Papa Weber were quartered. He saluted them with a mocking jeer.

"A message for the noble Herr von Strull," he said, and tossed a folded paper into the hut. "Otherwise, Papa Weber. Keep your eye on the Bat d'Af cantonments for the next hour, and you'll see some fun, you frogs of the Legion!"

He swaggered off again. Papa Weber picked up the folded paper, opened it, and read the scrawled words: *"Get ready to pay up the bet, full measure!"*

He crumpled the paper and threw it away, with anger smoldering in his eyes. Herr von Strull, eh? Garnot was keeping his word. He meant to tell the world about Papa Weber. God knows what he meant to do!

"What did the rat mean, about keeping an eye on their cantonments?" asked Karl.

"We'd better do it, and learn," Weber rejoined. "With those devils, anything is possible. They'd join the Chinese and fight against us, if they had the chance."

Later, Karl was to remember this prediction.

They saw the thing when it happened. A sudden commotion in the cantonments, in the outer works; whistles arose, shouts, a gusty wave of cheers and ribald comments, orders from furious officers disdained. A mutiny among the zephyrs? No. Something more strange, more amazing.

A corporal led off, and others followed him—eleven men in all, full armed. They left the lines at a trot, and inside five minutes vanished completely in the brush. Corporal Garnot and eleven men, going to attack the Bamboo Fort on their own!

They were gone; but behind them it was like smoking tinder to powder. As one man, the *Bataillon d'Afrique* leaped to arms. Officers came on the run, the Legion was ordered into ranks; buglers, ordinarily silent by reason of the proximity of the Chinese, blared out orders. The zephyrs were one vast confusion

of furious men, demanding to support their comrades. Only when the order was given to open fire on any who fell out of rank, did they sullenly submit.

Aides dashed back and forth between the lines and headquarters. Now and then, glimpses of Garnot and his eleven men were seen amid the brush, heading straight for their objective—an utterly impossible thing, it seemed. Their hand forced, the staff conferred hastily. At length came orders. Rations for four days—a yell greeted the word.

The zephyrs marched. The Legion marched. And there began a mad and desperate attack which was to last, not four days, but six.

Winding paths by ravines and defiles and jungled hillsides, by sun and rain; skirmishes with unseen Chinese placed in ambush, bullets streaming death into the white files. Onward and upward against incredible odds, by footpaths that not even mules could follow, or no paths at all. Days of it.

THEN, GAINING the Chinese positions above, quick rushes, and hand-to-hand work, and the surprise of bursting shells. The Chinese had their Krupps in place, and this would have ended matters once and for all, except for a typically Chinese incident. The first shells burst; but only the first. The later ones screamed in the air and did not burst. A few shells, sent with the guns, had fuses in place. For the others, fuses had

"You would," said Papa Weber. Just the two words, and
they lashed like a whip. The corporal leaped at him.

been delivered separately—and the Chinese did not know how
to put them in place.

The one little mountain-gun which was carried along and
put together on the heights, landed its first shell smack in the
Chinese battery. Gunners were blown into the air. The Krupps
were silenced. The positions were rushed.

And with a portion of the uplands in French hands, the days
of attack ended. The troops were utterly exhausted, and the
blinding rain of Formosa descended in a flood to halt the
advance and save the face of the staff. Now these upper positions

were consolidated and held. Nothing more could be done. The Dragon flag still waved on Fort Bamboo.

Once, during the fighting, Garnot and his men had been in full sight, climbing the lower scarps toward the fort; that was all. Three of the men were found, headless and mutilated corpses. The others came in, dispirited and half dead—all but Corporal Garnot. He had sworn never to come in, they said. Finding how mad and impossible was his ambition, he had kept on alone. By this time he was dead, or captured.

"And a good job," said Karl. Back in the Kelung quarters, he puffed at his pipe and nodded at Papa Weber. The zephyrs were holding the newly won positions, in the driving rain that fell day and night. "A good job. You're glad, no doubt."

PAPA WEBER looked at him, pawed the big beard, and shook his head.

"Glad? If it were true, I'd be relieved, perhaps; not glad. But I do not think that man is dead. He is too evil to die so easily. Wait and see."

They waited, waited a whole month; they could do nothing else. Sporadic fighting went on, but the hill paths were slippery mud, the skies opened to check any real efforts, and a horrible fear had begun to grip headquarters—fear of a major disaster here.

For, in the army, the dreaded cholera was taking toll, and fever with it.

Day and night the rain kept up interminably, blocking any operation. The positions gained were under sniping fire most of the time. The Chinese had received more troops, the French had not; reinforcements from Europe came slowly. The mortality among the officers had been enormous. Only one possibility remained: evacuation.

This meant a terribly black eye to French prestige. The only alternative seemed to be utter destruction of the whole force. A single battery of artillery might have effected this destruction, but the Chinese shells refused to burst. They still had no fuses in place. The only hope of saving face was to strike one sharp blow, win the positions on the circling heights, defeat the Chinese—and then clear out. But, if the rain kept up, if the cholera kept on, this would be impossible.

Companies of the Legion relieved the exhausted zephyrs along the outer defenses. Together, Papa Weber and Karl fought and smoked and endured. Together, they eyed the Chinese works being constructed here and there; the activity of the yellow men was amazing and disturbing. Papa Weber frowned, as they talked together one day.

"Unless we drive them out quickly, we're lost," he observed. "They're constructing new positions that will dominate the town and the bay. Once they get artillery up there, we're done for. Luckily, Corporal Garnot is totally ignorant of artillery."

Karl's eyes opened wide. "Garnot? What do you mean? We've heard nothing from him."

"Are you blind?" said Papa Weber scornfully. "Look at the positions they're laying out! Anyone can see with half an eye that some one who knows his business is directing those operations. Garnot reached his objective, that's all. Instead of losing his head, he used it."

"A Frenchman, fighting against the French?" gaped Karl.

"Bah! The devil has no nationality."

FEBRUARY WAS wearing itself out in storms. The cholera made worse inroads, hitting the Legion hard. The marines were reduced to skeleton companies. Day by day, the Chinese could be seen making progress. They were getting artillery up to their new positions now.

Then the news spread—not unexpected by Papa Weber and the Legion. The staff had decided to attack at all costs, with every available man.

Red sunset, clear moonlight; the rains and storm had ended, at least temporarily. Before dawn the columns were off and away. Radiant sunlight welcomed them. The objective was precisely that which Papa Weber had foreseen from the beginning;

*"Remember that corporal of the zephyrs who
let out that squad of eleven fools—and never
showed up again? We found him, dead."*

to capture the height called the Table, and then roll back the Chinese from the flank.

"Three days," said Weber, as they followed the winding paths. "Make up your mind to it, Karl. This is March 4th. On the 7th, we take the Bamboo Fort."

Karl merely grunted, as the first volleys rang out ahead....

All that day it was a long, savage, stubborn fight through the brush, but with no close work. The French prepared methodically for what must come, the Chinese consolidated their defenses along the crest of the Table.

"Tomorrow we'll have it hot," said Papa Weber, when they camped that night.

True enough, and a fine clear day. Off before dawn, the column splitting up, running into a hot fire as Chinese halted the advance and then fell back. On and on, part of the Legion working around; a road had to be hacked through the brush for the men with mountain-guns. Weber, at this work with Karl, paused abruptly and leaned on his ax.

"Karl! Did you hear anything? I thought I heard a voice calling me."

"Nothing," grunted Karl wonderingly.

THE WORK went on; at noon, the guns were in position and opened. The zephyrs led the assault, the Legion sustained them. They went into and over the defenses—a bloody, desperate, hand-to-hand affair. When it was over—the fort cleared, the routed Chinese in full flight and the Legion mopping up, Karl and Papa Weber came face to face.

"Well!" exclaimed Karl. "You were right. You are always right. I saw him."

"And I felt him." Weber showed his tunic, torn by two balls. "He did his best to get me, *ja!* Well, my friend, say nothing about this; no one else recognized him."

At four that afternoon, the Tricolor replaced the Dragon on the captured positions. To those down below in the town—within hearing distance—the bugles of the column saluted with the *"au drapeau"* call, announcing victory. The Table was captured.

THE NIGHT brought rain in a scant dash. The wounded were sent back to Kelung. With morning, stormy and cloudy, the operations went on; the ground ahead was occupied, the skirmish lines were pushed ahead, the Chinese lines were rolled back. All went forward methodically, but when evening came on with heavy rain, Karl perceived once again that Papa Weber had been right. The final push on Fort Bamboo would not come until morning.

That night, with the wind howling and the rain coming in gusts, Karl and Weber were on advanced post. It was past midnight. Karl, peering up at the precipitous heights facing them, shivered.

"It's an impossibility," he declared. "That ground is horrible.

*The zephyrs led the assault; they went into and over
the defenses—a bloody, desperate, hand-to-hand affair.*

Dawn is coming on, and the reserves haven't come up from
Kelung. The ammunition is nearly gone."

"The reserves will bring plenty," said Papa Weber calmly.
They were posted on the very edge of a deep defile. The opposite side, hot thirty feet away, was as fat beyond reach as the
moon. "The ram is passing, the stars are coming out. All goes
well."

"All goes well!" The words were flung back like an echo—
German words. The two men started, separated, took cover. A
mocking laugh came across the gulf to them.

"All goes well, very true! So it's you, Papa Weber!" came a voice they both knew. "Haven't you a word of greeting for me?"

"Traitor!" A guttural flood of German escaped Weber. It drew another laugh.

"Tomorrow I'll have better luck in sending you to hell," came the voice. "And do you know what'll happen? I'll fix you and your blasted Legion! And all the world will know who did it, too—Herr von Strull!"

An oath broke from Papa Weber. A shot made response, from opposite—the bullet came within half an inch of Weber's head. A mocking laugh, and then silence.

"That devil has some scheme," said Weber, wiping sweat from

his wide forehead. "He has some plan. He'll use his name, my name; he means—*ach, Gott!* I am sick, Karl. Call a relief."

The relief came. Papa Weber was sent off to the ambulance section. But when Karl followed, in the gray dawn, to see what was wrong with his friend, Papa Weber was not there at all. He had simply vanished from sight.

With the bugles sounding the advance, Karl had no chance to investigate further.

The reserves came up, ammunition was handed out, the column pushed forward up the slopes. It was incredible work. The Chinese maintained a heavy fire. Against it, the lines went up in two divisions, now descending into ravines, now pressing up steep hillflanks. Time after time, halts must be made to hack a way. Time after time, the only means of progress was by a bamboo ladder which the men must mount singly.

Yet they kept on, ever mounting. It was a face between the Legion and the zephyrs, and new bets were made, old ones were renewed, about that flag on the Bamboo Fort. By eight in the morning, one column was up, the other was halted. Up, and before the first Chinese entrenchments.

A terrible fire burst upon them. The first lines of the Legion were decimated, officers went down, but the others pressed on and over. At the third line of trenches, the Legion recoiled before the concentrated fire poured into them. A lieutenant and a handful of men won through and over. Others came up. At this instant, Karl perceived the figure of Papa Weber. He had suddenly appeared, over on the left, a squad of the Legion behind him. They mounted the parapet and poured bullets into the Chinese, who broke and fled.

BUT THE zephyrs, in an equally ferocious assault from the flank, won into the fort, and hauled down the flag.

"Name of the devil!" cried Karl amazedly, coming up to Papa Weber as he stood panting among the group who had come with him. "Where did you spring from?"

"He sprang just in time to get us here," cried the sergeant in charge, clapping Weber on the back. "Ha! We found him alone, and he showed us which way to come. And what do you think? Remember that corporal of the zephyrs who led out that squad of eleven fools—and never showed up again? We found him, too. Dead."

"Well, well, get to work and stop talking," broke in Papa Weber. The others scattered.

Karl came up to his friend.

"What does it mean?" he demanded. "You never reported to the ambulance section. Where did you go?"

Papa Weber was in bad shape. He had a bullet through one arm, his uniform was in rags from the thorns, and his face was gray with exhaustion. Perhaps not from exhaustion alone, for his eyes held a terrible inner anguish, and all his barriers were suddenly down. He spoke to Karl as to an old and trusted friend, without evasion.

"The job was mine; it had to be done. I was responsible for him, as he said; that is, in the beginning. I hold an honored name, Karl. The Legion is the only thing I have left in life. It was not for the sake of my name—it was for the Legion—"

He staggered, close to collapse.

Karl caught him, steadied him, helped him to where the surgeon was at work among the other wounded; and once there, Papa Weber slumped down into unconsciousness.

LATER HE was himself again, with all barriers up. Once or twice Karl timidly ventured on the subject, only to be rebuffed. Afterward, when they stood together at the rail of the *Tonkin* and looked back at the blue peaks of Formosa fading in the far distance, Karl made one more effort to understand.

"That day—you remember, after the Bamboo Fort was taken—you said some queer things to me. I'd like to understand. Then there was the night before, after Corporal Garnot spoke with us. Where did you go, off there in the darkness? You did not go looking for him?"

"Karl, you're a *dumbkopf!*" Papa Weber turned and surveyed

his old friend, that big splay beard of his all bristling. Then he smiled slightly. "Don't be absurd, my friend. Where did I go? I went off in the bush and was sick, but I fell in with the advance. With the third company. Look in the records; it's all there. Now, my friend, I command you never to mention the matter to me again. Never mention the name of Corporal Garnot again. It is finished, ended for ever. Leave it so."

And Karl knew better than to disobey.

PORSON'S VOICE fell silent. The picture of the two bearded Austrians of the Legion faded away; the men about the table stirred, lifted their glasses, exchanged glances and comments. A bad business, that Formosa affair, somebody observed; still, the Legion had done its work in the good old style—

"But—good Lord, Porson!" burst out Kramer suddenly. "It's plain enough now why you said Papa Weber was a great criminal. Do you actually mean that he killed this fellow, his own son, to save the Legion from dishonor?"

Porson gave him a level glance.

"You've heard the story," he said in his calm, dispassionate way. "You know all that I know; draw your own conclusions. It seems fairly evident to me. Not, mind you, that I think Papa Weber a criminal! Some might think him so, but I believe he was a great man. That's why I said 'a great criminal'."

"Oh, bother your play on words!" exclaimed somebody down the table. "There was no crime in that. Look at Jephtha and his daughter, or whatever the Bible story is; look at a dozen other such things in history. Yes, you're right. Criminal? Not a bit of it. One thing, though, I don't quite see. How the devil do you know so much about what happened and what was said? The Formosa campaign was long before your time."

Porson nodded quietly.

"True. However, there was one man in the Legion guilty of almost the greatest crime any Legionnaire can commit," he rejoined slowly. "I think we'd all agree that there's nothing so base or low-down in the old corps as to learn a comrade's story, gain his trust—and then tell. That's what Karl did—Papa Weber's friend Karl. Karl is dead long ago, and it's just as well. But Karl told me, and not in confidence either."

"Who was this Karl?" asked Casey, leaning forward. "What was his name?"

Porson smiled that tight-lipped smile of his.

"That," he responded pleasantly, "is one of the things we don't do, *mon ami.*"

FIGHTING THROUGH

"Fighting Through," the twelfth story in
this famous series, deals with a little-known
but desperate campaign in Tonkin.

DAD, THE date-pickers called him. An old fellow with
yellow-white whiskers and long untended hair and no
cleanliness to speak of. He showed up last year when the pickers
drifted up from Indio, and after the last picking he drifted back
again. I noticed he was one of those religious fanatics; he would
harangue the others by the hour, once started, about the Last
Judgment and so forth.

This year he showed up again when the first crop was ripe.
He dropped off a Los Angeles bus one day ahead of the gang,
and came up to the house. I was alone there, and he hitched
off his blanket-roll and asked if he should camp as before down
past the well.

"Camp where you like, Dad," I rejoined. "Take one of the
bunks in the *ramada,* if it suits you. Family won't be home for
a day or two."

"Gosh! I aint slept in a bunk in twelve year," he rejoined. He
looked at a bottle I had just thrown out—picked it up, and
blinked at it. "Hello! You do yourself pretty good. Nuits St.
George, eh? And the *clos* of '28 *mise au chateau.*"

I was astonished, for his French was beautiful. "You speak
French, Dad?"

"I was born French." He looked embarrassed. "Alsatian, that
is. Yeah, I was kind of unregenerate too, when I was in the army.
Aint nice to think about them days in China, for a fact."

"The French army? In China?" I calculated swiftly. "The Boxer troubles?"

"Nope, farther back than that." And he cackled. "I'm goin' on seventy-three, Mister, even if I don't look it. Nope, I was in the Tonkin mess. With the Legion. Second Company of the First Regiment."

I stopped short and stared at him, raking my memory. The Second Company? Only the previous night I had been reading about that company, in a book that Hamonneau sent me from his Legion library.

"Wasn't that Moulinay's company?" I demanded.

Dad was just about shocked white. He stood pawing his unkempt whiskers, his eyes getting larger and larger. Suddenly he found voice.

"Where did you ever hear of Captain Moulinay?" he demanded. "Yes, it was his company. I was with him when he was blown up."

"Then you were at Tuyen-quan," I said, wondering if he were lying.

"Yes," he said. "Yes. Where did you ever hear of it?"

"I was reading about it last night," I replied, staring at him harder than he was staring at me. The thing seemed incredible. "Tuyen-quan—why, that was one of the great episodes of the Legion's history! See here, can you cook?"

He blinked again, then grinned at me. "When you ask a Legionnaire if he can cook, you're just wasting breath."

"All right. Make yourself comfortable. I'm going to town and lay in a bit of wine, and some grub. You cook supper, and we'll make an evening of it. I want to hear about that siege firsthand."

Dad refused point-blank. He didn't want to drink wine, as it was against his religious principles; but he licked his whiskered lips wistfully as he said it. He didn't want to talk about his younger days, because they held only unregenerate memories; but all the same there was a hankering in his eye.

SO I went to town, came back with wine and steaks, and Dad pitched in with the brick oven out back—he just shook his head and looked scared when I showed him the electric range. And boy, could that old duffer cook! When the sun went down behind the date-palms and San Jacinto, we laid into a meal that would knock your eye out.

After about the third glass of wine, Dad wiped his whiskers and got communicative.

"Used to be some bad eggs in the Legion, back in those days," he informed me. "They used to say a tough soldier made a good soldier; that's not so nowadays. Was then, I think. About the worst excuse for a man I ever knew was in our company; but when the siege got going, he showed up different."

"Same old story, I suppose," was my comment, "about the bad *hombre* who turned out to be a hero in action and won his stripes."

Dad refilled his glass, and snorted in derision.

"Tripe!" he said. "Tripe! I'm talking about realities, m'sieur, not fiction. This fellow Hindmann was bad; he wanted to be bad, and he was proud of his badness. Why, he had got an Arab at Oran to tattoo a girl on his front, so that when he worked his abdominal muscles that girl did a dance—the worst kind of a dance, and not an Arab dance, either! That's the sort of low-down rascal Hindmann was. I knew him well. He hated Lieutenant Naert like poison, and Naert swore he'd have him sent to a punishment battalion—"

Dad worked his nose like Wallace Beery, wiped his whiskers anew, and declared it was good wine.

"Tell me about the siege," I said, judging the time ripe. A glint of shrewdness came into Dad's eyes as he surveyed me; then he sniffed the wine and tasted it, and rolled it over his tongue, and nodded.

"Sure. It'll have to be Hindmann's yarn, m'sieur, for I was sick most of the time, but I know all about that devil's doings."

He approved the wine once more, and then fairly let himself go.

YOU SEE, when the Black Flags and Chinese regulars jumped the place, nobody was much worried at first, even if they had surrounded us and cut off our communications. We never dreamed that fully twenty thousand of them were there, all well armed and with the express intention of wiping us all out.

Why should we worry? We had two companies of the Legion, one of native tirailleurs, thirty navy gunners, a third as many sappers, and half a dozen guns—close to six hundred men, all told. The place was strong. A hilltop citadel, the excellent buildings were surrounded by a stout wall with four demi-towers, halfway down the steep hill.

You would never have known the old Legion of north Africa; we had learned to dress for climate and jungle fighting. Some of us were from the Parrakeet Brigade, the sections uniformed in green drill for jungle use. All of us wore light trousers of native stuff, and the black *keo*, a sort of native blouse without collar. Our sun-helmets, too, were covered with blackish material. Only the blue cummerbund of the Legion remained, and the long cartridge-pouch across the breast.

No, we were not worried about any attack, until we made a reconnaissance and found an entire army coming in. We were surrounded and cut off, by then. When the Chinese showed up in force, planted a few guns to open on us, and burned the native town outside the walls, we knew we were in for something hot.

Three hundred yards away was a little hillock. Sergeant Bo-billot and eighteen men ran up a blockhouse there, intending to hold it; Hindmann was one of the eighteen. Surly and snarling as he was, Hindmann was a grand fellow when it came to actual work. Well, they built the blockhouse in five days, and held it for five days more. The enemy made direct frontal attacks at first, but soon learned better when our cannon showered them with grape. Then they settled down to a siege, and concentrated first on the blockhouse.

Five days those eighteen men held it, against twenty thousand. Against attacks, against bombardment, against sniping from trenches gradually coming closer. When the Chinese trenches were less than a hundred yards distant, the place was evacuated—a heap of ruins. Hindmann reached the citadel unhurt.

The fort itself, meantime, was entirely cut off from the rest of Tonkin. The enemy invested the place with trenches and siege lines at a distance of five hundred yards, and under a continual fire, day and night, pressed closer until they were actually within reach of the west and south walls. Scale those walls, they could not. Twice, during the hottest fighting, Lieutenant Naert felt the wind of bullets past his cheek—coming from behind. Later he looked up Hindmann and found him ugly with liquor. He had stolen brandy from the hospital supplies. The Lieutenant took him to one side.

"You've done well," he said, looking Hindmann in the eye. "Now you'll get detailed to a masonry party—you unspeakable dog, to steal what should be reserved for the sick and wounded! And you wasted two bullets today, which is between you and me."

Hindmann had ugly pointed teeth, like a dog. He showed them now, in a snarling grin.

"Next time, my lieutenant, there'll be no miss," he said, savagely refusing to deny the charge. It was something that could not be proved, of course. Naert tapped his revolver significantly.

"There'll be no next time, my honest fellow—for a while, at least. Report to Sergeant Bobillot at daybreak."

Bobillot was a veteran who knew all about building construction. Hindmann reported duly, and was the one unarmed and distrusted man in a squad of sixty.

Luckily, Commandant Dominé had had brought inside the place, before the Chinese lines came too close, the stones and rubble of a big pagoda, which had been knocked down. Now, with the desperate realization that it was a fight to the death against hopeless odds, and that this citadel could not be held forever, he set Bobillot to work building an inner defense, a parapet farther up the side of the hill, for last resource. The sixty men worked on this day and night, and Hindmann was worked like the dog he was.

Out beyond the walls were tents and gay flags; out under the walls pushed the Chinese lines, ever closer. On the walls men died, and were laid to rest in darkness along a burial ditch. The wounded were numerous; each stretcher was taken to the old powder-magazine—now transformed into a hospital—under a hail of bullets; and once bedded there, they could hear the bullets hitting the roof above them. Bullets everywhere; and for the sorry burials, the crack of rifles and the bang of cannon full-shotted.

IT WAS Hindmann who, on a trip to the pile of shattered masonry to bring up stones, discovered the new menace. Naert saw him standing, idle, sweating, bearded head cocked to one side, and strode up to him with acid command.

"Back to your task, you dog!"

"A dog can hear where others fail, my lieutenant," said Hindmann. "Listen! They're running mines."

Mines! That was why the Chinese lines had halted under the walls, why no fresh attacks were being made. The sound of pick and shovel was plain enough, now that attention was drawn to it. Sergeant Bobillot was hastily drawn from the work above, and put in charge of counter-mining; he picked Hindmann for his working party.

They worked furiously, driving a tunnel to meet that of the Chinese. On the tenth of February, it was evident that the Chinese were under the wall itself. The garrison was ordered to be ready, in case of an explosion, to close the breach and hold it. With an explosion imminent, Bobillot and his crew kept at work.

Next day, without the least warning, Hindmann's pick drove through into nothing. A Legionnaire behind him, Maury, shoved through the gap. They were face to face with the Chinese working party. A revolver spat fire, and Maury went down. Hindmann went at the yellow men with his pick, a wild yell on his lips, and they broke before him.

Bobillot scrambled through, recalled Hindmann, set frantically to work. Down came the unpropped roof of the tunnel. The men scrambled free—the opening was closed. But not for

long. Other tunnels were being driven. Next day the first mine went off with a roar, but the wall did not come down.

Hindmann was at work on the 13th, long before dawn, bringing up materials in case the wall was breached. Even in the darkness, bullets hailed in from the Chinese lines. Lieutenant Naert, who had charge of the party, came face to face with Hindmann and nodded to him.

"You've done well, lately. You'll have your rifle back today; see that you use it on the right people this time."

Hindmann snarled. "A dog doesn't forget."

At this instant—it was three in the morning—a sheet of flame split the sky. The ground shook. The southwest tower went up in a shower of rock; both men were sent sprawling by the concussion.

Here was a breach, with a vengeance!

The Chinese lines were rolling in. To meet them, despite the storm of bullets that hailed around, bamboo poles were planted; Legionnaires lined the walls, hasty parapets were built of loose stones. The shattering fire that was poured into the advancing lines had terrific effect; the Chinese melted, broke for shelter, and the assault failed.

Daylight showed the ruin, and thirty feet outside the parapet, a dead Legionnaire who had been blown out when the explosion burst. Corporal Beulin asked permission to bring in the body. Four men leaped to join him—Hindmann was the first. Unhurt, they accomplished the task under heavy fire.

"You have done well," Lieutenant Naert said again. "Stop snarling; fight!"

HINDMANN HATED him worse than ever, for somehow it got out that the Lieutenant had called him a dog, and the name stuck. Those pointed teeth of his made it seem apt. Jokes were flung at him from all sides, and he smarted under them.

Not that there was much time to smart, for the Chinese were now working fresh galleries, evidently determined to blow the entire west wall into the air. Desperately, the work on the hinder wall was pushed, and it came to an end. There were no new assaults, but the exchange of fire was continual. On the 17th, Captain Dia of the Tonkinese company was killed. Next day Sergeant Bobillot was wounded. The galleries were creeping in, and men could not be spared to drive counter-mines.

The list of dead had mounted. The hospital was crammed with wounded—badly hurt men, naturally, for walking cases kept on the job. The stench from the piles of unburied Chinese dead down the slopes was horrible. Birds of prey gathered there at any time the bullet-hail lessened.

ONE NIGHT Hindmann stole still more brandy, and it set fire to his brain. He was in Captain Moulinay's company, which had the guard that night. Toward morning, with all the devils of liquor and rebellion's fury riding him, Hindmann and a Pole named Baleski were together at one corner of the wall, and Hindmann refused point-blank to share any of the brandy he had stolen.

"Then drink alone and live alone, you dog!" said the Pole scornfully.

Hindmann flew at him, blind to everything. An attack was just then being made along the north wall, and everything here was quiet, ominously quiet. The dawn had come stealing up, with mist veiling the walls.

The two men were alone here. When Hindmann attacked him in mad ferocity, the Pole whipped up his rifle to parry. It needed no more than this for Hindmann to use his own weapon. The bayonets locked and thrust and stabbed, Baleski cursing furiously and Hindmann snarling like the dog they called him. Bullets lashed the air around, and one of them found its mark.

Baleski staggered backward. At the same instant, unable to check himself even had he so desired, Hindmann's bayonet jabbed home.

Even for Hindmann, it was a frightful moment as he stood there, breathing hard, and staring down at the dead man, his comrade. He was sobered in a flash, and across his brain and heart crept a slow, chilling horror of realization.

Not for what he had done; this was nothing to him. But for what would come of it. There was no earthly way he could cover up that bayonet-stab, and escape the penalty of it. Even though a Chinese bullet had killed the Pole, the slash was still there. Already the mist was lifting, the sun was coming up.

And then, suddenly, came discovery. A figure came striding through the thinning fog; it was Captain Moulinay himself, alone. At sight of Hindmann, with bloody bayonet, and the dead Baleski on the parapet, the officer halted sharply.

"Good God!" he exclaimed sharply. "It can't be possible—a man of the Legion, a man of my own company! Even you, Hindmann—even a dog like you, to be guilty of this—of killing a comrade!"

"It is true," murmured Hindmann stupidly. "A bullet killed him, but I stabbed at the same moment. We were fighting."

"Very well," snapped the officer. "You're under—"

Fifty feet away, the earth vomited fire and blood. A mine went up; then another. Then, almost at the same instant, a third. The whole west wall, for sixty yards of its length, was hurled into the air. As the debris showered around, the shrill yells of

Chinese rushing forward smote the silence. The attack on the north had been a ruse—here was the real assault.

"To the breach!" shouted Moulinay. "To me, every man—to me!"

HE WENT forward at a run. Hindmann, who had been knocked flat a dozen feet away by the concussion, scrambled up. Lieutenant Vincent and other men came on the run to help Captain Moulinay meet the assault. Hindmann, recovering his rifle, started to join them.

The earth spouted fire. He was sent rolling again, blood coming from nostrils and ears. A fourth mine had gone up.

Mechanically he staggered to his feet, found his rifle again, ran in to join other men who were coming on the run, led by the commandant himself. And what he saw caused a new and more terrible horror in Hindmann's brain. For that last explosion had killed Moulinay and a dozen other men, had wounded Vincent and twenty-five more—and the lines of Chinese were flooding over the breach.

Crash upon crash of volley-fire swept the yellow faces away. The commandant, coolly and quietly, was giving the orders. Hindmann fell into the ranks, loaded and fired with the others. The assault was smashed and sent reeling back, and broken. Bullets began to scream in once more, and shells began to burst. The crisis was past.

Baleski the Pole was gathered up with the other dead, and no one noticed or cared how he had died, it appeared.

Up in the citadel itself, at the crest of the hill, a grave was sunk for Moulinay, a ditch for the common grave of the others. Bullets were striking all around. The bodies, wrapped in mats, were lowered into place while the old chaplain, Boisset, recited prayers for the dead and then staggered back to his sickbed.

Hindmann stood looking on, with that same icy chill running from spine to brain. The liquor fumes were all gone now. The queer fact was impressed upon him that he would now be facing a firing-squad, at best, had not that fourth mine gone off when

As Hindmann stood staring down at the dead man, his comrade, he was sobered in a flash.... Suddenly came discovery: a figure came striding through the thinning fog.

it had. He was safe, because Moulinay and all these other men had perished; and for no other reason.

Somehow it weighed upon him fearfully. Bad as he was, Hindmann was far from being a mere hulking brute. He had in him the remnants of a soul, and also a certain imaginative power. These inner faculties played with the strange fact of his being alive because these others had died; they exaggerated it; they made the thing bulk large and larger in his mind. Perhaps his conscience had been wakened.

He moved out mechanically to his post, acted like a man in stupor, and hardly nodded when anyone addressed him. Sarbeck came along gayly—Sarbeck, finest marksman of the first company, Sarbeck, the handsome rascal who had a way with the women, and who had been the particular buddy of the dead Pole.

"Now for my daily Chinese!" he exclaimed, pausing to load. Each day Sarbeck leaped to the parapet, picked off a yellow man, and was satisfied. "This should be my twentieth. But I want one extra today, for Baleski!"

He leaped up, with a laugh, poised, flung up his rifle. It cracked.

"Ha!" he cried as he reloaded. "There's mine. Now—"

He doubled up and came down to the stones with a flop, a bullet through his brain. Hindmann looked on unmoved as they carried Sarbeck away. Why had he been spared, he thought, by the death of such men as Moulinay and the others—Captain Moulinay, whom everyone admired and loved?

That evening he was crouched by himself in a corner over his pipe, off duty, when the trim figure of Lieutenant Naert approached. He came to attention.

"At ease," said the Lieutenant quietly. "I wanted a word with you, Hindmann. I've just learned that some one must have heard me call you names, in anger. It was unworthy an officer. I'm sorry, and I apologize."

He paused briefly. Hindmann said nothing at all.

"One more thing," went on the officer. "I looked over the body of Baleski before it was wrapped up and buried. He was on guard with you. No Chinese got over the wall there; yet he had been thrust through—with a bayonet, apparently. I'm not asking you, Hindmann. I'm just telling you that I observed it."

IN THE darkness, Hindmann felt the sweat coursing down his cheeks, down his neck from the shaggy uncut hair.

"My lieutenant—" he said hoarsely, and paused.

Naert prompted him with a cool word: "Yes?"

A deep breath escaped Hindmann. "It was my bayonet," he said, and poured out the story, poured out the insensate details, without excuse or evasion. Why he did it, he was not at all sure. There was no need whatever; the Lieutenant might have suspected something, but knew nothing at all; and any one of a dozen lies might have served if questions had been asked about that bayonet slash. He finished, and stood silent.

"Why did you tell me this, Hindmann?" asked the officer in a low voice.

"I—I do not know," Hindmann faltered. "It is all so strange and terrible. The Captain knew, and is dead. Death wiped them all away to save me. It is something I cannot understand. Perhaps I did wrong to tell you. But I feel better."

Naert stood silent for a moment.

"After all," he said reflectively, "you did not kill Baleski. Perhaps you might more justly fear and wonder what caused that Chinese bullet to save you from murder! Well, this lies between you and me. It is forgotten. And I think," he added under his breath as he turned away, "that I perceive at last the advantages of the confessional!"

His figure melted in the darkness. Hindmann stood there trembling. He heard the voice of Naert again, speaking now to the men along the parapet:

"Aim low, remember. Don't waste bullets if they come; the ammunition won't hold out forever. Aim low—"

Hindmann wiped the sweat from his face and sank down again. He did feel better, as he said. The weight, the load was gone from his mind. Not that it had any permanent effect on him. Far from it! Late that same night he stole more of the hospital brandy, and finished up in the guardhouse.

However, there were no more references to the "dog." His comrades had gained too much respect for him; in the trenches, he fought like a devil incarnate.

THE NEXT day came a white flag from Luh Vinh, commanding the enemy, repeating an offer previously made of terms to the garrison. Now he even offered to let them march free with arms and baggage. The commandant made response with a cannon-shot; and when evening drew on with pitch darkness and a thin mist from the river, the Chinese came—this time by stealth, scaling the breached walls, pouring out silently from their trenches, suddenly rushing the sentries and flooding in at a dozen points. Sergeant-major Husband, with a section of the guard, met and held the assault. He fell. Sergeant Thevenet fell. The pickets were forced back.

With a handful of his comrades of the first company, Hindmann hurled himself into the mad confusion, bayonet at work. At the first shot, the Chinese lines had burst into light and sound, fireworks and bombs lighting the scene, a roar of gongs and drums cutting loose. Fight as they would, the Legion was forced back. The enclosure was pierced; the citadel was lost— when bugles sounded the charge.

In leaped Captain Cattelin with the reserves, bayonets sweeping the Chinese away, forcing them to give ground. It was bitter, hand-to-hand business, the sort of thing at which the Legion excelled all other troops in the world, with Bengal lights casting a lurid pallor from the broken walls. Bayonets against swords and long halberds and banging muskets, clearing the enclosure at last.

HINDMANN CAME out of it with nothing worse than a sword-slash across his chest—a slash that cut the tattooed

*Hindmann refused
point-blank to share
any of the liquor
that he had stolen.*

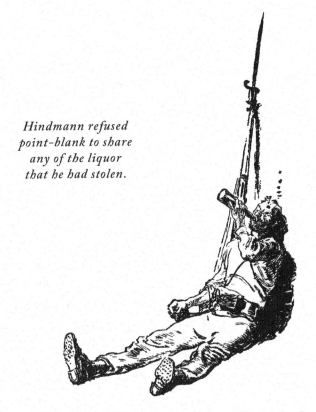

lady squarely in two, but did him no great harm. He was back
in line next day, when another mine went up and blew what
was left of the wall to smithereens. The whole west wall was
gone now, replaced by a parapet of bamboo; and the Chinese
were mining at the south wall to finish the job.

The ensuing days were a mad nightmare of furious and determined assault, shells bursting, rifle-fire sweeping the place,
battle by day and night, raids repulsed, cold steel more than
once employed. A third of the garrison were dead or disabled;
another third were wounded or sick. Officers fought alongside
the men, every rifle counting; most of the time, the volleys were
exchanged at point-blank range.

February was wearing away. On the night of the 27th, Hindmann was on guard when he heard French words from the trenches so close at hand.

"Not today, but tomorrow it'll come without fail!"

Others caught the ominous threat; the end was at hand. Morning found the trenches opposite manned by Chinese whose white cotton blouses bore a huge scarlet cross—mark of a death battalion, vowed never to retreat. The day dragged. With afternoon all sound of underground work ceased. The final mines were ready.

IT WAS at sunset that Hindmann found himself with a ravenous thirst. No longer could he steal from the hospital supplies. He had been on duty since dawn, was worn to the bone, and was ripe for anything. He fell foul of another Legionnaire; words came to blows, and in the midst appeared Lieutenant Naert.

"Madmen! Imbeciles! When we're all about to die, have you nothing better to do than this? You again, eh?" As he spoke, his gaze transfixed Hindmann. "Come with me. I want a word with you, my friend."

Hindmann followed him beyond hearing of the others. The Lieutenant halted, tapped his bandaged chest, and spoke in a low voice.

"You remember what you said to me, the night Captain Moulinay was killed?"

"Yes, my lieutenant."

"Thank God I'm not your lieutenant, except temporarily! Thank God I'm only filling a gap in your company of the Legion. Do you know why I say this, Hindmann?"

Hindmann did not know, and said so.

"Because," the officer replied, "I think there is a curse on you, my man. You said it yourself; Captain Moulinay and those others died, in order that you might live and go free. Those around you die or go into hospital. Your First Company of the regiment suffers horribly; the sergeants, the officers, the men—

dead! But you live. You live, and hate, and fight the world around you.

"And now," he added solemnly, as the two of them stood alone in the darkness, "all of us have death ahead. It comes this night; we know it. We're ready for it. If we can fight it off, we shall. But it doesn't threaten you, Hindmann. The bullets miss you. Not one of them bears your name. If every last man in this place perishes, you'll live on. Some men are like that—marked out by the devil for his own. Good night."

He turned and was gone.

Hindmann, with a scornful grunt, went to his place, flung himself down, and slept. Dreams plagued his sleep. A little after eleven, he came wide awake and sat up, with terror in his heart.

Those bitter words recurred to him, every one of them. What all the force of discipline and punishment could not do, Naert had done with a few words—reached the heart of this man and brought fear into it, and remorse. He thought of Naert, of the frank, simple young officer with whom he had had such strange dealings, and the wild wastage of his life uprose before him.

"It's not true!" he muttered hoarsely. "It might be true—but it's not. Marked by the devil? No! I'll prove it's not true—I'll prove it—"

THE EARTH shook. Flames roared upward; enormous masses of masonry showered over the entire hillside. A mine in the very center of the south wall had gone up, and thirty feet of that wall were one yawning gap. Before the ensuing silence was really felt, it was shattered by a tremendous fire opened by the whole Chinese line.

The end had come.

The Chinese were ready. As though trusting that the French would hasten to this new breach, they were waiting to assault the former openings where bamboo palisades alone resisted them. They poured up in waves, the death battalion in the fore, planted their black flags on the parapets; and—the Legion met them hand to hand.

Grouped at each threatened point, separated only by the bamboos, the grim bearded men of the Legion fought their last bitter fight. Hindmann flung himself into the thick of it recklessly, furiously, as though seeking the death that hung above them all, but it passed him by. When the bamboos went down, he hurled himself into the thick of the Red Crosses, his bayonet lunging and thrusting; if there had been a devil in him before, now there were ten devils urging him to new madness.

The minutes passed. Half an hour of furious, unceasing, point-blank fighting, that left men exhausted and staggering with weakness. The Chinese drew away, but not far. Over the walls came grenades, smoke-balls, fire-pots. The noise of drums and gongs redoubled; the hail of bullets drifted in from all sides. And with a rush, the reformed columns came back to the

assault—an assault as desperate, as determined, as unrelenting, as was the thinning line of men who met it.

But Hindmann went unscathed.

Another half hour of it, and another. The endless battle, the endless killing, the successive waves of fresh troops pouring up—Chinese regulars now, and shrieking Black Flags—went on interminably. It was past human endurance, but the bayonets on the parapet still flashed under the Bengal flares. If the Legion died, it meant to die on its feet.

The last of the reserves was in the line. The last of the wounded who could handle a rifle was at work; hand to hand, slashing, shooting, yelling—Hindmann was stark mad like all the rest of them here, giving hoarse yell for yell, thrust for thrust, reeling to and fro, staggering, still lunging with arms wearied past weariness, frenzied with such battle madness as the Legion had not known for years and would not know again for longer years. The Chinese masses poured up, died, were replaced. There was no cessation.

Toward three in the morning that furious and unrelenting assault was finally broken. Then, and only then, men looked around, sought for comrades, tended wounded and dying, realized with an incredulous comprehension that death would not come after all this night.

HINDMANN, THE wounded cared for, flung himself down like a dog indeed, his tongue lolling with sheer exhaustion. He was too stiff and sore and wearied ever to move again, it seemed—but suddenly his body jerked as though from a galvanic shock. He lay tensed, quiet; abruptly he came to his feet with shrieks of wild laughter, and pointed in the air.

"He's insane!" cried some one sharply. Orders rang out.

"Pull him down, two of you! Make sure of his rifle—"

Hindmann ceased his wild laughter as they rushed him.

"Wait, wait!" lifted his voice, imploringly. "Hold everything, comrades, and listen! There's the reason for their assault—it was their last chance. *Listen!* For the love of God, *listen!*"

Silence greeted his words. They listened; they heard a queer, far vibration.

"Cannon!" yelled somebody. "Cannon! A column is on the way, is fighting through—"

ACROSS THE table from me the voice ceased. The rumble of cannon-fire grew upon the air; an earth-shock was traveling down the valley. It hit us, sent the adobe house grunting, and was on its way and gone. Dad pawed his whiskers, reached out for the wine-bottle, shook it, and sighed regretfully.

"That there was right good wine," he said. "I guess it limbered up my tongue a mite, huh?"

I laughed. "Finish the story, Dad. Tell me what became of Hindmann."

"Him? Oh, he quit the Legion when his hitch was done. He

was changed, somehow. No more hell-raising. I heard tell he got religion, but I dunno. He was just a no-good skunk, anyhow. Well, let's clean up the dishes. I got to sleep and get up at them dates before the sun gets hot."

The curious part of the whole story came a couple of days later. A truck came along about noon, just in the heat of the day, to pick up the date lugs, and I went down among the trees to check over the number. Nobody was at work, naturally, at such an hour.

Sprawled out near the well, I came upon the figure of Dad, sound asleep. He lay on his back, snoring, his mouth open. I stared at him, struck by his old yellowed fangs; they had a queer look, as they protruded from his whiskers. Then I saw the reason. They were long and pointed, like the teeth of a dog. I only wished that at seventy-three I still might have a few stout teeth like those!

Then I noticed something else. Dad's shirt was torn open, and revealed a not too hairy torso—and it was highly colored. I looked closer, shamelessly, and beheld the tattooed figure of a lady; or to be precise, a female. One look was enough to convince me that if Dad were to wriggle his muscles a bit, that female would do a dance of the most unethical sort. And straight across that tattooed figure ran the white weal of an old scar, like a sword-stroke.

And realizing what it all meant, I turned and went away from there very softly. Not for the world would I have old Dad know that his secret had been revealed, and that I knew what had become of the Dog of Tuyen-quan.

GENTLEMAN ROYAL

"Gentleman Royal" gives you the strange drama
of an anonymous nobleman of the Legion
during its fantastic expedition in Siam.

THE OLD axiom about meeting all the people you know at three or four of the world's great crossroads has, like most axioms, a certain foundation of truth in experience. One of those arteries is Whitehall, in London. Another, oddly enough, is Westminster Abbey.

To prove it, I was standing in the Abbey one day, looking at the section of that historic floor devoted to the Unknown Soldier, and dodging the flocks of personally conducted tourists, when a man stepped up. I looked at him, and he at me, and our hands met.

"Pierre Dupré, of all people!" I exclaimed, regarding his stocky, grizzled figure in astonishment. We had met in Oran, two years previously. "Why, I thought you had retired with all the honors of a veteran Legionnaire to that little farm in Algeria!"

He sighed and smiled, and wrung my hand, all at once.

"No. So I proposed, but fate disposed otherwise—as usual. I'm living here—or rather, working here. I have a shop over in Whitehall Court."

"A shop?" I looked at him, puzzled. "No shops there, Dupré! That's a club building. I happen to belong to one of the clubs. What kind of a shop?"

"A hairdressing shop," he said, beaming at me. "Or in your American language, a barber-shop. That farm in Algeria—well, it is still waiting. I've never seen this church, so I dropped in to have a look around. I find you. Excellent!"

"It goes double," I rejoined delightedly. Pierre Dupré had been in the Legion since he was eighteen; he had been all over the world, knew everything and everybody, and had a trunk full of medals that would knock your eye out. Now he looked down and nodded.

"The Unknown Soldier, eh? Singular. That reminds me of my first enlistment, my first campaign, and a comrade I had there. In Siam, it was."

"Campaign, in Siam?" I exclaimed. "But France was never at war with Siam—"

He snapped his fingers joyously at me. "And I suppose you'll say the lost Dauphin of France does not lie in this very abbey? Come, I'll point out his tomb to you. That's another story, too. Never at war with Siam, eh? If you've time for a bottle of wine and a bit of sole in the genuine Marguery style—"

The challenge was accepted. I was curious to know about his unknown soldier, as he called the fellow. Dupré never evades life, but looks it squarely in the eye; and I knew his story would have a touch of the unpleasant, the unhappy, the gruesome—and would come straight out of the world's heart.

I N   A   little restaurant kept by one of his compatriots, who greeted Dupré almost with veneration, we settled down and shut out all London. There, in his brisk concise manner, Dupré described the incidents along the frontier of Siam, culminating in the killing of a French officer and his escort, which led to French action.

"That was in June of 1893," he went on. "Our fleet forced the river and blockaded Bangkok. By August, the Siamese accepted our conditions and there was no need for our troops who were on the way. The Marching Battalion of the Legion came, just the same, and disembarked at Bangkok along with our peace envoys. I was in the second company, and my chief friend in the outfit was André d'Ici. You may laugh at the

*"Glad I found you
Pierre," said Ici,
"you're going back,
so come along."*

name—*Here*, in English; and it was a little comic, being obviously assumed; but one did not laugh at the man.

"Well, there was no fighting to do, but there was a lot of mapping done, and when it turned out that my comrade André had been an engineer and could draw topographical maps, we were assigned to a survey party up the Mekong River, with headquarters at a place called Nampak, where there was a single white inhabitant among a couple of thousand Siamese. My comrade Ici got me taken along, you see. It was a soft, cushy job."

Dupré smiled reminiscently.

A man of mystery, this Ici. Tall, straight, handsome, with a blond mustache and an odd intent pucker about the eyes, something like Colonel Forey, if you ever met him. Ici never mentioned himself or his past history. His nationality was unknown; he spoke German, French and English with perfect fluency, but not until we had landed at Bangkok did any clue come, and then only to Dupré.

André d'Ici never received any mail, never wrote letters; he was completely wrapped up in his service with the Legion. He never showed his *livret militaire,* which would bear his true name, to a soul. On the first of each month, the battalion paymaster handed out to him a thousand francs, which he received without comment, and which he dispensed in wine for his section—naturally, the most envied group in the whole army.

The day after their disembarkation, Ici and Dupré were walking about the Siamese capital, looking at the temples and the strange sights, when they encountered an officer, an attaché of the British legation. He stopped dead, stared at Ici, then put out his hand with a quick smile. The two talked for a moment. Dupré did not understand their words, for he knew no English. They separated and went on again.

"So, my friend," said Dupré, who was young and foolish, "you are an Englishman!"

"No," rasped Dupré.
"We stick, she and
I; we'll get married
first chance."

Ici swept him an angry glance, then smiled.

"No, I am not," he said coolly. "But I was at Cambridge with that man we just met. You will do me the favor of not referring to this in future, Pierre. Now come along and see if we can find the famous white elephants!"

Pierre Dupré never again referred to the incident.

ANOTHER THING happened on the way upriver with the survey party. Ici had corporal's *galons,* but no point of discipline was maintained up here in the wilds; both he and Dupré were accepted for what they were. Thus it was not strange that one night when the general conversation fell upon the novels of Dumas, Ici took a hand.

Somebody had mentioned "The Three Musketeers," and dwelt scornfully upon the absurdity of such an infatuation as that of *Buckingham* for *Anne of Austria.*

"Much less," went on the speaker, "that the Queen should repay such a feeling! It's one of the major absurdities of an absurd story fit only for popular consumption."

"Your pardon," said Ici composedly. "The point is one of the great truths in a great novel, monsieur. It is not absurd. Parallel cases have happened in history since then; they even happen in our own generation. Today, however, the matter is usually hushed up."

His voice held an inflection of such real assurance, of so profound a feeling, that it startled his auditors.

"But," queried the officer, "what if there were to be a child?"

"Ah!" Ici smiled. "In that case, monsieur, the child would be very unfortunate."

The subject was changed, the argument dismissed; but Dupré remembered it. He was devoted to this handsome, genial, reckless comrade of his. If Corporal d'Ici said a thing was so, young Dupré affirmed it furiously. If Ici drank beer, Dupré would drink nothing else. It was a very real sort of hero-worship; and because the youngster had the right stuff in him, Ici repaid the adoration with a firm, deep friendliness. Perhaps it worried him at times, too. He was no paragon of virtue, by a good deal.

Settled in headquarters at Nampak, Dupré was put in charge of the place while the party worked out their maps. Consequently he had little to do, at times, and it was a bad thing for him, since the others were much away. He began to associate with Jean Legrand, the scrawny, cavernous danger-signal to humanity who was the one white inhabitant here. Legrand lived in a small compound and sold the vilest of imitation brandy to the Siamese, who took keenly to it. Also, Legrand lived alone, shunned other whites, would rant his brand of philosophy by the hour, and in the back room had two excellent rifles. He knew the jungle, the hills, the people, and there was a black devil in him.

Dupré thought the fellow quite a character, missing all the evil portents. Legrand had once been a gentleman—another bad sign which the young Legionnaire ignored.

"Your people will run into trouble yet," said Legrand, shaking his black head and glowering at Dupré from his deep-set black eyes. "No matter if they do have a Siamese escort. They'll run into trouble. Plenty of brigands and dacoits along the border here."

Dupré laughed. "So I've heard, but they'll not trouble our crowd."

H E G O T into the habit of going over every morning and having a chat, sometimes in the evening as well. Legrand introduced him to a charming native girl, aided him in a score of ways with his accounts and headquarters management, and learned that young Dupré was proud of the Legion but by no means pining to spend his life in uniform. In brief, the East had got into Dupré's blood—the East, with its luxury, its relaxed ethics, its dreamy ambition. Above all, the fact that Europeans could clean up a fortune here in a short time and retire for life. Legrand could retire if he so desired; he painted the possibilities in glowing colors, so far as others were concerned. He

"*Perhaps you woud write such a story, Legrand,
being what you are. But you never will!*"

showed young Dupré nuggets of gold, and queer flat gold coins and glittering stones.

"They're to be had!"—and he waved a skinny claw toward the jungle. "Retire? Why should I retire, and whither? Why, my little lascar, you're blind! Here's the true civilization. Back there in the cities, life's a fight, a battle, tooth and claw, and starve to death if you go down! Here, if you're old or invalid, the people work your fields for you, share their food with you, look after you. Here's one price on all merchandise. Suicide is unknown among these people—misery never pushes them so far. Savages, you call them? Well, give me such savages, rather than the civilization of Europe!"

HIS FAVORITE topic was this; he dilated on it at every opportunity, until he had the eager spirit of Dupré in a glow, and the eyes of the young man wandered over the distant jungle which was painted as a paradise, with obvious yearning.

The mapping party came in for a day of rest. Corporal d'Ici listened to the outpoured secondhand philosophy which Dupré had acquired, attempted to tear it to shreds with sarcasm, and only caused the younger man to fall into sullen silence. Then he tried another tack.

"Something's got into you, Pierre; what is it? You won't tell? Well, *mon vieux*, write that mother of yours a long letter. It helps. If I could only write mine!" As he spoke, his eyes warmed. "I appreciate what I lack. You fail to appreciate what you have."

Dupré grunted, and changed the subject to bandits. Ici laughed heartily.

"Bandits? Yes, plenty of them, but they'll not trouble us. They live off your charming savages; they're part of the picture. Raid here, raid there, steal and kill somewhere else—bah! Don't be a fool."

The others were off again, with new supplies. That night Dupré sat talking and drinking with Legrand and another man—a native chief, keen-eyed, hawk-faced, proud. A fine figure of a man. A chief from the jungle and the hills beyond, said Legrand; a free man, lord of his own lands, who was anxious to learn European ways and weapons. Gold was nothing to this man, and to prove it here were nuggets, gold pieces dug out of a ruined city, and half a dozen sapphires that blazed richly blue.

"Take them if you like—trade him a few cartridges," said Legrand, and Dupré effected the trade with shaking fingers, and pouched his wealth. When the chief had departed, Legrand chuckled scornfully at Dupré.

"What, excited about so small a matter? Come, come! If you weren't a slave of your so-called civilization, if you weren't bound to army service and were free to go into the jungle yonder, I'd send you to that rascal and you'd be a rich man in six months! Gold is nothing to him. What he needs is a soldier."

Dupré could not be expected to discern the true flavor of Legrand's philosophy, nor to check it against the action of the man in poisoning these admirable natives at a fabulous price with his vile rotgut brandy. Nor could he strip the sham trappings from the glittering distances opened to his view.

Here, far from the Legion's discipline, with the immensity of the world brought home to him, with the Mekong floods and the unknown jungles and hill country around, he was a ripe subject for Legrand's wiles. He had no fund of hard experience to lend him a cynic's vision; the glitter dazzled him. What one man did was of no moment in this wilderness. And here was the gold for the taking! It was not hard to dream a dream of glorious adventure, under such conditions.

I T   W A S   quite true that the hill chief wanted a soldier badly. Legrand was shipping in arms, smuggling them across the border; a soldier to go with them and direct operations would make that chief supreme in the hills. For that matter, Legrand himself was a bandit of parts and knew the dacoit trails well. The two rifles in his back room were not for hunting tiger.

So Legrand amused himself; but youth takes all things seriously. Environment made Dupré lose proper focus. The bare bald fact of desertion took on splendid trappings and seemed quite another thing, with the gleam of gold and jewels upon it. He failed to realize that gold and jewels were just as valuable to Siamese folk as to Europeans, and that most of the alluring vistas were plain and simple lies. How was he to know?

There was another thing. Legrand had evinced a singular probing curiosity regarding Corporal d'Ici. Here Dupré told nothing of what he himself guessed or suspected, which was indeed little enough. Legrand needed no urging, however; his first glimpse of the corporal, he readily confessed, had startled him.

One day Dupré found the man studying some pictures clipped from European magazines, pictures from which the titles had been cut. One of these he selected and handed to Dupré, with a leer in his deep dark eyes.

"Do you know who that is?"

Dupré shook his head. The picture showed a singularly handsome man of forty or fifty years, with a semi-uniform collar which betrayed no nationality.

"No. A Frenchman?"

"Not at all, nor an Englishman." Legrand fastened a glare of hatred on the picture. "Twenty years ago, before I came out here, I was in his service. Six or seven years before that, he had been in love with a queen, and she with him. There was a scandal. It was hushed, and nothing came of it." He struck the picture violently with his fingers. "Today this man is not only high in his country's service, but he is its Minister of War."

"What of it?" said Dupré with a shrug. Legrand eyed him a moment, then broke into a laugh and held up the picture.

"Nothing. Look at this again. Imagine Corporal d'Ici fortysix instead of twenty-six—I think you said he was about that age?"

"I did not say, but I imagine you've hit it closely enough."

"Imagine him with this beard.... Ah, you see?"

Dupré started, looked curiously at the picture, and nodded. "Yes, he does look somewhat like your statesman," he commented carelessly. "And I remember," he added with a laugh, "that people used to say my father looked like the Emperor Napoleon; but what of it? Such resemblances are everywhere."

"Even in Siam," said Legrand, nodding cynical assent, and tossed aside the picture. "So your friend gets a thousand francs each month, eh? Lucky fellow."

THIS CONVERSATION meant nothing, suggested nothing, to Dupré. His curiosity in regard to Ici was passive; he was not putting two and two together to check up with destiny. He never thought twice about it—just then.

What he did think about was what would happen if he skipped out to join that hill chief, five days' journey away. Nothing would happen to him, of course; he would not be pursued or followed. Nobody would care. He would be marked off as a deserter on the books of the Legion—and if he ever showed his face in French territory again things would be hot for him; but this seemed a small matter, weighed against fortune and wealth.

Three days after the corporal had come and gone again, Dupré plumped out the question flat-footed, brushed aside all evasive words, and got down to business with Legrand—who was delighted, and said so frankly.

"Now you're showing wisdom, my friend! I'm going to the hills myself in another three weeks; I have business there—shipments of opium, and rifles coming in."

"Three weeks would be too late for me," said Dupré, frowning over his drink. "I may be on the way to Tonkin by that time. Then—well, there's the matter of the girl. She'd go to the hills with me. She says so."

LEGRAND LAUGHED to see how Dupré was hooked and netted on all side's. That girl had worked well for him.

"Remember," he said, "there'd be no turning back! Six months from now we'll be the masters of an independent hill district. A bit of fighting, a bit of training from you, and with the rifles

I'm bringing in, my friend the chief will be sitting pretty. He needs me, and he needs you, and he'll pay well. When you're ready to clear out, you can always go over the British border into Burma, or up through Yunnan into China, and no questions asked. Do you want to go?"

"Yes!" blurted Dupré; and the die was cast. "But how?"

"Simple enough. I'll give you one of the native hunters here, who knows the trails. He'll guide you and the girl, if you want to take her. I advise against it; she'll slow your journey, and there are plenty of girls in the hills."

Dupré would not listen to this, for he was in love with the girl.

"Very well," said Legrand, with a nod. "Then take her. When do your officers come back here?"

"They've been gone three days—not for another week," said Dupré. "They expected to meet another party coming from the coast; ten days, they figured."

"Then," said Legrand, "suppose you get off tomorrow at noon. You'll be at your journey's end before they get back here, and there'll be no hurry about it. You might as well take the spare rifles and such other things as you can, from headquarters—"

"I'm no thief!" Dupré cried hotly. "I'll take my own equipment; nothing else."

"As you like." Legrand shrugged amusedly. "Be ready, then, at noon or a little after noon. Better tell the servants you're going off hunting."

So said, so arranged.

Legrand was going hunting himself, in another couple of days. He had no intention of being here when Corporal d'Ici and the others got back, for he knew very well that the natives would blab and the servants would blab, and he might get into extra hot water. It would be much simpler to go away and stay until the French had departed.

However, he got off a messenger immediately, telling certain brigands with whom he worked to meet Dupré and escort him to the hill chief. He wanted to make sure of Dupré, who would be invaluable to him in a dozen ways. A broken man who cannot go back makes a good servant, and as there were no restrictions on the opium traffic in Siam, Legrand wanted to go into it on a large scale, with liquor on the side and gun-running to fatten out the bank account. It mattered nothing to him that Dupré would be smashed for life.

Early the following afternoon, Dupré and the girl and the native guide got off, all three of them heavily laden. There was, of course, no haste....

It was close to sunset when Corporal d'Ici and a number of his native escort came into town. He had been sent on a hurry-up trip for certain spare instruments. He went straight to headquarters, found Dupré gone, found a short note Dupré had left for him, spoke briefly with the servants, and descended like a whirlwind on Legrand's compound.

Legrand, who had been comfortably swilling liquor, was given five minutes' warning by his servants. Finding that the corporal had returned alone, however, he laughed and laid his revolver in his lap, and waited with cool assurance. When Ici, in his black-covered helmet and black Tonkinese shirt, strode in upon him, he pointed to a chair.

"Welcome, Corporal! Sit down and have—"

"Where's Dupré?" snapped the corporal, breathing hard. His blue eyes were aflame, and that curious pucker of his brows was more pronounced. He was white about the lips, but Legrand disregarded these danger-signs.

"How do I know? I think he went for a little trip—"

"Don't lie," rasped Ici. "I got a note from him. He's my friend, and I want him back. You damned rascal, where is he?"

"Gone." The black eyes glittered. "Here, Corporal,"—Legrand pointed to the cut-out illustrations on his table as he spoke,— "look at these. Upon my word, you look just like this gentleman! A remarkable resemblance. Perhaps you've seen pictures of this lady before? Of course. A subject always has seen pictures of his queen."

The metallic acid of his voice, the significant thin-lipped smile, spoke volumes.

Corporal d'Ici looked at the features of the statesman, looked at the gentle face of the queen, and stood absolutely frozen for a moment. His bronze features whitened a little more, and his eyes lifted to the steady gaze of Legrand.

"What d'you mean, reptile?" he asked in a low voice.

"Come, be reasonable!" Legrand laughed softly and leaned back. "Forget about this foolish young private. He's gone with his girl—"

"I've heard about that girl," Ici said slowly. "And about your part in it all."

"Bah! Let the matter rest; Dupré has gone to make his fortune. You'd better let it rest, too." Menace crept into his tone. "Your memory doesn't go back twenty-six years or so. Mine does.... Think of the pretty story it would make for Paris journals, about a certain scandal now forgotten—how there was actually a child, and how that child, whose father is now minister of war in a certain country, whose mother is queen of that country, is now a corporal in the Foreign Legion!"

Under his bronze, the face of Ici became livid and taut as he listened.

"You'd never write such a story, Legrand," he said, his voice shaken.

"I would," Legrand affirmed with an oath. "And you'd better listen to reason—"

"Perhaps you would, being what you are," broke in Ici. "But you never will!"

Legrand's hand jumped to his revolver, but he was too late. His bullet merely chipped the corporal's shoulder, as Ici shot him through the head....

Corporal d'Ici went back to headquarters. To follow the jungle trails at night was an impossibility, of course. He arranged

for two native trailers to be ready to leave at dawn, arranged
for the spare instruments to be taken back to the party by the
native bearers, and wrote a brief note to go along:

> *I found the renegade Legrand has been plying Private Dupré
> with liquor. Dupré is ill of fever, and in delirium has gone off into
> the jungle. I shall bring him back.*

At dawn, he started with his two native guides, in light
marching order, rifle slung over his shoulders.

Dupré, meantime, had made a short afternoon's march,
camped for the night, and went on at daybreak. What with the
girl and the loads and an unhurried guide, he did not make any
speed—was not trying to make speed. Toward noon he ran into
a dozen armed natives, whom his guide knew; they were the
bandits Legrand had notified to meet him. Explanations consumed some time; the noon halt consumed more time. When
the march was finally resumed, it lasted only a scant half-hour,
because Corporal d'Ici caught up about then.

At sight of the bandits, his two guides hastily vanished. He

The rifle-butt stretched Dupré senseless; then the girl screamed blue fury and cut loose.

strode on across a long open glade. Dupré had halted in utter amazement at sight of him. The girl, who was the quickest-witted of the lot and knew what to expect, caught up Dupré's rifle and stood with wrath and fury in her face. Ici ignored her, plowed to a halt, and mopped his cheeks.

"Glad I found you, Pierre," he said abruptly. "We'll get going back, now. Legrand is dead."

"Dead?" Dupré started. "I'm not going back, you fool! Where'd you come from?"

"Never mind. You're going back, so come along."

The brown bandits scattered out through the brush.

"No," rasped Dupré hotly. "I'm done with the damned Legion and all the rest of it. Turn around and clear out. I'm off, understand? And there's reason enough." He put a hand on the shoulder of the girl, "We stick, she and I; we'll get married, with the first chance."

"You will, like hell!" said Corporal d'Ici. "You're coming back with me if I have to drag you by the heels!" He meant it, and showed that he meant it. He added his candid opinion of the girl; and he had learned enough about her to speak the very dark truth.

YOUNG DUPRÉ flew at him barehanded and smashed him in the face. Then the corporal's rifle-butt took him over the ear and stretched him out senseless. With this, the girl screamed blue fury and cut loose. Her first bullet went through Ici's sun-helmet with a spang. Her second bullet nicked his ear. He flung up his own rifle and shot her through the head, as unhesitatingly as he had shot Jean Legrand.

Then he stooped, picked up the senseless Dupré, and started back. And he went at a trot.

Before he was across the open space, he realized that the native bandits were after him. A bullet buzzed past his knees, then another—they were firing low in order not to hit Dupré. At the edge of the brush, the corporal lowered his burden to the ground, caught at his rifle, wheeled, and opened fire.

Those natives were caught full in the open, and before they made shelter in the grass, three of them were dead.

ICI TOOK the rifle-sling in his teeth, heaved Dupré up across his shoulders, and went trotting on along the jungle trail. Vengeful yells shrilled up behind him. Another open glade, and a long one, would have to be crossed after a hundred yards or so of the trail. There was no avoiding it, for he must stick to the trail. When he came to it, his breath was coming in long heaves, his eyes were bulging, but he kept up his steady trot. The yells from behind were closer now.

Straight out across the open space he headed, and was half over it before a gun banged and the bullet spatted through the grass beside him. He could not turn to look back without stopping. He went on. Another gun spoke, and he staggered in his stride, as a hot touch seared his thigh. He staggered again, and pitched forward. The figure of Dupré hit heavily and went rolling; but the corporal snatched at his rifle and came up firing.

One miss—a hit, another hit. The bandits scattered and stayed scattered. Once more Ici picked up his comrade and went on to the shelter of the brush, and then halted. No pursuit now. Dupré, jarred to life by that fall, sat up and blinked at him, as he made a hasty bandage for the bullet-scrape across his thigh.

"The devil!" Dupré abruptly recalled everything and came to his feet, wild-eyed.

"Take it easy, Pierre," snapped Corporal d'Ici. "Your girl's dead. Start anything, and I'll give you the butt again. Turn around—march!"

"Dead?" muttered Dupré.

"A bullet got her, in the scrap. It was a good scrap. March, damn you!"

Dupré broke, and went shambling along the trail with sobs in his throat. The world had gone to pieces for him, but Ici kept him going at a fast clip.

They came back into town after dark and went to headquarters. Dupré, dead beat, disheartened, dropped on his blankets, and Corporal d'Ici stood looking at him for a moment, then spoke.

"I've pulled you out of a dirty mess all around. Ask any of the servants about that girl of yours. Now that she's dead, you'll learn the truth. You're down as having an attack of fever. Now go to sleep and wake up sane! If I'd been a blasted fool, you'd have done the same for me."

Dupré waked up sane, sure enough: sane, disillusioned, shattered—but he had to pull himself together when he found Corporal d'Ici in delirium, struck down by the deadly jungle fever. Infection had got into his wounds, too.

That night Ici died.

Before the end, he was quite lucid. He looked up at Dupré, read the desperate things in the younger face, and the slight brave smile touched his lips.

"Don't think of it, *mon ami*," he said. "Suicide's a coward's end. It takes a brave fellow to face everything down without a word. You've nothing to die for, everything to live for—I believe in you. I know you'll come through big, a man of whom the Legion will be proud. Do this for me."

Dupré broke down. Ici pressed his hand and spoke again.

"That—candle. Bring it. And my *livret militaire*—"

Dupré brought the candle, and the little book, the military record no eye save that of Ici and a superior officer had ever seen. Ici, with shaking fingers, burned it in the flame.

As it burned, the page with the birth-record curled. Three words written there caught the eye of Dupré, though he did not try to see anything. Three words: *"Pas de mère."* "No mother."

When Ici closed his eyes and died, it was with a smile on his lips. And at the instant of death, his lips opened. By a grotesque and terrible irony, this man who had no mother of record, yet who must have known the whole secret of his birth, passed away with a little fluttering phrase upon his lips:

"Ah! My mother—"

AND THAT was all the story I heard in the French restaurant close to Whitehall. Dupré told the whole thing quite unconcernedly, as one recounts something so far in the past that its emotional angles are blurred.

"I think," he said reflectively, "that as he died, Ici must have seen and recognized that mother of his who had never dared to own him. That smile on his lips—I tell you, it was beautiful! It haunted me for a long time. So, you see, I've had an unknown soldier in my life, as I told you there in the abbey."

"And you never learned who Ici really was?" I inquired.

HE GAVE me a queer, penetrating glance, pushed back his gray mustache, and lit a cigarette.

"My friend, in those days I was young and foolish, as you may have inferred from my little anecdote. I might have inquired, I might have learned much; but I respected the secret of the man whom I had loved. It would have seemed a desecration to pry into the matter. Yes, I was young, ardent, idealistic! I vowed to myself over his dead body that I should make his words come true, make the Legion proud of me. Perhaps I've not succeeded very well, but as the proverb says: *on fait ce qu'on peut*—a fellow can only do his best. And do you know what I think?"

At my gesture, he went on to tell me, slowly.

"That smile, as he died—that smile of recognition as he saw his mother and breathed that sacred name—it haunted me, as I said. I don't care a damn for theology or arguments of any kind; but I do believe that when a chap comes to pass on, he sees something that no one else sees. He pierces the mystery. And when I get mine, I don't want anyone fussing around talking about my soul. All I want is to look up, somewhere, and see André d'Ici standing there waiting for me. And I hope— mind you, I don't expect it, but I hope—that he'll be standing at the salute."

Next day I met Pierre Dupré in his shop, and he was fearfully apologetic. He must have told me a lot of rot, he said; when he had a drop too much, he became sentimental—and was terribly ashamed of it afterward.

I assured him gravely that nothing of the sort had occurred, and he beamed again. The old rascal would have been frightfully upset if he knew how much of his own soul he had revealed in those last words of his.

THE KING'S PIPE

This grim drama of the Foreign Legion's little-known campaign in Dahomey, "The King's Pipe," is the fourteenth story in an already famous series

I WALKED INTO a blare of voices, a blue cloud of tobacco fumes, a redolent odor of the proper authority, and found myself in a gathering of "Anciens" of the Foreign Legion. Corrigan, whom I knew rather well, introduced me to the gang, as one who might be termed a friend if not a brother, and the talk went on. It was raucous and impolite.

"Gimme a *cibiche*—you smoked the last of mine, blast you!"

"I suppose you'll be sprawling under the table when Sidi Mahomet comes up?"

"Here's some Pernod; who'll have a caoudji with me? Allah! Don't take it all, you imbecile—"

However, toleration is the first law of society—toleration of Legion slang, of bawling oaths and insults given and taken in jest, of anything you please. Toleration, which men learn in a hard school.

The oldest man present said the least, until some one called on him for a toast. He was white-haired, thinly erect, vigorous despite his years. Corrigan leaned over to me.

"That's Wetzler—a Bavarian, I think. He was in the Legion before any of us. He has some of the damnedest stories you ever heard! Listen—"

Wetzler stood up, liquor banishing the pallor of his faded, lined cheeks, and raised his glass.

"Clink your glasses, comrades—to the Legion that destroyed the Amazons and dethroned a king, regardless of its own agony!"

If those final words, as I thought, held personal significance, it was lost in a roar of acclaim as the toast was drunk.

"What campaign was that?" some one demanded. "You mean real live Amazons—women fighting?"

"I do," said Wetzler dryly. "And could they fight! They were the bodyguard of Behanzin, king of Dahomey. They were armed with huge sabers, and when they chopped at a head, it went off *ker-flop*. They got in their daily exercise that way."

Somebody down the table grunted. "Oh, you mean that old Dahomey Campaign back in '92! A parade through the jungle for the Legion, a few casualties, and another slice of Africa under the Tricolor!"

Wetzler's eyes flashed. "It was no parade, my friend. A few casualties? Only a few hundred, true; but ten down with fever or dysentery for every one touched by a bullet. Tremendous losses, a march of sixty days on Abomey, the capital; every day of that march continual fighting, often hand-to-hand. And no jungle, either, but river marshes and tropical brush. And in those days, the Legion had adventurers in its ranks, man who played chess with kings for pawns, men who juggled life and death in either hand, and who laughed when they lost and paid!"

A ripple of applause greeted his peroration. He had something, that old fellow, and every one of us felt the power of him. My friend Corrigan spoke up.

"Wetzler, if there's a story back of all that, let's have it. We know the Legion of the war, of Syria, of Morocco; we're fed up with all that. Dahomey—that's a new one on me. What's the story, or is there one?"

More applause. As Wetzler looked around, decision came into his face.

"Yes!" he said almost defiantly. "A story to eat your hearts out—not my story, but that of Bauer. He was in my company; I knew him well. I know what happened to him. He had his head cut off—and yet he served with the Legion for another eight months and was discharged on our return to Algeria."

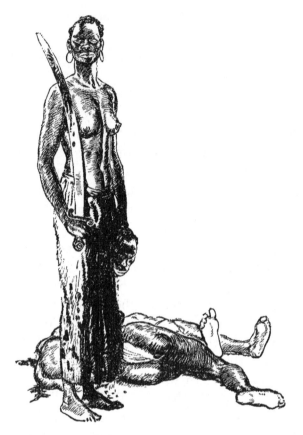

"What kind of a joke is that?" demanded a voice. "Are you serious? Or drunk?"

"I repeat," said Wetzler deliberately, "Bauer had his head cut off, yet was with the Legion in the rest of the campaign and may be alive yet for all I know."

"Oh! You mean magic, African magic, eh?" put in Corrigan.

Wetzler flashed him a look.

"I do not mean magic. I mean precisely what I say. The story's never been told, never been known, though snatches of it are in the records; it can do no harm to tell it now, if you want to hear it."

Everybody yelled assent, for those words of his had us all guessing. He stated a rank impossibility and had thrown out the only possible answer, that of magic or wizardry. And, while the wine of wizardry has always held allure for men, the necromance of the utterly impossible has always appealed peculiarly to the Legion. Yes, he had his audience, no doubt about that!

HE WENT on to tell about Bauer, one of those contradictory persons who appear destined for a hangman's noose, yet whose evil natures are lit by flashes of nobility. Bauer had a terrifically bad record, in a day when the Legion was noted for such records. It was no secret that his name was assumed; but as he himself had morosely observed, his whole family was devil-marked.

Bauer was a big, strapping fellow with a wide brow, intelligent eyes, powerful features. Beards were then popular, in and out of the Legion. Bauer wore his curly brown beard cut square, just below his chin, and he was hairy to the eyes.

He was given to strange moods of depression or uplift. He could be a joyous singing giant or an unutterable brute; usually the latter. Liquor maddened him, and in a drunken rage he was simply a destroying fury. Nobody loved him except the woman he had married shortly before the marching battalion left Algeria—she was the daughter of a quartermaster at Oran and should have known better. The day they embarked, she showed up with a black eye and bruised lips to wave farewell.

Bauer did not like the prospect of central Africa, and he hated everyone around him; he spent half the voyage in cells, becoming more and more embittered against Lieutenant Friant. Surprisingly enough, he knew a good deal about Dahomey, though he refused point-blank to say how he knew. So extensive was his knowledge that the higher command took cognizance of it and he was frequently detailed to give information regarding maps and routes and customs. But one day, when he was in expansive mood, the colonel put the question to him and he explained:

"One of my family is there, or was. He has written home volumes about the place; the letters have interested me."

The general hope in the company was that Bauer would remain permanently in Dahomey. He had another year of his enlistment to serve, which meant that he had made life hell to those around him for six years, and they were tired of it.

The Legion battalion formed part of the Dodds column, formed to march up-country and definitely to extinguish King Behanzin and his bloody capital of Abomey, just beyond his sacred town of Kana. Behanzin had all but pushed the French colony into the sea, was actually on the outskirts of Porto Novo, and the march would assuredly be a continual fight, at least until the holy town of Kana was taken.

Nor was it any march against black savages. Behanzin had an army of close to ten thousand warriors, trained by Europeans and armed with repeating rifles. Germans were all through this country, and according to barracks gossip German traders had given the king not only arms in plenty, but even a few Krupp guns. What Dodds could do with his little column was problematical. After leaving requisite garrisons, he had only the Legion, a few marines, and native troops—Senegalese and Haussas, some two thousand all told.

THREE DAYS before the march began, Bauer was summoned to headquarters to give information on routes. As there were no roads and the natives could not be trusted, his knowledge was valuable. He came back to barracks, after consuming a few drinks of palm-wine on the way, and came face to face with Lieutenant Friant, who perceived his condition and curtly ordered him to the guard-house.

Bauer, whom the heady palm-wine had turned into a perfect fiend, furiously tore open his cartridge-pouch, whipped a rifle from the rack, and fired point-blank at the lieutenant. The bullet missed Friant's cheek by an inch and slapped into the mud wall. Half a dozen of the Legion piled on to Bauer before he could fire again. They got him down, but he was foaming at the mouth, raving mad, and not until he was tied up could he be dragged off to the cells.

When he finally sobered up, he could remember nothing that had happened. His fate was perfectly clear, and he accepted it with sullen oaths; court-martial and execution....

The lieutenant, that evening, took his men aside and spoke with them, one by one—all who had witnessed the scene. Next morning came the court-martial. Bauer was brought in, surly, begrimed, with the look of a trapped animal. He mumbled a few inarticulate words and fell silent. For him, all was hopeless. Lieutenant Friant took the stand and spoke simply, clearly, quietly.

"The fault is really mine, for having issued loaded cartridges by mistake. They should have been blanks. In fact, Private Bauer must have supposed them blanks, as these were issued to all the men."

Surprise here, questioning of the other men; they all replied alike. Not, of course, that the officers trying the case were fooled by this talk of blank cartridges. They even eyed Friant and his Legionnaires with a certain cynical admiration, as though wishing him joy of his bargain.

And they were right. Bauer got off with a light sentence of cells and degradation; but far from expressing any gratitude, he cursed the lieutenant bitterly, with brutal and furious oaths, as soon as he could speak freely. And this won no love for him among his comrades.

The march began, and almost came to a sudden end at Dogba,

when four thousand of Behanzin's picked troops struck the
camp like a whirlwind at five in the morning. It was a complete
surprise. The Amazons, strapping black women with huge
sabers, led the attack. The camp was penetrated. For a moment
all was lost. Commandant Faurax gathered the Legion, and fell
dead. Raging, the Legion went into the blacks with the cold
steel, met the Amazons hand to hand, cleared the camp of the
enemy, and then attacked the four thousand. The black troops
were shattered and disappeared in the brush.

Bauer was led to where the king waited,
with his fearsome bodyguard of black
Amazons. Men were kneeling before him—
the leaders who had been defeated.

Bauer fought like ten, that morning; and in the days of constant brush fighting that followed, bore himself well.

The advance was stubbornly contested. The enemy cut off the lines of communication and the supply service was disrupted. The marsh-lands along the river were horrible, the higher brush beyond was sun-smitten. Sickness began to make heavy inroads. The convoys bringing up water were attacked daily. Colonel Dodds reluctantly decided to return to Akpa, reorganize the column, evacuate the sick and wounded, firmly establish the service of supply, and then finish the job. Kana and the capital, Abomey, were not far now.

Behanzin, at this recoil of the column, imagined it in defeat, and his black troops harassed the line of march night and day. The Senegalese suffered most. As usual, they had their wives and families along; not to fight, but to prepare their food, help in carrying their loads, take care of them if ill or wounded, and so forth. These people suffered. So did the coolies who formed the transport. So did the Legion, for that matter, since food had run out. The horses disappeared. The splendid mules brought from Algeria, worth upward of a thousand francs there, did not survive long here; those not killed by the climate went into the pots of the Legion.

It was a terrific march under the sun of the equator. With Akpa almost at hand, the crisis came when, for lack of porters, the Senegalese tried to carry the litters of the sick and wounded. They crumpled up. The column was halted, with a spatter of rifle-fire along front and rear where the blacks were attacking. It was Bauer who, with a rolling volley of oaths, broke ranks and waved an arm at his comrades.

"Come along, come along!" he bawled furiously. "Let the Senegalese fight for a bit. The Legion's good for other things."

The others got his idea, advanced on the litters, and the astonished officers beheld the Legion doing coolie work for the sick and wounded, all the rest of the way into Akpa.

Oddly enough, in all this marching and fighting, as the food failed and sickness hit, Bauer kept up to the mark. It was observed that he always had lemons on hand, would trade anything for lemons. He had kept his knowledge to himself, which made the other men furious, but lemons not only kept one in health here, they also gave a grateful breath to the sick and wounded. The very odor was enough to make a feverish man smile gratefully.

So, if Bauer was blessed for one deed, he was cursed for another; and he gave back curse for curse like a snarling beast. No one was sorry when he disappeared.

It came just before they reached Akpa. A furious tornado hit the column; black clouds, terrific wind that kicked up a dust-storm until they struggled blindly; finally rain in sweeping torrents. And all the time the *"pick-pock!"* of rifles along the skirmish lines where the native troops fought off the harassing blacks. Private Bauer was pricked off on the list of missing.

FIGHTING GUSTY rain and wind that bent trees and almost carried a man from his feet, Bauer stumbled into a gully, was knocked senseless, and revived to find himself being hauled out by grinning black soldiers. He fought, and was rewarded by a long slave-yoke of wood fastened about his neck, nearly bending him double with its weight, whips stinging his legs to urge him on.

In this fashion, he finished the march; not to Akpa, but to Abomey—a city of mud walls where heads grinned on spikes, of thatched huts and huddled mud houses, of the mud and timber palace of King Behanzin, fronting on a great market-square.

When they took off the yoke, Bauer flew at the blacks around him, hoping to make them kill before they tortured. He fought with the insensate ferocity of a beast, caught a spear from the nearest man, killed three of them before a club knocked him over. Then he was bound, and with blood besmearing his face and beard, was led through the huge square to where the king waited, among his five hundred wives and his fearsome body-guard of black Amazons.

A heavy black man wrapped in an old green silk dressing-gown, features wooden, cruel, impassive. A number of men were kneeling before him, an Amazon beside each one; these were leaders of his regiments whom the column had defeated. Behanzin lifted his hand. The sabers of the Amazons whirled, and the heads of the kneeling men dropped to the earth. The ground was blood-stained for yards around, from other executions.

BAUER WAS marched forward. Wiping the blood from his eyes, he saw the white-clad figure of a European among the group behind the king—a massive, heavily bearded man. This man spoke rapidly with the king, who gave a curt order. Instead of being handed over to the Amazon killers, Bauer found himself led away to a hut. Except for a chain that bound his ankle to the center-post of the hut, he was left free. Bowls of food were brought in. An Amazon stood guard at the door, and he was left in peace. Like the animal he was, he ate, washed the blood from his face, and fell asleep.

When he wakened, it was sunset, and a man sat smoking and watching him. It was the European he had seen behind the king.

Bauer sat up and blinked. The man was smoking a long native pipe whose bowl and stem were heavily and beautifully ornamented with worked silver. It caught the eye instantly.

"Ah!" exclaimed Bauer. "That's a pipe, a real one!"

"King Behanzin's pipe," said the visitor in German. "He gave it to me, as a mark of his favor. So you don't know me, Herman?"

Bauer's mouth fell open. His blue eyes widened. A low cry burst from him.

"You! No, no—not you, Hans! It cannot be—you're dead—"

The other smiled, leaned over to him, embraced him swiftly.

"So, brother Herman, I find you in the French army, the Legion! Yes, the last I heard from home, you had enlisted."

Bauer drew away. That touch of affection was more surprise than anything else; a remnant of boyhood, perhaps, when affection had existed.

"Ach!" he grunted, meeting the cold blue eyes, cold as his own. "And you, Hans! How is it that you're not dead? After your last letters came, there was word of your death."

"Politeness." Hans was of the same general build and air as his brother, had much the same voice. Without the beard, perhaps the two men would not have looked so much alike. The beard of Hans was a little more grizzled than the square-cut beard of Herman Bauer, but full, sweeping over his chest.

"Politeness to the family," he went on cynically. "I had an argument with my superior regarding a serious shortage in the funds of the trading-company. It came to blows. He got the worst of it, naturally, and I decamped. I was with an English company on the Niger for a year, then came over on my own to

Dahomey. I did well. Officially, of course, I'm dead. Here I'm Hans Schmidt, trader, assistant to the king, counselor, what you like! I've handled a lot of deals for him, such as bringing in guns and powder and cartridges. If I ever get out of this country, I'll be well off. That's in some doubt, thanks to your damned French. How I'll get out, without my identity being learned, is a problem. And now you have to turn up to complicate matters!"

"Complicate matters?" repeated Bauer.

"Yes. The king wants your head to put over the gate. I got him to postpone taking it until tomorrow, so I could get information out of you in regard to the French column. But tomorrow—" And he shrugged as he resumed smoking.

Bauer stared, and gulped hard.

"Eh? But if you're in favor with him, you can have me held as a prisoner, exchanged, anything!"

"Nothing," said the other, with a terrible finality. "No prisoners in this war, my honest brother. Behanzin wants a white head above his gate, and means to have it. With it, he'll win the war—so the fetich priestesses have told him. He's already convinced that the column has retired, beaten."

"Bah! Merely to reorganize, get rid of the sick and wounded, and make a dash for Kana and this accursed place."

Hans nodded. "So I thought, myself. And I must get away before your French reach here; they'd hardly treat me with consideration. Luckily, I speak French perfectly, also English, and my money's safe out of the country—"

"My God!" said Bauer. "And that's all you think about, when I'm to die tomorrow?"

"Be sensible," the other said coolly. "You've been dead, to me, for a long time. We needn't prate about brotherly love. I'd help you if I can, but it's out of the question. Even if I got you away from this town, you'd never get ten miles without being run down. I hope your comrades in the Legion have more affection for you than the folks at home. Or are you still a mad dog?"

Bauer snarled in response, and Hans laughed a little.

"The same, eh?" he resumed lightly. "You've never redeemed yourself and the family name, and you never will. I would if I could; but you'd not. That's the difference between us, my brother."

"YAH!" JEERED Bauer. "And you couldn't even if you would! You're officially dead at this minute!"

Hans chuckled amusedly. "Right; a good joke, too! However, I could clear out of here, go to Canada or America, and become a new man—simply because no one would ever be looking for me. I'd have money. I could go into business—"

"Why don't some of these blacks kill you?" snapped Bauer. "How can it be safe for you here, especially if Behanzin gets defeated by the whites?"

Hans held up the beautiful silver pipe.

"This—you see? The king's pipe is known everywhere; it's a sort of safe guard. No one would dare touch me, if I showed it."

"Then, why couldn't you let me take it and slip out of the damned place?"

Hans shook his head thoughtfully. "That has occurred to me; quite useless. Your escape would be discovered. Your charming guard is changed every three hours, and in three hours you'd not get far. In fact, if I save you from torture, I'll be doing all in my power."

HE WAS quite calm about it, quite definite. Beneath his impassive mien, however, was an equally definite stirring of anxiety, even emotion. Bauer divined this, and suddenly comprehended. If any earthly thing could be done to save him, his brother would do it; there simply was nothing. Next moment, this was proven.

"A message to Akpa?" he suggested. "If the French knew any white prisoners had been taken, they might—"

Hans shook his massive beard. "I sent off word this morning," he said quietly. "My messenger was turned back."

Bauer drew a deep breath and nodded.

"I see. Well, brother, I thank you; I understand…. Shall I see you again?"

Hans nodded.

"In the morning, yes. It won't be until noon; we'll have until then. Meantime, I'll try everything in my power. I've tried everything except threats—it isn't healthy to try threats with Behanzin. But I'll try them. Are more troops coming up to join your force, do you know?"

"A detachment of marines, yes."

"Good. Perhaps I can make the fool see reason. You know," he added gravely, "this king is what we, at home, would call a monster. He thrives on blood. *Auf wiedersehen!*"

Bauer found himself alone again. His eyes followed the square-shouldered figure, with the silver pipe in its hand.

Noon tomorrow, then. And now the evening was at hand. He remembered how the Amazons had lopped off those heads, each at one swift, sure stroke. He fumbled in his pocket for tobacco, and rolled a cigarette. His few belongings remained intact, for he had nothing that attracted black cupidity. He smoked thoughtfully, calmly. After all, no man could have a quicker, cleaner death—if only there were no torture!

When Hans, the following morning, came stooping into the hut and straightened up, the attitude of the two men was just the opposite of what it had been the previous day. Now it was the khaki-clad Bauer who was impassive, phlegmatic, absolutely cool; now it was the white-clad Hans who was nervous, agitated, his eyes bloodshot, his fingers unsteady as they clasped the silver pipe. At sight of the pipe, the Amazon on guard had admitted him at once.

"I've just been with Behanzin," he burst out. "There was a scene—a hell of a scene! He damned near had his women slice me on the spot! I used threats. I told him the French were being reinforced. The fat fool's been drinking. He's just killed twenty native prisoners, a couple of your Senegalese in the group. He's sending for you in ten minutes. *Ach, Gott!* It's frightful. I'm helpless—"

"Forget it, brother," Bauer said quietly, and smiled. "There's something you can do for me, if you will; change clothes with me. Then put on your white coat again, so you won't be in French uniform."

Hans stared at him. "Eh? Why?"

"I should like to die in clean garments, brother. It's a fancy of mine."

"So you don't know me?" Bauer's mouth fell open; a cry burst from him: "No, not you, Hans! It cannot be—you're dead—"

Hans obeyed, with tears glittering on his beard. He donned the army boots, the torn khaki trousers and shirt. His hand struck something in the shirt pocket.

"What's this?"

"My papers. Keep them." Bauer lit his last cigarette. "Now do something else for me."

"Anything. My God, if there's anything—"

"You'll do it? Give me your word of honor, brother."

"Of course!" said Hans in a shaken voice. "What, then?"

BAUER SMILED. "Calm yourself. You want to get out of this country; well, I'm showing you the way. Cut your beard square, like mine—you see? You have the clothes, the papers. You have the silver pipe which will get you safe away from here. Go back and join the Legion in my name—say that the blacks captured you, but you got away—"

"Herman! You're insane!"

"Quite the contrary. Half the Legion speaks French with an accent or speaks it very poorly. You've been a soldier. No one would question you for a moment. I've got a bad record; well, turn it into a good record, Hans! You couldn't manage it under different circumstances, perhaps, but here, on campaign, it'll go off like clockwork. Shave your beard entirely, if you like, later on. I've always worn a beard in the Legion—"

A tramp of feet. A dozen of the Amazons were marching up. He rose, calmly, and put out his hand.

"They're here. Good-by, brother! Oh, I forgot to tell you—so many things—"

They gave him no time to tell anything. The two men, embracing, were roughly jerked apart. Hans fell with his face in his hands, sobbing. Bauer marched out proudly and calmly, and everything was drowned in the yelling voices of the thousands of black folk thronged in the great square before the palace.

Next time Hans saw the face of his brother, it was on a spike above the palace gate. It speaks well for him, perhaps, that he risked a great deal to get that head down, and took it with him when he went by night, and buried it.

SOME DAYS later, Bauer came staggering into camp. The column was advancing from Akpa; he was picked up muttering in fever, and his appearance was regarded as miraculous. His story was disjointed, incoherent, but he had suffered much. And he had learned a great deal about the army of King Behanzin, about the fortifications at Kana, about everything the superior command most needed to know.

True, he had forgotten a great deal about things closer to hand. When he met Lieutenant Friant, the young officer halted and held out his hand.

"I'm glad you got back, Bauer," he said frankly, curiously. "Congratulations!"

"Thank you, Lieutenant," said Bauer awkwardly, but with a friendly glow in his blue eyes. "Thank you! It is like coming back from the dead."

The officer looked after him curiously. Assuredly, the fellow had changed!

Others found it so, too. In little ways, on the march, he just didn't know his way around; he was awkward, fumbling, uncertain. He seemed to have forgotten many things. All this was natural, with the touch of fever that was on him. The remarkable point was the difference in the man himself. All the old snarling animal had disappeared. Bauer was a man now, human. Doubtfully, hesitantly, some of his comrades began to like him a little....

They plunged directly into brush fighting. The column hammered straight on for Kana, the holy city of Dahomey. This was defended with desperate courage; the battle lasted three whole days, but the French were fully informed of the intrenchments, the disposition of Behanzin's army, and the terrain ahead. The hand-to-hand fighting was severe. The Amazons died with ferocity, but they died.

Bauer got his ticket home—a bullet tearing through his

chest, that landed him in a litter. As the wounded waited for the convoy to start back with them, Lieutenant Friant came staggering along, escorted by two men. An access of fever shook him. He was pale and flushed by turns, and halted, unable to go another step, while his men went to search for a litter.

"Ha, my lieutenant!" said Bauer. "Here's something that'll do you good."

Painfully, he twisted about, got a hand to the musette under his head, and drew out a lemon. The officer seized it with a gasp of gratitude, then checked himself.

"No, no! You need it more than I do, Bauer."

"Bah!" Private Bauer laughed a little, his white teeth flashing through that square, bushy beard of his. "I detest lemons, my lieutenant!"

And Friant bit into the yellow fruit with a sigh, as he sank down on the litter provided for him. He died three days later....

Bauer? Oh, he was tough! He got sent back to the base, and on to Porto Novo, and his wound healed in time. He had not even lost his pipe—a long pipe of beautifully worked silver about the wooden bowl and stem. One of the officers, recognizing it as native work, offered him a large sum for it, but Bauer only laughed.

"Pardon, but I can never part with this pipe! It is more than money to me. Where would I get another like it?"

"Where, indeed!" sighed the officer regretfully. "However, Bauer, when you get back to Algeria and your wife has a woman's say about that pipe—my offer stands good!"

This was Bauer's first intimation that a wife awaited him in Algeria.

AND THERE, to the general surprise of everyone, Wetzler ended his story abruptly. Voices poured at him to continue, demanding to know one thing and another. He held up his hand, with a shrug.

"Comrades! You say the Dahomey campaign was a parade,

eh? Well, let me tell you something. We came back to Oran, and before we had reached the Zouave barracks where the Dames de France had arranged a feast for us, we began to go to hospital. It's the truth! Not one of us was the same man. For weeks afterward, the men of the Legion were taken off to hospital—"

Corrigan lifted a lusty voice.

"Devil take your hospitals! What we want to know is what became of Bauer? And the wife of his brother?"

Wetzler shook his head. "I don't know. At the end of his enlistment he left the service. I imagine he married the wife who was waiting for him—surely, a woman would know the truth! Well, that's all."

It was disappointing. We had expected some grand climax, and there was none to the story....

When the party broke up, Corrigan drove home with me.

"If you're so damned interested in what happened to Bauer," he said to me, "why don't you ask Wetzler yourself? There's no doubt the old rascal knows, but he simply won't tell. He has a tailor-shop out on the west side of town somewhere—look it up in the telephone-book. Herman H. Wetzler is the name."

Well, I looked it up, found the address, and drove out there. I was curious enough to put the question to him.

I had to park at some little distance from his tailor shop, which was a small but comfortable-looking establishment. So I left the car and walked along to the shop, and paused to look in the window.

What a lucky pause that was! Inside, showing samples to a client, I saw Wetzler's spare, trim figure. A gray-haired woman came from the back room with some question. He turned to her, smiled, kissed her cheek affectionately, and came back to his client. And as he did so, I saw that he held a pipe in his hand—a long-stemmed pipe, of queer design, stem and bowl covered over with silverwork of curious form.

As I looked at it, the truth flashed upon me. This was the pipe of King Behanzin, of course!

So I went away without asking any question. I knew the answer already.

THE LITTLE BLACK GOD

This fifteenth story of the "Warriors in Exile"
series deals with the strange events of a
Foreign Legion expedition in the Sudan.

IN ST. Malo, that curious little walled town of the corsairs, the same today as when its rovers coursed the sea, you may see the towering, elegant houses built by the "armorers" or ship-outfitters, from their huge profits—houses all alike, huddled side by side within the circuit of the walls, identical from foundation to chimneypots.

From one of those houses I watched a funeral procession depart. Everybody was afoot, naturally, except the chief *dramatis persona;* and from those standing around I inquired the name of the defunct.

"Doctor Bistertt," some one told me. An odd name, I thought, and went my way.

Some months later, returning to St. Malo, I went to the sister-town of St. Servien one afternoon—five minutes, by tram. Here, tucked away in a twisting side-street, was a queer dingy shop holding everything from beautiful rapiers to Chinese books or brass pivoted handguns off old corsairs. The proprietor was a small grayish man, very amiable, very brisk and fond of a drink. I shall call him Charles.

Among other things, he showed me a jewel-box of carved dark wood, quite a handsome piece, and cheap. I bought it, and inquired whence it had come.

"I got it at a sale at St. Malo," he said. "The effects of an old surgeon were for auction on the sand under the walls. Here's another thing from his effects."

He showed me a small black fetich-figure of Sudanese work, very old and fine, but of such a nature that the customs would have confiscated it had I tried to bring the thing into America as it now was. However, the tiny figure had an instant fascination for me. The expression on the black carven features was diabolic; it had the charm of the ultra-horrific. I determined to buy it and, at least, take the torso home with me.

"How on earth would a doctor get hold of such a thing?" I asked idly.

"Oh!" exclaimed Charles. "Dr. von Bistertt was in the Foreign Legion, m'sieur. He got this in the Sudan. He was there, with the mounted company of the Legion. Often he has told me about it—you see, we were old friends. He buried my brother there."

Charles was just a trifle diffident, even after we repaired to the corner café. He hesitated to talk freely about Bistertt, and

"Then you are going to find out," said Bistertt. "Now!"

one drink followed another.... I touched on other matters. St. Malo is proud of its greatest son, Chateaubriand, who lies buried on one of the rocks jutting from the harbor, so we talked of Chateaubriand. I told Charles about an American restaurant which spells the name Chateau Briant, and he wiped his eyes with his laughter.

Presently he came back to Bistertt of his own accord.

"It is a horrible sort of story in its way," he said; "yet one gathers that you will comprehend much that cannot be said."

Having got this typically French sentence off his chest, he became more lucid. Bistertt, it appeared, had become a surgeon in Vienna, got into some kind of mess, disappeared, and enlisted in the Legion as a private, not letting out a peep about being a medico.

Charles then told me about his brother, another chap who made a mess of things and joined up with the Legion under the name of Lang. When, late in 1892, a company of four officers and one hundred and twenty men was picked from both regiments of the Legion for service in the Sudan, the two men were flung together and they speedily became friends.

Lang was a young fellow, while Bistertt was in his twenties, a quiet, retiring, laconic type of man, quite different from the fiery, impetuous Lang.

ONCE IN headquarters at Kayes, the Legionnaires were divided into flying columns aiding larger units in pursuit of Sultan Samory's brigands—"Sofas," as they were termed. The service was one of intelligence, of brush fighting, of guerrilla warfare. But at Kayes was a girl, the daughter of a Spanish half-caste trader; and the two friends would have to fall in love with Lola, of course.

In some ways she was a gorgeous thing, free, unmoral, with no inhibitions, and just close enough to the negro race to be imbued with all their superstitions. Her father was a furtive, greedy, fawning fellow, no good whatever. Whether she was any good or not, herself, she certainly possessed a flame of vivid beauty and an imperious will which brooded no obstacles. All who knew her were her slaves, from her father to the Legion; and most of them were glad to be her slaves.

One would naturally suppose that the cynical eye of Bistertt would shy from such an affair, and the more ardent Lang would be an easy victim. Real life, however, does not always correspond to theory. Lang had money in his pocket, and for a week was desperately and violently in love.

BUT WHEN a detachment of fifty men and two officers set off after a band of Sofas who were pillaging and burning, Lang had recovered from his mooning and was his usual brisk, impetuous self. It was Bistertt who carried a locket with a tiny picture under his shirt, and was more laconic, more wary, than ever. Lang read the symptoms aright.

"You'd better lay off that girl," he told Bistertt one night. "Just as one comrade to another."

The Austrian eyed him coldly. "Yes? You'd like to have me out of the way, eh?"

Lang shrugged. "I've had my lesson in that quarter. You can always see through a smoked glass if the smoke's rubbed off. Besides, I've picked up a few things. We're not the first troops to be in these parts, you know."

"What are you insinuating?" demanded Bistertt in chill fury. Lang met his gaze a moment, then turned away.

"Nothing," he said. "Except that rumors go around. Not true, perhaps."

"Correct," said Bistertt. "I tell you Lola is a rose in a dung-heap, and deserves to be better placed in life!"

"There's no argument," conceded Lang, who wanted no feud on his hands. "Forget it." But between them came a coolness; they were no longer inseparable friends....

The pursuit ended in nothing, except two or three men hit, a few sick. They rode back to headquarters, and prepared to go out with the Archinard column. And there Lola had a furious scene with Lang.

He had avoided her pointedly, but she cornered him. Now, a Frenchman such as Lang was, despite his borrowed name, almost intuitively sees through this type of woman. He may get his fingers burned, but if his pocketbook is burned as well, it reaches his heart on the instant. A Breton has eyes in his wallet, as the saying goes.

Charming as the girl was, excellent actress as she was, Lang was clear of the net and said as much.

"You and your precious father got my money," he stated calmly. "That, my dear, is your game; you worked it on that lieutenant of tirailleurs three months ago, and you've worked it on others. I'm not complaining; but I'm not coming back, either."

To his real surprise, she broke into tears. She possessed that singular youthful freshness, that engaging charm, which the French call beauty of the devil. Like many of mixed blood, she had a fleshly shell of unutterable loveliness. Any but a Frenchman and a Breton would have been instantly melted by her tears and her protestations of love, which sounded sincere enough. Any other man would have bartered his soul for an hour's love of such beauty. But not Lang.

"I don't believe a word of it," he said, though he did rather believe her. "Love me? Bah! You're no such fool. If you'd talked that way before I got my lesson—well, who knows? Too late now. My money's gone, and I'm gone."

She caught his hand and kissed it. Then, her eyes suffused with tears, she looked up at him.

"I can't blame you," she said brokenly. "But you're going back into the jungle, into danger. Will you accept a gift from me, a charm to ward off peril?"

Lang, being young, had begun to regret his own firmness, and was cursing himself for being cruel to her. He smiled a little and thought if this trifle would please the girl, well and good.

"With all my heart! But I don't hold much with religious charms—"

"Oh, this is a native charm!" she said quickly. "It has brought great good luck to my father, always. It was given him by the greatest witch-doctor on the upper Niger, and is centuries old. I'll steal it from him and give it to you—will you meet me tonight outside the barracks?"

Lang said yes to this, and parted from her in relief.

THAT EVENING he found Bistertt in savage humor. The queerest elements of human nature come to the surface when a soldier is far away from civilization in some dark corner of the world. This Austrian, with his background, would by all the rules be the last man to yield to superstition; yet now he gave Lang a deep, uneasy look, and spoke his mind.

"Bad luck ahead," he said in his jerky way. "Antonio says so."

"Antonio? Lola's father, eh? Better steer clear of that rascal," Lang advised. "I know he's hand in glove with Samory's agents. Headquarters have an eye on him. He's thick with every damned witch-doctor in the country, too."

"Precisely the point." And Bistertt sneered. "He says they all say the same thing—many dead on this coming expedition. He says Weber, the surgeon, won't come back. He says you'll stop a bullet. In fact, he's offered me a fetich charm of his own to carry; he says it's very old and of great power. I'm going to see him tonight, and get it."

Lang grinned to himself. He had no faith whatever in any of the African witch-doctors or fetich-workers. He had no faith in anything, for that matter, being at the wrong age to entertain much faith. So Lola was giving him her father's charm, and her father had offered it to Bistertt! Well, he would be the one to get it first, if Lola kept her word.

"What's this fetich charm like?" he asked.

"I don't know," said Bistertt. "Antonio has them by the score. He believes firmly in the things."

Lang chuckled again, but not outwardly. Behind the Austrian's manner he sensed a restraint, an angry agitation, and he wanted no trouble on his hands.

"Come," he said soberly, "don't worry about me, Bistertt. I'm cured of love, and so far as I'm concerned, you'll have a clear field with Lola. My word and my hand on it!"

"You mean that?" The other's eyes cleared, as he took Lang's hand.

"Faith of a Legionnaire!" exclaimed Lang; and they shook on it.

An hour later Lang went out to his meeting with Lola. It was not prolonged. She shook with sobs, to his distaste, and pressed a little package upon him.

"Guard it always!" she said brokenly. "My father is giving another to your friend the Austrian tonight. This is his chief treasure, and I stole it for your sake. Keep it, and you'll have luck."

He parted from her as quickly as possible; but to his annoyance, a passing corporal saw them there together, and was not slow to pass word around, which eventually got to the ears of Bistertt. Not immediately, however.

LANG PUT the little packet away among his possessions and forgot about it, save when he was packing or unpacking. To this detachment of the Legion, it was a lark to be mounted, to have a *bat* or a pack-mule to every two men; they cheerfully accepted all other privations, for the sake of this blessing, and covered ground like the devil himself.

They were off two days later on a fighting scout ahead of the column; and on the march Lang found Bistertt definitely hostile. He had heard of that meeting at night, an hour after Lang swore he had nothing more to do with Lola, and he was furious.

"Your word's worth nothing!" he snapped. "Listen to you? I will not. Keep your distance and speak to me only when you must."

Lang shrugged, and let the matter rest; he was only too glad it had not come to blows. Besides, he had troubles of his own.

Everything went wrong with him. His horse fell lame; a bullet damaged his canteen and it could not be well patched; his left eye caught a slight infection, and Surgeon Weber clapped a bandage over it; black marks began to blemish his record; and worst of all, his rifle developed trouble at the wrong times. Cleaning it, he discharged it when he could have sworn no cartridge was in it, and barely missed blowing his own foot off; as it was, his leg was badly powder-scorched.

Then they cornered the Sofas, cut them up, and the scrimmage was a hot one while it lasted. In the midst of it Andrews, an Englishman, was badly hit. Lang and Bistertt got him back to where the surgeon was at work.

"My friend, Lola didn't give you that fetich for any good," Bistertt told Lang.

"Not worth the trouble," said Bistertt. "His lung's punctured, and—"

He went on to tell in medical parlance just what was wrong with Andrews; and his words were true enough, for Andrews gasped and died before he finished speaking. Weber gaped at him.

"Eh? How do you know so much, Bistertt? Only a surgeon could—"

There was a *clump* and the surgeon toppled over with a bullet through his head.

An officer had heard the conversation, and he turned to Bistertt.

"You've been a surgeon? Then drop your rifle and get to work. You'll rank as surgeon the rest of the trip."

Bistertt obtained permanent rank as surgeon, in fact, and was an excellent one. It was typical of the Legion of that day, when the corps could produce anything from a prince to an artist, at a moment's notice.

Before the scrimmage was over, Lang stopped a bullet; a mere flesh-wound in his arm.

"You see? Antonio's prediction was a true one," said Bistertt, as he bandaged the hurt. "You're lucky, at that, Not even a sling necessary."

WEEKS OF pursuit, of hard marching, of occasional sniping and savage encounter, but nothing worthy of the Legion. Still everything went wrong with Lang, until it began to be whispered that he was under a fetich curse. One night in camp he came across Lola's packet, and opened it up.

He found a hideous little black wooden god, with a face so fiendish, so unspeakably malign, that it was fascinating. The savage workmanship was magnificent. The little figure was obscene; but wrapped about it like a doll's cloak was a fragment of khaki uniform cloth, dotted with knots of wool, cowrie shells and beads. Lang stared at it, frowned, remembered that Lola had once begged him for the tattered remnants of a uniform blouse; then he tossed the whole thing aside with a careless laugh.

He kept it, however. The hideous little god was attractive in its way.

A detachment of Hausas under a French officer, a gay blade recently out from home, joined the column to replace a convoy of sick and wounded who were sent back. Some days later a spy brought in word that Ali Segor, one of the Sofa leaders, was in a village a few miles away, with a dozen of his men. Instantly the Hausas and a dozen of the mounted Legion were sent out to round him up. Lang and Bistertt were among the dozen.

LANG HAD changed, during these weeks. His laughing gayety had deserted him; his cheeks had fallen in; his eyes were sunken; he looked twenty years older. There was nothing wrong that could be determined. An occasional touch of fever, but not enough to send him to hospital; yet the change was so marked that new murmurs arose among his comrades. Fetich work, they said. They had absorbed so much fetich talk that they were coming to believe in it.

They looked upon him as a doomed man. In this, they were encouraged by the blacks. How the talk started, no one knew; but the blacks avoided Lang like the plague.

The little force struck the village, caught Ali Segor napping, killed the Arab half-caste and some of his men, captured others, and counted losses. The young French officer of Hausas had a bullet through his ribs, not dangerously; and Lang, with his accustomed ill luck, was ignobly kicked by a mule, which made him vomit blood but did no outward damage. He was waiting to be examined by Bistertt while the latter bandaged the young officer's wound, and he saw what transpired.

As the officer's chest was bared, Bistertt stood frozen, staring at a locket and chain that was disclosed. The officer laughed.

"That? Oh, that's a gage of love, *mon vieux!* A girl back at headquarters. There—look at her picture! *Diable!* The thing cost me a thousand francs, one way or another; but she was worth it, I assure you."

He related a few details of his light love-affair with Lola. Bistertt listened, cold and still, then made a gesture and fell to work at the wound.

Afterward, Bistertt came and sat down beside Lang, lit a pipe, and after a moment asked:

"You heard? Of course. I don't blame you for going back on your pledged word to me, comrade; any man would go crazy for love of her. I would myself—but not any more."

"It's high time you were ready to talk of it," retorted Lang. "My word wasn't broken, Bistertt. Listen, if you want to hear how it happened—"

He told about having seen Lola outside the barracks, for a scant ten minutes. The Austrian heard him out, and nodded again.

"I see. I owe you the deepest apologies; I make them here and now."

"Nonsense!" Lang pressed his hand. "Forget it. We're comrades."

"What was the thing she gave you?"

Lang told about the little black god. Bistertt shook his head gravely.

"My friend, she hated you bitterly. Antonio hated you too. I'm glad you told me all this; now I'm sure of her duplicity. Oh, I've been silent, but I've thought a few things! And my eyes have been opened! Lola hated you because you would not come back to her. And she didn't give you that fetich for any good."

Lang smiled up at him. "Come! You don't swallow this fetich talk—you of all men?"

"I, of all men, would find something in it," Bistertt replied slowly. "I've looked into it, and there are things I can't explain or understand. Magic? As a scientist, I laugh at the idea. But primitive peoples have strange powers, my dear Lang.... Look here—there's a fetich priest in this village. Suppose I get him to look at your black god tonight, eh?"

Lang laughed assent.

He still laughed when, that night, the old black bag-of-bones admitted them to his foul-smelling hut, with an interpreter. Lang did not, could not, take all this mumbo-jumbo seriously. He was, however, deliriously happy that everything was cleared away between him and Bistertt, that the two of them were friends once more. This, to him, was the all-important thing.

THAT DAY the withered witch-doctor had seen the dreaded Ali Segor killed, his whole band killed or captured by these French, the new masters of the land. He had seen all the village fetiches overthrown, burned or destroyed. He was not only in terror, but he was cunningly ready to build for the future. Hence, he was amiable.

When the hideous little black god was disclosed, however, he very literally threw a fit. When Lang handled it contemptuously and spat upon it to polish the old dark wood a bit, the witch-doctor shivered, and stretched out a skinny claw and gabbled hastily. The interpreter turned a frightened face to the two white men.

"He says it is an image of the great snake god, Dambala. Some one who meant you harm has given it to you. This is a piece of khaki uniform wrapped around it, in which are sewn evil charms. Dambala will destroy the man who owned this piece of cloth, unless it is first destroyed and the god appeased."

Lang laughed at this; but Bistertt did not laugh. Looking grave, he spoke.

"Tell him to appease the god; I will pay what it costs. Tell him to destroy the piece of cloth."

The interpreter exchanged hasty words with the fetich priest, then translated.

"He says you must give him the image of the god."

"I will not," said Bistertt. "Tell him to do as I command."

An hour later, after witnessing an alleged magic ceremony that left them both unnerved, the two comrades departed. Bistertt carried the little black image.

"Here's your evil god or devil, if you want it back."

"Bah! Keep it, if it appeals to you," said Lang, and shivered. "I've lost interest."

"I don't blame you." The Austrian was very serious. "My friend, she gave it to you; she had that charm made; from that moment, you've had the worst run of luck I ever saw! And you tell me there's nothing in this fetich business?"

LANG SHIVERED again. "Devil take all of it! I've a touch of fever; get me a dose of quinine, before we turn in. And my side hurts like hell. Blast that mule!"

"Blast that accursed woman, rather!" said Bistertt in a low grim voice. "All you said of her was true, and I jeered at your warning. Well, comrade, I apologize again! And if anything happens to you—well, she'll answer for it."

"Don't be a fool," Lang rejoined. "A run of bad luck, sure; nothing else."

"Not at all sure," Bistertt said darkly. "Come along and get your dose."

Lang put down the quinine, and then managed a ghastly grin.

"If there were anything in your fetich theory," he said, "I'd have felt relief and gay spirits the instant that piece of cloth was burned! But I don't. I feel like the devil. Good night, my friend—it's good to be at one with you again!"

WHEN THEY came to turn him out in the morning, Lang was dead. There was a blue mark under his ribs where the mule had kicked him. With a start of recollection, Bistertt got out the little wooden image of the god and looked at the spot Lang had rubbed the night before. Sure enough, it was in the identical place of that blue mark—a spot in the wood.

*"Guard it always,"
she said brokenly. "I
stole it for your sake."*

With a curse, the Austrian put the little ugly image away,
carefully.

He was a man who took things hard; a cynical, deadly sort
of man, this Austrian. He could be cold and chill; he was a man
of few words; he made an ideal surgeon, for he seemed to have

no human sensibilities. This was a delusion, for still waters run deep, and he was very deep. This death of Lang horrified him to the bottom of his soul, and the cause of it.

That is, what he took to be the cause of it. He was earnest in his belief that the fetich people had something unseen but terrible behind them. The scientific brain in its ceaseless search for primal causes is the most gullible on earth, or the most cynical. On the premise that he has dissected a thousand brains and never discovered a soul, one surgeon may cynically deny the existence of a soul; while another will therefrom deduce a

The interpreter translated: "He says you must give him the image of the god." "I will not," said Bistertt. "Tell him to do as I command."

deeply mystic faith in the unseen and the unknown. Bistertt was of the latter type, in regard to fetich powers.

He actually believed that the bit of khaki cloth with its charms had been destroyed too late; that it had killed Lang; and that these fetich powers had been invoked by Lola for just such a purpose. This became a deep conviction, an obsession, with him. His eyes became more cold and bitter than ever.

All the while, the column was hard on the move.

Bistertt no longer wore the locket with the picture of Lola....

When the various detachments came together for the return, having marched three thousand kilometers and fought fourteen real encounters, without having put the Sofas out of business—when they came together, Bistertt received a letter from Captain Soutain. It was a letter Lang had given the Captain, to be delivered in case of his death:

> *I want you to know the truth about the woman who has be-witched you. Once we were friends, dear friends; if you receive these words, it will be after my death. I feel in my heart that I shall not return from this campaign. Because I love you, I leave you this legacy of the truth about Lola, as I have learned it. Rather, I should say, about her father. She is not so bad; it is Antonio who is evil. He is a spy for Sultan Samory, for the Sofa leaders. Nobody would believe this, just as you will believe nothing amiss about Lola herself—*

Bistertt read the accusations. They were deadly. No legal proofs, of course; nothing headquarters could act upon. But as Bistertt read, his eyes were opened. Now he knew why Lang had been given that devil-god with the evil charms, why he had been marked out for death.

Antonio and his daughter had learned that Lang was getting this information about them.

Bistertt said nothing at all. He tore up the letter and burned the scraps of paper. But he sat long over his pipe that night, brooding, and the expression in his face was not unlike the expression on the face of the little black wooden image. A letter from a dead man—"*because I love you.*" Well, there are hurts and regrets and savage thoughts too deep for words.

The weary column tramped into Kayes on May 3, 1893. Within the hour, word went around that the detachment of the Legion was homeward bound, that a ship would arrive at once. The mounted lark was all over.

That evening, still in his stained, tattered service uniform, revolver at hip, khaki-covered topee nicked by bullets and faded by sun, Bistertt came to the house of Antonio, adjoining the trader's store. There was a dance going on in town that night, and Lola was attending it with the young officer of Hausas, as Bistertt well knew; he had come, however, to see Antonio.

The furtive, swarthy half-caste received him warmingly, with great cordiality. The Austrian refused the proffered drinks, however.

"I have a present for you," he said, touching the package under his arm. "But not here; too many eyes around, Antonio. Can we go to the back room of your shop, where no one will see us? This is something very important."

"Of course, of course!" And with a leer the trader took up a lantern and lit it. "Come along. A little matter of loot, eh? I hear the troops brought back quantities."

"Correct," said Bistertt laconically.

He followed Antonio across the compound to the rear of the shop and warehouse, where the trader had a strongly built room that was thief-proof. They went in. The air was hot and musty, and a moth who had followed the light buzzled and flittered around the lantern on the desk. Antonio settled down, lit a cigar, and nodded.

"All safe. What have you?"

"Something extraordinary," said Bistertt. "It cost me a bit of money, too. Do you remember that some little time ago you gave one of your shirts to that fellow who works for you—a red shirt?"

Antonio laughed heartily, though in some surprise.

"Yes, of course! Poor Bojo has coveted that red shirt a long time. Well?"

With a shrug, Bistertt extended the package.

Antonio opened it with eager curiosity. A queer expression came into his face when thin red cloth came into sight, dotted with cowrie shells and knots of wool. His swarthy hue became an ashen gray when he saw it was wrapped about the black god Dambala. His eyes lifted in stabbing ecstasy of fear.

"*What*—" He swallowed hard on the word, tried again. "What is it?"

"So you recognize the procedure, eh?" Bistertt said grimly. "That's the thing I wanted to know. The snake-god is an old friend of yours, eh?"

"I—this—this is terrible!" quavered Antonio, flabby lines coming in his face as horror dilated his eyes. "You—you don't know what this means! Who gave it to you?"

"A friend of mine sent it to you," said Bistertt slowly. "Lang."

Antonio started at the word.

"No, no!" he declared with shrill emphasis. "He is dead. I saw his name on the list. I know he is dead!"

"You took good care he'd be dead," Bistertt rejoined coldly. "You had Lola give him this image of Dambala. You had it marked on the side by the fetich priest."

Antonio shrank back. "I—she—it was all a joke," he faltered. Then, with an effort, he drew himself up. "This is all nonsense. I am a good Christian. I have nothing to do with this fetich palaver. Only ignorant blacks believe in such things."

The Austrian grinned, without any amusement or humor.

"You gave me a charm that brought luck, anyhow.... Antonio, you're a damned liar. Lang had found out too much about your dealings with Sultan Samory. That's why you killed him with this damned thing."

"I know nothing about it, I tell you!" Antonio cried, sweat coursing down his jowl.

"Then," Bistertt said calmly, "you're going to find out—*now*."

In that solidly built, confined room, the sound of the shot was muffled. It drew no attention from the world outside.

DURING THE following morning Bistertt was hard at work on various papers which had to be drawn up, looking to his permanent appointment as surgeon. In the midst, one of his closest comrades came bursting into the room.

"Bistertt! Do you know what's happened? Name of the devil! That trader Antonio, you know him? Found with a bullet through his head. And in his hand a chain and locket with the picture of Lola—*mon Dieu!* And they say Lola has skipped out. And that young Hausa officer who's been sparking her, the one who was with us on the march—he has just shot himself in barracks!"

"Indeed?" said Bistertt coldly. "Best thing he could do, I fancy. That girl was no good."

"But I—we thought—you were in love with her—"

"Bah! As soon be in love with that thing." And Bistertt pointed to the little black image of the snake-god, holding down some papers.

The other turned, and crossed himself as he opened the door.

"You'd better burn that damned thing," he flung hastily over his shoulder at the Austrian, "before you get to looking too much like him."

When Bistertt, years later, received his discharge, he came to St. Malo and settled down there; but he had not burned the little black god. He lived alone, cold and sardonic as ever; and the Bretons crossed themselves when he went down or up the crooked streets, with talk of the evil eye.

And he died alone, with no one to mourn him except a few friends from Legion days, and those who respected his austere nature.

"OF WHICH," I said to Charles, "you were one."

He nodded thoughtfully. The charm of his story had departed; we sat again in the café at the corner, fingering our drinks. I looked at the little black god, which I had brought along, and my eye was caught by a distinct splotch on one side, under the carven ribs.

"Here," I said, thrusting it at him, "take the damned thing. I don't want it, after all."

"I knew you would not, m'sieur," he said. "But I had to be honest about it, and tell you the story. After all, you know, Lang was my brother."

And now I remembered that I had seen him tramping along after the black-plumed hearse of Bistertt, that day of the funeral. And noting his reverent touch as he folded a paper about the little black god, noting the queer look in his face, I wondered if he, like the Austrian, believed that fetich palaver.

Almost did I believe it, myself.

REILLY OF THE LEGION

This sixteenth of the colorful "Warriors in Exile" series
takes you to remote Madagascar and the Foreign
Legion's weird and little-known campaign of conquest.

PICARD FLUNG a book down on the table with a
horrible explosion of oaths. "This author has a Legionnaire
say *'Mon Caporal! Mon Sergeant!'* He even has some one say
'Mon Maréchal!' to a marshal. And I bought the book because
the blighter claimed to have been in the Legion!"

Campbell pulled over the book, glanced at it, and grinned.

"Oh, this fellow! The nearest he ever got to the Legion was
a girl in Bel Abbes who wasn't a bit particular. Why, Picard,
don't you know the Legion has branded this book a fake? So
has the French Government. You'll find some wonderful things
in it, sure—things we never knew when we were in the Legion!"

Picard cursed anew. But old Manukoff intervened calmly.

"Wait, my friends. The book is a fake, but not for the reasons
you allege. It is not actual, not human. It's a sensational lie. Still,
the language—"

Picard glared at him. "You served three hitches in the Legion,
Manukoff. Twenty-one years. Did you ever in that time hear a
private address a sergeant as, *'Mon sergeant?'* Of course you
didn't."

"But I did," said Manukoff. "And the other errors of speech
you're growling about, also. It was before your time, you young
fellows; it was in 1895, my first campaign, the Madagascar affair.
And I heard all these so-called errors in the book yonder take
place in real life. Of course, this does not excuse the wretched
fellow who wrote the book; certainly he never heard them. But

Reilly used to make those mistakes all the time. Reilly spoke French poorly. He seemed incapable of learning the language."

"An Irishman?" queried Campbell with interest. And the bearded Russian nodded.

"One of our recruits; we had many in the detachment. I remember seventeen deserted in one night as we came through the Suez Canal—overboard and ashore, you comprehend."

He puffed reflectively at his pipe. Campbell, who had served in the Legion cavalry, cocked a finger at the bartender. Picard, who had drawn all three together here in New York, calmed down.

"Madagascar! That campaign was a push-over, eh?" he observed. "Never was a slice of this earth won with as little effort!"

"Nor with greater suffering," said Manukoff. "The Hovas were not brave, true; we had no real combats, for the artillery usually broke up the enemy. Still, there were bullets enough. Every one of our hospitals buried twenty to forty men a day, and plenty of them from lead-poisoning, as you Americans say.... But more of the Legion committed suicide than were touched by enemy bullets. It was a continual suicide parade! Now, doesn't that make you stop and think?"

Picard nodded frowningly.

"Yes, of course. But this book—well, you've actually heard those classic errors of language in the Legion?"

"Often." The old Russian chuckled. "This Reilly, he was a cherub with red hair and an earnest resolve to make good. He had a fixed idea that it was proper to prefix 'my' whenever he addressed any kind of an officer. When we told him it was only used to certain ranks, he thought we were kidding him. The poor devil really understood little French."

Campbell grunted. "And I bet you raised hell with him in consequence."

"Why not? You know the Legion," said Manukoff. "There was mighty little sentiment in the Legion; or in the world either, back in those days. We grabbed Madagascar then, just as ev-

eryone was grabbing. Bah! This sentimental talk makes me sick. Look at Madagascar today, happy, civilized, prosperous!"

"That's one way of looking at it," Campbell said curtly. "At least we didn't massacre the natives in Madagascar."

"No; we lost more men than the Hovas did," assented Manukoff. "We made a fine up-country march, and then we were stuck; we had to stop and build a road so supplies could reach us. Those Hovas devastated the country and burned the huts as they retreated. We burned what they left, from fear of plague. And all the while we knew they had forty thousand well-drilled, well-armed men ready to jump us; easy enough now to say they were cowards, but at the moment we didn't know it. Then there was Reilly. We tormented him, yes; and he was a gadfly to us."

He paused, shook his bearded head, and told us about it.

AH, THAT red-head! Enlisting for glory, he had found none. Our artillery sent the Hovas scampering, so that except for sniping and skirmishes, we had no hand-to-hand work. Instead we labored endless weeks building the road so a light

column might push on to Tananarive, the capital, and finish the conquest.

Starvation, vermin, sickness, physical exhaustion—no wonder Reilly cursed the Legion! We played tricks on him, thanks to his inability to learn French. Oh, we made him suffer, be sure of that! When a recruit curses the Legion to its face, you know how we treat him. But Reilly was one of those stubborn little men who never know when they're licked.

He worked like a dog, and so did we. The sickness of Madagascar, you know, does not hit suddenly; it saps the life and energy gradually, eats away the endurance and the will to live. The filth of that land and its people was beyond description, and this of course helped to spread the contamination.

Under a broiling August sun, a sergeant addressed Reilly some question regarding the work. Reilly dropped his "1895 model rifle," as the men called the pickaxes, grinned and saluted, and responded: *"Mon sergeant—"*

The sergeant, himself a walking bag of fever-shot bones, snapped savagely and cursed poor Reilly as only a Legion sergeant can curse. He went on, leaving Reilly white and shaking with futile rage, while everyone else laughed.

That night Reilly disappeared.

This was not unusual. When any of the Legion went to hospital, he died there; it was logical, because a Legionnaire worked until he dropped, and had no energy left with which to fight death. The men did not think it logical, however. They thought it meant sure death to go to the hospital. Some disappeared, and patrols went out every morning to bring in the corpses. Or, as on this particular night, a shot would ring out, then another. Here one of the Legion, there an Algerian *tirailleur* perhaps. Men lay awake listening for the shots. They wagered on who would be the next suicide.

But Reilly did not turn up as a corpse. The paymaster cursed bitterly, since it was his job to establish the fact of death; and how to do this, without a corpse?

This did not worry Reilly a bit. He had deserted, and was glad of it.

He was one of those happy-go-lucky Irishmen who, in normal life, are liked at first sight. There was no crime in his past; an impetuous love-affair, too much drink, a romantic idea that the Foreign Legion offered glory—and there he was. Now his romantic notions had died, his face was gray and drawn, his eyes were older; but his cheerful smile still persisted. His sole ambition, as he slipped away in the night and headed for the hills and the Hova country, was to be done with the Legion forever.

"I'll die before I'll go back!" he muttered, over and over, until assured that his escape was an accomplished fact. Toward dawn he found an abandoned hut, and slept there until noon.

Then on again, and in the afternoon he walked into a native village and was at the crossroads of destiny.

The strapping brown natives in their white cotton robes were friendly. A party of Hova soldiers were friendly. Reilly was friendly; and everyone was quite happy, what with native liquor, a bit of song, and even a dance. Reilly was charmed to find that the natives, far from being bloodthirsty savages, were mild and amiable as their Polynesian ancestors; the village even possessed a church; and from what he could make out, his hosts were Christians.

THIS SCENE of more or less innocent merriment was rudely interrupted. The natives scattered; a horse pounded in and was reined short. Reilly, left alone, stared up at a black-clad man who sat his saddle like a centaur, and looked down at him with black angry eyes—a white man.

"Who are you? A French soldier?" came the rasping question.

"Devil a bit," said Reilly. "My name's Larry Reilly, and I'm wearing this uniform for my sins. And who may you be?"

The Reverend David Gwynne announced his name and missionary status with acerbity. He was not a pleasant man; and like most of the English missionaries here, he disliked the French conquest rather acutely. Unlike most of them, he had money and position, was able to import a saddle-horse and other luxuries, and believed in ruling his converts harshly. Which, for the Reverend Gwynne, was just a bit of bad luck.

"Are there no soldiers here?" he snapped out.

Reilly looked around.

"There were, but there aren't now," he said. "Apparently they didn't like your looks and skipped out."

"I'll not allow this carousing and dancing," began Gwynne, then checked himself and bit his lip. He was scarcely in a position to give orders, at present. "Look here, Reilly! Climb up behind me, like a good fellow. There's trouble at the mission; I've ridden ten miles to get help, and you'll be more good than all these natives put together. I take it you're a deserter from the French force?"

"Me? A deserter?" Reilly was admitting no such thing. "I got lost from the column and found this village; you'd not call that deserting! Trouble, you say? What kind?"

"The worst kind," rapped out Gwynne. "Queen Maorani's soldiers are looting the place, perhaps have burned it by now; my daughter's gone out of her senses; my wife's in danger of her life; and the Queen has threatened to murder me. I must get back with help. The sight of a uniform will accomplish wonders. Jump up, man, jump up!"

Reilly ran for his rifle, clambered up behind the missionary, and the horse started off.

Now, Reilly was nobody's fool. He had really tried hard to make good in the Legion, but he just wasn't born to it. He had picked up some Malagasy, had tried to learn about the natives and their ways, and was actually more at home with them than with the French. And with Gwynne, he was back among his own people. Disagreeable, harsh, hidebound as Gwynne might be, Reilly could at least understand him.

And Reilly could understand how so uncompromising a man might be scandalized daily by the easy-going natives. He knew, too, that local queens were scattered all over the island. One such queen and her ladies had met the Legion with open arms when it landed—so literally that even the French were taken aback!

AS THE big horse pounded on into the hills with its double burden, Gwynne gave some explanation of his plight. He lived alone with his family at this station, under the protection of Queen Maorani; but the Queen had finally tired of his everlasting interference with her pleasure-loving people, and had turned on him savagely. With the coming of the French, with their steadily advancing conquest, the island had been plunged into anarchy.

"Why she should want to kill me, I don't know," said Gwynne.

"What are you squirming about for?" asked Gwynne.
"Hang on!" But Reilly was getting rid of his uniform.

Reilly, who could perfectly understand it, and could even sympathize with the young Queen, grinned widely but made no comment as he jolted along.

"She's not a savage, really," went on Gwynne. "She's always been most pleasant to whites. We have many visitors from Tananarive, the capital. She has two white men in her town now; two godless rogues, I'm bound to say, who train her army and handle her artillery. She has no antipathy to whites in general—except, of course, to the French."

Reilly pricked up his ears. "Army? Artillery? Is she a big queen, then?"

"No, no; merely ruler of this hill district. But she has an army of two hundred men, well trained and armed. And half a dozen pieces of artillery. If I get you back in time, before the station has been sacked and my family murdered, the sight of another white man will give those rascals pause.... Here, what are you squirming about for? Hang on!"

But Reilly was getting rid of as much as possible of his uniform. Not that it would mean any particular danger to him from the natives; but if word got around of a white man in French uniform, particularly in Legion uniform, a day would come when the French would certainly gobble him up as a deserter. And he knew what that meant.

"You don't want to take a French uniform home with you, Reverend," he said shrewdly. "Then the natives would certainly lose their heads and wipe us all out. I'll get rid of this one; then you give me a suit of yours when we get there. I take it there was no actual attack before you left?"

"No," said Gwynne; "but it threatened at any moment. Unluckily, my interpreter and all my servants have run off, and I don't speak the language yet, with any fluency. In fact, I haven't wanted to learn it, because I've made our converts speak English."

Reilly blasted the stiff-necked Englishman—strictly to himself. Such a man, trying to win the souls of these laughing, gentle, indolent natives! He began to pull holes in the story, as the horse toiled on. It was not likely these natives would try to murder Gwynne and his family. Suddenly he recollected the two white men Gwynne had mentioned.

"Who's behind this attack on you? The Queen?" he demanded.

"Of course," said Gwynne over his shoulder. "And those two rogues who train her army. Schulte, the German, isn't so bad; but the other one should be strung up. He's a thorough scoundrel—an American soldier of fortune named Harrison, who has sold guns to the government at Tananarive and to the Queen here—a dissolute, godless rascal! He's the one who has driven my poor daughter out of her wits, hypnotized her, led her on to disgrace and ruin and everlasting shame!"

Big words for a few kisses, thought Reilly, and grinned again. He was beginning to get the proper slant on this missionary now. He had met quite a few missionaries in this island, and none of them had been of this stripe. Not that Gwynne was not an earnest, sincere man—he was just too earnest altogether.

"Not a bad idea, that, about your uniform," said Gwynne. "Yes, I can give you clothes. No use stirring up the natives more than necessary, I suppose."

REILLY WAS stripped close to buff and boots, by the time the mission was sighted. Gwynne did not come in through the queen's town, which was a huge collection of thatched huts and fruit-groves down the valley; instead he came in by a back trail that brought them out at the mission.

"They burned the church early this morning," he said bitterly.

The smoking ruins of it showed at one side. The residence, with its compound and sheds and gardens, remained quite untouched. Reilly reflected shrewdly that if murder was on the program, it would have been done when the church was burned. No natives were in sight; no maddened assailants were at hand; everything was drowsy with the peaceful repose of approaching sunset.

"No mob scene," said Reilly, slipping off, clinging to his rifle, looking about.

"Evidently the threatened attack is holding off. I'll put up the horse and then get you fixed up with other clothes," said Gwynne, and cantered off around the house.

Feeling rather puzzled, Reilly went to the veranda, slipped off cartridge-pouch and musette, and put them aside with the

*Starvation,
vermin,
sickness, physical
exhaustion—
no wonder
Reilly cursed
the Legion!*

rifle. He was not a pretty sight, with a blur of red beard covering his cheeks, and his unconventional garments. At a step from
within the house, he hastily ducked out of sight until Gwynne
reappeared; then Reilly followed him inside.

"Here are clothes." Gwynne threw open a closet. "Help yourself. If—"

FROM SOMEWHERE close by, a rifle crashed, then another; a wild yell sounded. Gwynne departed on the jump. Reilly, wondering if he were caught in some nightmare, clawed at the garments, found a shirt, climbed into a suit of regulation black ministerial garb, and hurriedly buttoned it in place. Another shot, and a burst of yells; he darted out, clumped down the hall to the veranda again, and grabbed for his rifle.

He saw Gwynne out in the open, facing the gateway, a revolver in his hand. At the gate was a mass of soldiers in white *lambas*, brandishing rifles and shouting something. One of them fired point-blank. The bullet slapped into the veranda thatch over Reilly's head; Reilly promptly went to one knee, aimed, and the shot crashed out. The Hova who had just fired whirled around and dropped. Two of his companions lugged off his body; the others vanished.

Gwynne turned and stalked back to the veranda, flourishing his revolver.

"I'm glad you have cartridges," he said. "I haven't one. I hoped to hold them off with this empty weapon."

Reilly grinned at him. "These natives puncture like a balloon," he observed. "The chances are they're still running."

"Thank God you're here!" Gwynne looked at him. "How shall I account for you?"

"Well," said Reilly, "I don't suppose you want to lie about it?"

"I never lie," Gwynne replied stiffly. "I detest lies."

"Then tell the truth. You just met me. I'm a beachcomber or something. Who cares?"

"My wife cares," said the other, and stalked into the house.

Reilly squatted there and laughed; he could not help it. The whole situation struck him as funny, deliriously funny. He was still laughing when, as he eyed the gate of the compound and the trees beyond, he caught sight of a man out there, a European in whites, cautiously reconnoitering the house. No natives in sight at all.

On impulse, Reilly left his rifle where it was, hopped up, and strode down past the flower-beds. The man outside had vanished. Reilly came to the gate, passed it, and halted.

"Come out," he said. "And sharp about it!"

T H E   M A N dodged out from behind a tree and approached him—a springy, lithe, lean man with a quick eye and a quick smile. Reilly liked him at sight.

"Who the hell are you?" said the stranger.

"Name's Reilly."

"Are you another sky-pilot?"

"Not by a damned sight!" And Reilly grinned. "Say, are you the godless American?"

"That's me, I guess. Tim Harrison. How—"

"Oh, I met up with the Reverend and came along to save him from massacre." Reilly chuckled. "He's the wrong kind of missionary. Glad to meet you. Shake."

Harrison shook hands, looking rather bewildered.

"Was it you who shot that native?" he said. "Well, you played hell. Lucky you didn't kill him. The Queen's hopping mad about it; she's liable to start real trouble."

"Lead me to her," said Reilly cheerfully. "I don't know what all this bobbery is about, but I can make a guess or two. I'll show her what the right kind of missionary is like, for a change. What about a drink before we meet the lady?"

Harrison surveyed him with twinkling eyes.

"Where'd you get the Irish accent?"

"Honestly," said Reilly. The other laughed and caught his arm.

"Come on, then! I don't know who the devil you are, or what, but you're okay."

"Which, I suppose, means you're satisfied? So am I," said Reilly. "If you're hoping to see the Reverend's daughter, she's probably busy right now soothing her mamma."

He said the word in the Irish way, and Harrison chuckled.

"We say *momma* in the States. Look here, stop in with me

and have a drink. Want to shave those whiskers before you see the Queen?"

"Not me. I'm growing a beard; reasons of State. And make my name O'Reilly, in case the French get here."

Harrison gave him a quick glance, a grave glance. "So? Okay with me. I hear the French have a walk-away; the Government armies just melt before them."

Reilly was puzzled by the American slang, but got the general drift. The town opened up before them, and he accompanied Harrison to the latter's quarters, a small house with two native servants. Harrison mixed a drink.

"Well, here's luck!" Reilly remarked. "Now, what's all the shindig about?"

"Poor Gwynne is a square peg in a round hole and doesn't know it," Harrison confided. "He's one of these harsh, uncompromising Britons—square as a die. The idea was to scare him out, what with the war and all. I should have had sense enough to know that an Englishman doesn't scare."

"Ah!" said Reilly sagely. "It takes an Irishman to do that. You don't know how to handle him. So you were back of it—and you in love with his daughter?"

"To save his life, you fool!" snapped Harrison. "The Queen has exaggerated notions of what a queen should be. She's capable of shooting him down, and dislikes him enough to do it. I want to get him out of here before the French arrive. That won't be many weeks off, and when they come, there'll be hell to pay. Schulte and I have everything fixed to lick hell out of those French."

REILLY CHORTLED. "With two hundred men and six guns?"

"You don't know me and Schulte—especially Schulte. Well, never mind all that. We've got to fix the Queen somehow. I don't want to see Gwynne murdered tonight."

"Let me talk to her," Reilly said. "Introduce me as the man who shot her warrior, and as a missionary. The right kind of a missionary. Tell her I've come to take Gwynne's place. I'll stay awhile, then get back and clear Gwynne out of here by morning."

"You fancy yourself," said Harrison dryly. "What about Elsie? And me?"

"Well, what about you?" Reilly gave him a look. "You wanted Gwynne gone; then what?"

"I get you. Yes, we've got things fixed up, if her folks get to the capital safely. I'd go along with them, meet her there, get married, and be back here to help Schulte."

Reilly stared. "Back here? She'd come back here with you— to fight the French? What kind of a woman is she, to want to come back into hell—"

"Forget it, forget it! We'll fix those French. And she's the right sort, true-blue and a yard wide," said Harrison. "All I'm worried about is you and the Queen and Gwynne. My God, what a sight you are in those clothes and with those whiskers!"

"You see that the Queen and I get a drink or two," said Reilly, "and trust your luck to the Irish, me boy. Lead on!"

Harrison shrugged and obeyed.

ABOUT THIS entire situation, the love-affair, the mock mob scene, the young queen who was capable of murder—was a grotesque flavor which Reilly thoroughly enjoyed. It was like the whole island, like the campaign itself, wherein armies fled at a few cannon-shot. And yet, behind all this *opéra bouffe* lay horrible grim reality, with death ever jogging one's elbow. Even Harrison's apparently puerile threat of destroying the French column with his two hundred men and six guns, struck Reilly as perhaps holding a certain frightful possibility. Harrison was that sort of man; he knew his business.

They went to the "palace," a widespread collection of huts surrounded by a stockade, in the center of the town. This was flickering with lights, seething with excitement. Schulte was here, and Reilly met him—a bearded German, very intent and earnest. Reilly was beginning to be afraid of men who were too earnest.

The Queen received them at once. She was a young woman, rather plump, very angry, a mixture of arrogance and dignity and effusive welcome. Her councilors squatted around her; a bevy of girls was at her feet. The appearance of Reilly created vast excitement. Harrison promptly introduced him as the new missionary who had shot the warrior, and left Reilly to save his own neck.

He did it efficiently. A few words of Malagasy, his amiable grin, his audacity—and he had captured the scene. In two minutes he was seated by the Queen; he kissed her ladies and her own royal lips, drank her health

"Leave everything to me," Reilly said.

with gusto, turned the place upside down with joyous zest, and conducted himself with a mad extravagance that left Harrison aghast. Yet it went over.

Reilly had no inhibitions. He promised anything and everything; with his magic gift of personality, he captured everyone from the Queen to the old councilors. An hour later he started back for the mission station with a dozen torchbearers, gifts of food, fruit, wine and flowers, and promises galore.

The arrival of this procession was singular. The Reverend David Gwynne was out at the gate, firmly convinced that

murder was at hand; he had Reilly's rifle, and came near shooting Reilly with it before he found all was peaceful.

"BUT WHAT does it mean?" he demanded, when the
natives deposited their gifts and withdrew. "I thought you had
run away—"

"It means plenty," said Reilly. With the island government
in chaos, with no chance of a reckoning facing him, he gave his
fancy free rein. "The Queen and those two godless ruffians,
Harrison and Schulte, intend to murder you and your family.
The council has more sense; the old men have things in hand,
at least for the moment. They want you to get off for the capital
in the morning. They'll furnish bearers, palanquins for your wife
and daughter, and so forth. They're sending messengers to the
government, asking that the Queen be deposed and that you
be placed in charge here. You present a similar request, and the
government will be only too glad to agree. Understand? You'll
be back here in a week or two, the Queen will go to her estates
in the country, and all will be quiet."

Gwynne was delighted. This project appealed to him as perfectly natural; it was the sort of thing he could understand, with
law and order and a proper respect for his dignity supplanting
what he called anarchy. He was overjoyed, and tremendously
grateful to Reilly, whom he took inside to dinner.

REILLY FOUND Mrs. Gwynne a quiet woman, plump
and fortyish; and met Elsie. His quick appraisal of her rather
dashed romantic notions. She was the cold type, level-headed
and blonde, with prominent teeth and a masterful eye. And the
gay Harrison was madly in love with her! Reilly gave up; it was
of a piece with the whole mad situation.

Reilly made no secret of the fact that he was remaining here.
He even promised to keep inviolate such effects as Gwynne
might want to leave until his return. When Gwynne went off
to pack, Reilly was smoking on the veranda, and Elsie came up
to him.

"Did you see Mr. Harrison?" she asked.

"I did," said Reilly. "He'll join you on the way to the capital, tomorrow."

"I don't think you told my father the truth," she said bluntly. "Queen Maorani would not let the council dictate to her. I don't like lies at all, Mr. Reilly."

"Faith, I'd cut off my right hand rather than lie to the likes of you," said Reilly. "So go get an ax and stand by to cauterize the wound."

She could not understand him at all, and went off in a huff to pack, which was what Reilly wanted....

Reilly was up at dawn to see them off. The bearers came as promised, with two native palanquins to carry the women. Gwynne shook hands with Reilly and rode off on his horse. When Jim Harrison showed up with a couple of guides, Reilly sighed and pitied him.

"Miss Elsie said to give you her love," he commented. "She's an angel."

"She's the most wonderful girl in the world!" said Harrison. "And she'll defy her father to marry me. Old man, you've accomplished a real miracle! I'm your debtor for life."

"God help you, I think you are," said Reilly. "When will you be back?"

"In three or four days. By the way, we had a courier this morning; a French column is advancing and will be here in a week to occupy the district. Fifty men of the Legion, a couple of hundred Algerians, some black troops and a mountain battery. Schulte hates the French like poison.... Well, I'm off. Good luck! You stand ace-high with the Queen,"

Reilly got out the big green umbrella that Gwynne had left behind, and headed for town.

HE STOPPED at the palace, invited the Queen and her ladies to hold a dance at the mission station that evening, then began a hunt for Schulte. One of the native officers finally led him three miles out from the town, and here he found the bearded German. What was more, he found the surprise of his

Beside one of the guns was a very obvious
missionary with red hair and whiskers.
He had a bullet through him.

life as well. Schulte, who had been drinking heavily, made no
secret of the matter.

"There!" he said, waving his hand. "There, my friend, look
for yourself and see what these damned French will run into!
My men have been working. Have some beer; I have a whole
barrel of it in the tent."

Reilly did not refuse. He needed a drink to steady him after
what he beheld.

In this one campaign, he had learned enough of fighting to
realize that Harrison had made no idle vaunt. This, the chief
road to the village, mounted along a pleasant valley and then
plunged into a ravine, very narrow at either end. Here Schulte
was posted, with his six masked and hidden guns that could

hurl death into the ravine. Here, at either end, were laid mines ready to blow in the road ahead and behind, bring down the side walls, hold any column trapped at the bottom until the last man was wiped out.

"Suppose they send advance scouts, as they will?" asked Reilly.

"They'll see nothing. They'll go on to the town and be killed there." Schulte let loose a blasphemous storm of invective against the French. All his calm was gone, and with the liquor in him, he was a different man. Even if most of his men ran away, he was capable of firing the mines and working the guns almost single-handed—and would do it.

Reilly invited him over to the dance that evening, and went home to make himself comfortable in the mission station. He was unable to do so.

Fifty of the Legion—his own former comrades! He was not thinking so much of their fate, as of what would happen to this little town and the amiable Queen and the friendly brown men here. The first French column would be destroyed, assuredly. But others would come, and swift revenge would be taken.

That night, amid the songs and dancing and the merriment, Reilly stayed surprisingly sober. He talked with Queen Maorani, with her ladies and councilors and chief men. He found there was no particular animosity against the French, no particular knowledge of them; but there was a childish greed for glory. Schulte had persuaded them all that the French could be wiped out at one blow. The Queen wanted to be the savior of Madagascar. Harrison, who had been fatly paid for arms and munitions, had seconded the blond-bearded German. And this Schulte had a fanatic hatred of the French, an obsession.

Reilly was not the man to neglect any opportunity of drinking, feasting and love-making. Before the night was over, he was a prime favorite with everyone, and half the court was sleeping off the carouse in and around the mission when the sun came up. Reilly, however, held his aching head and tried vainly to figure out some way of spoiling the plans of Schulte without revealing his own identity to the French. It was impossible. He could not send a note of warning, for he had no one to carry the message. Nor would he have dared send any note. Two natives, who had sold bullocks to the French, had been shot a couple of days previously. The Queen's army of two hundred men were eager to fight. They would run at the first artillery blast, of course, but that did not help Reilly now.

Vainly he cursed Schulte and Harrison, for leading these smiling, happy brown folk to certain ruin.

DAYS PASSED. Word came from Harrison: he'd been delayed, but would be back as soon as his marriage took place. Reilly, who had decked himself out in all sorts of clothes left behind by Gwynne, attached himself to the Queen and did his best to bring her mind to some reason and make her see the truth; he had scant success, however. With the men of her council, it was different. He managed to impress them to some extent.

So the brown folk laughed and loved and danced, and Reilly followed suit; but terror was growing in him: terror for them and all this sweet valley. He had no fear for himself. His beard had grown quickly; it made him look twenty years older, and he trimmed it to a point, with overhanging mustaches.

Still Harrison did not come, but another came one morning: a brown runner, spent and gray with exhaustion and horror. Columns of the French were advancing. The armies of the Government had broken in panic; the invaders had terrible cannon that spread death from miles away. Wherever they met resistance, they burned and slew without pity; their march from the sea was marked by a swathe of desolation. And the column heading this way was close behind. It would be here next day. Its advance scouts were not ten miles off.

THE TOWN hummed and buzzed; soldiers ran about; Schulte cursed the absent Harrison, and ordered his two hundred men out to their post. The Queen and her council were in panic, and Schulte, raging, turned upon Reilly.

"You damned Irisher!" he fairly foamed. "I've heard what you've been doing and saying—I know all about it! A French spy; that's what you are. Very well—I'll treat you to a spy's fate. Wait, curse you, till I get my revolver—"

He went off at a run.

Now, all this broke unexpectedly and swiftly upon Reilly. This was his first intimation that Schulte was on to his game. He had no weapon; only the Queen's bodyguard were allowed to carry arms in town. News that the French were upon them had the whole population in wild uproar. The army had promptly disbanded, and even the bodyguard of the Queen was ready to bolt *en masse*.

Reilly went up to the Queen, slipped his arm around her, and kissed her.

"Leave everything to me," he said. "I'll protect you from this crazy German and from the French. Don't run, but stay right here!"

Then he did the wisest thing possible. He abandoned the green umbrella, and went hell-bent for the mission and his rifle.

He got it, and started back to town. On the outskirts he heard several shots. A dozen horrified natives met him. Schulte had shot two of the army commanders and was herding as many as he could round up to reach the camp at the ravine. The German, obsessed by his furious determination, meant to push through his plan at all costs.

"Guide me to the camp ahead of him," said Reilly; and two of the natives obeyed.

He followed them blindly by hill paths and no paths at all. He knew now what he must do—the only thing he could do. He had his Legion cartridge-pouch, and his old rifle; a Lebel, 1893 model, magazine rifle. Schulte could spring the trap single-handed, true; and he would have enough terrified native soldiers,—more afraid of him than of the French,—to play holy hell with the column that was coming. And the advance scouts would be along any time now.

"The poor little Queen!" muttered Reilly, as he sweat and strode. "I'll stop that devil if I swing for it! Thank God, Harrison hasn't come back."

All the grim reality behind this laughing care-free dreamworld had suddenly emerged.

He reached the camp, the masked battery above the ravine, the places ready for the riflemen, and found it entirely deserted. Below, along the road, were coming a few parties of natives. His two guides descended the sharp slopes, exchanged a few words, and came back with the information that the French advance was close behind these fleeing folk.

Then the two guides took to their heels, and Reilly saw Schulte coming over the hill, driving a score of most unmartial soldiers ahead of him. With a sigh, he settled down by one of the Gatling guns and adjusted his sights.

It had all happened so suddenly! He had not been prepared for a crisis. And he could sympathize with the sheer panic of the pretty little Queen and her bewildered people. Upon this thought, he squeezed the trigger, and his first shot spanged out, the echoes volleying along the ravine below.

GRIZZLED OLD Sergeant Bauer of the Legion, with Manukoff and a dozen more of his men, and a group of Algerian *tirailleurs,* was feeling out the road and scouting the country as he advanced, hoping to occupy Queen Maorani's town without a fight.

When the first shot reached him, he took warning. At a half-dozen more shots, he sized up the situation and ordered his men to scale the heights above the ravine that lay just ahead. The Algerians to the left, he and his own comrades to the right.

"Apparently no one's firing at us," he said; "but nobody with rifles has any business up there when the column comes along below. We'll occupy the place for luck."

The shooting continued, then came to an abrupt end. Several native soldiers in their white robes came into sight, evidently making for shelter. Sergeant Bauer flushed them, and they froze in acute terror without firing a shot.

What he learned from them, made him send on his men at the *pas gymnastique,* rocks or no rocks. When he and the rest came up to the guns with a rush, only two men were in sight. Schulte lay dead, out in the open. Dropped beside one of the guns lay a very obvious missionary with red hair and whiskers. He was not dead, but he had a bullet through him.

In no time at all, Sergeant Bauer had all the information he needed from the prisoners, whom he set to bury Schulte. The guns were dismantled. A litter was rigged; and after Reilly's wound had been bandaged, the sergeant set out for the town ahead. He had a supreme contempt for all the armed natives in Madagascar, and was quite competent to occupy the town himself.

"AND WHAT'S more, he did it," concluded old Manukoff, pawing his big beard and glancing around the table at us, with his air of beaming delight. "The Legion did many such things, back in those days—"

I came back to reality with a gasp of dismay.

"But that's not all the story, surely?" I exclaimed. "And what has the yarn to do with a private addressing a noncom as *'Mon sergeant?'* "

Manukoff chuckled.

"Plenty, plenty!" he said. "You see, Reilly was taken to the palace, and the Queen herself took charge of him. Meantime, the sergeant had discovered the Legion cartridge-pouch and also the rifle—our regular issue Lebel rifle. He said nothing at the time, but he did a lot of questioning around town; and that evening he came to the hut where Reilly lay under care of Queen Maorani. He brought me along with him, because I had a bit of skill in surgery and was treating Reilly's wound. We found Reilly conscious, his wound doing very well, and nothing to worry about. Now, the sergeant spoke no English, but I did.

And I had been very good friends with Reilly before his desertion."

MANUKOFF PAUSED, with another chuckle.

"Sergeant Bauer looked down at him, asked a question, and Reilly disclaimed any knowledge of French whatever. The Sergeant cut loose, using me as interpreter. Reilly had deserved well; he had saved us, and possibly the entire column. If he was a missionary, the Sergeant desired to thank him. When I translated, Reilly looked up, and I saw the old cheerful grin come to his lips. And what do you think he said?

" '*Merci, mon sergeant!*' Just like that. It slipped out before he thought. The old Sergeant went red, then snapped an order at me. I followed him outside.

" 'Did you ever see that man before in your life?' he demanded.

"And then I did it." Manukoff grinned widely at us. "I myself uttered those classic words. *Jamais de ma vie!* I said. 'Never in all my life, *mon sergeant!*' And he stood there glaring at me. Then he turned away, and I saw his shoulders shake as he walked off."

Manukoff had really finished his story this time. He picked up his drink and swigged it, and called for more.

Picard leaned forward.

"So the deserter Reilly was never recaptured?" he asked. "Then what became of him?"

Manukoff sighed, accepted the fresh glass that was set before him, and lifted it high.

"I only wish I knew!" he rejoined. "You know, in that campaign we had a very true saying; A French soldier goes into hospital in order to get sent home; a *tirailleur*, in order to be cured; a Legionnaire, in order to die. Well, at least that wasn't true of Reilly. Whether he married the little Queen or not, I never heard. But anyhow—here's to Reilly of the Legion!"

We drank the toast standing.

A DEVIL IN THE HEART

"A Devil in the Heart" brings you back to the Foreign
Legion in its best-known field—the Sahara—
in a story deeply vital and wholly unusual.

THE HITCH-HIKER drew my attention, and I slowed down....Danger? Out in the middle of the desert? Of course. Like all prudent people, I refuse to pick up hitch-hikers; but somehow this man was different. He had a magnificent figure, a proud air, and his gray beard was as massive as the man himself.

Besides, I had a revolver, an old navy cannon, hitched to the emergency-brake handle.

So I took him aboard. Winnemucca was behind, and I was headed for Salt Lake City. He, apparently, was headed for anywhere. After an hour or so we got talking; his name was Kolbar. An Alsatian by birth, he said, but he had been wandering over the West for the past thirty years. He was sixty-two.

"I love the desert," he said simply.

We had grub and beer aboard, and along in the heat of the day drew out of the highway and set about eating in comfort. Kolbar was a proud fellow, sure enough. He had some bread and cheese himself, and would have refused my food, but I pressed it on him.

Then came a trick of destiny. I wanted to use up the old loads in the gun, clean it and reload it, and I hauled it out. When he saw that antique cannon of mine, his eyes lit up, and his expression made me smile.

"Ever use one?" I said, inviting him.

He took the weapon, laughed in his beard, strode over to a

clump of mesquite and hung on the bush the paper bag his
cheese had been in. I can remember now how the bag was all
smeared with grease-spots from the cheese. He came back to
me and swung around.

Without a word, he threw up the big revolver and let loose.
Five shots; and every one of them touched that paper bag. Yet
he shook his head sadly as he turned to me.

"Not so good," he observed. "Thirty-five years ago, I'd have
put every bullet through the middle of the bag. Just as I did
that day—"

His voice trailed off. He sat down on the car's running-board,
took the cleaning-things I had ready, and set about cleaning
the gun in a shipshape manner. Plainly, he knew how.

"What day was that?" I asked.

"September, the 2nd of September, 1903," he replied. "In a

desert like this, rocky and empty, a desert of little hills and deep ravines, a desert like hell itself and as full of devils. Yet the worst devils are those in a man's heart."

The bitterness of his words warned me to be careful.

"In what part of the world was your desert, Kolbar?"

"The southern Sahara," he said.

I sat up suddenly.

"Hello! On that date? You don't, by any chance, refer to the fight put up by Captain Vauclain's detachment of the Foreign Legion against the Moroccan Arabs?"

His eyes rested on me in astonishment. "You've heard of the Foreign Legion? I thought nobody knew anything about it, in this country. The Sahara is on the other side of the world!"

"I was down there a couple of years ago, by motor," I told him.

"Tiens, tiens!" He was still openly astonished. He sighed a little and wagged his massive beard. "By motor, imagine! Those terrific wastes where five kilometers meant agonies of march-

ing—well, I suppose the world changes. Even the Legion changes."

"Then you were in the Legion?" I said incautiously. He stiffened.

"No! Not at all. But I knew a man who was. Forster, a Swiss; a big man, like me. He was in the Legion, and he hated it. The Legion was brutal, in those days. Men deserted. They chose death rather than their seven years of hell. Forster was one who skipped out. He was in Vauclain's mounted outfit—ninety men of the Legion and thirty Spahis, who were escorting some six hundred camels with ammunition and supplies to the post of El Aschad. Eleven groups of *sokhars;* exactly 572 camels, to be precise."

I got out what remained of the beer. He took a bottle, drank, sighed again.

"It's a queer story," he said thoughtfully. "Forster hated the Legion and had made all arrangements to desert. He and a Pole named Zinken were going together. They had some money; with their mules, some water and grub, they counted on getting clear across to the Spanish colonies on the coast. They intended leaving on this night of September first. They knew that hostile Arabs were somewhere around, but no one suspected that a column of such strength would be attacked."

Kolbar paused, lit a cigarette, and began to laugh.

"Two other men were with the column, and I wish you could have seen them!" he went on. "One was Père Simon, a bearded Franciscan in his brown robe; the other was a Protestant chaplain, Jalert, who was authorized by the Minister of War to go where he pleased. They were magnificent, those two! On Sundays, they held services on the opposite sides of whatever camp they were in. They did no proselyting; they were with the army to serve. But this night something funny had happened. You see, Jalert was all for prohibition, and would try to get the men to sign the pledge; he had quite a bit of luck, because no one wanted to displease him and it was easy to scrawl one's name and make him happy—"

THE TWO of them were talking, low-voiced, when at eight o'clock Captain Vauclain ordered the fires out; the march was set for two in the morning, the last stage of the weary march to the post of El Aschad. The men slept. The camels, at one side, grunted and stirred. Only the outposts watched and awaited the midnight relief.

Lines of burnouses by high saddles marked the sleeping Spahis, the wavy croups of their horses touched by the starlight. Beyond were the six-man tents of the Legion, their mules grouped to the rear. Here over their dying fire the two chaplains talked business.

PÈRE SIMON was gaunt, indefatigable, earnest. He wore only sandals, brown robe and a musette bag with his few personal belongings. Another bag, containing all his religious articles, was carried with the baggage. Jalert was thin also, but a rather jolly fellow, and quite a surgeon at times. Just now he was chuckling at Père Simon's complaint.

"You signed up that rascal Forster," the Franciscan was saying, "to drink nothing for fifteen days. But today, he got into my bag and drank all my communion wine. I've traced it to him."

"And you'll have him punished?"

"Don't be absurd. You know me better," snapped Père Simon.

"Ha! Well, I have a complaint to make, also," said Jalert. "You were talking with that rogue of a Pole, Zinken, about your experiences along the Rio de Oro, to the west, and the Spanish colonies there."

"Yes. Zinken was much interested in our work. In fact," said Père Simon, "he studied for the church in his youth and he made some valuable suggestions."

"His interest," Jalert said dryly, "isn't what you think. He and that rascal Forster are scheming to desert. Zinken was worming out of you information about the trails and water-holes in that country."

"Impossible!" Père Simon growled in his beard. "Desert? On active service? It would be death, whether they were caught or they got away!"

"Little they care," said Jalert. "I know the symptoms; so do you. Now, I have a certain sympathy for Forster. He has a good streak in him. It's not apparent, but I'm convinced it's there."

"Hm!" grunted Père Simon. "I, at least, am much concerned in keeping Zinken from making a corpse of himself. Desertion! Why, it's utter folly, at this moment! Where are those two rogues? We might have a word with them now."

"Impossible." Jalert jerked a thumb toward the rocky height above. "They're on outpost duty. Tomorrow, by all means, and before we end the march at El Aschad. I fancy they'll skip out from there. I did have a word with Forster about it, and he said it was none of my blasted business, but he didn't deny the intention of deserting. Both of us ought to go at them together."

"An excellent idea," said the Franciscan. "We must get the thought out of their minds before anyone else suspects it. Actually, it's a question of saving those two fools from themselves!"

They worked together perfectly, those two. They knew how to calm the stormy hearts of rancor or despair that beat under the Legion uniform. And when bullets were flying, their work was as much under fire as with the hospital unit.

In this case, they were a few hours too slow. Forster and Zinken were relieved at midnight, but did not show up in camp. When the whistle of Captain Vauclain sounded at two o'clock, they were far away. Not a difficult matter, since from midnight on, the camels had been loading and preparing for the march, making plenty of disturbance. It was three o'clock when the Spahis filed out to scout ahead and on the flanks, and the march began.

The hundreds of camels were strung out over four kilometers; behind them swung along the column, in square. The captain

"Desertion?" grunted Père Simon. "Why, it's
utter folly! Where are those rogues?"

had trouble with the guides, who were inefficient; the stars had
been veiled by high fog and the night was pitch black. That two
men were missing, the officers did not know.

THE MISSING men were well away. At a distance from camp with the mules they had secured, they halted to confer. Forster, bearded and massive, was by nature the leader. The Pole, Zinken, was a shrewd, raw-boned fellow.

"As I see it," Forster said, "stick to our plan and head south, in advance of the column; they'll look for us everywhere else. We can skirt El Aschad, replenish our water at the wells there tonight, and head on. Agreed?"

"Agreed," said Zinken, a man of few words. "Lead."

Both of those men knew the Legion. They knew how to march, to fight, to conduct themselves in all emergencies; they knew how to suffer, and how to die. But, in the Legion, one moves always by order. Now they were in the desert, in starless night, where there was no road or track to follow. And neither of them knew the desert, or had a compass.

They went on and on. The eastern sky was graying, when Zinken halted, with an oath, and pointed.

"Look! There's the east. We've been heading west, not south!"

Forster, looked, cursed, and acquiesced. He swung to the south, now, but he knew that in four hours they might have gone horribly amiss. It was, perhaps, half an hour later that he halted, and in the grayness of dawn held up a hand.

"Listen!"

They were on a rocky rise. Somewhere, not far distant, and to their left, lifted a dull murmurous confusion, felt rather than heard. Zinken lifted his head and sniffed.

"Ah!" he said, under his breath. "Camels! Below, and upwind from us."

A guttural, piercing voice came to them with three Arabic words: *"Allah i samah!"* followed by a low echo of laughter, a jingle of accoutrements. They stood frozen. Spahis, scouts! The murmurous sound was the sluff-sluff of camels by the hundreds. Here, almost within reach in the darkness, marched the column!

Forster echoed those Arabic words, an exclamation in common use.

"Allah will pardon! Well, Zinken, we've been fools; we've circled around. Those are the right-flank scouts who just went past, below us. We can still circle and come back into the line of march ahead of the column—"

"And be seen by those damned Spahis?" said Zinken. "Or by others? No. We've bungled it. Better lay a course southwest, and avoid El Aschad altogether. Hit away from the column on an angle."

They headed the mules back, and struck off at once.

"Those Spahi scouts are the ones to get after us," said Forster. The Pole grinned nastily and slapped his rifle. They both detested the Spahis.

By six o'clock the full daylight had arrived, and they could advance with no more apprehension of losing their direction. As they were going down a long slope, Zinken uttered a low exclamation and checked Forster.

"Look back at the skyline—I thought so!"

Forster obeyed. Two mounted figures appeared there for an instant, then came forward and were lost to sight. No others showed. Below, and ahead, broken country descended to the vast level plain of El Ascherak. Forster, who had carried a map tucked away for weeks past, nodded to the other.

"Two Spahis, eh? Very well. I want to have a look at this map anyhow. They're a mile behind us, at least. Here are rocks. Why not rest before we kill them?"

"Agreed," said Zinken.

They took the mules among high rocks, tethered them out of sight, and settled down to a cigarette and a wait, their rifles ready. Forster had spread out his map and was studying the broken ground far ahead, when a low word broke from him. He seemed frozen. The Pole looked, his eyes focused on the distance, and he jerked out a grunt.

Moving shapes were there, fifty, sixty, a hundred of them at least, flitting across their field of vision and disappearing.

"Arabs, and at the gallop!" muttered Forster. "Damned queer! If they—"

Suddenly he dived for his map, stared at it, looked up at Zinken, wide-eyed.

"Name of the devil—look at this! They can be going only to El Aschad, or else to cut the column's line of march. Eh? And—"

Excitement spewed color into the lean browned cheeks of the Pole.

"Right!" he exclaimed. "And spurring fast. Why? A hundred, at most."

"I get you." Forster nodded. "Not enough to attack the column—spurring, therefore, to join others and be in at the death. Suppose we don't kill those two Spahis after all, but send 'em back to warn Vauclain?"

"Vauclain be damned," spat the Pole. "I'd like to see the whole outfit wiped out. Why let those Spahis take in news of us?"

The two looked at each other; their whole natures clashed, in this one look.

FORSTER FLUSHED under his bronze. "We'll have to warn the column," he said slowly. "It's but common decency. We've bunked with those men. It was just about here, three years ago, that a Legion convoy was attacked, ambushed, decimated. We must warn 'em."

"I'll be damned if I will!" said Zinken.

"You'll be damned if you won't," Forster rasped. "I mean it."

As always, when actually on the march and on campaign, the mounted companies of the Legion were given great latitude

in equipment and uniform. Forster, for example, wore a *chechia*, known in the Occident alone as a "fez"; this Zinken disdained because, as he claimed, he was a good Christian and refused to wear headgear that all over the Orient pointed to its wearer as a believer in Allah. Zinken wore Arab footgear instead of shoes, as being more comfortable. Forster had replaced his shirt with a Saharan *seroual,* and under it had a revolver hidden. He was an expert with the weapon.

"Those two Spahis get stopped for good, here and now." Zinken walked toward the two rifles, thirty feet away.

"I say not," rejoined Forster, not moving, but getting out his revolver. "Zinken, for God's sake listen to me! I won't let you do it."

The Pole strode on and picked up his rifle. He swung around, his eyes on fire.

"You damned fool!" he blazed out. "It would spoil everything for us. My skin comes first. To hell with the Legion! I'd like nothing better than to see the column shot to pieces."

"I wouldn't," said Forster. "I say you sha'n't do it! Those Spahis must take in the warning to Vauclain! We can get away all right—"

"We can't, damn you!" snarled Zinken.

Neither of them took note, so absorbed were they in each other, that the two figures coming from the rear were now in plain sight among the rocks.

"I'll stop you if I must!" And Forster flew into a rage. "Do as I say, you damned Pole! I'm giving orders here—"

Zinken saw the revolver whip up. A scream of fury burst from him.

"Murder me, would you?" He flung up his rifle and fired.

Forster's revolver merged its voice with that of the rifle. Furious, the Swiss fired again and again; Zinken's one bullet had touched him, it was life or death now. So rapidly did he pull trigger that the hammer clicked before he realized what he was doing. Zinken's rifle exploded again, the bullet going into the sky; then the Pole crumpled and fell in a heap. All five bullets had hit him in the forehead.

FORSTER RELOADED the revolver, and walked forward. He looked down at the dead Zinken; all the fire had gone out of his face, his eyes were dull and vacant. He still stood there, staring down, when the two riders approached. He glanced up at them listlessly, then surprise grew in his gaze.

Not Spahis after all! Instead, Père Simon and Jalert.

He reached down and covered the face of the Pole. The two men of religion, who had actually witnessed the shooting, dismounted and came up to him.

"Keep going," he said in a dead voice. "You must warn Vauclain. Arabs—"

"You killed him!" accused Jalert. "We saw you do it! But he fired first. Man! You're hurt! Then he hit you!"

Forster waved him away. Père Simon was gazing at him curiously, and now produced a canteen. He shoved it at Forster. "Drink," he ordered, and Forster obeyed. Cognac and water. "Better than stolen wine, eh? Take off that *seroual*. Here, M'sieur Jalert! What do you think of it?"

Forster bared his torso. Jalert looked at the wound under the arm and laughed.

"Bah! A mere touch. Forster, what were you fighting about? Here, you fool; stand still till I get a bandage on!"

"We thought you were two Spahis—you're on horses," said Forster dully, while the pastor expertly applied a bandage. "We had seen the Arabs, a hundred of them; going to cut off the column, evidently. I wanted to warn Vauclain—and he didn't. That's all."

Suddenly he blinked, wakened. "Hello!" he went on. "What are you two doing here, anyway?"

Père Simon rubbed his beard.

"Hm! Looking for you two deserters. We caught sight of you, and followed. It was only Providence that guided us."

"You're coming back to duty," said Jalert with authority.

"Go to hell," snapped Forster rudely. "I'm doing nothing of the sort. But someone must warn the column. Get off, do you hear? No more nonsense about me going back."

"Vauclain has scouts," Père Simon rejoined. "Let him look to his own business. Ours is with you. We're taking you back with us—to duty, Forster!"

Forster saw that he was quite serious about it, and went off into a bellow of laughter that held no mirth whatever.

"Back to duty, eh? Back, to be punished for desertion—punished for killing this swine at our feet! *Nom de Dieu,* what an optimist you are!"

"Come, be sensible," intervened Jalert sharply. "Your explanation of this matter is quite sufficient; besides, we saw Zinken fire first. As to desertion, I doubt whether it's known yet by any of the officers. And even that, perhaps, can be arranged. Your desire to warn the captain will atone for it. Not that there's any need of warning."

Forster sobered abruptly.

"Messieurs, there's acute need for warning," he said gravely. "Vauclain depends on the Spahis for warning of any ambush—ahead and on the flanks, quite as should be. But how do those Spahis scout? We've seen them along the march. We men in the ranks know more than the officers. Those Spahis act as though on campaign service around some little peaceful outpost of the Tell; they make a promenade, instead of making a careful

inspection of the terrain. Why, they'd ride straight past any ambush without seeing it!"

HE LEFT them and went back to the map he had been studying. Picking it up, he rejoined them, glanced at the sun-bright sky, and shook his head.

"Look." He pointed to the map. "Here's the column, march-ing south, straight on to the immense plain you can see from here. An ambush in any of those ravines opening on the plain would catch the column like rats. Get off with you! Warn Vau-clain!"

"You're going with us," said Père Simon with stubborn in-sistence.

Forster blinked at him. He could not make these two men see the thing as he saw it, understand the urgent need of action as he understood it. The memory of those Arabs hurtling across the distance flickered in his brain; a groan escaped him.

The last Arab pitched down, rolled over, came up with his knife—and Forster gave him the last bullet, between the eyes.

"Come, my son," went on the Franciscan more gently. "You were guilty of a moment's rashness in deserting—"

"A moment carefully planned and long awaited," snapped Forster.

"No matter. Destiny has intervened; Providence, I should say." And Père Simon pointed to the dead man. "The circumstances will pardon you; I answer for it. You've served three years. There's good stuff in you. Forget this madness, come back and serve out the balance, face your duty like a man and not like a coward!"

"To hell with it," said Forster; and desperately, he faced them. "Look here, I know what I'm about. I can make the Rio de Oro country, I can make it alone, and I'm going to do it. I'm built for it; I've thought it all out. Climb on your horses. I'll get our mules."

"What do you mean to do?" queried Jalert.

"Accompany you back within reach of the column and send you in with warning, or fire a couple of shots as warning," said Forster. "Then make my get-away. And no more of your blasted arguments!" he added savagely. "Move!"

He slung his own rifle over his back and, after thoughtfully

taking the money and personal effects of the dead Zinken, he
went to where the mules were hidden. With two mules, he
reflected, his escape to Spanish territory was certain.

He mounted, pushed the mules hard, and the two horses
followed. Despite the peril, he headed down for the plain, there
picked up the tracks of the Arabs he had seen, and swung off
to the left on this trail. Here was sand instead of rock; vast
dunes of sand glittering ahead in the level light of sunrise, the
grim rock range rising abruptly to the left as they curved along
its front. No Arabs were to be seen. These raiding tribesmen
from across the Moroccan border knew their business.

ABRUPTLY, A rocky spur showed ahead. To the right,
circling it, went the Arab trail. Forster eyed the rocks keenly.
Not high; undoubtedly a mere jutting outpost of the hills. He
decided to gamble, and turned to the other two.

"We'll go straight across there; the mules can make it," he
said. "No back talk! Follow me. We'll save time and distance,
if I'm right. If your horses can't keep at it, dismount and lead
them."

He pushed his mules straight at the long rocky slope, following a faint ravine which came down from the saddle of the
spur.

Except for this faintly defined wash, the mules could not
have made it, but here was fair footing, even for the horses. It
was a rush and a scramble, until at length Forster was up. The
undulating crest beyond showed nothing, and he pressed ahead,
to find the crest of the spur wider than he had believed. The
frightful possibility that he had lost the gamble chilled his
blood. If, after all, this were not a short cut—

Ah! He drew rein, as the other two slowly overtook him.
Père Simon called:

"Forster, I'm afraid this leads nowhere."

"No! I was right." Forster's voice held an urgent ring. "We
can go a little farther, then we must leave the animals. Look!"

Straight ahead, he pointed to a faintly discernible tinge of yellow rising in air.

"Dust, fine sand," he explained. "It's from the camels. Come along! We'll cut into the very path of the column. Another ravine, no doubt."

A few hundred yards farther, not even the mules could cross the rocky expanse ahead. All four animals were tethered and left. It was not far now. Forster could even catch glimpses of a wide ravine that debouched at an angle into the plain.

This became more clear, as the nearest intervening rocks were passed. The three men scrambled on. Forster, with a grunt of dismay, looked at his watch; nine o'clock, The sun was beating down hotly. Suddenly, almost as by magic, they rounded a pinnacle of rocks and found themselves at the head of a little ravine that broke down abruptly upon the scene. They were within five hundred yards of the column itself.

Exclamations burst from them—of surprise, from the other two, of abrupt dismay from Forster. However, he reflected swiftly, he was safe enough. He could make his way back out of sight, retrace his steps to the animals, and get off with horses and mules together, long before any pursuit could catch him up…. All this in the mental flash of an instant.

To the right was the draggling convoy of camels, trudging into the plain. Here ahead was the Legion, dismounted, in deployed line, getting its breakfast. The Spahis were ahead, moving slowly, negligently.

"You see," panted Jalert, "you were entirely wrong. There are no hostiles in sight anywhere. There's no place for any ambush—"

"Thunders of heaven! Look at that!" burst out Forster. He pointed at a deep gully which made a semi-circle across the mouth of the ravine, a hundred yards from the camp. "Look at that gully, at the heavy brush which fringes it! Those Spahis passed right by. But from here, from above—"

"Ah! Glints of metal!" exclaimed Père Simon. "Yes, yes! And some movement there, too. You were right! The gully is deep enough to hide horses and men alike. Come, Jalert! We'll get in with warning—"

"I'll give it first. No time to waste." Forster unslung his rifle. He fired twice, in air.

HE WAS half a minute too late. As he was in the act, puffs of powder-smoke lifted from far beyond, where a group of the flanking Spahis must have come upon a number of hidden Arabs. The group went down in a scramble of men and horses. Two emerged, heading back at a gallop.

The alarm had been given. On the instant, the Legion broke into motion, caught up rifles, and fell into line. To the left, spurting figures came out of the gully; a gasp broke from Forster as he saw them. Men by the hundreds—three hundred, four hundred—opening a terrible fire on the section of the line there. Ahead, the gully vomited up more robed figures, pouring in a fire on the other sections.

"It's an army!" cried Jalert, agony in his voice as he watched. "Look! Captain Vauclain is deploying his section behind the mules—he's down—"

Père Simon watched, with horror in his bearded face. Vauclain was down. Another and another officer was down—all of them were down. The men were falling. But they were firing, too. An incoherent word of dismay and consternation escaped Forster, a cry of sheer terror, as he pointed.

FROM BEHIND the first sand-dune, eight hundred yards away, a second Arab line appeared at a gallop. Not three or four hundred of the enemy, but double that number!

"Sergeant-major Tissier is down," broke out Forster. "Look! There goes Sergeant Dannert. And Montes—and Lieutenant Hansen—all the officers are gone—"

The three watched, seized by a paralysis of futile despair. Everything was happening in a moment. Despite death striking into their ranks, the Legion was rallying upon two little rocky knolls which commanded all the ground around. The wounded were transported there. The third section was almost destroyed; some of them reached it. The fourth section fixed bayonets and charged the Arabs, but the charge was broken. The survivors opened a fire by volleys that had tremendous effect. The second section deployed and attacked the Arabs to the left.

All this, it seemed, in no time at all. One sergeant and two corporals remained to command the groups of the Legion, but these groups were now in action, in motion, with cool and precise attack and recession. One group, with the Spahis, seized the higher ground to the left. The others joined on the two little knolls where the rocks gave good shelter. The wounded were brought in. The position was consolidated, and the Arabs were unable to attack in the face of the savage fire poured into them.

"And we are not there to help the poor souls!" muttered Père Simon.

"You can't get there," snapped Forster. "Look—we're cut off!"

The moving flood of Arabs had surged forward. Now some of them occupied the ground below the little ravine where the three stood. Half a dozen of them came up the ravine itself. One of them looked up, saw the three. With a savage yell, the group came rushing forward, firing as they came.

"Give me your rifle," said Jalert calmly. "You have the revolver."

"True," said Forster, and laughed. "We'll have a share in this business after all, eh? Don't fire yet. Père Simon! Cover, man— take cover!"

He shoved the Franciscan to one side, behind a rock as the six wild Moroccan tribesmen came, knives out, guns waving, eyes rolling. Jalert fired, missed. He fired again and then staggered as a bullet hit him. The rifle escaped his hands, but he had dropped one of the six.

Forster whitened, stood firm, waited. He had six bullets in the revolver now, every chamber ready. They were not forty feet away, and rushing on. Thirty feet—the revolver exploded. Shot after shot, rapid, cool, unhurried. The last Arab pitched down ten feet away, rolled over, came up with his knife—and Forster gave him the last bullet, between the eyes. Six of them sprawled in a trail of death. Not one bullet had missed, except Jalert's first shot.

"Apparently your prayers have produced a miracle, Père Simon," said Forster ironically. "See if Jalert's dead."

LUCKILY, JALERT was only scraped by a bullet that had stunned him.

Forster brought in one good rifle from the scattered weapons of the dead Arabs, and gave it to the Franciscan. He took a poorer one for himself; good enough, however.

"Now, gentlemen, you're about to fight," he said gayly, cheerfully. "If we dislodge the Arabs below, you can go straight through to what's left of the force, yonder. I think you're badly needed. Apparently, this little side-issue of the fight has escaped the notice of those Arabs underneath us. Come along! Fire when I give the word. When they run, you make a break for it. Our men will cover you, depend on it, and you'll get to the position safely. A lot of men are dying over there who need you."

Jalert nodded, and tugged at the bandage about his head.

"Ready," he said. He clapped Forster on the shoulder, looking him in the eyes. "If I don't get through, I want you to know that I respect you."

"And," said Père Simon, lifting his hand, "my son, accept my blessing."

Forster looked from one to the other with a hard gaze.

"All right," he rejoined, "but just remember one thing; don't tell anyone what you know about me. Ready? Let's go."

He led the way down the little ravine.

The group of Arabs who had taken cover below, thirty or more in number, had opened a galling fire on the Legion position, which was fairly close. They had it in flank and were somewhat above.

When three rifles opened a sudden burst of fire on them from behind, panic swept them. Two of those rifles were deadly enough. Père Simon, if he could not shoot well, could at least shoot fast, and did. With yells of terror and surprise, the Arabs broke and ran for it. Bullets from the Legion position swept them as they ran.

Then came the surprising sight of a gaunt man in a brown habit, and a bareheaded man in whites, legging it for all they were worth. A sudden cheer rippled up from the men of the Legion, a cheer of recognition and wild applause. Their fire redoubled, and the two runners came through—puffing but safe enough.

Forster, sitting among the rocks, lit a cigarette, viewed the mouth of the ravine below, sighted an Arab stealing forward, and calmly dropped the man.

"And that," he said, coming erect and drawing back to cover, "is all I can do. It's enough, perhaps. Comrades, Private Forster salutes you—and goes about his own affairs."

HE DID not neglect to despoil the six dead Arabs, before making his way back up the gully to the rocky elbow; there, he was beyond sight of the scene. He came safely to where the four animals had been left. There he packed everything on the mules, mounted one of the horses, and took his departure, with the three lead beasts trailing behind.

Descending the hillside to the sandy plain below, he drew rein. A crackling mutter of rifle-fire came over the rocky spur to his ears. Even now, hesitation took him. He knew what was happening there, what would happen. The Legion would defend itself all through the blazing day, until relief came from El Aschad. Every rifle would count. And he was turning his back upon that scene.

He shrugged. "No. I'll never again have such a chance," he muttered…. "Serve out that seven years of hell? Not much!"

And, with a deep breath of decision, he put in his heels and rode away.

THE STORY was finished, the beer was finished, and the cigar I had given Kolbar was finished. We were back in the Nevada desert, and Kolbar was sadly wagging that great gray beard as he came to the end of the story.

"It's no very heroic tag to the yarn," I observed.

"Perhaps not," he assented mildly. "You see, it's real. Things aren't so very dramatic in real life, as a rule."

"How did you learn so much about it, anyhow?"

He hesitated, then made awkward response.

"I met Forster some years afterward and he told me the whole thing. He—well, he was unhappy about it. He said those two men of God were right; there was a little devil of remorse in his heart. He never forgave himself. I think he came to a bad end."

He rose abruptly. From the car, he took the little pack he had carried slung over his massive shoulders. I glanced at him in surprise.

"Where are you going?"

"Back." He jerked his thumb along the way we had come. "A trail branched off the highway, a quarter-mile back. I'm going to take it and strike off into the hills. I don't like these highways; too many cars. Thanks for everything, Mister. It's been fine. Maybe we'll get together again another time."

He nodded to me and went striding away.

At first, I did not realize why he had left so suddenly. I cleaned things up, had a smoke, and got the brakes adjusted a bit. Then, preparing to depart, I caught sight of something. It was the paper sack, still hanging on the mesquite clump, pierced by bullets. And it caught me up with a round turn.

He had noticed it, of course; he had gone, quickly, before I suspected anything. Now I remembered what he had said:

"Thirty-five years ago, I'd have put every bullet through the middle of that bag. Just as I did that day—"

The day he had killed Zinken, of course, and turned his back on the Second Regiment Etranger.

ABOUT THE AUTHOR

H. BEDFORD-JONES is a Canadian by birth, but not by profession, having removed to the United States at the age of one year. For over twenty years he has been more or less profitably engaged in writing and traveling. As he has seldom resided in one place longer than a year or so and is a person of retiring habits, he is somewhat a man of mystery; more than once he has suffered from unscrupulous gentlemen who impersonated him—one of whom murdered a wife and was subsequently shot by the police, luckily after losing his alias.

The real Bedford-Jones is an elderly man, whose gray hair and precise attire give him rather the appearance of a retired foreign diplomat. His hobby is stamp collecting, and his collection of Japan is said to be one of the finest in existence. At present writing he is en route to Morocco, and when this appears in print he will probably be somewhere on the Mojave Desert in company with Erle Stanley Gardner.

Questioned as to the main facts in his life, he declared there was only one main fact, but it was not for publication; that his life had been uneventful except for numerous financial losses, and that his only adventures lay in evading adventurers. In his younger years he was something of an athlete, but the encroachments of age preclude any active pursuits except that of motoring. He is usually to be found poring over his stamps, working at his typewriter, or laboring in his California rose garden, which is one of the sights of Cathedral Cañon, near Palm Springs.